The Landloper
The Romance Of A Man On Foot

By

Holman Day

Double 9
BOOKS

The Landloper
The Romance of a Man on Foot
by Holman Day

ISBN: 978-93-62766-41-0

Published by

DOUBLE 9 BOOKS

2/13-B, Ansari Road
Daryaganj, New Delhi – 110002
info@double9books.com
www.double9books.com
Tel. 011-40042856

ABOUT THE AUTHOR

Holman Francis Day, an American author, was born in Vassalboro, Maine. The Holman Day House, his residence in Auburn, Maine, is on the National Register of Historic Places. The Rider of the King Log, based on his book, was filmed in 1921. Along Came Ruth, based on his play, was filmed in 1924. Day married Helen Gerald, the only daughter of Amos F. Gerald, a railroad engineer, and Caroline W. Rowell. She died in 1902 at the age of 32 and was buried at Maplewood Cemetery in her father's birthplace of Fairfield, Maine; Day, on the other hand, was buried in Nichols Cemetery in his hometown of Vassalboro, Maine, after dying in 1935. He graduated from Colby College (class of 1887) and worked as the Union Publishing Company's managing editor in Bangor, Maine, from 1889 to 1890. He was also the editor and owner of the Dexter Gazette in Maine, a special writer for the Journal in Lewiston, a Boston Herald representative, and the managing editor of the Lewiston Daily Sun. From 1901 until 1904, he served as the military secretary to Maine Governor John F Hill. He moved to Carmel-by-the-Sea, California, in the 1920s.

CONTENTS

I
IN THE DUST OF THE LONG HIGHWAY

The man who called himself Walker Farr plodded down the dusty stretches of a country road.

He moved leisurely. He neither slouched like a vagabond nor did he swing with a stride which indicated that he had aim in life or destination in mind. When he came under arching elms he plucked his worn cap from his head and stuffed it into a coat pocket which already bulged bulkily against his flank. He gazed to right and left upon the glories of a sun-bathed June morning and strolled bareheaded along the aisle of a temple of the great Out-of-Doors.

He was young and stalwart and sunburnt.

A big, gray automobile squawked curt warning behind him and then swept past and on its way, kicking dust upon him from its whirring wheels.

He gave the car only an indifferent glance, but, as he walked on, he was conscious that out of the blur of impressions the memory of a girl's profile lingered.

A farmer-man who had come to the end of a row in a field near the highway fence leaned on his hoe-handle and squinted against the sun at the face of the passer-by. Then the farmer shifted his gaze to the stranger's clothing and scowled. The face was the countenance of a man who was somebody; the clothing was the road-worn garb of a vagrant.

"Here, you!" called the farmer.

"I hear you," said the man who called himself Walker Farr, smiling and putting subtle insolence into the smile.

"Do you want a job?"

"No, sir."

"Have you got a job?"

"Yes, sir."

"What is it?"

"Chopping down well-holes that have been turned inside out by a cyclone."

The man in the highway flashed a wonderful smile at the farmer and passed on. The farmer blinked and then he scowled more savagely. He climbed the fence and followed, carrying his hoe.

"Look here, you! There ain't no such business."

"Send for me next time you have a well turned wrong side out and I'll prove it."

"You're a tramp."

Farr sauntered on.

"You're a tramp, and here's what we are doing to tramps in this county right now!"

Beyond them in the highway men were delving with shovels and hacking with mattocks. The men wore blue drilling overalls, obtrusively new, and their faces were pasty pale.

"We have taken 'em out of jail and put 'em doing honest work," said the farmer. He pointed to guards who were marching to and fro with rifles in the hook of their arms. "Here's where you belong. I'm a constable of this town. I arrest you."

The young man halted. His smile became provokingly compassionate as he stared down at the nickel badge the farmer was tapping.

"So you represent the law, do you?" inquired Farr.

"I do."

"It's too bad you don't know more about the law, then. I have neither solicited alms, trespassed on private property, begged food, nor committed crime in your little kingdom, my good and great three-tailed bashaw. Here is a coin to clear the law." He exhibited a silver piece. "I am sorry I cannot remain here and help you mend your ways—they seem to need it!"

He went on past the sullen gang of pick and shovel, treading the middle of the broad turnpike.

"Ain't that a tramp?" asked one of the guards.

"I don't know what he is," confessed the farmer.

The man who called himself Farr turned a corner and came upon the same automobile which had overtaken and passed him, contemptuously kicking its dust over him, a few minutes before he arrived at the farmer's fence.

A rear tire was flat and a young man who was smartly attired in gray was smacking gloved hands together and cursing the lumps of a jail-bird-built road and the guilty negligence of a garage-man who had forgotten to put a lift-jack back into the kit. Two women stood beside the car and looked upon the young man's helplessness.

"Enter tortoise, second scene of the ancient drama, 'The Tortoise and the Hare,'" Walter Farr informed himself.

His amused brown eyes noted the young man was obviously flabby.

"Here, you! Help me prop up this axle," commanded the charioteer.

"You do not need help," suggested Farr. "You need somebody who can do the whole job."

The glance he gave the young man, up and down, conveyed his full meaning.

"Well, I must say that's saucy talk from a hobo," declared one of the women.

"Mother!" warned the third member of the party.

Farr turned his cynical gaze from the older woman to the younger—from the bleached hair and rouged lips to a fresh, pure, and vivid loveliness. He saw her profile once more.

"No one has remembered to say 'please' yet," the girl informed him, meeting his gaze. "I say it, sir!"

He bowed and went straight to the roadside and picked up a bit of plank on which his searching eyes rested.

He gave it into the gloved hands of the car's owner, he slipped off his own sun-faded coat and rolled the sleeves of his flannel shirt above his elbows, and then, with shoulder thrusting up; and arms straining, he heaved the car high enough so that the flabby gentleman could set the prop under the axle. And when the gentleman began to dust his gloves and to search for spots on his gray immaculateness, Farr dug tools from the box and proceeded to the work of replacing the tire.

The girl stood near him and regarded him with interest. He looked up when he had the opportunity and found her eyes studying him. She was entirely frank in her gaze. There was nothing in her eyes except the earnestness of a scrutiny which was satisfying curiosity.

When the work was done the owner offered money.

Farr refused with curt decisiveness.

"Well, have a drink?" invited the debtor.

"I do not use liquor."

The autoist emptied his cigar-case into his hand and offered the cigars to Farr, who had just tugged on his coat.

"I do not smoke, sir."

It was not declination with humility; the manner of the man of the road contained a hint that anybody who drank or smoked was no better than he should be. The girl studied him with renewed interest.

"Don't stand there and try to put anything over on me," advised the man in gray, showing resentment. "What can I do for you?"

"You might thank the man, Richard," declared the girl, tartly. She turned to Farr.

"He seems to have forgotten 'thank you' as he forgot 'please.' May I make amends? We thank you!"

"And now I am in your debt," said the rover. He bowed and walked on.

When the car passed him the girl turned and gave him a long look. He waved his hand. The dust-cloud closed in between them.

"Kat Kilgour! That's a tramp! I'm amazed!" said the elder woman, observing the look and the salute.

"Yes, this world is full of surprises," agreed the girl, sweetly.

"But your own eyes told you that he was a tramp."

"There isn't any doubt of it, is there, if you used your eyes?" demanded their escort.

"We'll consider that the eyes have it—and let the matter drop," said the girl—and her tone was not sweet.

The man of the keen brown eyes and the faded garb fared on.

He plucked a rose from a wayside bush and carried the flower in his hand.

"Your sister just passed this way," he informed the rose in whimsical fashion. "I don't suppose you and I will ever catch up with her. I go very slowly, but you may journey along with me."

II
A HOME-MADE KNIGHT-ERRANT

The wayfarer who called himself Farr came down the long hill and turned the corner of the highway where the alders crowded to the banks of the narrow brook; they whispered to one another as the breeze fluttered their leaves. He drank there, bending and scooping the water in his palm. He bathed the rose and stroked its wilted petals.

"Too bad, little one!" he said. "The long road is a killing proposition, and I'm afraid I had no business inviting you to go with me. Your sister must be a long way ahead of us."

The rocks were cool where the alders cast shade, and he sat there for a little while, watching the drift of tiny flotsam down the eddying current and observing the skipper-bugs skating over the still shallows on their spraddled legs.

There was a pleasant hush all about. The bubbling ecstasy of a bobolink floated above the grasses of a meadow, and near at hand a wren hopped about in the alders and chirped dozy notes. Peace and restfulness brooded. The man at the brook leaned low and thrust his head into the water and then rose and shook the drops from his thick thatch of brown hair. He did it with a sort of canine wriggle and smiled at the thought which came to him.

"A stray dog!" he muttered. "Of as much account—and he'd better forget the sister of the rose. Here's a good place to put imagination to sleep—here's a place where all is asleep."

He went on around the curtain of the alders.

There was a big old-fashioned house near at hand. Its walls were weather-worn, its yard was not tidy. The faded curtains at the windows hung crookedly. The glass of the panes was dirty. The entire aspect of the place indicated that there was no woman's hand to make it home. It was commonplace and uninteresting.

But the front door was flung open suddenly with a screech of rusty hinges.

Then came backing out of the doorway a very old man—a bent and wrinkled old man with long white hair which trailed down from under a broad-brimmed hat. He was dragging a coffin, single-handed. The free end of the solemn box bumped down the wooden steps with a hollow clatter that suggested emptiness. There was a woodpile at one side of the yard. The old man tugged the casket over the litter of chips and dropped the end. He wrenched an ax from its cleft in a chopping-block and caved in the top of the coffin with the first blow.

The man Farr, observing from the road, saw that the casket was empty. The old man continued to bash and batter.

The wayfarer, before the destruction was begun, had time to note that the coffin was a remarkably fine specimen of cabinet-maker's work. There were various sorts of wood inlaid with care, and the fretwork along its sides had been jig-sawed with much pains spent in detail, and the pilasters were turned with art. But the old man battered at all this excellence with savageness. It was evident that he was not merely providing kindling-wood—he was expending fury.

It was an affair that demanded undivided attention from the observer in the road; but a man came around the corner of the house just then and Farr promptly gave over his interest in the aged chopper.

The new arrival was clothed cap-a-pie in armor.

He stood quietly at a little distance and gazed from under his vizor on the energetic old man at the woodpile.

Farr noted that the armor was obviously home-made. The helmet, though burnished and adorned with a horse's tail, had the unmistakable outlines of a copper kettle. The cuirass could not disguise its obligation to certain parts of an air-tight stove. But the ensemble was peculiarly striking and the man in the road took a quick glance around at the New England landscape in order to assure himself that he was still where he supposed he was.

Farr went to the fence and folded his arms on the top.

The old man, resting a moment, seemed to feel that intent regard from behind and, without turning his body, hooked his narrow and bony chin over his shoulder and swapped a long stare with the stranger.

"Well," inquired the venerable chopper, "what is on thy mind, sir?" His tone was sour.

"Seeing that the question is direct and remembering that age deserves the truth, I'll say that I was thinking that this seems to be an ideal location for a private lunatic-asylum, and that guests are allowed to enjoy themselves."

"I will have thee to understand that I have sat for thirty long years at the head of the Friends' meeting in this town and never has it been said that my wits are cracked. Furthermore, this is none of thy affair. Move on."

Farr merely shifted his feet and took an easier pose at the fence.

"Feeling as I do, it will not trouble me much to come over there and take a chop or two at thee," warned the old man.

"I didn't know that Quakers ever allowed their feelings to get so highly spiced."

"Along with thee, tramp!"

"You see, my dear sir," drawled the man in the road, "I am out in search of peace of mind. If I should go on my way without understanding what this means my itching curiosity would never allow me another good night's sleep. A word from you to soothe curiosity, and then I go!"

"Thee has seen me knocking into pieces a coffin. Is there anything strange in seeing me knock into pieces a coffin I have made with my own hands?"

"No, sir. That is quite within your rights. But why? From what little I saw of it it seemed to me to be a mighty fine piece of work."

"It was," stated the old man, a bit mollified. "Walnut with bird's-eye maple inlaid."

"May I ask if it was made for anybody who died lately?"

"I made it for myself—I have had it by me for twenty years! Seeing that thee must stick thy nose into my business!" His tone was pettish and he stooped down and began to toss splinters and broken boards upon the woodpile.

"Then I suppose it was—er—sort of out of date," suggested Farr, blandly.

"I see thee is minded to tease me—the world is full of fools." He straightened as best he could, propping hands on his hips, and divided angry gaze between the man at the fence and the armored figure. "I am not going to die—I have decided to stay alive. I have a fool on my hands."

"Father, I think thee had better choose thy words a bit better in the presence of a stranger," advised the man in armor.

"Can't thee see that he is a fool?" demanded the old man.

"I don't think I want to venture an opinion, sir. I'll simply say that your son's choice of a summer suit seems a little peculiar. But, of course, every man to his liking!"

The old man walked down to the fence. He was crooked at the waist and his legs were hooked with the curves of age, but he strode along with brisk vigor. His gaze was as sharp as a gimlet, though the puckered lids were cocked over his eyes with the effect of little tents whose flaps were partly closed. He put his face close to Farr's.

"Thee is as cheeky as a crow and as prying as a magpie and I venture to say thee is a roving scamp. But I may as well talk to thee as to anybody."

With armor rattling and squeaking, the son started toward them.

"I do not care to have thee talk about me, father," he warned.

Farr noted that the son had eyes as keen and as gray as those of the elder. The armored citizen was sturdy and of middle age and the face under the vizor revealed intelligence and self-possession.

The father paid no heed to the son.

"Has thee traveled around the world much?"

"Yes, sir."

"Thee has met many men?"

"Many and of all sorts and conditions."

"Then I want to ask thee what thee thinks of the good wit of a man who declares that he will go forth into the world, faring here and there, to try to do good to all men, to try to settle the troubles between men, free of all price?"

Farr turned gaze from the father to the earnest countenance of the son, and then stared again into the searching eyes of the old man. Prolonged and embarrassed silence followed.

"Thy looks speak louder than words," declared the father. "Thy eyes say it—he is a fool."

"It may be as well not to say so with thy tongue," advised the son. "I might not be as patient with a stranger as I am with my father. He is wholly practical, without imagination, and so I excuse him."

"I offer no comments," said Walker Farr with a frank smile which won an answering flicker from the face under the vizor. "I do not understand."

"I would not expect a vagabond to understand anything or to be brave enough to say what he thinks," piped the father. He turned on his son. "Here's a scalawag of a tramp. Go along with him and be another such."

"I may be a peripatetic philosopher, for all you know," said Farr, teasingly. "There are knights in fustian as well as knights in armor."

"I think thee is of more account than thy clothing indicates," stated the son, regarding the stranger keenly. "And thee carries a rose in thy hand. Little things tell much."

Farr put the flower into his pocket. "Don't fool yourself about me," he said, roughly.

"Thy speech has betrayed thee," insisted the other.

"I have met crib-crackers who were college men—and pocket dictionaries are cheap. And so good day to you, gentlemen."

"Wait one moment!" appealed the man in armor. His face softened when he approached his father.

"We have talked much and there is no more to say to each other now. I have served here patiently many years. If I leave thee for a little while there is old Ben to wait and tend. And I will come back after I have done my duty."

"I will stay alive so that I can bail thee out of prison," his father informed him, sourly. "Go on, thou fool; learn thy lesson! The world is all right as it is; it will cuff the ears of meddlers. But go on!"

"I would rather thee would show another spirit at parting—but have it thy way," returned the son, with Quaker repression of all emotions. He came forth from the gate.

"I am going thy road," he informed Farr, "because all ways are alike to me. I would be pleased to talk with one who has journeyed. Thee may have good counsel for me. May I walk with thee?"

The wayfarer opened his mouth and closed it suddenly on a half-spoken and indignant refusal of this honor. He pursed his lips and his thick brows drew together in a frown. Then, as if in spite of himself, he began to smile.

"I will be no burden to thee," pleaded the home-made knight. "I have had my armor for a long time and have practised walking in it."

"But why the tin suit?" expostulated Farr.

"I will explain as we walk."

"Well, come along!" blurted the wayfarer. "Nothing more can happen to me, anyway."

"So thee has found one of thy own kind to follow about in the world?" inquired the father, tauntingly. "Feathers on the head and rattles in the hand! Cockahoops and fiddle-de-lorums! Thee'll be back soon with thy folly cured after I have bailed thee from the calaboose! Then thee'll stick to thy forge and be sensible!"

Farr noted a small shop by the roadside as they started off.

"My father is a good man, but practical—wholly practical," said his new comrade of the ways. "From my good mother I derive imagination. My life has not been happy here. But work has helped."

He pointed to the shop. Over the main door a faded, weather-worn sign advertised "Eastup Chick & Son, Blacksmiths." On the gable was a newer sign heralding "Jared Chick & Father, Inventors."

"I am Jared Chick, my friend."

He talked slowly, pausing to pick words, phrasing with the carefulness of the man of method, talking as those persons talk who have read many books and use their tongue but seldom. Farr found much quaintness in the solemn man's discourse.

"My father put my name on the sign when I was young, and it pleased me. I put his name on the other sign when he was old and it did not please him, though I have insisted that he must share in all credit which comes to me. But my father does not possess imagination. I am sorry he lost his temper to-day and broke up his coffin. Not that I approved of having it in the house all these years, but he was very proud of it. He made it soon after my mother died. I think, now that he has destroyed it, he will live many years longer. He is very strong-minded."

"I'm glad to have my suspicions confirmed," said Farr.

"He was extremely angry when his eldest brother died at eighty. He stood over him in the last moments and made us all very uncomfortable by telling Uncle Joachim that there was no need of his dying—that if he would only show a little Chick spunk he could stay alive just as well as not and would not go fushing out just when he was most needed in the Friends' meeting."

"Considering that the old fellow was eighty and probably felt like quitting, seems as if your father was rubbing it in just a little."

"Perhaps he was a mite harsh, but there is another side of it. There were only three of us left of the Friends' society to go to the old meeting-house on First Day so that it might not be said that after one hundred years we had allowed the society of the fathers to perish in our town. Thee may have noted that my father and I still use the plain language, keeping up the ways of the founders. My father sat at the head of the meeting, my Uncle Joachim was next to him on the facing seat. I am the only worshiper. I am not fitted to be a minister. My father, when Joachim died, had no one with whom to exchange the hand-shake at the end of the meeting."

"And now he's losing his congregation?"

"Yes, my friend, and so my father blames me for going, just as he blamed Uncle Joachim for dying. He has the meeting much at heart."

"What will he do for a crowd after you go away?"

"He will continue to sit at the head of the meeting, sir."

There was silence between them for some time. The blacksmith clanked on his way sturdily.

"He will still sit at the head of the meeting! Only a little fire is left there, sir, but he will not allow it to go out as long as he is alive to blow the bellows of devotion."

"Look here, Brother Chick," demanded Farr. "I don't want to be prying or impertinent, but what's your idea?"

"I'm not ashamed of anything I'm going to do. Even though it is a very strange plan, as the world would look at it, I'm not ashamed of it. A very few words will tell you: I'm going out among men and spread the gospel of mercy and forbearance, teach the lessons of peace, urge men to forgive instead of fight—showing them that courts of law are more often the devil's playground than the abode of real justice. I have worked hard, I have read many books, I have stored information in my mind, I have laid up money enough. You behold my armor—I have wrought at it patiently for a long time."

"Expect to have 'em throw things at you?"

But the blacksmith, replying, gave no sign that he resented this brusque humor.

"It is well known that it is hard to attract the attention of the world from its own affairs. For instance, if I had stood in the yard to-day, dressed as a plain man, thee would have passed on thy way—providing father had been chopping up kindling-wood instead of a coffin. If I had stopped thee and started to explain my views thee would have paid little attention to me. Isn't that so?"

"It's so."

"Well, then, thee have my theory and know my plan and have noted how it has worked," said Mr. Chick.

"I don't want to discourage you in a good thing, but how long do you think a policeman would let you stand on a street corner?"

"I shall find places where I can deliver my message without offending."

"There's another point—a rather delicate point to consider, Brother Chick. There are plenty of persons who are a bit dull when they are examining a man's motives, but who think they are almighty smart in detecting a man's mental failings; when somebody does anything they wouldn't do they say he's crazy."

The blacksmith turned his serene face and smiled at Farr.

"I appeal to thy good judgment, sir. Would thee, after talking with me, even if I do wear iron outside my wool garments, send me to an asylum?"

"No," acknowledged Farr, "I don't believe I would send you to an asylum."

"Thank thee! I believe thee can speak quite generally for the average man."

"But the armor scheme—it's a little risky, Friend Chick."

"But it has been the trade-mark of unselfishness ever since the days of the Crusaders," declared Mr. Chick. "Why shouldn't its significance be revived in these modern times? At any rate," he added, with Yankee shrewdness, "it's necessary to give the world quite a jump these days before it will stop, look, and listen."

"Some advertising concern will make you an offer that will pull you into camp your second day out, if you're not careful. You've certainly got a good idea of the business."

"I am sincere. I am not trifling. I have pondered on this for a long time. I shall be misjudged—but I shall not be afraid!"

III
KNIGHT-ERRANTRY TESTED

The two marched on, side by side, and Walker Farr, piecing in his mind, from the scraps he had heard, the entire history of the Chick family, indulged the whim of Jared and forgot for a moment the grotesque figure presented by his companion.

"No, I am not afraid!" repeated the new apostle of world harmony.

But it became promptly apparent that Mr. Chick could not communicate his intrepidity to other creatures.

Around the bend of the road came a sleepy horse, stubbing his hoofs into the dust, dragging a wagon in which rode a farmer and his wife.

The horse became wide awake at sight of Mr. Chick.

With head up, eyes goggling, nostrils dilating, and mane erect, the animal stopped short on straddled legs. Then he snorted, whirled, took the wagon around in a circle on two wheels in spite of the farmer's endeavors, and made off in the opposite direction, the driver pulling hard on the reins, hands above his head, elbows akimbo.

"It occurs to me, Friend Chick," said his companion, after the outfit had disappeared, "that in planning this pilgrimage of yours you have failed to take everything into account. If that farmer-man and his wife pile into the ditch and break their necks, then all your general mediating in other quarters will hardly make up for the damage you have caused right here."

"The world is full of problems," sighed the man in armor. "There seems to be a hitch to about everything!"

After a few moments the farmer came pelting into sight on foot.

"What in the name of bald-headed Nicodemus do you call yourself, and what are you trying to do?" he shouted. "It's only by luck and chance and because the webbin's held that me and my wife ain't laying stiff and stark in the ditch."

"I am sorry," said friend Chick with dignity.

"Get a hoss used to bicycles, flying-machines, red whizzers and blue devils, and then along comes something else that ain't laid down in the back of the Old Farmer's Almanick! You there, the one that ain't crazy, what's this thing you're teaming round?" the farmer demanded, addressing Farr.

"In this case I am not my brother's keeper," stated the young man.

"Well, where is his keeper, then? He needs one." He walked around Chick and rudely rapped his whip-butt on the breastplate. "If I wasn't afraid of spraining a toe I'd boot you from here to hackenny, you old two-legged cook-stove!"

"If there has been damage done, I'll pay for it."

"There isn't any damage and I'm not looking for anybody's money. But there *will* be damage unless you get out of this highway. If you're in sight when I drive my hoss past here again I'll lick you, even if I have to use blasting-powder and a can-opener to get you out of that suit."

Jared Chick went apart into the bushes and Farr accompanied him.

"This is a rather vulgar and discouraging adventure for high ideals to run into so soon," averred the younger man.

"I am not discouraged."

"I'm afraid you'll be even more greatly misunderstood."

"I don't expect silly old horses to understand me. My appeal is to men."

Farr sniffed scornfully. "You'd better let men alone," he advised.

"The world needs pure unselfishness," insisted Chick.

"The purer it is the more it is misunderstood. I have tested the matter. I know."

"Then you yourself would not go forth into the world and do good to men, without calculation and without price?"

"I don't think I would," declared Farr, dryly. "And I am so little interested in the matter that I think you'll have to excuse me from further talk about it. You have just had one illustration in a crude way of how the world misunderstands anything that's out of the ordinary."

"Have you any advice to give me?"

"Not a word. I'm not even able to give myself sensible counsel. Good day to you!"

"Then you do not care for my company longer on the way?"

"I do not. Excuse my bluntness, but these are parlous times for wayfarers and I cannot afford to have a tin can tied to me as I go about."

"And you are absolutely selfish?" called Chick.

"I think so," replied Farr from the highway, getting into his stride. "When I see you again I expect you'll be wondering why you ever were altruistic. That will be the case, providing you wear that armor any longer."

Jared Chick from behind his bush called, appealingly, "But I fear I shall never see thee again and I have some questions to ask of thee!"

"Oh, I promise to look you up somewhere in the world. If you keep on wearing that suit it will be easy to find you."

The man in armor leaned against a tree and pondered.

"A strange young man, and callous and selfish. But there is truly something under his shell. I would relish putting some questions to him."

Then Jared Chick plunked an ash staff from a pile of hoop-poles left by a chopper and went on his way along shaded woodland paths, avoiding the main highroad. He decided that it would be better to go by the roundabout way and show himself on the streets of town instead of on a rural turnpike where countrified horses did not take kindly to a real knight-errant.

"It was a good place back there for sleeping," reflected Walker Farr, remembering the brook, singing over the stones, the whispering alders, the old-fashioned house, and the somnolent landscape. "That man who has been living there until the day of his emigration has certainly been asleep for a long time and is sleeping soundly now; he is having a wonderful dream. The nightmare will begin shortly and he will wake up."

After a time Farr came into a village, a hamlet of small houses which toed the crack of a single street. It was near the hour of noon and from the open windows of kitchens drifted scents of the dinners which the women were preparing. All the men of the place seemed to be afield; only women were in sight here and there at back doors, pinning freshly washed garments on lines, beating dust from rugs, or, seen through the windows, were bustling about the forenoon tasks set for patient household slaves in gingham.

At one back door, his back comfortably set against a folded clothes-reel, was a greasily fat tramp, gobbling a hand-out lunch which a housewife had given to him.

Under a little hill where the road dipped at the edge of the hamlet here sounded clink of steel on rock, suggesting that men labored there with trowel and drill. There was complaining creaking of cordage—the arm of a derrick sliced a slow arc across the blue sky of June.

The fat tramp held up his empty plate and whined a request and the hand of a woman emerged from a close-by window and placed something in the dish.

Farr slowed his steps and looked at the tramp, and a woman in a yard near by stared over the top of a sheet which she was pinning on the line and scowled at the new arrival.

"I wonder if I'm considered as the Damon of that Pythias?" Farr asked himself, smiling into her frown. "But Damon is nomad spelled backward! I wish I dared to ask her for a piece of that pie cooling on the sill."

Just then, over the clink of metal under the hill, above wail of straining pulley, rose the screech of a man in agony, the raucous male squall whose timbre is more hideous than the death-cry of swine.

Then came a man running from the valley under the hill.

"It's your husband, Mrs. Jose," he panted, turning in at the house where the fat tramp ate with his back against the clothes-reel. "You better go! I'll telephone for a doctor."

She ran, white-faced, gasping cries. Other women ran. The spirit of helpfulness and curiosity to know what had happened set wings on the heels of the little community. The messenger telephoned and followed them.

The fat tramp set down his plate and glanced to right and left and all about. Then he shuffled into the deserted house and after a brief stay hastened out with his pockets crammed and bearing garments in his arms; he scuttled away with sagging trot across the fields.

Farr saw him go and did not pursue.

"Yonder goes the spirit of the age," he told himself, with sardonic twisting of his lips. "When Opportunity knocks, knock Opportunity down. Embrace Opportunity, but be sure it's with the strangle hold. The directors of a robbed railroad make a more dignified getaway than that porcine pedestrian is making—but it's the same as far as the stockholders are concerned."

He went on slowly toward the hollow under the hill.

The procession met him—a limp man, moaning, borne in the arms of his sweating mates, women trotting alongside and crossing the road, to and fro, like frightened hens—clucking sympathy.

Farr found a half-finished stone bridge under the hill. A paunchy boss with underset jaw and overhanging upper lip was profanely urging his helpers back to their jobs.

"Fifteen minutes before knock-off time—fifteen minutes! You can't help that man by standing around and doing his grunting for him. Get busy!"

The men lifted their tools slowly and sullenly.

"It's hell what can happen when you're fifteen days behind on a contract, with county commissioners waiting and anxious to grab off a penalty," declared the boss, to nobody in particular. "One man bunged, and four to lug him home, and the rest of the crew taking a sympathetic vacation!"

Farr, sauntering, swung off the highway down the lane leading to the temporary bridge.

"Here, you long-horned steer, want a job?" called the contractor from his rostrum on the granite block.

"No, my Sussex shote, I do not!"

"Damnation! You dare to call me names, you hobo?"

"Yes," returned Farr, quite simply.

"Well, quit it. I need men here. You're husky. Two dollars a day, even if you're not a regular mason."

"No."

He drawled both the affirmative and the negative and there was something subtly insolent in his tone—something that aroused more ire than a cruder retort would have accomplished. He turned his back on the cursing man and went on down to the bridge. He waited there for a time and watched the drift of foam on the fretted waters. The steady burbling of the stream made him oblivious to other sounds and he did not hear the two men approach. They leaped on him and seized him. One of his captors was the paunchy man, and his hands were heavy and his fingers gripped viciously.

"No wonder you wouldn't work! You're making your living in an easier way."

"What is the occasion of this effusive welcome to your city?" asked Farr.

The man who held one of the captive's arms was panting. He had run at top speed from the house to which he and his mates had borne the injured man.

"You thief! You sneak! Eat a man's grub, his hard-earned grub, and steal when his wife's back is turned!"

"Of all dirty work this job is the worst," declared the big man.

"She gave you all you could stuff into yourself, you loafer. You ransacked when her back was turned. You even stole her husband's Sunday suit. Where is it?"

"I saw a fat tramp running away into the woods," returned Farr, quietly. "He was carrying articles in his arms."

"You're the only tramp in sight around here," insisted the contractor. "Where did you hide the plunder?"

"She said she fed a tramp. She left him at the back door. You're the sneak," indorsed the panting emissary.

"If you will take me back to the house you may get some new light on the affair," suggested their captive. "You need not drag me there. I'll go with much pleasure."

The mistress of the despoiled home, red of eyes, hurrying from her sink with a cold compress in her trembling hands, viewed Farr from her back door.

"That isn't the man. I never saw him before. Oh, he is in awful pain. Why doesn't that doctor get here? But there doesn't seem to be anything broken. He took my pocketbook, too, with two dollars and twenty-seven cents in it. And it's every cent of money we've got by us. And it may be weeks before he can go to work again. Troubles don't come singly. That mis'able, fat, greasy thief! After I had fed him—even gave him pie!"

"As I told you, gentlemen, it was a fat tramp. I saw him run away into the woods."

"If you call yourself a man why didn't you chase him?" inquired the contractor, with disgust.

"I took no interest in his affairs—no interest whatever," stated Farr, with languid tone.

"You don't care much what happens to anybody else, you hog!"

"My interest in other persons is very limited."

"You'll stand by and see one of your kind run away with the property of poor folks, will you? You meet him later and get your whack?" asked the big man.

"No," said Farr, mildly. He directed compelling gaze into the eyes of his detractor. "And you do not think so yourself."

"Perhaps not. But you're worse. You have just said it. You're a selfish renegade!"

"Peculiarly selfish, hard, and unfeeling."

"And wouldn't turn your hand over to do a good turn for anybody?"

"I don't think so."

"I'll tell you what I think *I'll* do—I'll detail four of my men to ride you out of this town on a rail."

"I wouldn't call them off their jobs if I were you! I overheard you say that you are short of time and men. By the way, you offered me a job. I'll take it."

The contractor blinked and hesitated.

"If after a half-day you find I'm not worth the money I'll pass on and you'll have a half-day's work free."

"Get on to the job, then."

Through the open door Farr could see the woman of the house wringing cloths at the sink.

He stepped to the door and addressed her. "Madame, will you take a boarder? I'm going to do your husband's work on the job yonder. I will pay liberally. In your present difficulties the money may help. I'll be small trouble."

"We need the money terribly," she said, after pondering. "Yes, I will take you. In the face you do not look like a tramp!"

"I thank you," said Farr. "If you will give me some food in my hands I'll take myself out of your way."

That afternoon Jared Chick came over the hill where the trowels clinked and the great derrick complained with its pulleys. He carried his armor on his back.

He stopped and watched for some time his former companion of the road, who was sweating over his man's toil.

"May I have sixty seconds off to speak with that man yonder?" Farr asked the contractor. "It partly concerns your business."

The big man nodded surly assent.

"Thee sees I have taken off the armor for a time. I will wear it in the city where horses and people are not so silly. What is thee doing here?"

"I have no time to talk about myself, Friend Chick. I want to ask you if you are still of the same mind about your mission?"

"I am."

"Then throw down that hardware and come to work on this job. A man has been hurt here—his wife is in need. Earn some money and give it to them."

"But my mission concerns the world—the wide world."

"Real selfishness's chief excuse! Here's something ready to your hand. Will you do it?"

"But thee told me thee would not go forth and do good!"

"No matter about me. I am not a professional knight-errant! Will you do this?"

"Ten seconds more!" warned the boss.

"I cannot change my plans so suddenly," protested Chick.

"A knight-errant should not have plans! My time is up and I have work. Good-by, Friend Chick!"

The young man went back to his task and the Quaker passed on, muttering reaffirmation of his own high aims.

"And how could I expect a vagrant to understand?" he asked himself.

The vagrant toiled two weeks at his heavy task and when the man Jose was about again the volunteer slipped away without farewell.

He left on the table of his under-the-eaves bedroom in the Jose house all the pay he received for his work, to the last penny.

"He wasn't what he seemed to be," ran the burden of Mrs. Jose's various disquisitions on this strange guest. "He ate his vittles and asked no questions, and was out from underfoot, and was always willing to set up with my husband and give me a snippet of rest and a wink of sleep; and he read out of little books all the time—he had 'em stuffed into his pockets. And there needn't anybody tell *me*! He left all his pay on the table, every cent of it, and stole away without waiting for no thanks from nobody!"

IV
FARR, THE FAT TRAMP, AND
A SUIT OF CLOTHES

On a balmy forenoon a jovial-appearing old gentleman went jogging out of the mill city of Marion and along a country road in his two-wheeled chaise. He sat erect and he was tall above the average of men, and he was very neat in his attire.

"I wish," he mused, "that the men who could really appreciate a good outfit of clothing and could use the same properly were not so infernally touchy. As it is, cranky human nature drives me out on an expedition like this—and I'm afraid I am just as cranky as the rest of 'em, otherwise I wouldn't be doing this!"

The old gentleman hummed a song under his breath and slapped his reins against the flanks of the plodding horse to keep time. He came into a piece of woodland. He seemed to take cheery and fresh interest in this place. He poked his rubicund face out from the shadow of the chaise's canopy and peered to right and to left. There was a smile in his puckery eyes. When there were trees ahead of him, trees behind him, and trees all about he pulled his old horse to a standstill.

He listened, squinted quizzically through the glass of his chaise's rear curtain, and then climbed down. From a box at the rear of the vehicle he secured various articles of clothing and draped them over his arm. There was a frock-coat, not too badly worn, trousers in good repair, waistcoat, and a shirt. He also took out of the box a pair of shoes and a hat. With this load he went to the roadside and began to rig out a fence-post. When the garments were hung on it and the broad-brimmed, black, slouch-hat had been jauntily set on top of the post, anybody could see that the old gentleman was thus disposing of some of his own extra clothing. He was wearing a similar hat and a frock-coat, himself, and the decorated post took on a bizarre and slouchy resemblance to its decorator.

He went back to the chaise and found a nickel alarm-clock in the box. He wound this up carefully and propped it on a rail of the fence near the clothing.

Before he could escape from the vicinity of the exhibit and get into his chaise a wagon came rattling around the bend of the road. There were firkins and jars in the rear of this wagon and the driver was plainly a farmer-man.

He pulled up short and then saluted the old gentleman with a stab of forefinger at his hat-brim.

"Any trouble, Judge?" he inquired, affably.

"None at all," replied the old gentleman, edging away from the fully garbed fence-post.

"Airing 'em out, hey?" A jab of the forefinger toward the garments.

"No, leaving them out."

All at once the old gentleman appeared to remember something else. He took off his hat and produced a placard. He straightened it and stuck it into a crack in a fence-rail. Its legend was "Help Yourself."

"You're giving them clothes away, are you, Judge Peterson?"

"I am leaving them here for any one who chooses to take them. Do you want first pick, Jolson?"

"Not me! I ain't taking charity hand-me-downs from any man, Judge. If it's a polite question, why are you giving away your duds this way?"

"I think you have just answered that question, Jolson. I offered you these clothes. Your nose went into the air. Other men have acted in the same way in the past when I have offered to give a fellow a good suit. I don't want to hurt other folks' feelings. I don't want to have my own feelings hurt. So, let any man help himself when no one is looking."

"I'll take the alarm-clock, if you say so," volunteered Jolson. "It'll help to rout me out of bed at milking-time."

"No, you cannot have the clock, Jolson. I have tinkered it so that it will purr a little every half-hour. It will call attention to the clothes. You see, a good many men rush through life without looking to right or left, and so they miss a lot of opportunities."

Jolson clucked to his horse and rattled away down the road, muttering sour remarks.

The old gentleman, with the air of a man who has satisfied his philanthropic ambitions, climbed into his chaise and followed the farmer.

The brisk breeze flirted the tails of the frock-coat and the trousers legs tried out a modest little gig as if some of the jocose spirit of the old gentleman had remained with the garments he had discarded.

There were several passers before another half-hour had elapsed.

The trousers kicked out quite hilariously when a young couple drove by in a buggy. The girl was pretty, and companionship with her might have suited even a judge's garments. But the young man and the girl were quite absorbed in each other, and the trousers kicked and the frock-coat flirted ineffectually.

A peddler's cart passed very slowly, but the driver did not look up from a paper filled with figures.

There were others to whom the judge's garments offered themselves mutely, but no one glanced that way and the clock was discreetly silent. The breeze died down and the trousers and the coat hung with a sort of homeless, homesick, and wistful air. One might have thought they were trying to conceal themselves when the next person appeared, so still were they. He was not an inviting person—not such a new lord and master as a judge's garments might be expected to welcome.

He was grossly fat and his own trousers were lashed about his bulging waist with a frayed belt; his coat was sun-faded, a greasy Scotch cap was pulled over to one side on his head with the peak hauled down upon his ear, and he scuffed along in boots that were disreputable. Surely, a most unseemly and unwholesome character to be wrapped in the habiliments of a judge! But just then, with that cursed inappropriateness of inanimate things, the clock jangled its alarm.

The tramp—there was no mistaking that gait and that general air of the vagrant—snapped himself about, located the noise, stared at the post, and then hurried to it. He made sure that there was no one in sight. He scooped all into his arms, climbed the fence and trotted into the woods. He kept looking behind him as if he feared pursuit. It was plain from his disturbed demeanor that he was much perplexed and was chased by the uncomfortable thought that he was stealing this property. He bestowed so much attention behind him that he paid but little attention to what was ahead of him, and so he ran down into a little bowl of a valley among the trees and stopped short there, for he had come upon a man.

It was the man who called himself Walker Farr.

The man was kneeling beside a tiny fire, toasting bread on the end of a beech twig. He held the twig in one hand and an open book in the other. He looked up without changing his position when the tramp came charging down the hillside.

He had wide-open, brown eyes, this man in the hollow. The eyes were not merely wide open on account of surprise at this irruption—one could see that they were naturally that way—keenly observant eyes. He had hair as brown as his eyes; his cap was on the ground beside him.

But the tramp was not taking account of the attractions of this stranger; he was more interested in searching for flaws.

He had been frightened at first sight of the man—for the tramp had the timidity of his kind; now he began to feel cheered. This stranger in the hollow had not been shaved recently, his clothing was unkempt, his shoes bore the marks of a long hike. He was cooking in the open—plain indication of the nomad.

"Well, I say, bo," chaffed the tramp, shifting from fright to high spirit with the hysteria of weak natures. "I'm sure glad to see one of the good old sort. I didn't know what I was dropping in on when I fell down that hill. But it's all right, hey? I'm on the road. My name is Boston Fat, and my monacker is a bean-pot."

The brown eyes moved slowly from the grinning face to the garments heaped in the man's arms. They were cold and critical eyes and there was no humor in them.

"I do not do business during my lunch-hours, my man. I do not desire to change tailors just yet and I do not buy stolen property."

His chilliness did not dampen the other's good nature.

"Oh, that's all right, old top. I'm no thief. These clothes were hung on a fence-post just above here on the road. I reckon they were only waiting for first-comer."

He dropped the shoes, cocked the hat on his head, and began to fumble the garments. The placard dropped out of the folds of the coat and the man at the fire craned his neck and read aloud: "Help Yourself."

"Oh, that's what the paper says, hey? I never learned to read any of the modern languages," confided Boston Fat. "I was too much taken up with the dead ones at Harvard. Well, comrade, now you can see for yourself that I didn't steal this mess of moth-food. There was the sign right on it saying,

'Help Yourself.' It was there, even if I couldn't read it. Instinck told me them clothes was for me. I took 'em and came in here."

He shook out the garments one by one and hung them on a bush, chattering his comments. He set the ticking clock on a stump.

The man at the fire slipped a piece of meat between two slabs of toasted bread and began to eat. He still held the open book in his hand but his eyes were watching the tramp.

The vagrant was orally appraising his find, exhibiting the wisdom of one who has begged garments at back doors for the purposes of peddling them to second-hand shops.

"A moucher," observed the man at the fire. He continued aloud, evidently and sardonically exercising his vocabulary, plainly enjoying the amazement he provoked by his style of language. "The spirit of a stray cat at midnight, the tastes of the prowling hyena! The fat thief I saw running away into the woods! When such as these began to take to the road, knight-errantry vanished from the face of the earth. The varlets borrowed the grand idea of care-free itinerancy and debased it, as waiters borrow a gentleman's evening dress for their menial uniform, and drunken coachmen wear the same head-gear that a duke wears to a wedding! Why prove evolution by searching for a man with a tail? The performances of human nature must convince any thinking man that we have descended from apes!"

The astonished tramp stared for a short time at this person who employed such peculiar language—then mumbled an oath and shook his head.

He began to try on the frock-coat, paying scant attention to the other's monologue. The coat was a ludicrous misfit; it would not meet over the bulging belly; its tails dragged on the fat man's heels.

"If I happened to stand handy by when a Kansas cyclone ripped the insides out of a clothing-store only the boys' sizes would drop in the same county with me," grumbled the tramp, working his arms out of the sleeves.

"The coat was plainly built for a gentleman," stated the man at the fire. "Therefore it is of no value to you."

Boston Fat surveyed the stranger with a vicious glint in his little eyes, as a pig might stare at a man who had struck it across the snout.

"Good afternoon, perfesser," he sneered.

"Why 'professor,' my frayed and frowsled Falstaff?"

"There you go with it—showing yourself up out of your own mouth! Words a yard long—words that would break a decent man's teeth! You're one of these college dudes out on the road getting stuff to write into a book. I've heard about your kind. And that kind is getting too thick and plenty and you're putting slush all over the real profesh. Quit it and go back to college. Don't use me for your book."

This was reciprocation of derogatory sentiment with a vengeance!

The man at the fire sat back on his haunches. He finished chewing his mouthful, regarding the tramp with a languid stare that traveled from crown of his head to tip of his battered shoe.

"The only thing about a book that you would be good for," he said, "would be for use in a volume of this sort." He tapped the book in his palm. "Your anatomy could supply the binding. It is bound in pigskin."

The tramp squealed an oath in the falsetto voice that the weak and the flabby possess and took one step forward. The man at the fire came to his feet and stood erect. He was tall, and the brown eyes talked for him better than threats or bluster. The vagrant shifted his gaze from those eyes and backed away.

"If I hadn't been penned in a pie-belt jail all winter up North, and all the strength starved out of me," he whined, "you wouldn't call me a pig and get away with it."

"A person who forces himself into the presence of a gentleman who is dining mustn't expect compliments," stated the stranger.

"You ain't a tramp—not a real one," snarled Boston Fat.

Farr's eyes glistened; he smiled; he continued to play on this ignoramus his satiric pranks of mystifying language:

"More of your lack of acuteness, my fat friend. Because I do not patter the flash lingo with you, you appear to take me for a college professor in disguise. *You* are not a real tramp. You are a bum, a loafer, a yeg. You never traveled more than two hundred miles away from Hoboken—the capital city of hoboes. Have you ever hit the sage-brush trail, hiked the milk-and-honey route from Ogden through the Mormon country, decked the Overland Express, beaten the blind baggage on the Millionaires' Flier? Hey?"

The sullen vagrant blinked stupidly.

"Or have you made the prairie run on the truss of a Wagner freight, or thrown a stone at the Fox Train crew, or beaten the face off the Katy Shack when he tried to pitch you off a gondola-car?"

"I don't know what you're chewing about," sneered the fat man.

"Probably not, for you are not a true man of the road. You disgrace the name of nomad, you sully an ancient profession. I'll venture to say you don't know who Ishmael was."

"Who said I did?"

"Not I, because I'm not a flatterer. I am going to follow the example of the man who cast pearls before swine—I'm going to cast you a pearl from one of my own poems. You may listen. It will pass your ears, that's all. You cannot contaminate it by taking it in, so I repeat it for my own entertainment, to refresh my memory:

> *"Of the morrow we take no heed, no care infests the day;*
> *Some hand-out gump and a train to jump, a grip on the rods, and away!*
> *To the game of grab for gold we give no thought or care.*
> *We own with you the arch of blue—our share of God's fresh air.*
> *One coin to clear the law, a section of rubber hose.*
> *To soften the chafe of a freight-car's truss, our portion of cast-off clothes,*
> *And the big wide world is ours—a title made good by right—*
> *By mankind's deed to the nomad breed with the taint of the Ishmaelite.*
> *Some from the wastes of the sage-brush, some from the orange land,*
> *Some from God's own country, dusty and tattered and tanned.*
> *Why are we? It's idle to tell you—you'd never understand.*
> *To and fro*
> *We come and go.*
> *Old Father Ishmael's band."*

He leaned back and laughed in the tramp's puzzled face.

"Well, what's the answer?" scoffed Boston Fat.

The other man talked on, humor in his eyes, plainly enjoying this verbal skylarking.

"I'm afraid I cannot waste time and breath on you in an attempt to answer the riddle of the ages, to explain the wanderlust that sent forth the tribes from the Aryan bowl of the birth of the races, my corpulent bean-pot. Your blank eyes and your flattened skull suggest a discouraging incapacity for information."

"I don't know what you're gabbing abut. But there's one thing I do know. I'll tip 'em off at the next insane-asylum I come to that I met you headed north." The tramp gathered the articles of clothing from the bushes and got down on his knees and began to fold them.

The man of the brown eyes stepped forward, laid down his little book, picked up the frock-coat and pulled it on, the fat man squealing expostulation. With serene disregard of this protest Farr buttoned the coat, smoothed it down, and then straightened his shoulders.

"You may see that it was built for a gentleman and that it fits a gentleman, friend pork-barrel."

"You shuck it off and pass it over, that's what you do," yelped the tramp. "It's my coat."

"It was perfectly apparent that it was not your coat when you tried it on."

"I tell you I found it hanging on a fence-post just above here."

"That was merely by accident, and you should have passed on and left the garments for one whose frame was fitted to wear them. You illustrate the curse of modern society. Men are so filled with the greed of getting that they grab misfits simply out of passion for possessing."

"I've stood your slurs ever since I got here, but I'll be jobeefed if I'll stand for your swiping my property."

The man of the brown eyes smiled. His whole demeanor showed that he was more than ever hugely enjoying his own verbosity—the florid language which was both maddening and mystifying the tramp.

"Further evidence of your mean nature: a gentleman resents an insult that steals away his character much more quickly than he resents an act that steals mere property. In that little book which I have just laid down Shakespeare speaks trenchantly on that matter: 'Who steals my purse steals trash . . . but he that filches from me my good name robs me . . . and makes me poor indeed.'"

The tramp gave over his work of folding, and awkwardly and cumbersomely got upon his feet.

"You take off that coat and hand it over. It's mine—I found it. I can stand a crazy man's gab, but when any one tries to do me out of what's my own I'll fight."

"May I ask what you're going to do with these garments of a gentleman which have fallen into your hands by accident?"

"I'm going to cash 'em in at the nearest second-hand shop, that's just what I'm going to do."

"Just as you sold the Sunday suit you stole from a poor man! My friend, I was insulted that day on account of you. You owe me something!"

Just then the alarm-clock purred a brief signal.

Up to that time the air of the man with the brown eyes had been that of banter, of impish desire to harry and confuse by stilted language the ignorant stranger who had come blundering upon him.

He stared at the clock, looked down upon the frock-coat, and then surveyed the other articles of clothing. He scowled as if he had suddenly begun to reflect. Seriousness smoldered in the brown eyes. That tinkling touch of metal against metal seemed to change his mood in astonishing fashion.

"Ah, it may be morning again, O my soul!" he cried with such tense feeling in his voice that the tramp surveyed him with gaping mouth and bulging eyes, as one stares at a person suddenly become mad.

"I will talk to you though you will not understand! Once upon a time the world was ruled by men who were ruled by omens. Man was then not so wise in his own conceit. His own soul was nearer the soul of things. He was not a mere gob of bumptiousness covered with the shell of cocksureness. He was willing to be informed. He sought the omens of true nature—he allowed Fate to guide him. He was not a pig running against the goad of circumstances, unheeding the upflung arms of Fortune, waving him toward the right path. He was simpler—he was truer. He felt that he was a part of nature instead of being boss of nature. Well, I have got nearer to true nature since I have been in the open. I am in contact with the soul of things. I am no longer insulated. I am not reformed, I am simply ready once again to grab Opportunity. So you think I am crazy, do you?"

"They had a gink in a padded cell in the jail where I was last winter and he didn't take on much worse'n you," stated the tramp.

"As a brainless observer you may be quite right. I may be a lunatic. I feel much like one just now. It is lunacy to go climbing back to a level in society from which I have been kicked. But as I knelt there by that little fire, before you came, yearning sprang up in me—and I had thought all that sort of yearning was dead in me. A moment later came habiliments of a gentleman, borne in the arms of a wretch who could not wear them. There came Opportunity. Then the jangle of that clock signaled Opportunity—and there was a throb in me as though my sleeping soul had rolled and blinked at the sunlight of hope and had murmured, 'It's morning again.' Such are omens, when one is ready to heed."

He set his teeth, clenched his fists, and by expression and attitude showed that he had arrived at a decision of moment. He walked close to the tramp. "I will admit, Friend Belly-brains, that you came upon Opportunity before I did this day. But tell me again, are you to make no further use of said Opportunity than to run to an old-clothes shop and exchange for a few pennies that which will help to make a man?"

"They are mine and I'm going to sell 'em," retorted the sullen vagrant.

"I am sorry because you have no wit—no power to understand. Otherwise you would gladly lay these garments in my hands and bid me Godspeed. You don't understand at all, do you?"

"Look here, are you trying to frisk me for these duds?"

"It's all a waste of breath to explain to you that Providence meant these things for me. You are not acute enough to understand close reasoning. I could not show you that, for the sake of a few coins, which would do you only that harm which would come from their value in cheap whisky or beer, you might be wrecking the future of a soul that is awake. I simply tell you that I shall keep the clothing for myself. Perhaps you can understand that plain statement!" The brown eyes became resolute and piercing. "Even if I had money I would not pay you for these garments. Money does such as you no good; it may bring you trouble. My dear Boston Fat, I cannot afford to let you prejudice my future, which, so instinct tells me, is wrapped up in those poor things of wool and warp." He snapped a finger into his palm and extended his hand. "Give me that hat and then pass on about your business."

The tramp backed away. His little blinking eyes expressed both fear and rebelliousness. More than ever did he resemble a pig at bay. The black hat, set on top of his greasy cap and topping with its respectability his disreputable general outfit, added a bizarre touch to the scene between the two men.

"You think now that you are the injured party," calmly pursued the man of the brown eyes. "You haven't intelligence enough to take my own case into account. You are injured because you are losing a few coins—but I may be injured in all that gives life its flavor if I do not grasp this opportunity." Both raillery and earnestness dropped out of his tones. He became merely matter-of-fact. "I'll make it plain. Trot along about your business, fat one, or I shall proceed to pound the face off you and then kick you a few rods on your happy way. You deserve it as a thief—I worked two weeks as a stone-mason on your account. Do you get me?"

For answer the infuriated vagrant rushed at him and kicked.

With one hand the stranger plucked the hat from the tramp's head and sailed it to a place of safety. With the other hand he grabbed the attacker's ankle before the foot hit him and with a jerk he laid the tramp on his back.

The victim fell so helplessly that the concussion knocked the breath and a groan out of him.

The man of the brown eyes had moved languidly and had talked languidly till then. When he grabbed the foot he moved with a sort of steel-trap efficiency and quickness. He promptly straddled his victim, seated himself on the protruding abdomen, and began to beat the man's face. He battered the flabby cheeks and punched his fists into the pulpy neck. He ground his knees against the fat flanks and redoubled his blows when the tramp struggled. After the squalling falsetto had implored for a long time, the assailant at last gave over the exercise.

"Are you licked?" he asked.

"Yes," whined the tramp.

"You have stolen—in most dirty style. I whipped you for that job. Now will you stay licked for some time?"

"Yes."

"You'll go on about your own business, will you, without any more foolish talk about those garments?"

"Yes."

"Are you sorry you stole from that good woman who fed you?"

"Yes."

The man of the brown eyes swung himself off his prostrate victim, as a rider dismounts from a horse, and the tramp sat up, moaning and patting his purple face.

"I never had no luck, never," he blubbered. "I was kicked out of jail before the weather got warmed up, I was thrown in last fall just when the Indian summer was beginning. When other fellows get hand-outs of pie I get cold potatoes and bannock bread. I have to walk when other fellows ride. I'm too fat for the trucks and they can always see me on the blind baggage. I'll keep on walking. I never had no luck in all my life."

He rolled upon his hands and knees and then stood up. He started away, wholly cowed, whining like a quill-pig, bewailing his luck.

"Luck!" the man of the brown eyes shouted after him in a tone which expressed anger and regret. "What do you know about luck, you animated lard-pail? A thing like you is in luck when he is in jail where there is no workshop. Better luck than that is too good for you. Hold on one minute! Turn around and look at me."

The tramp obeyed. The stranger pounded one of those hard fists on his own breast.

"I say look at me! No matter what I was once! But to-day you found me cooking bacon over three sticks and ready to fight for another man's cast-off clothes. And in between whiles I have hiked every path that the hobo knows between the oceans. Now jog on and think that over and keep your jaw shut on luck! I say jog on! Don't look back. Forget that you ever saw me."

He waved angry gesture and took two steps as though to enforce his command with his fists.

The tramp jogged on at a brisk pace. He hurried to the highway and set out on his shuffling pilgrimage, rubbing his aching face and muttering to himself.

V
THE GIRL WHO GUARDED HER LIPS

The brown eyes of the victor watched the tramp out of sight and for some moments surveyed the nick in the undergrowth where the fellow had disappeared.

There was no anger in the eyes. There had been none while their possessor had been pummeling the wretch. He had beaten the man up in a calm, methodical and perfectly business-like manner.

When at last he turned and looked at the clothing he smiled whimsically.

"The perambulating pork-barrel thinks I am crazy," he mused, looking at the frock-coat. He had stripped that garment from his shoulders and had tossed it on a bush when he had decided on combat. "If I should stop to argue the matter with myself just now I should find myself flattering his good judgment. I have robbed a poor devil for a whim. Thank God, I went at it brutally and frankly. There was no 'high finance' sneak-thieving about that job. I sent him away with his face smarting. They sent me away with my soul black-and-blue."

He gathered the garments, picked up the shoes, put the hat on top of the pile on his arm, and went farther into the woods, following the course of a tiny stream of water. This stream led him to a pool. It was tree-bordered, it was a center gem in a dim alcove in the forest, it was as secret as a private chamber. The pool was glassy, for the winds were still in the tree-tops.

The man laid down his burden. He stripped off his own well-worn coat and shirt, and secured a razor and stick of soap from the scattered articles he dumped from the coat pocket. He kneeled on the brink of the pool, leaned over and shaved himself carefully, using the glassy surface as a mirror. Then he put off his other clothing, the mean garments of a vagrant, and plunged into the pool.

When he came forth from the water and dried himself with his discarded shirt, he revealed himself to the birds whom his splashings had attracted to the branches above the pool. If the birds' twitterings were comments on his appearance, they must have been admiring comments. The man's skin was white and he was lithe and tense and muscular. Breeding showed in him as it shows in the muscles and conformation of a race-horse. When he was dried he threw down the makeshift towel and combed his shock of brown hair with his fingers. Now that the bristle of beard was off his face he looked younger.

From the pile of clothing he selected his outfit, garment by garment. The jovial humor of the judge had provided complete equipment for a man. In the breast pockets of the frock-coat there were a clean collar, a necktie, and a freshly laundered handkerchief.

By the time he had finished his dressing the pool was still and glassy once more. He flirted out the handkerchief, holding it by one corner, and swept the soft fabric around and around the crown of the black hat.

He carefully set the hat on his head and leaned over the pool and took an interested peep at himself.

"You are a fool in this matter," he informed the reflection. "And I wonder why you are determined to persist in the folly. The man Chick's tin suit cannot bring as much trouble to him as this garb of respectability may bring to you. For no man can step up to that poor Quaker and touch his shoulder and say—"

He broke off. He began to search through his discarded garments and to stow his few possessions into the pockets of his new attire.

"All folly!" ran his thoughts. "I am consumed with it all of a sudden. I have ranted to a tramp. Now I rant at myself. I am sloughing the rags that have protected me. All folly!"

His searching fingers, groping to the deepest corner of a pocket, found the crumbling fragments of a dried rose. He narrowed his eyes and surveyed it as it lay in his palm, and then made as if to toss it into the pool. But he checked the gesture. He set his chin in his hands and communed aloud with himself after the fashion of those who hold aloof from mankind:

"Folly, little sister! I may as well be truthful! Two dark eyes which gave me the first honest, unafraid, and frank gaze I've had from a maid in two years, two red lips which said 'Please' and 'Thank you'! A flash of a glance behind her which called me, even if she did not mean it as a call—and so, on I fare in a lunatic's dream. Own up! I have dreamed that some day I will see her again. And down in the depths of me stirs that impulse of the male which makes the peacock spread his feathers and silly man perk in front of a mirror. Why not give in to the sense of heredity once in a while even though it means beating up a tramp and making myself more of a mark for human eyes?"

He rolled the old clothes into a bundle and stuffed them under the roots of a tree. Then he strolled away leisurely, and when he as in the wider stretches of the wood where the light was better he pulled a small book from his pocket and read as he walked.

The volume was *Sartor Resartus*. His eyes happened to find this passage and he smiled as he read:

All visible things are emblems. Hence clothes, as despicable as we think them, are so unspeakably significant. Clothes, from the King's mantle downward, are emblematic not of want only but of a manifold cunning victory over want. Men are properly said to be clothed with authority, clothed with beauty, with curses and the like. It is written, the Heavens and the Earth shall fade away like a vesture; which indeed they are: the time vesture of the Eternal. Whatsoever sensibly exists, whatsoever represents spirit to spirit, is properly a clothing, a suit of raiment, put on for a season and to be laid off. Thus in this one pregnant subject of clothes, rightly understood, is included all that men have thought, dreamed, done, and been; the whole Eternal Universe and what it holds is but clothing; and the essence of all science lies in the Philosophy of Clothes.

From time to time he looked down upon himself complacently.

When he came near a glade in the wood he heard the chatter of the voices of a merry party and he saw picnickers, men and women, gathered about hampers. Automobiles were parked at a little distance, and he made a detour to avoid the scene.

He emerged upon an animated tableau of modern nymph and modish satyr in a close-by forest aisle. The girl was flushed and disheveled and was resisting a young man who had pushed aside her veil and was kissing her with ardor. She beat him back with her gloved hands and eluded him, but he caught her to him with more of rough passion than tender affection.

"We are engaged to be married," he insisted. "Why shouldn't I kiss you? Don't be a prude!"

She thrust her protesting palms against him and set her arms rigidly and held her head away, not with coyness, but with indignation and fierce rebellion.

"I love you! My God, can't you understand?" he gasped. "I can't keep my hands off you. You can't handle a man as you're trying to handle me. I must have some affection from you!"

"Richard! I'll not endure this! I am insulted!"

"My kisses an insult? I'm no ice-water lover. You set me crazy. I can't help myself."

She wrenched herself from his grasp and faced him, her face filled with outraged fury.

Farr had started to leave the scene. He stopped. The girl was the girl of the red lips and the dark eyes.

"Don't touch me!" she cried. "The only promise you have had from me, Richard, is the one my mother has fairly forced from me. I am trying honestly to like you. I will please my mother and you if I can."

"That's a devil of a thing to say to a man who loves you as I do," he declared, with anger.

"That is all I can say just now. But if you use me again as you would pull and haul a girl of the streets, I'll despise you. I give you warning."

"What sort of books have you been reading, Kate?" he asked, sarcastically. "Where did you get your idea of what love-making is? They don't sing serenades under windows these days. They don't kiss finger-tips and write mush poems. I am going to tell you a few things you ought to know, as a girl engaged to be married."

Farr stood close by them and in plain sight, but their absorption in their struggle had left them attention only for each other. He knew that if he started away while they were talking his presence would be promptly noted and undoubtedly misjudged.

He set his finger between the leaves of his book and took his hat in his hand.

"Your pardon!" he pleaded. "I stumbled here quite by accident. Please suspend conversation on private matters until I can walk out of earshot."

He stared straight into the eyes of the girl and once more received from her that frank and wondering gaze which had touched him so strangely when he had seen her first on the broad highway. His face was white under the tan. His hands trembled as he replaced his hat. In his heart he was saying farewell to her and his eyes expressed some of his emotion.

"You may take your own time, sir," said the girl. "This gentleman and I have finished our conversation." She passed Farr, looking him up and down with increasing curiosity and dawning recognition, and when her escort called to her impatiently, she caught her skirts around her and ran toward the glade where the others of the party were chattering over their hampers.

The lover started away slowly and sullenly on her trail, with only a glance at this blundering stranger.

"No, they do not sing serenades under windows any more—nor has the stone age returned with its love-making manners," remarked Farr, his lips trembling and his emotion still in his eyes. "There are some manners which were worse, however, than knocking maidens down with clubs."

The other man snapped himself around on his heels.

"Damn you, you're that fresh hobo! I don't forget a man who shoots off low-down sneers at me. Here! You come back here! I want to ask a few questions, my man."

Farr continued on his way, opening his book.

"If I ever see you again—" blustered the lover.

"I sincerely hope that will never happen," remarked the stranger, without turning his head. "Instinct of the purely animal sort tells me that if our paths cross in this life it will be very bad for one or the other."

When Farr was in the highway he fumbled in his pocket and found the withered rose. He tossed it away among the roadside bushes.

But after he had gone on his way for some distance he retraced his steps and hunted in the bushes for a long time on his hands and knees until he found the poor little keepsake.

He put it carefully into the deepest pocket he could find in his newly acquired habiliments and trudged on down the world.

VI
A MAN ON FOOT AND A MAN IN HIS CHARIOT

A blatant orator, haranguing passionately, attracted two new auditors.

A tall young man sauntered to the edge of the little group in the square and listened with a smile which indicated cynical half-interest.

An automobile halted on the opposite side of the group. A big man sat alone in the tonneau.

He began to scowl as he listened.

The young man continued to smile.

The big man was plainly a personality. He was cool and crisp in summer flannels—as immaculate as the accoutrements of his car.

In face and physique the young man was plainly not of that herd near which he stood.

His glance crossed that of the man in the car; he met the scowl with his smile.

Like a kiln open to the hot glare from a brassy sky or an oven where the July caloric blazed like a blast from the open mouth of a retort—such that day seemed Moosac Square in the heart of the cotton-mill city. High buildings closed in its treeless, ill-paved, dirty area. The air, made blistering by the torch of the sun, beat back and forth between the buildings in shimmering waves.

In the center of the square the blatant orator balanced himself on a stone trough which was arid and dust-choked. He harangued the group of unkempt men; sweating, blinking, apathetic men; slouchy men; men who were ticketed in attire and demeanor with all the squalid marks of idlers, vagrants, and the unemployed.

The man on the trough was of the ilk of the men who surrounded him. His face was flaming with the heat and with his vocal efforts. Perspiration streamed into his eyes, his voice was hoarse with shouting, but he had the natural eloquence of the demagogue. He was delivering the creed of the propaganda of rebellious poverty, the complaints of the dissatisfied, the demands of the idle agitators. He spiked his diatribe with threats flavored by anarchy. He pointed to policemen who had taken refuge in strips of shade which had been cast grudgingly by the high buildings. He reminded his hearers that those policemen had just driven them out of the tree-shaded parks. There the selfish rich folks were loafing under the trees. Poor folks were herded down the street and were forced to hold this meeting in that Gehenna, so he averred.

The man in the automobile muttered impatient words. Then he shouted, breaking in on the impassioned anathema which the orator addressed to the rich: "Stop lying to these men—stirring them up. The parks are for the people. You can go there—all you men can go there—if you'll go without making a disturbance."

"If men in these days open their mouths to speak for their human rights it's a disturbance," retorted the demagogue. "If we go up to the park and sit there and tremble like rabbits you rich men will let us stay there—perhaps! But we don't have as many rights there as the rabbits, for the rabbits are allowed to step on the grass."

"You've got to obey the law like other citizens—you will not be allowed to disturb decent and respectable people. You and men like you must stop putting foolish notions in the heads of loafers in this city."

"Then put something into our mouths—give us food. Why are we loafers?"

"Because you won't go to work. I'll give every able-bodied man here all the work he wants. Apply at the office of the Consolidated Water Company—now."

"What's the work?" inquired a man in the crowd.

"Digging trenches for water-pipes. How many men want that work? Hold up hands."

"It ain't work for human beings in this weather," snarled the man who had inquired. No hands were raised.

"That's your style!" blazed the big man. The policemen had sauntered into the square and their presence was reassuring. He stood up and began to lecture them.

"And them's the kind of lord dukes that's running this country to-day—own it and run it," growled a slouchy fellow who stood near the tall young man. "They ain't willing to give a poor man a show."

"He has just offered you a show—all of you," stated the young man.

"Yes, a Guinea job for white men."

"You're picking a poor excuse for being a loafer, my friend."

"Who says I'm a loafer?"

The young man shot out his hands and grasped the fellow's elbow and hand. The arm was flabby, the palm was soft. He doubled back the fingers and exhibited the palm to the crowd.

"I don't find any labor medals here, men. Is there anybody in the crowd who can show some?" He released the struggling, cursing captive.

"What's labor medals?" inquired a bystander.

The big man was still denouncing them from his car, but the group paid little attention now.

"Callous spots in the place where a working-man ought to wear them. And that place isn't on the tongue."

"Are you sneering at us because we can't get a job?"

"You're a loafer yourself, and anybody can see it," declared another.

The young man raised his arms, showing them his palms.

"I carry a few labor medals," he returned, curtly.

"Why ain't you on your job? The lord dukes won't give you one?"

"*When* I work and *where* I work is my own business, so long as I don't beg food at back doors."

"Do *we*?"

They had crowded around him and menaced him with murmurings and glowering gaze.

"I should say so," he replied, giving them an indifferent going-over with his cold eyes. "You carry all the marks."

Then he shouldered his way out from among them, displaying the air of one who found further discourse unprofitable.

He strolled leisurely in the direction of the big man in the car. The crowd he had left stared after him without presuming to voice taunt or reply; there was something compelling about him.

As Farr approached the automobile its owner stopped talking and stared at the tall stranger with some apprehension. Then the big man beckoned unobtrusively to a policeman. It was evident that Farr was not of the same sort as the ruck of men from among whom he had just emerged, nevertheless he had come from among them. The lordly man in the car had observed him moving in the group, for Farr had loomed above the heads of the others; what he had been saying to the malcontents the big man had not been able to hear, but he guessed.

"Some sort of sneak has been stirring up the fools in this city lately," the aristocrat informed the officer who came promptly to the side of the car. "Who is this fellow coming?"

"I never saw him before, Colonel Dodd."

"Stand by! He is going to tackle me and make a grand-stand play in front of his gang. His clothes give him away—a loafing demagogue!"

But the tall man did not pause at the car or even glance at the dignitary who occupied it. He seemed to have lost all interest in the occasion. He yawned as he passed the automobile and started away across the square.

"Here, you! You big chap!" called Colonel Dodd, promptly emboldened.

Farr halted and turned, his countenance showing mild inquiry.

"What do you mean by coming into a peaceable city and stirring up labor troubles?"

"Have I done so?"

"You have just been mixing and mingling with those men, talking to them. I know your kind."

"Ah, a gentleman of keen discernment!"

"I have seen you before—you fellows with long-tailed coats and short-horned ideas. We don't want your kind in this city!"

"I seem to have made a prompt sensation without trying to do so," returned Farr, meekly. "I have been in your city less than fifteen minutes, sir!"

"You're a traveling labor-agitator, aren't you?"

"No, sir."

"But I just saw you circulating among those men. Your rig-out shows your character!"

"You mean these garments I wear?"

"Certainly! A frock-coat helps out your pose before an ignorant public."

"He stole that coat from me," squeaked a fat man, standing at a little distance, scrubbing a torn sleeve over his grimy, sweat-streaked face. "He picked it fair off'n my back. I have follered him to show him up as a robber and a fake. That's so help me!"

Riotous laughter from all the listeners followed that declaration; a glance at the tubby tramp and survey of the tall young man whose contours fitted the garments made the fat man's assertion seem like a huge joke.

"I can prove it!" squalled the vagrant.

"Beat it! Get out of this city!" commanded a policeman. "If you don't we'll have you on the rock-pile. What ye mean by such guff?" He flourished his stick and the tramp hurried away.

"It's no use," he whined. "Grab and bluff! Him what can do it best always wins. That's the way the world goes!"

"When I took these clothes off the back of my vanishing friend I felt that they would make a change in my life," stated Farr, with a smile which provoked more laughter. "But I did not dream that they would bring me such prominence in so short a time." He bowed to the man in the car.

But Colonel Dodd was angry and insistent and did not join in the merriment.

"I say you are a labor-agitator. Any man who won't go to work himself has no right to be stirring up other workers against their own interests. You may as well own up to me, my man. These men standing around here know what you are—you have been talking with them. Outside of stirring trouble, you don't work, do you?"

"Oh yes, my lord!"

There was smiling mockery in the tone, almost insolence. He seemed to be willing to display to the rich man the same lack of respect he had displayed to the poor men who stood near and listened to this colloquy.

"Oh, you do?" Colonel Dodd raised his voice. "Listen sharp, my men! Do you want to be led around by the noses by a man who doesn't work? This gentleman is going to tell us what his job is!" He sneered when he said it.

"I am an assiduous toiler in my profession, your excellency. I am surprised that as an employer you do not recognize a real worker when you see one."

This tone of raillery and this stilted manner of speech promptly caught the fancy of the throng. The men crowded more closely and the orator on the trough was silent.

"What do you work at?"

"I am an architect, your gracious highness."

"Less of that insolence in the way of names, my friend! An architect, eh? Well, what did you ever build?"

"I laid out Dream Avenue in the boom city of Expectation and built on that thoroughfare a magnificent row of castles in the air. If you had a bit more imagination I might try to sell you something in my line. But it is useless, I see! Farewell!"

He swept off his broad-brimmed hat with a deep bow, backed away a few steps, and bowed again and went on his way. The crowd guffawed. This baiting of the city's labor magnate had most agreeably scratched their itching sense of resentment.

"I don't know who that josher is, but I hate to lose him out of town," confided the orator on the trough to those near him.

"I never saw that fellow before, but I'll pinch him if you say so, Colonel Dodd," volunteered the policeman. "Do you make complaint?"

"No," snapped the colonel, glowering on the broad back which was swinging across the square in retreat. He told his chauffeur to drive on.

When the car passed Farr the colonel flicked cigar ashes which alighted in a spray of dust on the sleeve of the frock-coat.

"Bah!" said the colonel, shooting the young man a scowl.

Farr gave in return a smile, but it was not a particularly genial smile.

The young man went on his way leisurely; by his gait, by his frequent and somewhat prolonged pauses at shop windows, by his indifferent starings at traffic and pedestrians, it was plain that he had little of moment on his mind.

He bought a penny glass of water at a corner kiosk.

"Do you mind telling me," he asked the vender, "Who is Colonel Dodd of this city? I am a stranger and I have just overheard the name."

The man grinned. "If it wasn't for Colonel Symonds Dodd I wouldn't be making much of a living here, selling spring-water. He is president of the Consolidated."

"And that means?"

"Why, it means that he is boss of the water trust that owns the system in this city and in all the other cities and towns of this state. And they pump all of their water out of the rivers because the lakes are so far off, and nobody drinks that water unless he has to or don't know any better. Colonel Dodd? Why, he bosses the whole state, they tell me."

"I gathered that he was important," said the young man, and walked on.

He was held up in the passing crowd at a street corner for a few moments because a parade of some half-dozen automobiles whirled past. The cars were decorated with banners, and the wild flowers and other spoil of forest and field in the arms of the ladies indicated that this was a party returning from a picnic in the suburbs.

"Would you mind telling me," asked Farr of the policeman who was guarding the corner, "who that young man is—the one there in the gray automobile?"

"With the bleached blonde and the pretty girl?" asked the officer. "Oh, that's Colonel Dodd's nephew—Dicky Dodd. Of course you know who the colonel is."

"Yes," said Farr. He opened his mouth to ask another question, for the policeman seemed to be of the obliging sort. Then he closed his lips resolutely and marched along.

"What's the use?" he muttered. "Two dark eyes and a red mouth—and I am almost forgetting how to be a philosopher."

Farther down the city thoroughfare he met one who had claimed to be a philosopher. It was Jared Chick, stalking along the sidewalk in his homemade armor. He held a box of stove-polish in one hand and a brush in the other, and as he strolled he was giving his corselet and such parts of the armor as he could handily reach a glossy coat—a gleaming and burnished surface. On his helmet in place of a crest Knight Chick bore aloft a metal banneret inscribed, "Invincible Stove Polish."

"And the mission?" asked Farr, halting his quondam companion, who had been too intent upon his business to pay heed to passers.

"I find thee changed, and no doubt thee, too, finds me changed," sighed Mr. Chick.

The mouth of an alley between high buildings afforded a retreat and the breeze blew there fitfully, and Mr. Chick stepped to that oasis of shade in the glare of sunshine.

"I have been obliged to modify my mission in some degree. I must confess that to thee," he said. "This is a strange and wicked world."

"Didn't you know it before you gave up a good blacksmith business to go out in the hot sun and suffer torment, all for nothing?"

"It is very hard work," acknowledged Chick, showing his flushed and streaming face under his vizor. "If I were not used to the fires of the forge I think I would fall down and die. But I must keep on."

"But you are simply an advertising-sign."

"I have modified my mission. I have not given up, however. I will tell thee! I found a man beside the way—a man who had been drinking strong waters and whose pockets had been turned wrong side out. So I took him to a tavern and I sat with him through the night, and nursed him when he suffered, and revealed my mission when he awoke. 'I am out to do good to all men,' I told him, and he searched through his pockets with blasphemy, and he said that I had done him—and he haled me before the court, and the judge said that no man could publicly profess such disinterestedness and escape suspicion, because people in these days are all looking for the main chance. So he did not believe me and he sentenced me to the jail. But a good Samaritan interceded for me and took me from behind the bars, and now in the spirit of gratitude I am repaying him; he makes and sells this stove-polish."

"That man is evidently shrewd in business and a good advertiser," commented Farr.

"I find that I get along much better in the world," asserted the knight-errant. "Now that I carry an advertising-sign my armor attracts no rude mobs. I can go abroad and do good to a foolish world; I can use the stipend my good benefactor allows to me for my work and I can help poor folks here and there. Therefore, I am content with my modified mission. Is thee more at peace with the world?"

"I ought to be, after hearing you say that *you* are contented," said Farr, with irony.

"Thee has manifestly improved thy condition, so I observe."

"It often happens in this world, Friend Chick, that the sleeker we are on the outside, the more ragged we are within. I think I'll move on. I might say something to jar your sense of sublime content. I'd be sorry to do that. Real contentment is a rare thing and must be handled very carefully."

"I fear thee loves thyself too much," chided the Quaker. "Affection for somebody might make thee happy, my friend."

Farr choked back the comment that occurred to him in regard to love and walked away.

VII
THE RAKE WHICH GROPED IN DARK WATERS

The afternoon was waning, but the hot bowl of the sky seemed to shut down over the city more closely.

Farr held to the shaded sides of the streets, and yearned for a patch of green and a tree and its shade.

At last he came into a section of the city where vast mills, one succeeding another in rows which vanished in the distance, clacked their everlasting staccato of hurrying looms, venting clamor from the thousands of open windows. A canal of slow-moving, turbid water intersected the city and fed its quota of power to each mill. The fenced bank of the canal was green; and elms, languid in the fierce heat, gave shade here and there with wilted leaves. The masses of brick which inclosed the toilers within the mills puffed off tremulous heat-waves and suggested that humanity must be baking in those gigantic ovens.

A high fence interposed between the canal and the street; the mill lawn which extended between the canal and the shimmering brick walls was also inclosed. Signs posted on the fence warned trespassers not to venture.

A bridge carried the street across the canal, and Farr stood there for a time and watched the swirl of the water below. Then he sauntered on and surveyed the expanse of mill lawn with appraising and envious gaze.

The young man climbed the canal fence, exhibiting more of his cool contempt for authority by helping himself over the sharp spikes with the aid of a "No Trespassing" sign. The sickly odor of raw cotton came floating to his nostrils from the open windows. He strolled to the head of a transverse canal which sucked water from the main stream. A sprawling tree shaded a foot-worn plank where an old man, with bent shoulders and a withered face, trudged to and fro, clawing down into the black waters with a huge rake. He was the rack-tender—it was his task to keep the ribs of the guarding rack clear of the refuse that came swirling down with the water, for flotsam, if allowed to lodge, might filch some of the jealously guarded power away from the mighty turbines which growled and grunted in the depths of the wheel-pits. With rake in one hand and a long, barbed pole in the other the old man bent over the bubbling torrent that the rack's teeth sucked hissingly between them. Bits of wood, soggy paper, an old umbrella, all manner of stuff which had been tossed into the canal by lazy folks up-stream, he raked and pulled up and piled at the end of his foot-bridge.

"Hy, yi, old Pickaroon!" came a child's shrill voice from a mill window. "There's a tramp under your tree."

The old man raised his head from his work at the rack.

"You must not come on dis place," he cried, with a strong French-Canadian accent.

"Who says so?" inquired the stranger, putting his back against the tree and stretching out his legs.

"I—Etienne Provancher."

"And I—my worthy alien—I am Walker Farr from Nowhere. Now that we have been properly introduced I will sit here and rest. I am here because I love the soothing sound of babbling waters on a hot day. Go about your work. I'll watch you. I love surprises. Who knows what next you'll draw forth from the depths of fate?

"I can have you arrest!" cried the old man.

The uninvited guest took off his broad-brimmed hat, laid it across his knees, and ran his hand through his shock of brown hair; it curled damply over his forehead and, behind, reached down nearly to his coat-collar, hiding his tanned neck. In some men that length of hair might have seemed affectation. It gave this man, as he sat there uncovered, that touch of the unusual which separates the person of strong individuality from the mere mob. Then he smiled on old Etienne—such a warm, radiant, compelling, disarming sort of smile that the rack-tender turned to his work again, muttering. His mouth twitched and the crinkles in his withered face deepened.

Walker Farr found a comfortable indentation in the tree-trunk and settled his head there.

"How much do you get a week for doing that, Etienne?" he inquired, with cool assurance.

The old man glance sideways sharply, but the smile won him.

"Six dollaire."

"After supporting your family, what do you do with the rest of the money these generous mill-owners allow you?"

"I never was marry."

The young man looked up at the mill windows where childish heads were bobbing to and fro.

"That was poor judgment, Etienne. You might have married and have a dozen children now, working hard for you in the mill. Just like those children yonder."

The old man came to the end of his foot-bridge and flung down his rake and his pike-pole.

The sudden emotions of his Gallic forebears swept through him. His features worked, his voice was high with passion.

"Ba gar, I don't sleep the night because I think about dem poor childs. Dem little white face, dem arm, dem leg—all dry up—not so big as chicken leg. And all outdoor free to odder childs—not to them childs up dere." He shook his fists at the mill windows. And some child who saw the motion, getting a hasty peep from a widow, squealed, "Hi yi, old Pickaroon!"

"It doesn't pay to get too excited over the sorrows of the world, my friend," drawled the young man under the tree. "It doesn't do any good; and then somebody calls you names. I was something like you once. But I've changed my philosophy. I have hypnotized my altruism. Now I'm perfectly happy."

Etienne stared without understanding these big words. But he had often told himself that he never expected to understand Yankee speech very well. He worked alone; he lived alone in his garret in the tenement block; he talked but little with any person. But this young man with the wonderful smile seemed to inspire him to talk—even to the extent of revealing his secrets.

He lowered his voice. "Thirty year I have work here. I live way up in the little room. Bread I eat with lard on it. It costs little. Of the six dollaire I save much. Ah, *oui*! Hist! Not for me I save it. Ah, *non*! To the priest I give it. To the good priest. And the poor childs what are sick—he send 'em to the farm—to have some outdoors. But I don't sleep the night because I think the dollaire come so slow—and so many poor childs are sick."

He picked up his rake and pike and went back to his labor.

The man under the tree did not lose his smile.

"Yonder is a brand of altruism that cannot be hypnotized or modified like Knight Chick's, I fear," he muttered. "You'd have to hit it on the head — kill it with sticks! And my definition of philanthropy has always been, 'giving away something you don't want in order to get yourself advertised.' Etienne is interesting. He is the only philanthropist I have even found who will eat lard instead of butter so as to save more for his philanthropy." Now his smile grew hard. "Don't dare to open your eyes, Altruism," he commanded. "I saw the lids quiver a minute ago while that old man was talking, but remember you're hypnotized."

He saw the rack-tender lay down his pike so as to give both hands to his big rake.

He was pulling at something heavier than the ordinary flotsam — something far below the surface of the water. At last it broke through the black surface of the turbid flood. To Walker Farr, glancing carelessly, it seemed like a bedraggled bundle of rags with something white at the end.

"You come help, m'sieu'," called old Etienne. "It is a dead woman."

Together they pulled the rake's dread burden slowly up the bars of the rack.

"You seem pretty cool about this," gasped the young man.

"It is no new thing. Many drown themselves — they drown in the canal so they will be found. Women and girls, they drown themselves. So! Help me carry her."

Farr gazed down on her after she had been laid on the canal bank. She was young, but thin and work-worn.

"Weaver," commented old Etienne, laying back on her breast one of the hands he had lifted. "There's the marks on the fingers where she have tie so many knots so quick."

There was a key on her breast; it was secured by a cord that passed out of sight between the buttons on her waist. Farr stooped and pulled on the key. A folded paper came with the key; the other end of the cord was tied around the paper.

"You must not — it is for the coroner," protested Etienne. "I know the law — I have drag up so many."

"My besetting sin is curiosity," declared the young man, his calm impertinence unruffled. He pulled the wet paper from the noose of the cord. "We'll read this together."

"I cannot read," confessed the rack-tender. "You shall read it to me." His little black eyes gleamed now with curiosity of his own. "I shall be glad to hear. The coroner he never read to me."

The water had spread the ink and spotted the paper, but Farr was able to decipher the missive. He read aloud:

"'My head has grown bad since my husband died. It is grief, the awful heat, the work at the looms. They said if I would give my little girl away she could go to the country and grow well. But I could not give her up for ever. I could not earn the money to send her to board. I could not earn the money except to buy us bread here in the tenement block. And my bad head has been telling me it's best to kill myself and take her with me. So I kill myself before my head grows so bad that I might take away my little girl's life. It belongs to her and I hope she may be happy. Will somebody take her and give her happiness? It is wicked to kill myself, but my head is so bad I cannot think out the right way to do. This is the key to the room in Block Ten.

"'MRS. ELISIANE SIROIS.

"'Her name is Rosemarie.'"

Walker Farr finished reading and stared into the glittering eyes of the old man.

Etienne Provancher swore roundly and furiously—the strange, hard oaths that his ancestors had brought from the Normandy of the seventeenth century.

"So you shall see—it is as I have say." He shook his fists again at the mill. Its open windows vomited the staccato chatterings of the myriad looms. "It chews up the poor people. Hear its dam' teeth go chank—chank—chank!"

"The Gallic imagination is always active," said Farr, joggling the key at the end of the cord and eyeing it with peculiar interest. "But in this case it seems to picture conditions pretty accurately. I wonder just what a visitor would find inside the door that this key fits!"

"You shall go tell them at the office of the mill," commanded Etienne. "Tell them they have killed another. They will telephone for the coroner. I will give the paper and the key when he come." He held out his hand. "It is the law."

"I have a natural hankering—sometimes—to break the law," affirmed the young man. "I feel that fatal curiosity of mine stirring again, Friend Etienne. I will send the coroner. But coroners love mysteries. If we give him the letter it will take all the spice out of this affair. Let's make him happy— he can drag out the inquest and give his friends a long job on the jury." He smiled and started away, shaking his head when the old man protested shrilly. "Better say nothing about this letter and the key. You'll get into trouble for letting a stranger come in here and carry away evidence. Better keep out of the law, Etienne." He grabbed the "No Trespassing" sign for a hand-hold and climbed over the fence. "I'll come back and tell you, Etienne. But keep mum," he advised.

"It is his smile—it makes me break the law," mumbled the old man.

VIII
THE KEY TO A DOOR IN BLOCK TEN

Walker Farr gave the first policeman—a fat and sweltering individual—a piece of gruesome news and in return casually asked the location of Block Ten.

The policeman grudgingly growled the information over his shoulder while waiting for the station to answer the call from his box.

The young man, taking his time, found the place at last, one in an interminable row of tenement-houses, all identical in structure and squalor, bearing the mark of corporation niggardliness in their cheap lumber and stingy accommodations.

The hallway that Farr entered was narrow and stifling—stale odors of thousands of dead-and-gone boiled dinners mingled there, and a stairway with a greasy handrail invited him. The key bore a number. He hunted till he found a room, far up, flight after flight. Through open doors he saw here and there aged women or doddering old men who were guardians of dirty babes who tumbled about on the bare floors.

"Either too old to run a loom or too young to lug a bobbin," Farr informed himself; "that's why they aren't in the mill."

Old folks and babes stared at him without showing interest.

No one looked at him when he opened the door in which the key fitted.

He stepped in quickly and closed and locked the door behind him.

It was a little room and pitifully bare, and it was under the roof, and the ceiling slanted across it so sharply that the young man, tall above the average, was compelled to bow his head.

A little girl, a wraith of a child, pale with the pallor of a prisoner, hardly more than a toddler, sat on the floor and stared up at the intruder, frozen, silent, immobile with the sudden, paralyzing terror that grasps the frightened child. Pathetically poor little playthings were scattered about her: a doll fashioned from gingham and cotton-waste, makeshift dishes of

The Landloper The Romance Of A Man On Foot | 59

pasteboard, a doll-carriage made from a broken flower-basket with spools for wheels. The man who entered saw all with one glance and understood that here in this bare room this child had been compelled to drag out the weary hours alone while the mother had toiled. Here now the child waited patiently for—for that water-soaked bundle, with the white, dead face, that lay on the canal bank waiting for the coroner.

And when he realized it and saw this and looked down on that lonely, patient, wistful little creature making the best shift she could with those pitiable playthings, something came up from that man's breast into his throat. He had not supposed he had any of it left in his soul—it was tender, agonizing, heartrending pity.

She still stared at him, terrorized. Probably she had never seen any face come in at that door except her mother's.

His pity must have given Walker Farr a hint of how to deal with this frightened child. He did not speak to her. He made no move toward her.

He smiled!

But it was not the smile he had given the fat plutocrat in the automobile, nor yet the jocular radiance he had displayed to old Etienne. It was such a smile as the man had never smiled before—and he realized it. He did not want to smile. He wanted to weep. But he brought that smile from tender depths in his soul—depths he had not known of before—and tears came with the smile.

Before that time the lines in his face had fitted the smile of the cynic, the grimace of banter, of irony and insolence. But the strange glory that now glowed upon his features came there after the mightiest effort he had ever made to control his feelings and his expression.

He smiled!

In that smile he soothed, he promised, he appealed. Then when he saw the tense expression of fear fade away he smiled more broadly—he provoked reply in kind. And slowly upon the child's face an answering smile began to dawn—little crinkles at the corners of the drooping mouth, little flickerings in the blue eyes, until at last the two beaming faces pledged—on the part of the man tender protection, on the part of the child unquestioning confidence.

But he said no word—he dared not trust his voice.

He went down on his knees cautiously, her smile welcoming him now.

He held out his hands. She hesitated a moment and then gave into them her chiefest possession—her rag doll. It was as if she had pledged her faith in him. He danced the doll upon his broad palm, and the child's eyes, dancing too, thanked him for the courtesy he was paying to her dearest friend.

But Walker Farr realized that something strange and disquieting in the case of a man who believed himself a cynic was stirring within him. That hostage of the doll was not sufficient to satisfy the sudden queer craving. The knowledge of the hopeless helplessness of that little girl throbbed through him. The memory of the spectacle of what he had left on the canal bank made the pathos of this little scene in the garret doubly poignant as he looked into the child's eyes. Never, in his memory, had he invited a child to come to him.

Now he put out his hand—and it trembled. She snuggled her warm little fist into his grasp. And then she scrambled up and came and nestled confidingly against him. She couldn't see his face then, and he allowed the tears of a strong man who is overcome before he has understood—who wonders at himself—he allowed those tears to streak his cheeks and did not wipe them away.

Walker Farr was too perturbed to soliloquize just then in his philosopher's style, but he did realize that some part of his altruism had come out of its trance.

And after he had knelt there on the floor for a time he rose and took the child in his arms and sat down in a creaky rocking-chair and crooned under his breath, and was astonished to find that she had gone sound asleep. He stared into the dusk that was gathering outside the dormer window and wondered what ailed him.

He had heard many feet thudding on the stairs below. The workers were returning. The beehive was filling. There were many voices, clatter of dishes, chatter of patois.

He wondered how well the woman Sirois was known in the house—whether she had relatives—how soon somebody would come and beat upon the door.

He wondered just what disposition was made of children left in this manner.

If the woman had relatives who were forced to take the child it meant more of this horrible tenement life. The child in his arms was pale and thin; her bones seemed as inconsiderable as a bird's.

He did not know much about children's homes, orphanages, institutions for the reception of the homeless, but it seemed to him that such a tiny, frail little girl would be very, very lonely in such a place.

The skies grew dark without. He was cramped because he had sat for hours in one position, fearing to waken her. But when he moved she did not waken—he did not understand how soundly childhood can sleep. He laid her on the foot of the narrow bed and looked about the room, shielding a match with his hands. He had resolved to carry her out of that fetid, overcrowded babel of a tenement. Where? He did not know. He hunted to find her belongings. He found a few clothes. There was no receptacle in which he could pack them. He folded them and crowded the articles in his pockets. He stuffed in the doll and the rude playthings and hooked the basket doll-carriage upon his arm. She did not waken when he picked her up. He tiptoed down the stairs and nobody noticed him, In his own dizzy mind he could not determine whether he felt most like a thief or a lunatic. At any rate, he found himself walking the streets of the mill city at ten o'clock at night, carrying a little girl in his arms and all her earthly possessions in his pockets.

It came over him at last that the longer he kept her the more uncertain he became as to what disposal he should make of her, or else he was more loath to part with her; he didn't exactly know which.

Then she woke and spoke for the first time. "Me is te'bble hungry—and firsty," she mourned.

"Good Lord! What's the matter with me?" grunted the young man. "If I had found a cat or a dog, the first thing I would have done would be to give 'em something to eat. I reckon I must have thought I had picked up an angel." To her he said, smoothing her hair with his free hand. "We'll have sumpin for baby's tummy mighty quick." He flushed at sound of that baby prattle from his lips. But it had popped out in the most natural manner possible.

He headed for the nearest night lunch-cart. He entered with his burden.

He elbowed aside men who were eating sandwiches and pie at the counter. With complete and rueful knowledge as to the extent of his resources, he ordered a bowl of bread and milk—"the best you can do for a hungry kiddie for ten cents," he added.

"Anything for yourself?" inquired the waiter.

He shook his head and paid for the child's supper with his whole capital, two nickels. He held her on the end of the counter and, awkwardly but with tender carefulness, fed the bread and milk to her with a spoon. A healthy man's hunger gnawed within him and the savor of coffee from the big, bubbling urn tantalized him. He tipped the bowl to her lips and she drank the last of the milk with a happy little sigh, and he went out into the night again, carrying her in his arms.

He understood all the suspicions that policemen entertain in the case of night prowlers, and knew that they would be particularly and meddlesomely interested in one who prowled with a child in his arms. The child began to whimper softly. Her interest in the stranger who had won her with a smile, her slumber in his arms, her feast in strange surroundings, had kept her child's mind busy and pacified till then. Now she voiced childhood's unvarying lament—"I wants my mamma!"

He soothed her as best he could, promising, giving her all manner of assurance regarding her mother, wondering all the time what was to be done. Why had he interfered? Why had he taken upon himself the custody of this mite, so trifling a weight in his arms, but now resting—a giant of a burden—on his responsibility? He did not know. He owned up to that ignorance frankly. But he walked on, carrying her, and put away from his thoughts the sensible alternative of placing her in the hands of those duly appointed to care for such cases.

He told himself that, as a stranger in the city, he would not be able to find a refuge—an institution that time of night—and he knew that he was lying to himself, and wondered why.

The impulse that directed his course toward the canal was rather grim, but he remembered the tree which had been sanctuary for him that day. He carefully lowered the little girl over the fence and climbed after her. And she did not call any more for her mother because this strange new scene seemed to impress her and fill her with wonderment. She stared up into the dim, mysterious, rustling foliage of the tree for a long time. She patted her hands upon the grass as if it were something she had never seen or felt before. She seemed to be making her first acquaintance with Mother Nature—claiming the heritage of outdoors that children so intensely covet. The sloped ceiling and the walls of the attic room had been sky and landscape for her. She peered into the still waters of the canal and saw the stars reflected there, and cocked her ear to listen when sleepy birds stirred above and chirped in their dreams. And then she fell asleep again and he tucked her within his coat to keep from her the dampness of the faint mist rising from the canal.

The dawn flushed early and she woke when the birds did, and found so much to interest her—ants who ran up and down the tree, funny bugs that tumbled, robins who bounced along the sward on stiff legs—that she did not ask for her mother nor seem to find at all strange the companionship of this tall man whose face was so kind.

And so Etienne Provancher found them when he came with his rake and pike-pole at six o'clock, the hour when the great turbines began to grunt and rumble in their deep pits.

"It is Rosemarie—I found her in the room," said Walker Farr.

The old man came close and gazed down on the pallor and pathos of this little snipped who still stared at the new wonders of outdoors.

"Anodder one, hey? You found her lock up?"

"Yes, and I brought her away—and I don't know just what the matter is with me, Etienne. I have not been inclined to put myself out for anybody in this world—man, woman, or child—of late years. I had made up my mind to let the world run itself."

"It is the way the rich man say—he do not care. But the poor man should care—he should try to help odder poor man. He should care."

"Oh, there are things that can happen to make a man stop caring. But I brought her away, just the same. I—I woke up—or something. I have been awake all night—I have been thinking—I had nothing else to do. Insomnia has made me insane—one night of it!" He laughed when the old man blinked at him. "I'm so crazy that I want you to help me find some good woman who will take this child to board in a comfortable home."

"Who'll pay?"

"I'll pay. Oh, I am completely crazy—I'm going to work—earn money to pay her board."

"I know a good woman near by—she have leetle house, cat, plant in window."

"That's the kind."

"I will tell you where she live. You shall say you come from Etienne Provancher and it will make you good for her." He paused, raised a brown finger, then went on. "But you shall not know where she live onless I may pay half the board money for the poor little one. We have been togedder in it—I tell some lie to the coroner—we must be togedder in help the childs."

There was firm resolve in old Etienne's face and tones.

"Partnership it shall be, my old boy," agreed the young man, heartily. "I'm no pig—I won't keep a good man out of a real picnic." He rose and swept the child into his arms. "Give me the address and hand her over the fence to me. I'll have to quit being nurse and find a real job. By the way, Etienne, I heard a fat man weeping yesterday because he couldn't get men to dig dirt for the Consolidated Water Company. He seemed to take a great fancy to me. Where's their office?"

He received both the information and the child after he had climbed the fence. Etienne was able to point out the little house of sanctuary from where he stood—and he waved his rake reassuringly from a distance when the good woman came to the door, answering Farr's knock. He danced into the house with the child, behind the good woman, who had answered Etienne's signal with a return flip of her apron; he was trying to bring a smile to the little face.

"You'll have to lie to her more or less about her mother, good woman. Etienne and I will tell you all about it when there's time. When she asks about her mother just give her something to eat and lie a bit." He set the child upon the table where the good woman was making fresh cookies. He piled the little toys about her. "I'm going to market, to market to buy a fat pig, and I'll be home again, riggy-jig-jig," he declared in a singsong that fetched a chuckle from the waif, and she followed him with a smile as he hurried out. "That smile will sweeten a day's work in the trench," he assured himself. "I sure am some foster-father when I get started!"

A listless clerk at the Consolidated office gave him a ticket to be delivered to the foreman of construction—the foreman sent him out with other men on a rattling jigger-wagon. By being very humble, and with the aid of his smile, he succeeded in begging a corned-beef sandwich for his breakfast from a workman on the jigger who was carrying his lunch to work. He ate it very slowly so as to make the most of it.

The new trench was in a suburban plot which had just been opened up by a real-estate syndicate. It was a bare tract, flat and dusty, and the only trees were newly planted saplings that were about as large as fishing-poles. How the sun did beat into that trench! But Walker Farr threw off his coat and used again his ready asset—his smile. He smiled at the boss who sneered at the style of "fiddler's hair" worn by a dirt-flinger—smiled so sweetly that the boss came over later and hit him a friendly clap on the shoulder and said, "Well, old scout, here's hoping that times will be better!"

"I'll take her out on the bank of the canal this evening before bedtime and we'll have a lark," reflected Walker Farr as he toiled in the hot trench. And he stopped quizzing himself as to the whys of this sudden devotion to a freakish notion. He seemed to know at last.

IX
THE GIRL FROM TADOUSAC

When the noon hour came Farr went and sat under a spindling tree and began to read in one of his little books, dismissing thoughts of hunger with the resoluteness of a man who had suffered hollow yearning of the stomach and knew how to conquer it.

But he could not escape the keen eyes and kindly generosity of the fraternity of toilers.

"A topper down on his luck a bit—see his clothes," said the foreman, and he took tithes from willing men who were eating from pails that were pinched between their knees; he carried the food to the young man.

Farr accepted with gratitude, ate with thrifty moderation, and hid what remained in the pockets of his coat; it would serve for his supper.

He ate that supper after his day's work was done and after he had laved his face and hands in the overflow from a public fountain in a little square.

Then he hurried to the house of the good woman.

She was busy with her dishes in the kitchen and Rosemarie was on the knees of a young woman who sat and rocked in one of the sitting-room chairs.

Farr entered by the kitchen door and stood there, looking in with some confusion on the girl and child.

"It is only Zelie Dionne; she is my boarder," the woman informed him. "She is a good girl and she has the very nice job in the cloth-hall of the big Haxton mill. She lives with me because I was neighbor of her good folks in the Tadousac country, so far away from here in our Canada. Come! I make you acquaint. You shall see. She is a good girl!"

Zelie Dionne rose and acknowledged the introduction with a French girl's pretty grace. A bit of a flush lighted the dusky pallor of her cheeks when Farr bent before her. The bow in her hair was cocked with true Gallic chic and her gown was crisply smart in its simplicity. Her big, dark eyes were the wonderful feature of her face, and Farr looked into them and seemed to lose a bit of his cool self-possession; he faltered in speech, groping for words in the first commonplaces.

"You must talk together. I must work," said the good woman. She hurried back into her kitchen.

The child ran to Farr and climbed upon his knees.

"You have been good to Rosemarie. I thank you," he said. "I suppose the good woman has told you how it has happened."

"Yes, when I came at noon." Her tones were peculiarly sweet and compassionate. A touch of accent gave piquancy to what she said. She looked at him meaningly. "I have been talking to our little Rosemarie and she will not cry any more for her good mamma who has gone up to the green hills because she is sick and must rest. So Rosemarie will be patient and live here and I will be play-mamma."

"Yes, play-mamma," agreed the child. "Good play-mamma! Two mammas! But only one papa!" She put up her arms and tucked them about his neck and snuggled down with a happy sense of complete understanding of his protection. At last, so it seemed to her, she had recovered the father she had never known. Poor, little, caged bird, her release from that lonely prison was dated in her happy consciousness from his appearance in the doorway, and all things had been well for her after he came—sunlight, the trees, the blue sky, and tender care, and the companionship of human beings. Therefore, the rush of a love her child's comprehension could not analyze had gone out to him.

Farr returned with significance the look Zelie Dionne's dark eyes gave him.

"I found the note. It made me go a-meddling. It left a legacy to somebody—and I accepted—without understanding why I did so." He stroked the child's curls.

"I did not understand at first—when Madame Maillet told me," she confessed, with a smile. "Old Etienne came at noon to tell her and she has told it to me. It is very sad—but yet it is comical when I look at you. But as I look at you I understand better. You have a good heart. I can see!"

"I am only a strolling stranger—here to-day and there to-morrow," protested Farr. "I think the heat must have affected my head. It has been very warm lately. But when I saw her—" He choked suddenly.

"Oh, it is easy to understand," said the girl, reassuringly. A mist of tears came across her big eyes, though her mouth did not lose the wistful smile. "The poor folks help one another—and they understand."

"It wouldn't be right to give her to an orphanage," insisted Farr. "She has missed too much already. Of course I don't pretend to know what a little girl needs—but I am willing to be told."

"I will tell you and I will help."

"I think old Etienne and I need you in the partnership—as adviser. I thank you."

Then came the old Canadian, his wrinkled face tender with solicitous interest, and he chuckled when he welcomed the new member of the firm.

"Ah, Mam'selle Zelie she shall help us the very much in what we do not know," he informed the young man, and continued, while the dark eyes flashed protest: "I am of the Tadousac country, and she is a good girl, for I have know her all the years since I trot her on my knee when she much small as the petite Rosemarie. I can tell you how she dance down the meadows in the ring-a-rosy play and how she—"

"Phut! Your tongue is as long as your rake and it goes reaching down into other folks' affairs, old Etienne! What cares this strange gentleman for what happened in Tadousac? Go use your key instead of your tongue. Unlock your little door so that Rosemarie may walk on the cool grass beside the canal."

The old man grinned and started away.

"We're going out where the birds will sing good night to you," Farr told the child and lifted her off his knees. But at the door she stopped and turned to Zelie Dionne, who had not risen.

"Come, play-mamma!"

"I will wait here till you come back, Rosemarie."

But the child was coaxingly insistent, holding out her hand.

"I think it is because she has been so lonely all her life," suggested Farr. "Now that she has found friends she wants them to be with her in her little pleasures. May I presume enough to add my invitation to hers?"

She came and the child walked between them, holding their hands.

"One papa and my play-mamma!" she said, looking up at them in turn.

Mother Maillet came to the kitchen door and waved adieu with her dish-towel.

"Ah, the family!" she cried. "Yesterday it was not—to-day it is. And grandpere marching off ahead!"

"Old folks and children—they say embarrassing things," remarked Farr when they were on their way.

"One must be silly along with them to be disturbed by such chatter," said Zelie Dionne, tartly.

They followed old Etienne through his little door and walked along the canal bank where the waters were still and glassy, for the big gates had been closed and power lay motionless and locked in the sullen depths till morning. The sunset behind the big mills glowed redly through the myriad windows.

They walked slowly because little Rosemarie found marvels for childish eyes at every step, and even the cool carpet of the grass provided unfailing delight as she set slow and cautious footsteps into its yielding luxuriance. The old man plodded ahead, muttering and frowning as he peered down at the flotsam in the motionless waters.

The silence between the two who accompanied the child continued a long time and Farr found it oppressive.

"I have never been in Canada," he said. "I am sorry you did not care to have Etienne talk about your home. I would like to know more about that country."

"He was talking about me instead of my home in Tadousac. I am not so important that I am to be talked about."

"Where is Tadousac?"

Her vivacity returned, her dark eyes glowed. "Ah, m'sieu', you should go there. It is in the country of the good habitants where the St. Lawrence and the Saguenay meet. And now, as the sun is setting, the people are resting under the wide eaves of the little white houses, looking up where the hills are all so blue, or off across the wide bay. The white houses are very small and they crowd along the road, and the farms are narrow, and there is not much money in the homespun clothes or in the old clock, but the good world is wide about them and the people are not sad like those who sit yonder."

She pointed across the canal to rows of wooden tenement-houses many stories in height; on narrow porches, nicked one above another, and on fire-escapes which were slowly cooling after hours on the forge of the sun, men, women, and children were packed, seeking a breath of fresh air.

"They stand at loom and spinner and slasher all day," she said. "They are too tired to walk afar to the parks. They wait there for good air to come and it does not come."

"I don't understand why they flock down here from Canada—why they stay," he declared, bluntly.

"Ah, you look at me when you say that!" she cried, arching her brows. "You hear me talk about the sunset over the meadows and the hills, and you wonder why I am not there? Well, listen! There are fourteen sons and daughters of Onesime Dionne—that's my father—for all the habitant folks marry young, and the priest smiles and blesses the household when there are many children. And girls are not of much account in the house. The sons claim and receive their shares of the arpents of land when those boys are grown and married. The girl may marry—yes! But what if the right one does not ask? What if the right one has a father who says to him that he must obey and marry one the father has chosen? All kinds of things can happen in the habitant country, m'sieu'. So, then, the girl is less account in the house. And the letters come back from the girls who have gone down into the mills in the States. The pictures come back showing the new gown and the smart hat—and so!" She shrugged her shoulders and tossed her free hand. "One more girl for the big mill!"

He stared at her with some curiosity.

"You ask yourself which one of those things happened to me, do you not?"

"Perhaps," he confessed.

"I talk little about myself. I talk about the habitant girls. I am fortunate. I do not breathe the air where the looms clack. I inspect in the cloth-hall because I have sharp eyes and nimble fingers."

"But you came here alone—it is strange. I mean, do not the father and mother and all the family move here, usually?"

She lifted her chin and gazed at him with pride in her mien.

"If you go to Tadousac you shall find that my father owns a large farm and that one of his grandfathers was a captain with General Montcalm, and many Dionnes have lived on the land that was given to a brave man. I came to the States because I wanted to come. My people did not come."

She clipped the last sentence in a manner that suggested to Farr that there was no more to be said on that topic. But she went on after a time in softened tones.

"It is not strange that so many came to the States, sir. The farms of Beauce, of l'Islet, of the Chaudiere, were so crowded. Years ago, the old folks used to tell me, the boys began to drive the little white horses hitched to buckboards across the border in the early summer, and the boys were strong and willing, and the farmers who laughed at them and called them Canucks hired them for the hay-fields just the same. And they slept in the haymows and under the trees and worked hard and brought back all their money. Then the big mills needed men and women and children, and the Yankee girls would not work in the mills any more. You must understand how it was: Ouillette, who had worked in the hay-field, would hear of the work in the mill, and the Ouillettes would sell and go to the city. And as soon as they had seen the lights and the theater and the car which ran with a stick on a wire, and had earned their first pay and had bought Yankee clothes they wrote home to their cousins the Pelletiers and the Pelletiers sat nights till late talking excitedly—and then they sold and came, and so it has gone on and on—the endless chain, one family pulling on its neighbor, down the long way from Canada to the States. But it may be all for the best. I am not wise in such things. But when the sun bakes and the fever comes and the children die in the tenements, then I wish the fathers and mothers were back on the little farms and that workers of some other race than the habitants were chained to the looms in the big mills. That may be a selfish thought, but my own people are dear to me."

Farr was not in the mood to argue the economic side of that question with this girl who had so tersely told the story of two generations of mill-toilers. With that little waif between them, victim of the industrial Moloch which must roll on even if its wheels crushed the innocent here and there, he permitted sentiment to sway him. In fact, for a day and a night he had surrendered to sentiment and had found a strange sort of intoxication in the experience. His heart was with the humble folk and pity was in him—pity which was uncalculating and in which his cynicism was dissolving.

And when the stars were mirrored in the still canal and the grass was damp with the dew, they walked back to the house of Mother Maillet and little Rosemarie murmured her bit of a prayer and was tucked in bed.

"I hope that some day I may go to Tadousac," said Farr to the girl, before he passed out of the good woman's house. "I would like to see the sunset, for you have praised it."

"Ask for the house of Onesime Dionne, second beyond the big parish cross. It will be easy to find, and the sunset is very grand from the porch under the eaves."

Farr went along with the old man and they walked slowly. Their way took them down narrow streets between the high tenements.

"Yes, you shall find it very grand at Tadousac—and M'sieu' Dionne is an honest man," declared Etienne. "Now and then in the thirty year I have been visit up there in Tadousac, and I sit those day and whittle for the children and then little Zelie trot on my knee with the others. So I know the story of those place. And all the people up there don't care if I know, because I listen and am glad to know, and sometimes I can give advice, for I have live long on the States where great matters are happening. But Farmer Leroux would not listen to me when I advise about his good son Jean and Zelie Dionne. Farmer Leroux is a good man, but he is a hard man when his ugly mad get stir. And the children up there do what the father tell—because that is what the cure preach and it is the way of the habitants."

"The old, old story—the Montagues and the Capulets on the banks of the river of the North."

"I think I know something what you mean, m'sieu', though I don't know your friend you speak about. But if he say to his son, 'Ba gar, you don't marry no girl what I don't like her fadder because we have hosswhip one anodder t'ree or two time when we have fuss over line fence—or crowd our wagon when we go to market'—why, then that's your friend. And it start from there and grow into big thing, so that all the cure can say it don't make no friend of them. So they wait—Jean and Zelie! Ah yes, they wait!" He put his finger beside his nose and winked. "They love. They get marry some nice day. But now!" He flirted his gaunt fingers. "They say nottings. I maself say nottings. But I see some very queer look in Jean Leroux's eye when he say to me as I meet him at the gate of his fadder's farm, 'And how carries Zelie Dionne herself these days?' And though he look high over the tree and chew the straw and look very careless, ah, I see the big tear in his eye and hear him choke in his throat."

"It's played out and old-fashioned, this letting old folks manage young folks that way just to satisfy old grudges," scoffed Farr. "If they are in love they ought to get married and tell the old folks to go hang!"

Etienne stopped and gazed quizzically at the young man who thus expounded the law for lovers.

"I think you have in you none of the understanding of the French habitants who have live the three generation on one farm so that a young man, no matter if he love a mam'selle so very much that all the bread he eat taste ashes in his mouth—ah, he cannot say 'I will leave—I will go!' For then that young man must turn himself to be anodder young man—and the habitant does not so change."

"I may be a poor judge," acknowledged Farr. "I have never yet taken root in the soil of any one place."

"And I think, mebbe, the girl you do not understand! Is it to stay in the home and hear every day about you love the pig of a Leroux, bah? No, no, m'sieu'! That's too proud, is Zelie Dionne. And so is Zelie Dionne too proud to take a son from a home that do not want her. So they wait."

"It's a tough old world, Uncle Etienne," said Farr. "Why, even I, lord of my own affairs as I am, don't know where I'm going to sleep to-night. Do you have a boarding-place?"

"I have my little room on the block up there—my room and my place at the big table. It is not grand. But there is place for you—and anodder little room. If you like you shall come and I will speak good for you."

"All right, Etienne! Take me along and speak good for me."

It was another such place as Block Ten. It was a crowded and stuffy warren, and the basement kitchen advertised itself with stale odors in all the corridors. But Farr was glad to stretch himself upon the narrow bed. He owned up to himself that he was a very weary bird of passage and confessed to his own heart, just as frankly, that he was a captive in the frail grasp of a little girl—and he did not try to understand.

X
POISON FOR THE POOR

It proved to be an amicable and satisfactory partnership between Etienne Provancher and Walker Farr and dark-eyed Zelie Dionne.

When the days were pleasant the old man kept the little girl with him out of doors on the canal bank. She did not trouble him by running about. Her long days of confinement in the attic room had accustomed her to remain quietly in one place. She sat contentedly in the shade and watched the bugs in the grass and the birds in the tree above her. In the cool of the evening she trudged along the canal bank with Farr and the play-mamma until eyes grew heavy and little feet stumbled with weariness and it was time for bed. Rainy evenings they studied the alphabet or he read to her from picture-books in blazing colors, and after a time she remembered all the stories and made believe read them to him.

He worked in the trench and looked forward impatiently to Saturday nights when the clerk came along with the pay-envelopes; there were so many things in the stores that would delight the heart of a little girl who had never had any toys except a rag doll and a broken flower-basket. Then there were pretty dresses to buy. The taste of Zelie Dionne took charge of that shopping. When he bought the first one—one that was white and fluffy—and Rosemarie walked out with him she displayed such feminine pride in fine feathers that he looked forward to future Saturdays nights and new dresses with anticipatory gusto. If one had questioned him he could have told weeks ahead just what his plans of purchases were, for he canvassed all the possibilities with the play-mamma who knew so well how to get value for a dollar—who knew the places to buy and whose needle helped to much.

It was a wicked summer for those who were doomed to the mills and the tenement-houses. The heat puffed and throbbed over the lashing machinery. The slashers seemed to spit caloric. The spinning-frames tossed it off their spindles. The looms fairly wove it into the warp. The thick, sweet, greasy air seemed to distil cotton-oil upon the faces of the workers. The nights proved to be no better than the days. The stuffy tenements gulped in the hot air of midday and held it as a person holds his breath. All the folks came out upon the little platforms that were ranged, story after story, above each other. They gasped for air in the narrow spaces between the high buildings. The stars above those narrow spaces did not sparkle and suggest coolness; they seemed to float above the hot earth like red cinders.

Every day the undertakers' wagons came "boombling" down the narrow canyons of streets between the "Blocks," for the people were dying. The little white hearse was a more frequent visitor than the rusty black one; the ranks of the children were paying the greatest toll to death.

"But we shall not worry about our Rosemarie," old Etienne told Farr. "Under the shade on the green grass she shall stay where outdoors can paint her cheeks the very fine color."

But when the old man called for her at the good woman's house one morning something else than the sun had painted the little girl's cheeks—they were flushed with fever. He told the good woman to send straight for the doctor, and went to his work much disturbed.

Later in the day the yard overseer, passing the rack, saw that the man was working with furious energy. He was even reaching out his rake to capture floating stuff before it touched the bars.

"This seems to be your busy day, Pickaroon," suggested the overseer.

"I make believe this old rack to be a good friend of mine and that the float stuff be sickness come at him—so I work hard to keep it away."

The overseer went along about his business, commenting mentally on a Frenchman's imagination.

When the big mill bells clanged the noon hour Etienne hurried to the good woman's house. The city physician had been there and had left medicine—two tumblers of it. He had hurried in and had hurried away and had been curt and brusk and had not told her what was the trouble, so the woman reported. But the child had been sleeping.

She was drowsy all that evening while Farr held her in his arms and Etienne sat near by with Zelie Dionne, ministering solicitously.

"Her cheeks are not so hot," said the young man many times. He talked hopefully to reassure himself as well as the others, for he had been dreadfully frightened when he had come from his work. Fright had trodden close on the heels of much joy—for the superintendent of the Consolidated had taken him out of the hot trench that day and had appointed him boss of twoscore Italian diggers, doubling his pay.

"I have been watching you," the superintendent told him. "You're built to boss men. What kind of a bump was it that ever slammed you down like this?"

The answer the superintendent got was a smile which put further questions out of his mind.

"No, her cheeks are not so hot," affirmed Farr when he laid her in her bed that night. "She will come along all right."

But at the end of a week languor still weighed on the child. There were circles under her eyes and her cheeks were wan, and she did not clap her hands with the old-time glee when he brought her new toys; the playthings lay beside her on the bed and invited her touch—staring eyes of dolls, beady eyes of toy dogs—without avail.

"It is the queer way of being sick," lamented the old man. "The doctor mebbe not know, because he very gruff and do not say. I think I know what may cure her—it has been done many time.

"Away up in the Canada country there is the shrine of the good Sainte Anne de Beaupre. There she stand in the middle of the big church and she hold her little grandson in her arm—the little boy Jesus. So she feel very tender toward poor, sick childs. Ah, I have seen her many time—I have seen childs healed there and made so very smart—all cure. She loves little childs. *Oui.* All about her feet are short, small crutch where she has cure childs. The piece of her wrist-bone is there in the sacristy—it look like a wee scrap of some gray moss under the glass. And it cure when the good priest say the word for her. I know the way to the shrine of La Bonne Sainte Anne—I will go with the little Rosemarie and she shall sing and dance after that."

For a moment the cynical smile of the skeptic etched itself at the corners of Farr's mouth—the flash of the nature the young man had hidden during recent weeks.

He turned to Zelie Dionne and found her regarding him with grave eyes.

"It is as M'sieu' Etienne says," she assured the young man. "La Bonne Sainte listens very tenderly when the children come to her. She is good to all, but her spirit leans over the poor little children and comforts them."

"You have been there?"

"Many times, sir. It is not only the sick body that the good Sainte Anne heals—she comforts anybody who is in much sorrow—she tells the right way to go. There are many roads to take in this life—and if any one goes to her with prayer and humble soul she will guide. Ah, it is true, sir."

There was earnestness in her features and conviction in her tones and it was plain that Zelie Dionne was speaking out of the depths of her heart, and Farr remembered what old Etienne had said about the son of Farmer Leroux.

"Yes, she will lead to the right way and make all well in the end," asserted the girl. "And, most of all, she is kind and gentle to the little children."

Between her and the wistful old man Farr divided tolerant and kindly gaze.

"I believe in more things than I used to," he said. "I'm willing to admit in these days that things I do not understand may have truth in them. The doctor is not making her well. But it is a long way to that shrine."

"It is a long way, so! But I am very scare for her as she lie here all day. I will carry her very tender—on the railway car—on the big boat. The good Sainte Anne is everywhere, too. She will help."

"If faith can move mountains it ought to heal easily one poor, little toddlekins," muttered Farr.

A new doctor came the next day, a breezy young man, a talkative and frank young man, the assistant of the over-worked city physician, whose municipal duties had obliged him to take on helpers.

"I shall ask him, hey—about the shrine?" whispered Etienne to Farr while the doctor was examining the child.

"Yes; he'll be more patient with you than with me."

"And do you think that pretty soon she can go on the railway if I be very careful, good docteur?" asked the old man, wistfully, apologetically.

"Go where?"

"On the pilgrimage to the shrine of the good Sainte Anne in the Canada country."

"Don't you realize what this case is?" demanded the young physician.

"He have not say—he hurry in, he hurry out."

"You the grandfather?"

"No!"

The doctor turned on Farr.

"Father?"

"No."

"Then I can talk right out to you two. This is a case of typhoid that will be fatal in twenty-four hours. There's no use lying about it."

Old Etienne's mouth and eyes seemed to sink deep into his wrinkles, as if Time had forced him suddenly to swallow an extra score of years. He looked at Farr's blank and whitening face, and as quickly looked away.

"Break it to her grandmother," advised the doctor, nodding toward the kitchen where the good woman was at work.

"But you don't know what you say," stammered the old man.

"It so happens that I do, my man. I've been handling too many of these cases to be fooled. Why, I've got more than fifty cases of typhoid in this city—just myself."

"But she has had sun and fresh air—on the canal bank where I tend the rack."

"Sun and fresh air can't cure victims of the poison that is being pumped through the water-mains of this city," snapped the doctor.

"Water-mains!"

The doctor turned and stared at Farr, for the husky croak of his exclamation had not sounded human.

"That's what I said. You can't have lived very long in this state not to know what we're up against on the water proposition."

"I haven't lived here long. But about the child—it can't—"

"Why, this Consolidated Company is owned by Colonel Dodd and his politicians—and they own all the city and town water systems in this state," said the doctor, no longer interested in his patient—exploding with the violence of imprudent youth. "They boss mayors, the aldermen, the politicians—boss the governor himself. That's because they've got the machine and the money. They've got a lot of money, because they won't wake up and spend it to lay lines far enough to tap the lakes in the hills.

They tap these rotten rivers at our back doors, pump poison through the mains, sell it at prices that yield them twenty percent dividends. They say the water is all right—and back it up with analyses. I say it's all wrong."

"And you damnation doctors are letting this go on—letting folks drink poison—telling us when it's too late!" shouted Farr, purple replacing the white in his face.

"Well, the folks up-town who have got wisdom and the money buy spring-water and mineral water. All the doctors don't agree that the river is responsible for the typhoid. With the governor and the legislature bossed by Dodd and his associates, and the city governments tied up by them, and the banks taking orders from the syndicate in case any town or an independent company tries to borrow money and install a water system, and the mill corporations and the tenement-block owners all in cahoots, a crusader who expected to get anywhere in politics or make money out of his business would stand a fine and dandy show, now wouldn't he? And the most of us in this world are trying to get ahead either in business or in politics." He snapped the catch of his little black case. "Forget what I have said, you two. I hold my job through politics. I'm apt to talk too much when I get started. But don't drink city water, no matter if Colonel Dodd's analyses do give it a clean bill."

Farr caught him at the door, restraining him with a heavy hand.

"You stay here, don't you let that baby die. By the gods, she sha'n't die!"

"My staying will do no good, my friend. The little girl is death-struck already. It's quick work with the children. Sometimes we can bring the grown folks through. Get another doctor, if you feel like it, but I've got to keep moving—there are lots of folks waiting for me in these tenements."

He shook off Farr's hand and hurried away.

Old Etienne stood by the bedside, gazing down on the little sufferer, closing and unclosing his shriveled hands as if he were grasping at straws of hope, dragging the depths of his soul for reassurance even as he dragged his rake in the black waters of the canal.

"The whippersnapper lied about her. Because she's a baby he won't bother," stormed Farr. "I'll ransack this town for doctors—I'll find one who knows his business." He tiptoed to the bed and laid tender palm against the child's cheek. "I say her face isn't as hot as it was," he persisted. "Where can I find a doctor with gray whiskers, Etienne? That young fool doesn't know."

"There are many wise old docteurs in the long street named Western Boulevard—they live in the big houses—but they don't come to the tenement folks."

"One of them will come this time even if I have to lug him on my back."

He began to search for his hat, not remembering where he had tossed it in the haste and eagerness of his arrival at the good woman's house. He did not find it readily and he rushed out bareheaded.

"The sun and the air they do no good! It is the poison water—and the poor folks of the tenements they do not know!" muttered the old man. "That is what he say?" He went to the kitchen sink and unscrewed the faucet. He sniffed and made a wry face, then he ran his thin finger into the valve-chamber. He hooked and brought forth stringy slime, held it near his nose, and groaned. "The poor folks do not know. They who ask for the votes of the slashers, the weavers, the beamers—the men of the mills—they who ask votes do not want the poor folks to know, because the votes would not be given to them who sell poison in the water," he told the astonished good woman who had watched his act.

"I am careful about my kitchen—I am neat—I wash everything, Etienne," she assured him, sniffing at the slime in the sink, overcome by confusion, her housewife's reputation at stake.

"Yes, but you cannot wash the souls of them dam' scoundrels who send that water through the pipes to the poor people who can buy no other," he raged. "This is not your blame—you did not know." He pointed his finger, quivering, dripping with the slime, at the child on the bed. "They have murder her! With this!" He slatted his finger with the gesture of one who throws off a noisome serpent.

"But I drink the water—it hasn't made me sick," she protested.

"You—me—odders that are all dry up—tough old fools—we ought to die and we don't," he raged, stamping back and forth across the kitchen, waving his arms. "We have been poison so much we do not notice. But the poor little childs—the young folks that die—die in these tenements all the time—and we see the white ribbons hanging from the doors, so many place every day—the poor young folks with life ahead and much to live for even down here—they are poison and they do not know! Oh, le bon Dieu! Boil dem dam' devil in hell in the water they have sell to the poor!" He stopped, shocked by these words he heard coming from his mouth, and crossed himself contritely. "But I look at her—I hear what the docteur say—I talk and I cannot help!" He staggered into the room where the child lay, and sat down in a chair and held his face in his hands.

It was an aged and somewhat unctuous physician whom Farr brought. The doctor pursed his lips and puckered his eyebrows above the little wraith who minded him not at all, lying with eyes half closed, plucking with finger and thumb at the bedclothing.

"With a bit stronger constitution—if she were a little older—Take the case of an adult—"

"Say it short," growled Farr, clenching his fists as if he wanted to beat indulgence for the child out of the hide of the world. "I'm paying you for her life."

"I have nothing to sell you in this case—therefore there can be no pay." He leaned over the bed and smoothed the moist, tangled hair away from the child's brow. "I can only *give* you something, my friend. I give you all my sympathy. This baby is departing on a long journey, and I'm Christian enough to believe that the way will be made very smooth for the feet of little children. That's the faith of an old man."

There were both earnestness and tenderness in his tones—the smugness of the physician was gone. He shook Farr's hand and went out of the room, treading softly.

And the next day Rosemarie's tiny fingers stopped their flutterings and she went away—somewhere!

XI
THE LORDS OF THE CITY

Walker Farr would not allow the tiny body of Rosemarie to be carried away in the white hearse. In his grief he had not been able as yet to dissociate the identity of the child from the poor little tenement in which her spirit had dwelt for the few barren years of her life; it seemed to him that she would be very lonely in the white hearse. He rode to the cemetery, holding the tiny casket across his knees. There was only the one carriage—it was sufficient to carry the friends of little Rosemarie: one Walker Farr and old Etienne and play-mamma Zelie Dionne.

The rack-tender sat opposite Farr and nursed a bundle on his knees. He had wrapped it surreptitiously.

The two men sent Zelie Dionne back to the city in the carriage. But they waited beside the grave until the sexton had finished his work; Farr felt an uncontrollable impulse to wait till all was ended, as he had always waited every night till the little girl was sound asleep and tucked up in bed in the good woman's house. He sat crouched on the edge of a turfed grave, elbows on his knees, his hands clutched into his shock of hair.

After the sexton had departed, tools on his shoulder, Etienne unwrapped the bundle. He began to arrange the child's toys on the grave.

"It is as the others do—the fathers and mothers of our faith in the tenement-houses," he explained, wistfully, to the young man. He pointed to other graves in the vicinity, short and narrow graves. Toys were spread on them, too. They were the poor treasures of dead children. The toys had been left there in the vague, helpless yearning of parents who strove to reach their human consolation beyond the grave.

Farr gazed on these pitiful memorials of the children—from those graves to the new mound which covered Rosemarie. The ache that had been in his throat for so many hours grew more excruciating. He realized that a father in those circumstances would weep, but he did not feel like shedding tears, and he was ashamed of himself for what seemed lack of something within himself. What he felt then, what he had felt ever since that young doctor had passed sentence of death was surly, bitter rancor—the anger of a man who is robbed.

"Look all around at the graves," said Etienne, tears in his wrinkles. "I know something better since I take off that faucet. Not all the martyr die when the lion eat 'em up and the fire burn 'em; there be some martyr these day, too. And sometimes, mebbe, some man what have the power will come here and see all these poor little grave and then he go and choke the lion what eat all these poor childs."

"What kind of man would that be?" pondered Farr. At that moment he had little faith—much less faith than usual—in the decency of any human being; and for many years his faith in humankind had been expressed by a contemptuous snap of his finger.

To sit there longer and look at that fresh earth with the pathetic toys sprinkled over it was a torment his soul could not endure.

He arose and hurried away and Etienne followed him. They trudged in silence back to the city—Etienne to take his rake and pike-pole from the hands of the man who had substituted at the rack, and Farr to resume surly domination over his sweating Italians.

"The martyrs," Etienne had called them. The notion of that stuck in Farr's brooding thoughts.

He tried to look deeper into his own heart than he had ever looked before and explain to himself just what motive had attracted him to the child in the first place; he had never been especially interested in children before. He found himself muttering, "And a little child shall lead them," without understanding just why this child had led him so strangely.

If one Walker Farr had understood it at all and had been able to explain it to himself, he would have penetrated the mystery of the dynamics of love—the great gift to humanity that God has not seen fit to expose in its inner workings. Therefore, Farr strode here and there in the hot sun, spurred his diggers with crisp oaths, and on the heels of his profanity muttered to himself, "And a little child shall lead them."

The tile boss of the Consolidated, whose crew was following the trench-diggers, accosted Farr, after several inspections of his lugubrious countenance.

"Don't you think you need to be cheered up a little?"

Farr scowled at him.

"I don't know what has disagreed with you, but you're certainly in a bad way," pursued the boss. "Go up with the crowd to City Hall to-night and hear 'em open up the police scandals. Plenty of free fun for the heavy-hearted! There are about half a dozen fat cops in this city who'll be fried to a crisp on both sides, and the sound of the sizzling will be pleasant in the ears."

"I'm not interested."

"You will be, if you tend out. The hearing is before the mayor and the whole city government. Nothing very hefty in the way of charges—only loafing in beer-coolers during the heat of the day, spending their time chasing the labor-agitators out of the parks, and letting burglars keep house all summer in the mansions up-town while the owners are away at the seashore. It's all more or less of a joke."

"Why don't the mayor and aldermen of this city attend to duty instead of jokes?"

"Oh, this city is run so smooth that there's nothing to do in the summer except stage a little farce comedy at City Hall."

"Let me tell you that there's something to be investigated in this city that isn't a joke," raged Farr, his bitter ponderings blossoming into speech.

"What's that?"

"Murder going on every day in this damnable town."

"Well, I guess if there was any murder going on which we didn't hear about, even from our fat cops, it would be investigated, all right. What's the matter with you?"

"I'm glad now you told me about that hearing to-night," stated Farr, ignoring the other's curiosity. "I'm glad I know when and where to locate the mayor and his men in session. I'll find out if they propose to waste the people's time hearing funny stories about policemen and are going to let murder go on while they are laughing."

He strode away, cursing at his workmen as he tramped along the side of the ditch.

Farr knocked at the garret room of Etienne early that evening.

"I want you to come with me," he commanded.

The old man obeyed without questions. As they walked along the streets Farr did not volunteer information. He was grimly sure that if

Etienne should receive an inkling of what was expected of him the old man would not stop running until he had crossed the Canadian border.

They were ten minutes worming their way through the press that packed the corridors of City Hall. Groups were bulked at the doors admitting to the aldermen's room—men thatched against each other and overlapping like bees in a swarm at the door of a hive.

But the young man was tall and his shoulders were broad and he kept uttering the magic words, "Room for witnesses!" In his own consciousness he knew that what he should attempt to testify to that night was not on the slate, but the crowd accepted him as one of those from whom they anticipated entertainment, and allowed him to pass—and Etienne, holding to his young friend's coat, followed close and made his way before the throng could close in again.

The hearing began and progressed, and there was much laughter when the delinquencies of certain fat policemen were related—it was a free-and-easy affair—a sort of midsummer fantasy in municipal politics—a squabble between ward bosses who had become jealous in matters of the distribution of police patronage.

Walker Farr, standing against the wall of the audience-chamber, did not laugh. He was busy with thoughts of his own. This bland fooling in municipal matters while stealthy death, protected by city franchise, dripped, so he believed, from every faucet in the tenement-house district, stirred his bitter indignation. Etienne Provancher stood beside him, and the old man did not laugh, either, because he did not understand in the least what those men were talking about. And he was very uneasy, wistfully awe-stricken, hardly daring to touch with his hands the polished oak at his back. He was in the great *hotel de ville* whose exterior he had stared at many times without presuming or daring to enter the broad portals.

Then there came a recess while the mayor examined papers at his desk. The aldermen leaned back in their chairs with lighted cigars.

"Etienne," whispered the young man, deep resolve thrilling him, his eyes blazing into the wondering gaze of the old man, "those men who sit behind those desks can do something to save the children and the poor folks in the tenements. But they must wake up, these men here must. You and I must try to wake them up!"

Etienne's eyes opened wide. He did not in the least comprehend how he could serve.

"I know you will not desert a friend, Etienne. I know you'll stand behind me. I know you love the children. So be a brave man now!"

The next moment Etienne was so frightened that he feared he would drop where he stood, because the young man raised his voice so that it rang through the great hall and all eyes were turned that way.

"Your honor the mayor, and gentlemen; I am a stranger here. But I humbly ask permission to address you."

"If you are a witness in the police matter you will be called on in your turn after the recess," stated the mayor.

"I am not a witness in the police matter. I am here on other business."

"There is no other business before this meeting."

"But there should be, sir, for the business I have come on is a dreadful matter. It is a matter of life and death."

A hush fell on those in the chamber, and the mayor and his aldermen leaned forward, staring apprehensively. They had been warned that there were dangerous labor-agitators in the city. Many meetings had been broken up by the police at the request of Colonel Dodd, president of the Consolidated Water Company, and other employers had backed him. This tall young man had startled them with his sudden outbreak.

"It is a matter, gentlemen, which concerns every man, woman, and child in this city—vitally concerns them every hour of the day—every hour they are awake. You say you have no other business now except this silly police investigation. For God's sake, wake up and attend to real business—save the people's lives. Here you are in session and here are the people to listen."

"State your complaint. Be very brief," commanded the mayor.

But Walker Farr, it was plain, possessed craft as well as courage; he realized that curiosity, properly tickled, will make men more patient in listening.

"First, I want to call a witness. I am not known to this city. But I have here a man whom many of you know, I'm sure, for he has stood out in plain view of a street where many pass, and has worked there for thirty years. It is Etienne Provancher."

Several men laughed when Farr pushed the old man into view. There was a murmured chorus of "Pickaroon."

"It's for the children—the poor folks—for the memory of our little girl," hissed Farr in the old man's ear. "Will you go to your bed to-night—the night of the day we buried her—knowing that—you are a coward? These are only men. We must tell them so that they will know. Speak! Tell them!" He set his firm clutch around the trembling old Frenchman's arm and held him out where all could see.

"I do not know how to talk here—to so much man—to the lords of the city," stammered the miserable old man, licking his parched lips, scared until all was black before his eyes.

The hush was profound. Men curved their palms at their ears, wondering what old Pickaroon could have to say in City Hall.

"Remember what we have left up there—in the cemetery—the poor children in their graves," muttered Farr, again bending close to Etienne's ear.

Then, thus reminded, thus spurred, all his Gallic emotion bursting into flame in him suddenly, the old man felt the desperate resolution that often animates the humble and ignorant in great emergencies. The little ones had been martyrs—why not he? That thought flashed through the tumult in his brain.

"Yes, since you all hark for me to speak I will speak," he declared. "Messieurs, I am a poor man. Not wise. It is very hard for me to talk to you. But I have been to-day up where the little children are bury—so many of them, with their playthings on the graves. I went to take there anodder little child, poor baby girl. I leave her there with the odder ones—so very lonesome all of them—their modders cannot sing them to sleep any more."

"This is irregular," cried the mayor. "What do you want?"

"Nottings for maself," cried Etienne, passionately shrill in his tone now. "But I have to ask you, masters of this city, how much longer shall you send poison down the water-pipes to the poor folks and the children in the tenement blocks? It is poison that has kill our little Rosemarie—and all her life ahead! The doctor say so—and he say I cannot understand about the rich man, why he do it. But I understand that the childs are dying. I say you shall not sent that water—if you do send it I will bring here the fadders who have lost their babies and the modders of the babies." His lips curled back in his excitement and froth flecked his mouth. "Sacred name of God! We shall tear that poison-factory up from the ground with our bare hands!"

"Officer, put that man out of the room," ordered the mayor.

"Won't you listen to us?" shouted Farr. "You are the chief magistrate of this city. You and these aldermen are the guardians of the people. Are you going to sit there in those cushioned chairs and let a crowd of rich assassins murder the poor people?"

Men hissed that speech.

The mayor rapped his gavel furiously.

"This is no matter to be brought up here at this time. You're slandering honorable men, sir! We have other business."

"Can there be any other business as important as this?"

"Put both of these men out, officer."

"Are you and these aldermen owned by the water syndicate, as report says you are?" cried Farr. "Look here, you men, men in this room and at the door! This is your City Hall—these aldermen are elected by your votes. Aren't you going to demand that the people be heard in this matter? Don't you know that typhoid fever is killing off the children in this city—and that poison water is the cause of it?"

"It's rotten stuff to drink—we all know that," cried a voice. "But there'll have to be a change in politics in this state before they'll give us anything else."

Two policemen elbowed their rough way to Farr and Etienne.

"The big chap is right—it's about time to have this water question opened up, Mr. Mayor," called another voice.

"Open it up in a legal and proper way, then," snapped the mayor. "Go to the law."

"That's it—go to the law—go to the law," jeered another. "And we'll all be dead and the lawyers will have all our money before the thing is decided."

There were more hisses.

But an outburst of indorsing voices indicated that many men in that chamber understood more or less of the political management behind the Consolidated Water Company.

"If a thing is wrong, change it. What better law do you need than that?" asked Farr, disregarding an officer's thumb that jerked imperious gesture.

"When you know a little more law you won't be ignoramus enough to come into a public hearing and try to break it up. You'd better go and study law," said the indignant mayor. He pounded his gavel to indicate that the recess was over.

"I'll take your advice," replied Farr, towering over the policeman and vibrating his finger at his Honor. "If you hadn't found law so handy in your own case you wouldn't forget yourself in your excitement and recommend it to others. If we've got to fight the devil we'd better use his weapons."

Men shouted approval all around him.

"Clear the room," ordered the mayor. "Everybody out!"

"Keep your hands off," Farr advised the officer nearest him. "I'll go without any help. I have found out that I'm only wasting my time in this place."

In the corridor men pressed around him. Some of them insisted on shaking his hand. Others shouted commendation. Still others exhibited only frank curiosity in the stalwart stranger. And others were clamorously hostile.

"By gad! If you wanted to start something you took the right way to do it," affirmed one of the throng.

"You showed good courage," declared an elderly man with an earnest face. "Some of the rest of us have tried to do something in the past. But those who didn't have much power were either kept out or kicked out of any office in city government or the legislature—and those who did amount to something were gobbled up by the machine. The machine can pay. Working for the people isn't very profitable. So I'm afraid you won't get very far."

"You needn't worry about that chap not getting along all right," remarked one of the group—but his indorsement was ironical. "He's a construction boss for the Consolidated, and he went into that hearing to start some kind of a back-fire. Shrewd operators—the Consolidated folks."

The men about Farr pulled away from him and there was considerable malicious laughter in the crowd.

"So we see the game, even if we don't catch on to the meaning of it just now," said the observant one.

Farr squared his shoulders. They stared at him with fresh interest and a bit of additional respect. They saw in him something more than a mere popular agitator—a disturber of a municipal hearing; he must be a trusted agent of the great political machine, executing a secret mission.

"You're right—I have been working for the Consolidated," he admitted in tones that all could hear.

"Move on! Get outdoors! Clear this corridor—all of you," shouted a captain of police who had come hurrying up from down-stairs and had taken command of the situation.

The crowd began to surge on, following Farr.

"I went to work digging in their trenches because I struck this town on my uppers and needed the money—needed it quick. I was promoted to be a boss. But I want to tell you now, gentlemen, that I do not work for the Consolidated."

"I reckon you're right," said somebody. "I just overheard a man telephoning to the superintendent about you—and if I'm any judge of a conversation you are *not* working for the Consolidated. Not any more!"

"I'm sorry you're going to leave the city," lamented the elderly man. "We need chaps like you."

"I'm not going to leave the city."

"You might just as well," counseled one of the bystanders, "after what you said in that hearing. If you get a job in this city after this you'll be a good one!"

When they were outside City Hall, Farr waited for a moment on the steps. Etienne, still trembling after that most terrible experience of his placid life, pressed close at the young man's side.

"Will all you gentlemen please take a good look at me so that you'll know me when you see me again?" invited the ex-boss for the Consolidated.

They stared at him. His face was well lighted by the arc-light under the arch of the door.

"I am not a labor-leader, nor a walking delegate, nor a politician, nor an anarchist. You men go home and unscrew the faucets in your kitchens, take a good sniff, and pull the slime out of the valve. Then remember that the mayor and aldermen of this city wouldn't listen to me to-night in the Hall that the tax-payer's money built. Also remember that a little later they will listen to me. Gentlemen, my name is Walker Farr. I'm going to stay here in this city. Good night."

XII
AT THE FOOT OF THE THRONE

As usual at nine-thirty in the afternoon, the big tower clock on the First National Bank building in the city of Marion pointed the finger of its minute-hand straight downward.

As usual, at this hour, as he had done for many years, Colonel Symonds Dodd eased himself down from the equipage that brought him to his office. This day the vehicle was his limousine car.

In view of the fact that Colonel Dodd owned the First National block the big clock seemed to point its finger at him with the bland pride of a flunky in a master. It seemed to say, "Behold! The great man is here!"

Colonel Dodd was never embarrassed when fingers were pointed at him wherever he went. If a man is lord of finance and politics in his state he expects to be pointed out.

When he stepped from his car he carried in his arms, with great tenderness, a long parcel which was carefully wrapped in tissue-paper. He always carried a similar parcel when he came to his office. Each morning the gardener of the Dodd estate laid choice flowers on the seat of that vehicle which had been chosen to convey the master to the city.

Colonel Dodd coddled the long parcel with the care a nurse would have bestowed on an infant—but he kicked his fat leg clumsily at an urchin who got in his way on the sidewalk. A college professor of Marion happened to be passing at the moment and saw the act and knew what the colonel was carrying in his arms. The professor made a mental note of fresh material for his lecture on "The Psychological Phenomena of the Bizarre in the Emotions." The professor had just met a woman wheeling a cat out in a baby-carriage.

The doctor had advised exercise for the colonel—a small amount. The colonel toilsomely climbed the one flight of stairs to his office. That was his daily quota of exercise.

A little man with a beak of a nose was waiting in the corridor and hastened to unlock a door marked "Private," and the colonel went in, and the little man locked the door and tiptoed down the corridor to the general offices.

Before he removed his hat Colonel Dodd carefully stripped the tissue-paper from the damp flowers. There were two huge bouquets. He set these into vases of ornate bronze, one on each end of his desk. He patted and stroked the flowers until they appeared to best advantage. He stood back and bestowed affectionate regard on them. No human being had ever reported the receipt of such a look from Colonel Symonds Dodd. It was rather astonishing to find softness in him in respect to flowers. He seemed as hard as a block of wood. He had a squat, square body and his legs seemed to be set on the corners of that body. His square face was smooth except for a wisp of whisker, minute as a water-color brush, jutting from under his pendulous lower lip.

He hung up his hat and stood for a moment before a massive mirror. The report in Marion was that he stood before that mirror and made up his expression to suit the character of a day's business.

Then he sat down at his desk and stuck a pudgy finger on one button of a battery of buttons.

A girl entered with a promptitude which showed that she had been waiting for the summons.

He did not look up at her. His gaze was on one of the bouquets.

She brought a portfolio and packets of letters all neatly docketed.

His salutation was merely, "Miss Kilgour." Colonel Dodd did not deal in many "Good-mornings." It was also reported in Marion and the state that his stock of urbanity was so small he was compelled to expend it very thriftily. He certainly did not waste any of it on his office help. He might have afforded at least one glance at the girl, for she was extremely pretty. Still another report in Marion was to the effect that he had selected Kate Kilgour as his secretary as the final artistic touch to the beauty of his private office in order that he might have a perfect ensemble. She did seem, so far as his interest in her went, to be only a part of that ensemble which he occasionally swept carelessly with his gaze—he reserved all his intimate admiration for the bouquets.

She laid his "Strictly Personal" letters on his fresh blotter.

She sat down and began to read the business letters aloud, not waiting for his orders to begin. It was her daily routine, business transacted as Colonel Dodd wished it to be transacted—crisply, promptly, directly.

He dictated replies, usually laconic, even curt, as soon as she had finished each letter. His eyes were on the flowers as he talked.

When the letters were finished she retired with her portfolio and her notes, the thick carpet muffling the sound of her withdrawal.

After he had slit the envelopes of his personal correspondence and had read the contents the colonel pushed another button. The little man who had been waiting in the corridor slipped edgewise in at the door. He was thin and elderly and his knob of a head, set well down on his pinched shoulders, had peering eyes on each side of that beak of a nose. When he walked across the room his long arms were behind him under his coat-tails and held them extended, and he bore some resemblance to a bird. In fact, one did not require much imagination to note resemblance to a bird in Peter Briggs—many folks likened him to a woodpecker—for he flitted to and fro in Colonel Dodd's anteroom, among those awaiting audience, tapping here and rapping there with the metaphorical beak of questions, starting up the moths and grubs of business which men who came and waited hid under the bark of their demeanor.

"Seventeen, Colonel Dodd. Five for real business; twelve of them are sponges."

"The five?"

"Chief Engineer Snell of the Consolidated, Dr. Dohl of the State Board of Health, the three promoters of the Danburg Village Water system."

"Send in Snell."

Engineer Snell did not sit in the presence of his president, nor did the president ask him to sit.

"Briggs tells me the Danburg men are here."

"They're waiting out there, Colonel Dodd."

"Quitting?"

"I don't think so—just yet. They look too mad. I gave 'em the harpoon in good shape, as is usual, but I didn't expect they'd run here so soon. Thought they would flop a little longer."

"They got their poke from Stone & Adams yesterday afternoon, did they?"

"Yes, Colonel. My report to Stone & Adams showed that the Danburg plan of levels is faulty, that their unions are not up to contract, that their station and pumps are inefficient for the demands. So Stone & Adams had to tell 'em that their bonds were turned down."

"Do you know whether they have tried another banking-house yet?"

"I don't believe they have had time, Colonel."

"But such fellows always do try. Their banging in here on me so quickly looks a little irregular. In business, you know, Snell, if you tie a tin can to a dog and he runs and ki-yi's, that's perfectly natural and you can sit back and wait for nature to take its course. If the dog doesn't run, but sits down and gnaws the string in two—then look out for the dog."

"I must admit they're coming here sudden after their jolt. They look mad. But I figure they must have quit. The jolt was a hard one, for Stone & Adams had been leading 'em on—according to orders."

The colonel stared at a bouquet.

"Have you got your other report—the side report—in shape for me to get a hasty idea? If they have come here with a proposition—want to quit and cover themselves, I need information right now."

Engineer Snell laid papers on the desk. He proceeded to explain.

"If you don't feel you have time to go over it—don't want to keep the Danburg crowd waiting—I can tell you that the plant is pretty nearly all right. So much all right that you can afford to slip 'em a couple of thousand apiece on top of what they have already spent. I don't suppose you want 'em to holler too loud. I can tell you that Davis, Erskine, and Owen—those men out there—are cleaned out. They have put in all their ready money. They were depending on Stone & Adams for the first instalment from the bonds, so as to take up some thirty-day notes and pay bills due on material."

Colonel Dodd meditated, pulling on his wisp of whisker.

"It's one thing to encourage enterprise in this state—it's another thing to be everlastingly paying rake-offs to local promoters who grab a franchise when we're not looking and then hold us up. I don't want to hurt the Danburg men. But my stockholders expect certain things of me and it's about time men in this state understand that we propose to control the water question. Snell, you go and talk to those Danburg men like a father to children. Send them in here smoothed down and we'll do the right thing by them."

He signaled for Briggs and told him to admit Dr. Dohl.

The doctor, chairman of the State Board of Health, was a chubby man with a tow-colored, fan-shaped beard. He sat down and sprung his eyeglasses on his bulgy nose and drew out a package of manuscript.

"Colonel, I have felt it my duty to write a special chapter on the typhoid situation in this state for the report of the State Board of Health."

"Very well, Doctor." The colonel was curt and his tone admitted nothing of his sentiments.

"DO you care to listen to it? It rather vitally concerns the Consolidated Water Company."

"You don't blame us for all these typhoid cases, do you?"

"No, sir—not for all of them."

"Why blame us for any of them? Our analyses show that we're giving clean water. How about dirty milkmen and the sanitary arrangements in these tenement-houses and all such? It's the fashion to blame a corporation for everything bad that happens in this world."

"We have placed blame on milkmen where any blame is due," stated Dr. Dohl. He tapped his manuscript. "But I have spent considerable of my department's money in making a house-to-house canvass, tracing the sources. The man before me *guessed*. I have made *sure*! Colonel Dodd, the Consolidated water is pretty poisonous stuff these days."

"What's the matter in this state all of a sudden?" snapped the colonel. "I am told that a lunatic almost broke up our city government meeting the other night, shouting that the Consolidated is trying to poison folks. You're too level-headed a man to get into that class, Dr. Dohl."

"I'll allow you to set me down in any class which seems fitting from your point of view," replied the doctor, stiffly. "But if that lunatic, as you call him, got an angle-worm or a frog's leg out of his tap I don't blame him for breaking up a meeting of the city government which will tolerate the water which is being pumped through the city mains just now."

"We're working on the filtering-plant—it will be all right in a little while. It got out of hand before we realized it," said the colonel, now a bit apologetic.

"In this crisis your filter amounts to about that!" The doctor snapped a pudgy finger into a plump palm. "The river-water in this state has been poisoned. You must go into the hills—to the lakes, Colonel Dodd."

"You don't mean to say that you recommend that in your report, Doctor?"

"Absolutely—emphatically."

"Without stopping to think of the millions it will cost my company to build over its plants?"

"It has come to a point where it isn't a question of money, Colonel."

"We can't afford it."

"Then let the cities and towns of the state buy in their water-plants and do it."

"Good Jefferson! Don't you know that every city and town in this state where we have a water-plant has already exceeded its debt limit of five percent?"

"Do I understand you as intimating, Colonel Dodd, that there is no help for this present condition of affairs?"

"Look here—I'm neither a Herod nor a Moloch, even if some of the crack-brained agitators in this state will have it that way," protested the magnate, with heat. "Are you going to print that report before you have given us time to turn around?"

"With one hundred deaths a day from typhoid fever in this state, Colonel, that matter of time becomes mighty important."

"Look here, Dohl, don't you remember that it was my indorsement that gave you your job?"

"I do, Colonel Dodd. But I'm a physician, not a politician."

"I see you're not," retorted the colonel, dryly. "But you're a member of our political party, and you know that the Consolidated and its associate interests are the backbone of that party. There are a lot of soreheads in this state, and we're having a devil of a time to hold 'em in line. Every savings-bank in this state, furthermore, holds bonds of the Consolidated. Do you want to start a panic? You've got to be careful how you touch the first brick standing in a row. Dohl, you leave that report with me. I'll go over it. I'll take the matter up with the directors. We'll move as fast as possible."

The doctor hesitated, stroking the folds of his manuscript.

"You're not doubting my word, are you?" demanded the colonel.

"No, sir!" Even the physician's sense of duty did not embolden him to persist under this scowl of the man of might.

The colonel took the document from Dr. Dohl's relaxing hands and shoved it into a pigeonhole of the big desk.

"You must understand that pipe-lines to lakes cannot be laid in a minute as a child strings straws, Doctor," admonished the magnate.

"Do you propose to lay lines to the lakes, Colonel? I need to throw a little sop to my conscience if my report is delayed."

"Everything right will be done in good time, Dr. Dohl. I will proceed as rapidly as possible, considering that the law, finance, and politics are all concerned. As you are leaving," he added, giving his visitor the blunt hint that the interview was over, "I must draw your attention to the fact that if you bludgeon the Consolidated with a report like this it may be a long time before we can move in the matter. You'll only scare the banks and set the cranks to yapping. Just remember that you're a state officer and have a weighty responsibility to your party and to financial interests."

Dr. Dohl went away. He sourly realized that he was only a cog in the big machine; that for a moment he had threatened to develop a rough edge and start a squeak, but the big file had been used on him. It had been used on many another of the State House cogs, as he well knew. Responsibility as to his party! Safety and sanity in regard to financial interests! He knew that these talismanic words had been used to control even the lords in national politics. He departed from the Presence, muttering his rebellion, but fully conscious that a political Samson in modern days made but a sorry spectacle of himself when he started to pull down the pillars of the party temple.

He continued to mutter when he walked through the anteroom.

Most of the men who waited there had faces as lowering as the visage which Dr. Dohl displayed.

The doctor had not lost all faith in his own fearlessness and rectitude of motive, but he was obliged to acknowledge to himself that just then he was a rather weak champion.

"However, I'd like to lay eyes on the sort of man who can unjoint this devilish combination of politics and law and finance," he informed himself, trying to justify his own retreat.

His eyes, in passing, swept a stranger.

The stranger was a tall young man with wavy hair and brown eyes. He sat patiently, nursing a broad-brimmed black hat on his knees.

"I'd like to see that man!" repeated Dr. Dohl, mentally, sugar-coating his disgust at his own weakness.

If mortal man were gifted with prescience Dr. Dohl would have stared out of countenance the tall young man who sat on a bench in the outer office of the state's overlord and nursed a broad-brimmed hat upon his knees.

XIII
THE CODE AND THE GAGE OF BATTLE

"I appreciate zeal in public affairs," mused Colonel Dodd, gazing at the door which Dr. Dohl had closed behind him. "But once there was a retriever dog who chased his master with a stick of dynamite that had a sputtering fuse."

He set his broad hands upon the arms of his chair, derricked himself up, and went over to the mirror. He peered at himself and seemed to rearrange his countenance, much as a woman would smooth the ruffled plumage of her hat.

"We're not murderers," he informed the composed visage which the mirror held forth to him. "But we haven't got to the point where we're letting lunatics who break up city government meetings, or crank doctors, tell us how to spend a million or two of the money we've worked hard to accumulate. There's getting to be too much of this telling business men in this country how to run their business. If we're peddling typhoid fever in spite of what our analyses tell us, then we'll go ahead, of course, and clean up." Colonel Dodd was willing to acknowledge that much to himself, surveying his countenance in the mirror. "But we'll continue to run our own business," he added.

Then he sat down again in his chair and pushed a button. "Briggs," he directed, "send in those three men from Danburg."

He whirled his swivel-chair and sat there at his desk, his rectangular front squared to meet them.

The three men who came in were of the rural businessmen type, and their faces were not amiable. Two of them halted in the middle of the sumptuous apartment and the third stepped a couple of paces ahead of them. He carried a huge roll of engineers' plans under his arm.

"My name is Davis, as I suppose you know, Colonel Dodd," he reported.

"Have seats, gentlemen."

"We are tired of sitting," stated the spokesmen, with sour significance.

"I understand, Mr. David. But mornings are very busy times for me. I was attending to appointments made beforehand. You made no appointment, and I was not expecting you."

There was silence, and the three men glowered on him. It was evident that settled animosity emboldened these country merchants even in the presence of Colonel Symonds Dodd.

"I was not expecting you, I say."

The colonel's demeanor displayed a little uncertainty; he had rather expected suppliants. He knew what a nasty blow had been dealt these men the day before.

"Probably not," assented Davis. "You expected that after Stone & Adams yanked the gangplank out from under us yesterday we would put in at least one day tearing around to other banking firms, trying to place our bonds."

"Why—why—Well, if Stone & Adams—You naturally wouldn't take the verdict of one banking-house on a matter of bonds, would you?"

"Look here, Colonel Dodd, we understand you—clear way down to the ground—and we may as well save wear on our tongues. And first of all we have come right here to save shoe-leather. We have come straight to headquarters. Do you suppose we're going to gallop around this city to bankers after the word has gone out about us? Not much! We are here in the captain's office, and you can't fool us about that."

"I never heard such—" the colonel began to sputter.

"I know you never did—and it's getting your goat," asserted the blunt countryman. "We've got a plain and pertinent question to put to you—do you intend to ram us to the wall in our water deal?"

The head of the state's water trust simulated anger perfectly, even if he didn't feel it. And there was astonishment in his anger.

"What have I to do with your dealings with bankers?" he demanded. "Probably your plant isn't up to pitch."

"That talk doesn't go with us, not for a minute, Colonel Dodd," shouted the undaunted Davis. "You're talking to business men, not to children. We offered to leave the matter of our plan to any three engineers in this state. Why is it that Stone & Adams refuse to take the word of anybody except your man, Snell?"

"They probably want the word of the best consulting-engineer in the state."

"But he's your man."

"He is our man because he is the best. We hire him for our work. But we do not control his opinions when he is consulted by others. Oh no! And I want to tell you, my men, that I refuse to listen to any more such talk from you."

"Then call in one of your political policemen and have us put out," invited the unterrified Davis.

"Build your plant right and your bonds will sell. Our bonds sell when Mr. Snell reports on our plants."

"We'll save our strength in the matter of building plants and running around trying to place bonds with brokers who have been tipped off by the money trust of this state. We propose to get it straight from you first. You can't fool us for one minute, I repeat! We'll have our last wiggle right here. Will you take your hands off our affairs?"

"I haven't put my hands *on* your affairs," shouted Colonel Dodd, furious at being baited in this amazing manner. Never before had any visitor dared to raise his voice in that office. "You're crazy."

"You're right—we are—pretty nearly so. Myself and these two neighbors of mine have tied up every dollar we can rake and scrape to build a water-plant for our little village and give our folks clean water from a lake, not the rotten poison you would pump out of our millstream for us. We have tried to do this for our town and make an honest dollar for ourselves. Now you have got us lashed to the mast, financially, so you think, and you propose to step in and gobble our franchise. That's enough to make men crazy."

"Get out of my office!"

"You grabbed the franchise and common stock of Westham that way," declared Davis. "You scooped in Durham and Newry and a lot of others. But I'm here to warn you, Colonel Dodd. Danburg is going to choke you if you try to swallow it. We are only countrymen, and we know it. You have always done all the bossing and threatening in this state up to now. But I tell you, Colonel Dodd, there comes a time when the rabbit will spit in the bulldog's eye. If we three go out of this room in the same spirit in which we came into it something will drop in this state. We shall have a story to tell."

Colonel Dodd swung his chair around and faced his desk.

"Gentlemen, let's not get excited," he appealed. Ostensibly he reached for a pencil. He also pushed a button he had not touched before that day. Then he came around slowly on the swivel of his chair. "You have mentioned certain towns, Davis. Those towns have water systems that are a part of the Consolidated, to be sure. But the men who promoted those plants and were unable to complete them came to us and begged us to step in and take the burden off their hands." While Colonel Dodd talked he kept glancing, but in an extremely unobtrusive manner, at a huge and magnificent Japanese screen that occupied one corner of his office. "It is easy enough to start ventures in this world, Mr. Davis. An inexperienced man can do that. But it most often takes experience and a lot of money to install a successful water plant."

"We want to get down to cases, Colonel Dodd," insisted the spokesman. "We haven't come here without posting ourselves. We know how you have talked to the others. But you can't bluff us. You propose to steal our plant, such of it as we have been able to build to date. One word from you to the money gang takes the hoodoo off us. Now talk business! Do you propose to pot us like you have the rest?"

The heart of the big rose in the center of the screen flashed once with a glow that was imperceptible unless one had been gazing at it, watching for a signal. Colonel Dodd understood that Miss Kate Kilgour had entered through a low door and was behind the screen, ready with note-book and pencil. He leaned back in his deep chair and interlocked his pudgy fingers across his paunch.

"I assure you I have not the least interest in your projects as to the Danburg water system, Mr. Davis, Mr. Erskine, Mr. Owen." He dwelt on the names. "The Consolidated has plenty of its own business to attend to."

"But I say you are trying to run *our* business, too—no, ruin it!"

"Do you realize, Mr. Davis, that you are accusing me of criminal conspiracy—making a statement that might go hard with you in a court of law? You have accused me of trying to discredit you with banking-houses. Can you produce any proof except your foolish and unjust suspicions? You have been made angry by a refusal to handle your bonds. I don't sell bonds. I build and operate water systems."

"The same old game," sneered Davis. "Your water syndicate, the railroads of this state, the banks, the politics—they're all snarled up together like snakes in winter quarters. I say, if you pass the word our bonds will be taken. If you don't do it, I'm going to trot out of this office and expose your highway-robber system."

"In one breath you threaten me because you say I'm interfering in your affairs. In the next breath you threaten me because I refuse to interfere. You are making dangerous talk, Davis. I may call the courts to pass on that threat. There is only one proposition I can make to you—and that's strictly in the line of my business. If you are tied up financially—are at the end of your resources and must have help—I'll give you my aid in getting the Consolidated to take over the Danburg plant at a fair valuation."

"Is that the best word you've got for us?"

"I have made you an honorable business proposition."

"That your final talk?"

"Absolutely."

Davis found words inadequate for his boiling emotions just then. He advanced on Dodd, who shrank back into his chair. Davis whipped the long roll of plans out from under his arm, held the roll by one end, and swung it like a bat-stick. But he did not strike at Dodd, as the magnate seemed to apprehend.

He swung over the colonels' head and swept the top of the desk clean of everything; vases, bouquets, *objets d'art*, all went rolling and smashing to the floor.

Colonel Dodd ducked low and held his square head in his hands as if he feared that the next assault would be on that. But Davis led his associates out of the room through the door which Briggs had flung open, summoned by the crash in his master's holy of holies.

For the first time, perhaps, in the history of that private office the door leading into the anteroom was left open and unguarded. Briggs ran into the room, his coat-tails streaming, his inquisitive beak stretched forward. On his heels followed the tall young man who had been waiting in the anteroom. It was Walker Farr, who closed the door behind him, shutting out the curious anteroom clients who flocked and peered.

When the colonel lifted his head he found himself looking squarely into the eyes of this tall young man whom he in no way remembered.

Briggs went down on his hands and knees and began to pick up the debris.

One of the bouquets had rolled to the colonel's feet, and he stooped with some difficulty, recovered it, and laid it across his knees. He gazed past Farr with a frown—with a significant, dismissing jerk of his head. The young man turned in time to see the capitalist's handsome secretary. The amazing riot in the sanctuary of her employer had brought her from behind the screen. Uncertainty and alarm were in her eyes and excitement had flushed her cheeks. Against the background of the gorgeous screen she seemed a veritable apparition of loveliness, and while Farr stared, frankly admiring her, recognizing her, exchanging that startled recognition with her, she disappeared.

"How do you dare to come into my private office in this fashion?"

"I have waited in that anteroom every day for ten days, trying to get an audience. The door was open just now and I came in."

"It's your own fault if you haven't seen me. I see men who have business with me and who send in an explanation of that business."

"So I have been told by that man," stated Farr, pointing to Briggs, who was groping about on the carpet. "But my business with you couldn't be discussed through a third party."

"Now that you're in here, what is that business?"

"I'll tell you first what it is *not*, so that there won't be any misunderstanding in your mind about me. I am not here to borrow money, beg money, ask for work, ask for a personal favor of any kind, solicit a political job, nor have I anything to sell to you or to give to you. So, you see, my business is different."

With a quick motion he brought out a parcel which he had held concealed in the broad-brimmed hat.

Briggs straightened up on his knees and remained thus, seemingly paralyzed, staring at the parcel.

The capitalist sank back in his chair, his face growing greenish white.

"Don't you throw that bomb!" he gasped. In his panic he was not able to deduce any other explanation for the presence of this stranger who had so strenuously disclaimed all reasonable motives for his visit. He quailed before this man who seemed to be a dangerous crank—for Farr's attire was out of the ordinary and his eyes were flashing and his poise was that of a man sure of himself.

"What do you think I have here in this package?"

"Dynamite!" mumbled the magnate.

"It's worse."

Colonel Dodd rolled his head to and fro on the back of his chair, shutting his eyes in vain attempt to find somebody to whom to appeal for help. He started a furtive hand in the direction of the battery of buttons.

"Keep your hands in your lap," commanded Farr. "I say that what I have here in this package is worse than dynamite." He tore the paper and disclosed a half-dozen faucets that were still dripping with slime. "You know now what I mean, Colonel Dodd. This is the stuff your water company is pumping through the pipes in this state."

The president of the Consolidated straightened in his chair, but he had been thoroughly frightened.

While Farr talked on the colonel seemed to be gathering himself—recovering his voice.

"It's a mighty bold act for me to come in here like this, Colonel Dodd. I understand it. I'm a poor man and a stranger in this city. Just consider me a voice—call me Balaam's ass if you want to. But I've come up from the tenement-house districts where the children are dying."

"What do you want?" The magnate discharged the question explosively.

"Pure water in the city mains."

"Whom do you represent?"

Farr hesitated. Colonel Dodd scented possible political strategy in this visit, and was controlling his ire in order to probe the matter.

"Come, my man. Out with it! Who commissioned you to come here?"

"I'll not claim that I have any powers delegated to me, sir."

"How did you dare to force your way in here?"

"Considering what kind of a man I was a few weeks ago, I'm having pretty hard work to explain to myself what I'm doing, sir."

The colonel knotted bushy brows. This person seemed to be playing with him. "Who told you to come here?"

"The soul of a little girl who was named Rosemarie."

Colonel Dodd came out of his chair, thoroughly angry—and yet he repressed his anger. This person, more than ever, seemed to him to be a crank with vagaries.

Farr put up a protesting palm. His tones trembled, and into them he put all the appeal a human voice can compass.

"I know I astonish you, Colonel," he added. "I astonish myself. I'm not much on self-analysis. I don't know just what has come over me the last few weeks. But they do say the Deity picks out queer instruments when He wants things done. Man to man, now, forgetting you're a mighty man and I'm a small one, won't you say you'll give the people of this state pure water instead of poison?"

"You don't think you can stroll in here and coax me to build over the whole Consolidated system, do you?"

"That isn't the idea at all, sir. Treat me simply as a voice—a jog of your conscience—a reminder. I'll go away and you'll never see me again."

"If you think the cranks in this state can influence me in the least item about running my own business you're the worst lunatic outside the state asylum," declared the colonel, with passion.

"You mean that what I have asked on behalf of women and children hasn't had any effect on you?"

"Not the slightest. Get out!" In his present mood Colonel Dodd would not admit to this interloper that he planned reforms, and in that moment he unwittingly created his Frankenstein's monster.

Farr retreated a couple of steps and bowed. "Colonel Dodd, in my part of the West we fellows had a little code: help a woman, always, everywhere; tote a tired child in our arms; and, in the case of a man who announced himself an enemy, give him fair notice when it came time to pull guns. Better get your weapon loose on your hip."

He bowed again and went out.

Briggs rose from his knees and his master snapped an angry stare from the door that the young man had closed softly behind himself.

"What kind of a resort is my office getting to be? Do you know who that devilish fool is, Briggs?"

"No, sir. He has been hanging around here, that's all I know. I kept at him." He made a little dab of his woodpecker beak. "But I couldn't find out anything from him."

"Well find out from somebody else, then. And get judge Warren on the 'phone for me."

When the bell rang and the colonel heard the voice of the Consolidated's corporation counsel greeting him on the wire he ordered the judge to come over at once.

"Hell has just burned through here in three small patches," stated the colonel, grimly. "The sooner we turn on the Consolidated hose, the better."

In the early dusk of a summer evening Mr. Peter Briggs stood at the edge of the sidewalk of one of the squalid avenues of the district of the tenement-houses of Marion. His hands were behind him, propping out his coat-tails. He kept peering at the gloomy stairway of a house near at hand. Take the gloom, his attitude, and his sooty garb, and he gave a very picturesque impression of a raven doing sentinel duty.

At last a tall young man came down the stairs which Mr. Briggs was watching and strolled off leisurely up the avenue, stopping here and there to chat, nodding to this man, flourishing a hand salute to that man. The young man apparently had nothing whatever on his mind except to enjoy a stroll in the summer evening.

Mr. Briggs watched him out of sight without moving from his tracks. Then he withdrew both hands from under his coat-tails. In one hand was a note-book, in the other hand was a pencil. Mr. Briggs made an entry, closed the book with decision, and snapped an elastic band around the covers. Then he made off toward his home. He lived up-town in a section where there were fewer smells and better scenery. He determined that this should be his last tour of surveillance. He had found his trips into the nooks and crannies of the Eleventh Ward to be very distasteful employment for a man who had served Colonel Dodd for so many years in the sumptuous surroundings of that office in the First National block.

He asked himself what would be the use of hunting for any more information regarding such an inconsequential individual as one Walker Farr? He wondered why this crank had impressed Colonel Symonds Dodd sufficiently to stir up all this trouble for himself, Peter Briggs. The fellow had come from somewhere—nobody in Marion seemed to know. He had been discharged from the employment of the Consolidated. Now he was going about, warning all the people to boil the city water they drew from the faucets. He seemed to be a crank on the water subject, so Peter Brigg's note-book recorded.

The book also recorded that this queer Walker Farr strolled about the streets in the poorer quarters, "currying favor": so Peter Briggs expressed the young man's evening activities in the note-book. That seemed to be all there was to it. At any rate, Peter Briggs decided that he had finished his quest.

Thereupon he had snapped the elastic band with vigor and made up his mind to tell Colonel Dodd the next morning that chasing that worthless fellow around or thinking that such a fellow could do anything to interfere with Colonel Dodd was poppycock. Peter Briggs hoped he would dare to call it "poppycock" in the presence of his master—for he was thoroughly sick of being a sleuth in the ill-smelling Eleventh Ward.

He did dare to call it poppycock. And Colonel Dodd shrugged his shoulders and forgot one Walker Farr. The fellow seemed inconsiderable—and Colonel Dodd found other matters very pressing.

For one thing, those three men from Danburg had brought suit against both Stone & Adams and the Consolidated Water Company and had engaged as counsel no less a personage than the Honorable Archer Converse, the state's most eminent corporation lawyer, a man of such high ideals and such scrupulous conception of legal responsibility that he had never been willing to accept a retainer from the great System which dominated state affairs. Colonel Symonds Dodd feared the Honorable Archer Converse. It was hinted that the Danburg case would involve charges of conspiracy with intent to restrain independents, and would be used to show up what the opponents of the Consolidated insisted was general iniquity in finance and politics.

Colonel Dodd outwardly was not intimidated. He sent no flag of truce. He decided to intrench and fight. He cursed when he remembered the interview with the Danburg triumvirate.

"Under ordinary circumstances I would buy them off in the usual way," he informed Judge Warren. "But that damnation lunatic raved at me with all the insults he could think of—then he up with his dirty bunch of plans and knocked my flowers on to the floor—yes, sir, that was what the mad bull did—he knocked my flowers on to the floor!"

And Colonel Dodd emphasized that as the crime unforgivable.

XIV
THE MATTER OF DOING WHAT ONE CAN

It was from Citizen Drew that Walker Farr heard the story of Captain Andrew Kilgour.

Citizen Drew was the elderly man with the earnest face who had been first to commend Farr that evening at City Hall when he and old Etienne had made their pathetically useless foray against bulwarked privilege.

Folks in Marion who knew Citizen Drew had forgotten his given name. In his propaganda of protest he called himself "Citizen." He built carriage-tops in a little shop where there were drawers stuffed with political and economic literature, and he read and pondered during his spare hours.

Farr sought out Citizen Drew and sat at his feet, with open ears.

For Citizen Drew knew the political history of his state, the men concerned, their characters, their aims, their weaknesses, their virtues, their faults—especially did he understand their faults—their affiliations with the Machine, their attitude toward the weak; he had followed their trails as the humble hound follows big game.

Therefore, Farr, a stranger in that land, seeking knowledge with which to arm his resolve, went and sat with Citizen Drew and learned many things.

Sometimes loquacity carried Citizen Drew a bit afield from the highway of politics, and when he touched on the case of Captain Andrew Kilgour Farr's heart thumped and his eyes glistened. For Drew prefaced the bit of a story with this:

"I never knew Symonds Dodd to do anything toward squaring a wrong he had committed except when he gave Kate Kilgour a fine position in his office. And there are those who say that he was only showing more of his selfishness when he hired her; he wanted the prettiest girl in the city to match his office furnishings."

"I have seen her," said Farr, trying to be matter-of-fact. "I—I sort of wondered!"

"Her father was a friend of mine. He was a good man. And the Consolidated money couldn't buy him. His people were Kilgowers in Scotland and he was a man not given to much talk, but he was willing to let me run on, nodding his head now and then while he smoked. He was an honest man and the best engineer in the state, and he kept his own counsel in all things. And he showed me the Kilgower coat of arms—and he didn't show that to many. He was no boaster. He was proud of his people, but he used to say that it made but little difference who the ancestors were unless the descendants copied the virtues and tried to improve over the faults. There was a Kilgower who went down across the border and gave himself as a hostage so that the clan might gain time—and he knew that he would be hung—and he was. But he saved his people. And I wish you would remember that, Mr. Farr, for it explains a bit the state of mind of Andrew Kilgour.

"He wouldn't sell himself for the gang's dirty work—he made honest reports. So they did for him, Mr. Farr. And he couldn't afford to have them do for him, because his wife was vain and a spendthrift and he let her waste and spend because he was a good and simple man when it came to the matter of a woman's domination over him. That's the curse on strong men—they are tender when it comes to a woman. She wasn't worthy of him, his wife. It's the daughter who has his honesty. I think if she knew who had done for her father she would not stay in Symonds Dodd's office. But the gang does for a man most often without leaving the trail open when they run away and hide.

"He would come here and sit with me and smoke and was very silent. I knew there were debts and I knew well enough that the woman wanted him to sell himself.

"He raked and scraped money—he sold everything of his own, his instruments and all. He took out every cent of insurance that money would buy. Then he put prussic acid in a capsule—a shell of salol, I believe they said it was—so that the work of the poison would be delayed, and he swallowed the capsule on the street and went into an office and sat and chatted with friends and joked and laughed much more than was his habit till at last his eyes closed and his face grew white and he fell out of his chair upon the floor stone-dead, and never uttered a groan.

"It was brave work. They called it heart disease, but it's not easy to fool insurance people. They took him out of his grave and proved suicide—and they did not pay a dollar of insurance to his family. They were not obliged to. The policies were new and the suicide clause let the companies out. So he left only debts instead of twenty-five thousand dollars. However, I say it was brave work."

"It would have been braver to stay and face it," blurted Farr.

"But Andrew Kilgour had a code of his own—a state of mind some of us could not understand—the example of an ancestor. We are not all alike. Many cannot stay and face trouble. You might be able to do it—you seem to have a level head!"

Farr grew pale, his hands trembled on the arms of his chair, and then he got up and marched across the little shop to the window, turning his back on Citizen Drew.

"You told them in City Hall that you would stay here and fight," pursued Citizen Drew. "That is brave work."

"I'll be much obliged to you, Citizen Drew, if you'll leave me out of your catalogue of heroes. And I take back what I said about his facing it. I hadn't any right to make any such comment."

"So the girl went to work in Symonds Dodd's office and his nephew is courting her. I hope he doesn't get Andrew Kilgour's daughter. He never went after any other girl honestly. I have looked into this case because I was Andrew's friend. Young Dodd wants to marry her and the mother is helping him. But I know that rapscallion, Mr. Farr. I can't believe that Kate Kilgour will be caught by him."

"He has a fine position, they tell me," said Farr, still gazing out of the window.

"The Machine made old Peleg Johnstone state treasurer, and he doesn't know bonds from biscuit. Colonel Dodd put in his nephew as chief clerk, and old Peleg is a figure-head, smoking his pipe in the back office and resting his wool-tipped boots on his desk. Oh, I know the bunch of 'em, sir. I can tell you the inside of things. Young Dodd takes orders from his uncle and runs the treasury. All the state's money is in the Dodd banks on the checking-account basis—and the gang is letting it out at six percent. Tidy little profit! And nobody to say a word, even to ask how Richard Dodd finds so much money to spend. But that's the principal wonder in the world, Mr. Farr—how your neighbor gets his money to blow. Jones, Smith, Brown, and Robinson—they stand and look at one another and ask the same question. And folks in the Eleventh Ward are even asking me how you get your living," added Citizen Drew, smoothing his curiosity with a bit of jocoseness.

"I have been working in this city—doing good, hard work," stated Farr, moving toward the door.

"Yes, but you have been discharged."

"I understand how it is you know so much stuff to tell me," returned the young man, smiling. "Well, Citizen Drew, I'm going to take the first job that offers itself. Tell 'em that!"

"I'm glad of it," said Citizen Drew, with blunt heartiness. "If you have set out to do anything among the plain folks you've got to be at work in the open, earning honest wages, or they'll suspect you. They have been fooled too often by fakes and loafers. But since you advertised yourself in City Hall you may find jobs a little hard to land. It's pretty much of an air-tight proposition, Consolidated influence."

"I have somebody looking after my interests in that line, Citizen Drew. I'm not worrying." He opened the door. "In fact, there are two mighty helpful chaps whom I'm going to associate with more or less from now on."

"Bring 'em with you and let me know 'em. Can't have too many in a good cause."

"I'll bring them—but they are pretty hard to understand—rather slow getting acquainted—lots of folks have no use for them," said Farr, starting down-stairs.

"What are their names?" asked the inquisitive citizen, eager for more additions to his general stock of information.

"I'll tell you later."

But Farr named them to himself when he was on the street.

"Chance and Humility—I hope you are going to stick by me from now on," he muttered. "Chance, you have led me into a queer position and into a strange state of mind. Humility, you are helping me to understand. Now, Chance, what have you to say to me?"

It was more of the fantastic whimsy with which Walker Farr played.

His eyes, searching the street after this challenge to Chance, beheld an ice-wagon rumbling past. It was a neat-looking cart, painted white, and bore the advertisement, "Crystal Pure Independent Ice Company."

Another wagon, painted dirty yellow, followed. It was a Consolidated ice-cart; Farr knew those carts with their loads of river-ice.

The spectacle of something which promised rivalry to that yellow cart piqued his interest. His mood welcomed the first adventure which Chance presented. He had found Chance playing peculiar pranks with his affairs in the days just past.

He hurried in pursuit of the white cart and accosted the driver.

"Where can I find the manager of this company?"

"He's up at Coosett Lake this afternoon, sir." The man was respectful. The stranger's garb and demeanor impressed him. "The trolley will take you pretty near it. Take a car in the square—a Halcyon Park car."

Without canvassing the matter further Farr took the car.

He decided that it was a most comforting sensation, this abandoning his problems to Chance! It saved so much fuss and worry.

He found the little lake at the limits of the park area—a hollow among the hills.

Men were busy at the foot of the slope over whose crest he marched. He saw several rough buildings at the edge of the lake, plainly makeshift ice-houses. One was a new structure and the other two were old barns which had been "darned" here and there with new material, and their yawed sides were propped with joists. Men were loading ice upon carts; the translucent cubes flashed in the rays of the sun.

During the process of his little crusade he had become acquainted with the conditions in the city of Marion and he knew that the Consolidated folks controlled the ice-supply as well as the water. They held an iron grip by legislative charter on all the riparian rights along the river and allowed no one else to operate an ice-field. He had seen and sniffed the unwholesome slime which a melted cake of Consolidated ice deposited.

When he found opportunity he accosted a man in corduroy. He was a big chap, bronzed by the sun, and Farr singled him out as the manager because he had been directing the other workers while he toiled himself.

"It's a little business of my own," said the man. "I have started in independent."

"I had thought the Consolidated had control of everything."

"They would control everything if they could. They wouldn't let me run my carts through the city streets if they knew how to stop me. I worked for them fifteen years, lugging their dirty ice on my back, up stairs and down, and I know that crowd. I don't understand much of anything but the ice business, mister, whoever you are. But I wouldn't lug any more of that ice into homes. I put my savings in here, every cent, hired these barns and a shore privilege, and I'm selling clean ice. But I'm going to lose every blamed cent! It's no use. I can't buck 'em. Excuse me! It's no interest to you. My mouth runs away with me when I get talking about that gang."

He went back to the barn to help his men shift a runway.

Farr waited patiently until he was able to speak to the busy man again.

"I don't mean to bother you, sir," he said, humbly. "But I am interested in this proposition of yours. I have worked for the Consolidated, myself. I was discharged because I stood up and damned their water before the mayor and aldermen."

"Say, I heard something about that!" cried the iceman, displaying prompt interest and admiration. "The boys said it was good work."

"I mention it merely to put myself right with you."

"Then say on ahead, my friend!"

"Do you tell me you can't make a go of this?"

"I'm afraid I can't. It's a half-mile haul for me to the nearest siding. The railroad folks don't give me any better rate than they're obliged to—and you know why that is! And I have to have another set of carts for the city delivery. And no capital to work with! I'm up against a crowd that has all the money, plenty of equipment, and has its supply right at the back door of the city—and it belongs at the back door! But you know what the buying public is! The only reason why I have lasted is because my old customers gave me their business and are sticking pretty well."

"My friend," declared Farr, putting his hand on the shoulder bent and ridged by many years of ice-toting, "lots of men who are making money as missionaries are not doing half the good in the world you're doing. You're certainly showing some of the citizens of Marion the difference between good ice and frozen gobs of pestilence."

"A fellow needs grit, grace, gumption, and a lot of missionary spirit to fight what I'm fighting, mister. I ain't going to say anything about a lot of obstacles the syndicate has put in my way. Those were to be expected in the way of regular business competition. But you can see I have only got limited resources here, and I can't afford a big outfit in the city. Sometimes I have run short, the best I could do—and it's mighty little sleep I have. And the Consolidated drivers have refused to sell ice to anybody who has been buying of me even when mothers have pleaded so as to keep milk for sick babies from souring. That's orders from headquarters! You wouldn't think that the same big chaps who boss the governor of the state would get down to such nubbins as that, eh? But they do—that's their system. They used to tell me that it's the only way a big syndicate can keep its grip—never leave a bar down! Yes, sir, they have blacklisted my customers until they'll be good and give the Consolidated a yearly contract. More than that, they pass word along that I'll be out of business by another season and that folks who have bought of me this year will be given the go-by next! Can you beat it?"

"Are you going to sell out to them?"

"No," said the iceman, grimly. "There are two good reasons: I won't sell and they won't buy. They will kill me out so that nobody else will be encouraged to try the scheme again."

"I want a job," stated Farr, curtly. "I want to work for you. Give me a place on one of your carts in the city."

"Say, look here," blurted the other man, frankly astonished, "you look more like a gent than an iceman!"

"No matter what I look like. The main question is, can I lug ice? Feel of my muscle!"

"It may be a poor outlook for your pay—working for me," warned the proprietor. "And if you ever want another job in Marion you may be blacklisted. I don't want to get you into a scrape."

"I can't be in any worse scrape than the one I am in now. Haven't I just told you who I am?"

"Oh, I know that! I reckon you're the same fellow. But, see here, mister, I'm one of those simple kind of galoots—and the less a man knows the more suspicious he is. You ain't wanting to work for me just because you need a job!"

"I do need a job! I have spent the little money I had by me after I was fired by the Consolidated. I had some special expenses—the funeral of a—a friend," he added, wistfulness in his tones. He drove his hand into his pockets and exhibited a few small coins in his palm when he pulled his hand out. "That's my cash—every cent of it!"

"Sure! I see it. But money's easy enough to come at by a fellow like you when he needs it. You haven't come across all square with me yet!" It was not mere inquisitiveness; it was the insistence of a plain man who wanted a definite peg on which to hitch the first warp of association. "You've got to handle money of mine," he went on. "I'm in a tight place and I have got to have the right men tied up with me. I wouldn't have to ask one of those boys yonder why he wanted to lug ice. But you ain't no ordinary slouch, mister. You don't do things—not many of 'em—unless you've got a good reason for same." It was the instinct of ingenuousness. "Keep it all to yourself if you want to. But in that case you'll have to excuse *me!*"

Farr did not hesitate. He smiled.

"You're a down-on-the-ground fellow who may be able to understand the thing better than I do myself," he declared. Again he put his hand on the bent shoulder.

"You didn't break loose from a good job and start this ice business here simply to make more money, did you?"

"Well, I've got a family to support and I wanted to make some money, of course, but I thought it was about time to have less relics, germs, curiosities, microbes, and general knickknacks left in ice-boxes after the ice had melted. So I went out of the frozen museum business, mister." His voice softened suddenly. "We lost a little girl a year ago last summer. Typhoid!"

"I lost a little girl—a friend," said Farr, patting the shoulder. "It's this way with me—What is your name?"

"Freeland Nowell."

"Mr. Nowell, I have poked more or less fun in my life at men who claimed to have missions. Perhaps that was because those men drew my attention by advertising their missions loudly—and, therefore, I concluded that all men with licenses to cure this and fix that and regulate the other were fooling themselves or else were bluffs. But all of a sudden I have waked up to something. I believe that any human being who isn't doing a little something on the side to help somebody else in this life is mighty miserable. I believe that the average sort of folks are doing it—keeping it quiet, in most cases, perhaps. I thought I had a mission and I stood up in your city government and advertised it and made considerable of an ass of myself."

"Well, it was all right one way you look at it," said Nowell, with the caution of the honest citizen. "But, of course, you got the stigmy put onto you of being a crank and a disturber and you don't get nowhere! It ain't gab and holler that does it! If talk sets folks to thinking—that's all right, so far as it goes. But a lot of these chaps set their mouths to going and let their hands lay crossed in their laps and then wonder why the world doesn't get better because they have asked it to be good."

It was sagacity from the humble observer.

"Mr. Nowell, I don't want to be quite as lonesome in this world as I have been," said Farr, with earnestness. "It's an awful feeling, that! A man can be lonely for a time and crowd down the hankering to be in the march of honest men where he can touch elbows and be a part of things. I see you look at me! That's right—it's queer stuff to be talking to you." He pondered for a moment and went on. "Queer thing, eh, for a fellow to wake up all of a sudden—a fellow of my stamp—and want to do some real good in the world? Well, it surprises *me*, and it would surprise you a whole lot more if you knew me better. We won't try to analyze the feeling. I've given up trying to do it." He paused and his brown eyes surveyed the blinking iceman with a quizzical appeal in them. "That's a pretty long preface, Mr. Nowell. It ought to lead up to some very important request. But it doesn't. I simply want a job on your ice-cart. It will give me the best opportunity I know of to go into homes and tell mothers to boil the water which comes out of those dirty taps; after I unscrew the faucets I won't have to argue much. I told Colonel Dodd in his office to look out for me! That may have been bluster. I am a nobody. But I'm on his trail, and there is one thing I can do to start with! I can help save the lives of a few children. That's all! I'll be following my new motto. Will you give me the job?"

"I sure will," declared Nowell, heartily. "If I don't know when a man is talking rock-bottom to me, then it's my own fault. When do you want to go to work?"

"Now."

Nowell gave the new man's garments a disparaging side glance.

"You look more as if you was going out to preach instead of deliver ice. But I can fix that if you're busted, my friend. You slip off that coat and help here till we're loaded. Then ride into the city on the freight-car and tell any one of my men to give you the overalls and jumper I left hanging in my stable office."

In this fashion it came about that Farr that day was riding on an ice-wagon in Marion, learning his route. A red-headed youth who was nursing an ice-pick wound in a bundled-up foot served as guide and driver and spotted the "Crystal Pure" cards propped here and there in windows, mutely signaling the household needs. With zestful complacency, and with secret enjoyment in being allowed to "team" this chap who looked and talked like a "nob," the youth allowed Farr to do all the work.

The route took in many apartment-houses of the city.

The labor was muscle-racking. In most cases there were stairs to climb. He stood, sagging under his burden, till chests were cleared by the housewives or sluggish maids. He discovered that the iceman was considered a fair and logical butt for all the forenoon grouches of the kitchen. Women complained querulously that the ice dripped on the clean floor, or that the piece was not up to the twenty-cent piece delivered by the other company, or that he was late, or he had not had his eyes about him the day before or else he would have seen the card.

On numerous occasions he was obliged to carry a piece of ice back down-stairs to his cart and exchange it for a piece of another size and price. He received no apology in such cases; he was tartly informed that he ought to have common sense enough to know what was wanted in that house. In other cases, the mistress of the apartments turned him from the door and explained with entire lack of interest in his long climb that the card had been left up by oversight—the chest had been filled the day before.

And at two places sharp-tongued women would not allow him to enter, frankly stating that icemen were too dirty creatures to allow inside the door of a respectable house; the women received their ten-cent cubes in pans and slammed the door in his face.

And through all this Farr preserved his smile.

In this slavery, tongue-lashed by fretful women, sweating under his burden, he was happy; he could not account for it and did not attempt to, but he knew it. He accepted the situation.

He received rewards enough to fortify his resolution.

A motherly woman asked him to wait a moment and she mixed for him a glass of lemonade. That gave him an opportunity to say a few words to her about drinking-water, modestly and deferentially. She was interested, and he showed her what the guilty faucet of her tap held in concealment.

And he saw that she was shocked and after he had warned her he asked her to tell all the other women whom she knew. She promised to bring the matter up in her sewing-club.

"And even the fussy women," he told himself, as he plodded back to his cart, encouraged by his first experiment, "if I keep calm, if I keep smiling—I shall find my chance to say something to them after a time."

A fresh doughnut was given to him by a maid who smiled up at his manly good looks approvingly, and he was very grateful, for his breakfast had been a meager one because he had barely enough small coins to make a jingle in his pocket.

The maid gasped affrightedly when he showed her what was in the faucet, and immediately set on water to boil to supply the bottles in the ice-chest.

Furthermore, the maid stated that she knew many other maids who would be glad to know about such a dreadful thing, and that she would have a word to say to them on the way to Sunday mass and back.

Farr began to understand more clearly what can be accomplished by a lone voice, carrying a gospel which can be backed and illustrated by signs and wonders.

"I'll have them listening to me yet," he pondered. "I'll never say another unkind word about a woman's tongue."

Colonel Symonds Dodd flashed past the ice-cart that afternoon in his limousine.

Farr laughed aloud at the humor of a thought which occurred to him: he reflected that he would like to behold Colonel Dodd's face and hear Colonel Dodd's remarks if somebody told that gentleman that the man before whom he had quailed and grown pale was now starting what the man believed was a more effective assault on the dynasty than even a whole car-load of dynamite bombs could make, even if they were exploded in all the Consolidated reservoirs. The remarks which would entertain, so Farr pondered, would come when the colonel was informed that the assault consisted of a lone iceman making talk to women in kitchens.

"However," said the iceman to himself, as he checked a nick in a ten-cent cube at the back of his cart. "I hold that my new motto is all right, and old Etienne will indorse it, and he knows what self-sacrifice consists of. It isn't rolling up your eyes and folding your hands and saying, 'What can I do?' It's saying, 'I'll do what I can!'—and then keeping your hands busy!"

XV
WHEN A MAID IS COY

Mr. Richard Dodd came wooing.

He waited in his gray car at the curb in front of the First National Bank block until Kate Kilgour issued forth into the afternoon sunshine.

He called to her, holding open the side door.

"I just had to see you," he told her. "I have come down from the capital, doing forty miles an hour. You're more precious than all the money I have locked up in the vaults."

He did not find in her eyes any of that acclaimed glad love-light which eager lovers seek. On the contrary, Miss Kilgour made just a bit of a face at him and was distinctly petulant.

"I do not want to ride, Richard. I enjoy my walk. I need it after a day at my desk."

"But I'm going to take you on a long ride into the country. We'll have dinner at Hillcrest Inn and we'll—"

"I'll go straight home, if you please."

"Then come in here with me."

"Oh, if you insist!" She said it with weary impatience.

"Are you tired?"

"Yes."

He drove slowly. "I don't want you to work any more. You know I don't. You know how I feel. Kate, I have published our intentions of marriage."

Her demeanor till then had been marked by tolerance, a bit pettish. Now she turned on him the indignant stare of offended womanhood.

"Richard, I have not given you permission to do that."

"But you are going to marry me!"

"Some day. I will tell you when. I am not ready."

"You are playing with me."

"I am not so frivolous."

"But why do you keep putting it off?"

"A woman who gives herself has the right to say when it shall be."

"My God!" he raged. "I wish you would wake up."

She did not answer.

"You don't know what love is. You won't let me touch you."

"I suppose that your experience has qualified you, Richard," she returned, half humorously, half scornfully.

"We are going to be married. Your mother is anxious for you to marry. I am going to tell my uncle to hunt for another secretary."

"Be careful how you take liberties with my private business," she warned him, sharply.

"You need somebody to take care of it for you. You have promised to be my wife. You can't give me a single good reason for waiting any longer."

"But I intend to wait."

He drove along in angry silence and they left the car together at the Trelawny Apartments. The car had made a detour in reaching the curb— avoiding a white wagon at the rear of which an iceman was briskly pecking in twain a cake of ice.

The girl glanced sharply at the man and turned her head when she reached the sidewalk in order to survey him more closely. The iceman, peering up at the windows to locate such signal-cards as might be visible, lowered his gaze and intercepted the girl's scrutiny. Color came into her cheeks, but she frowned as if resenting his stare and hurried into the vestibule, her lover at her heels.

"Look here, Friend Myself," reflected Walker Farr, "it's time you woke up!" He sighed and swung a chunk of ice upon his shoulder. "But what else can I expect? Come on, Humility, and give me a soft word or two. I was hoping I'd never see her again."

"Youse take those two front numbers—ten and twelve—Mrs. Kilgour and Mr. Knowles," advised his helper. "Package-entrance is around behind."

Farr toiled up the stairs, carrying one ice cube on his shoulder, with another swinging from tongs. There was but one door to the Kilgour apartment and the girl and Dodd stood in front of it; they had evidently waited in the corridor after emerging from the elevator, and the young man was detaining her, talking earnestly.

The girl opened the door with her latch-key, and with an apology he stepped in front of the pair and entered.

"Well, I'll be—" blurted Dodd. "So that's what he is—a cheap, low-lived iceman!"

Mrs. Kilgour came into her vestibule and led the way to the kitchen, for Farr stood irresolutely in the doorway, awaiting directions as to his burden. Following her, the young man noted her house-dress, beribboned over-much, her rouged face, her bleached hair, and wondered how such a woman could have beguiled Andrew Kilgour, as he felt he knew that sacrificing hero from what Citizen Drew had said.

"Say, that's the plug-ugly who insulted us in the woods. I'll never forget that face," stormed Dodd, making no effort by lowered tones to conceal his sentiments from the iceman. "Where else am I going to run across him? He needs a horse-whipping. If there weren't ladies present I'd give him one."

"The man seems to be minding his own business," said the girl, coldly.

Farr heard her. There was a hint of contempt in her tones, and the young man humbly accepted the scorn as directed toward him. He lifted the ice into the box and received his coin from the languid woman, who seemed to pay as little heed to his presence as she did to Dodd's threats.

She seemed to be more especially interested in herself, and when Farr departed was fondling into place the masses of her hair before a mirror in the vestibule. Through the space formed by the portieres he saw Dodd reaching eager hands to the girl, her presence having apparently charmed away his thoughts of vengeance.

The iceman went humbly on his way.

He was meditating on the sacrifice of Captain Andrew Kilgour; he remembered that stalwart men are willing slaves of the weakest women. He wondered how much of the honesty of the father was in the daughter. He tried to console himself by insisting that it was not there. He had had only a limited opportunity to study Richard Dodd. However, he was convinced that his unflattering estimate of that young man was surely justified; and so certain was he that the character of Dodd must be patent to all he went back to his tasks with a lowered estimate of the girl who would select such a man as husband. And yet out of the dust of the highway the profile of her face had touched him as his heart never had been touched before; he had plucked the rose and had plodded on behind the little sister of the rose. He wondered what strange impulse had touched him. She must be merely like all the rest. Her graciousness in that first meeting had tempted him to believe that she was different. Now some consciousness, equally as intangible, suggested to him that she was selfishly selling herself for ease. His thoughts were pretty much mixed, he acknowledged. But as he went on, bearing his burdens, listening to the petty tyrants who may ruthlessly taunt the man who comes in by the back door, he was aware that he had full need of much ministration from his new friend, Humility.

In the sitting-room of the Kilgour flat Richard Dodd was telling the mother that he had made application for a marriage license.

"And I have waited long enough," he declared. "Mother Kilgour, you must convince Kate that we are to be married within a week."

And he gave the mother a look which made her turn pale and twist her ringed fingers nervously.

"Kate, what is the use?" she pleaded. "You are acting like a child. You love Richard. You know you love him. You tell me often that you love him! Richard is such a dear boy!" She said this fawningly, with evident intent to placate the sullen young man. Her tone, her air suggested the nervous embarrassment of a debtor who seeks to put off a creditor with flattery and fresh promises. "Now be a darling child and say that we'll have the wedding next week without any fuss or feathers."

"I am not ready to get married, and I simply will not be married just yet," declared the girl, her red lips compressed.

"You don't love me!" complained Dodd.

"I like you, Richard," admitted the girl, frankly, without any coquettishness. "I have never cared for anybody else. You have been good to me, except when you were foolish."

"Foolishness—that's what she calls being so much in love with her that I can't keep my hands off her," said Dodd to the mother. "Mother Kilgour, you haven't talked to Kate as you should. She doesn't know what love is."

"Oh, I'll find out all about it, and then we'll be married—when I'm ready to become a wife," said the girl, with an indulgent smile. "All at once

I'll wake up, just as you have been begging me to do, and then we'll simply run away and be married and live happily for ever after."

"I don't like this stalling," growled Dodd, brutally.

"I'll leave you two children together," said the mother. "I'm sure you'll come to an understanding." She went away, showing relief.

"Sit down here on the divan with me, sweetheart," pleaded the young man.

But without removing her hat she went to the piano and began to play.

"Please come!" he entreated.

She smiled at him over her shoulder and made a pretty *moue*.

Muttering an oath of passion he leaped up, hurried across the room, and began to kiss her fiercely.

He crushed back with his lips all her protests; standing over her, he held her upon the piano-bench until by main strength and with all the force of her resentment she tore away from him.

"And now you are going to blame me because I can't help it," he gasped.

"I don't in the least understand why normal persons can find any pleasure in that kind of folly."

"Is your idea of loving anybody rubbing noses like Eskimos?"

"I'd endure that kind of loving in preference to that kind of kissing, Richard. That isn't love which you're offering—not the kind of love I want. I am going out for my walk—you filched it from me. No, I'm going alone. Go and talk with mamma, if you like."

She escaped the clutch he made and hurried out and to the elevator.

Flushed and angry, Dodd made his way to an inner room where Mrs. Kilgour was reading a novel, sunning herself with feline indolence. She put the book by with evident regret.

"Oh, Kate, has so much poise!" she lamented, breaking in on the young man's complaints. "She is so like her father. No one except myself could do anything with him at all. Sometime it was very hard for me! He would set his mind and his teeth! But I always won in the end."

"Well, go ahead and win now," commanded the surly lover. "You are simply letting this thing run along."

"I know Kate's nature, Richard. It's only a matter of the right time."

He sat down at her feet on the end of the couch.

"The time is here—now!" he told her. "I insist that you make Kate understand. I have been patient and reasonable for a year. You have promised me that you will bring everything around all right. Why don't you do it?"

"But delivering a daughter into marriage isn't like delivering groceries on order!" Her tone showed a bit of impatience. "Be reasonable!"

"I don't want to say anything to hurt your feelings, but we must get down to cases. I'm not asking you to deliver anything to me except what was promised long ago—promised by Kate herself. And you know what you said when I loaned you five thousand dollars to help you save those stocks. Excuse me, Mother Kilgour, but I can't always control my nature; I've been in the game with the bunch for a long time and I'm naturally suspicious—I have seen a good many chaps trimmed, and I don't propose to have anything put over on me."

"You are insolent and cruel," she cried, her cheeks pale.

"I don't mean you—I believe you want to help me. But it's time to be up and doing. She doesn't give me one good reason why she will not be married right away. It's only jolly and putting it off."

"But you are twitting me about the service you have done me! I am not selling my daughter!"

"That isn't it at all! But you must agree that I have been good to you. I want you to be a friend to me. But I don't get anything that's definite. If this thing drags on and on the first thing I know some fellow will come along and she'll fall for him. That's the girl nature!"

"You are talking about my daughter, Richard! She has her father's disposition and she is true blue. She has given her promise and she will keep it."

"When?" he demanded, curtly.

"I can't drive her."

"You said you could," he insisted. "You said a year ago when I advanced that money that you knew just how to handle her."

"Are you going to keep twitting me about that money?"

"No; only I'm going to say that you haven't even told me about what stocks you were protecting. You haven't said anything about repaying the loan, Mother Kilgour. It has been a sort of general stand-off all around for me. Hold on! I'm not making a holler! But I like to be taken in right. I'm a Dodd, and I can't help playing to protect myself."

"It will come around all right, Richard. You don't know Kate as I do. I understand her because I understood her father. She is rather self-centered. But she is romantic underneath! But you know you're so sort—sort of—well, just a business man—so matter-of-fact. A girl like Kate needs to be stirred—her poise shaken—something like that!"

"Lochinvar business, eh?" he sneered.

"It must be something a little bit out of the ordinary to hurry her, Richard. Go away, please. Let me think. I have an idea. I must spend a little time on it."

"How much time?"

"Oh, I don't know just how much. Be patient."

"Mrs. Kilgour, if this thing cannot be put through by you I want you to say so. I'm at the end of that patience you're appealing to. I won't be fooled."

"You don't need to say that you're Colonel Dodd's nephew," she retorted. "You have all the family traits."

"Well, there's one I haven't got: I loaned you five thousand dollars without taking security—and that's the act of a good friend. Excuse me, but I've got to speak of it—you need a little reminder. Four days from now I'll have my marriage license from the city clerk. And when I have it in my hands I shall come to you and shall expect that you'll do your part."

"I will," she said.

"How? I want plain statements from now on."

"I will write you a letter to-morrow," she faltered. "I will give you directions what to do. You'd better not come here till—till I have it all arranged. You know what they say about absence!"

"I know what they say about a good many things. But I want something besides say-so."

"I will tell you in my letter what to do. Then you follow instructions."

"I don't like to go into a thing blind. What is the plan?"

"Oh, if I tell you all about it you'll go and do something to spoil it," she protested, impatiently. "A woman knows about such matters better than a man does. I will write to you at the State House. Now be patient!"

"I'll be going before you preach any more patience to me," he said, sourly. "I might be provoked into saying something you won't like."

After he had gone she rose and touched up her cheeks.

"The fool! They are all alike," she muttered, viciously. "They pay. They never forget they have paid. Then they stand with their hand out—and just remember that they have paid. I am glad I bought this novel," she added, taking the book from the couch and settling herself to read. "The woman who wrote it must have known human nature. If the plan worked in the case of the girl she writes about it ought to work in the case of Kate. If it doesn't it will be his fault because he has hurried me so. A poor, persecuted woman can't do everything."

And she applied herself to her recently discovered manual of procedure in the case of stubbornness in a maid.

XVI
FARR HAS A VISION AND CLOSES HIS LIPS

Walker Farr put aside papers upon which he had been working since he had eaten his modest supper, and pulled on his coat and went forth into the evening. He strolled up one of the streets in the Eleventh Ward of Marion, manifestly glad to be out among the people.

He stopped at the curb and hailed the driver of a truck-wagon which was loaded down with kegs and jugs.

"Marston," he said, when the driver halted, "it's good to see the noble work going on."

"Yes, and now that the babies aren't dying off so fast old Dodd's newspapers are claiming that the new filtering-plant is doing all the good, sir."

"Well, it shows that our work is worth while if they're claiming it, Marston. But we'll wake up the folks all in good time. Do what we can for first aid, that's the idea! The people are waking up to what we're doing. And they are waking up in other places. I took a little run up state last week. Five other cities are going to try this co-operative scheme of getting good water to the poor folks until something better can be done."

"You've got a head on you," commended the driver. "It's a little tough on tired horses to work at this after a day's trudging on regular business, but my nags seem to understand what it's all about—honest they do. I have hauled five hundred gallons this week. But I'd like to haul old Dodd up to Coosett Lake and drown him, if it wasn't for spoiling water that the poor folks are drinking."

Farr shook his head and walked on.

He was a rather striking figure for a New England city as he strolled along. It did not seem to be affectation for this man to wear a frock-coat without a waistcoat, a flowing black tie setting off his snowy linen. The attire seemed to belong to his physique and manner.

Women smiled at him in friendly fashion; men gave respectful and affectionate salutation.

Soon he stepped off the street into a room where a group of men were waiting for him, so it appeared, because they all rose when he entered.

He called the little meeting to order promptly, informing them that he would detain them only a short time.

"I rise to make a motion," said a man at one stage of the proceedings. "There have been so many volunteers in the work and the folks have been so ready to pay for real water in place of that stuff we get from the taps, that three hundred dollars have accumulated in the treasury. We all know that there is just one man who had been responsible for this whole plan and has given his time and has run about our state and hasn't charged anything but expenses for doing it all. I move we give that sum to Mr. Farr—wishing it was more."

The speaker was loudly applauded.

Farr was so quickly on his feet and spoke so promptly that he clipped the man's last words.

"A moment, my friends, before that motion is seconded." He held up his hand and checked their protests against what his air told them. "Because my little plan has succeeded better than I hoped is not due to me, but to the generous co-operation of good men who have given their time. We are saving the babies, thank God! But do you know what else we have done by our hard toil and our devotion? We are propping up the Consolidated Water Company in this state. Understand me! I am not attacking that company because it is a corporation. If it were now making preparations to pipe down to us clean water from the hills I would gladly go on giving my time to this cause in order to help the case of the Consolidated. But the men in control are deliberately shutting their eyes to the real situation. Now that folks aren't dying, they claim all the credit—when we know the credit is due to weary men who go on working after their day's toil is over. It isn't right—it isn't just! My friends, I have got hold of a bigger thing than I reckoned on when I started out to wake those poison-peddlers up. Now that we are cleaning up the typhoid, the Consolidated is simply riding on our backs—refusing to see the real truth. If they give Marion pure water it will be only at more exorbitant rates, because the nearest lake is twenty miles away. I'm not an anarchist—I want to see capital get its just reward. But when a syndicate takes a franchise from citizens and makes them pay over and over for what was their own the citizens have a right to rise in self-defense. When we force the Consolidated to give us what we're paying for—pure water—they evidently propose to make us pay for what they call our cheek in asking." He paused for a moment, and his smile succeeded his earnestness. "I beg your pardon for saying 'we.' I must remember that I'm still a stranger in this city."

"I'll have to dispute you there," interposed a man. "You're one of us. And we're going to prove it to you a little later."

"My friends," went on Farr, "until the cities and towns of this state own their own water-plants and take their own profits they will be paying double tribute to a merciless crowd."

"But we can't own our plants till the millennium, sir. There's that five-percent-debt-limit clause in the constitution."

Farr smiled—this time wistfully. "I've—I've had a sort of vision in regard to that," he said. "I don't dare to explain myself just now, friends. It may be only a vision—but I think not. I'll not say any more at present. I did not intend to say as much. What was on my mind when I got up was this: I will not accept that money in the treasury—on no account will I take it. Because I believe that strange days are coming upon us soon in this state—days when we shall need money. Keep that nest-egg and guard it." He picked up his hat and started for the door. "The meeting is adjourned," he informed them. He smiled at them over his shoulder in such a manner that they wondered whether he joked or was in earnest. "Guard well that money—for the only way my vision can be realized, I fear, is by turning this state's politics upside down, and that will be quite a job for a rank outsider fighting Colonel Symonds Dodd—and fighting without money. Good night!"

Men whom Walker Farr met as he strolled ducked amiable greetings. They grinned admiringly after him as he passed on.

If a woman asked in regard to him or a stranger in the ward questioned a native they were informed with gusto that he was "the boy who stood in City Hall and talked turkey to the mayor and all the bunch, and said a good word for the poor people, and twisted the tail of the Consolidated and lost a good job doing it—and that's more than any alderman would do for those who elected him."

At a street corner children of the poor were dancing around a hurdy-gurdy. Farr gave the man at the crank a handful of change and told him to stay there and keep the kiddies happy. Shrill juvenile voices promptly proclaimed his praises to all the neighborhood, and mothers and fathers beamed benedictions on him from windows.

He stopped at another street corner where a dozen youths were congregated. They were heavy-eyed, leering cubs, their hats were tipped back, and frowzled fore-tops stuck out over their pimply faces—types of youths whom modest girls avoid hurriedly by detours.

"Boys, folks are writing to the newspapers complaining that young chaps are insulting girls on the street corners of Marion. But it must be those high-toned loafers up-town. You're not up to any of that business down here, of course."

"None of us would ever as much as say 'shoo' to a chicken," protested one of the group.

"You're Dave Joyce's boy, aren't you?"

"Yes, sir."

"The fifty men he bosses at the ice-house like him because he's square. Here's a good motto: 'Square with the boys and nice to the girls.' But keep off the street corners, fellows, or they'll get you mixed up with some of that masher gang."

The Joyce boy pulled his hat forward and marshaled the retreat from the loafing-place.

"Naw, he ain't no candidate, nuther," he informed his associates when they were out of hearing. "He ain't canvassing for no votes. My old man says he ain't. He ain't a four-flusher. He's the guy that stood for the poor folks up at City Hall and doped out the spring-water stuff."

At the side of a street where traffic raged to and from the city's Union Station Farr came upon two shriveled old ladies who were teetering on the curbstones, waiting tremulously for an opportunity to cross. They put down into the roaring street first one apprehensive foot and then another, like children trying chilly water. The big fellow offered an arm to each and led them safely across.

"You're a real knight-errant, sir," squeaked one of the two, looking up into the kindly face.

He laughed, doffed the broad-brimmed hat with a low bow, and strolled on his way.

"Knight-errant," he muttered, still smiling. "Guess not. They don't have 'em these days. The stories about 'em read well. Wonder what kind of a feeling it was that started those boys off on the hike! Perhaps there wasn't enough doing in politics. It must have been a fine game, though, rescuing distressed damsels. And all for love and not for pay!"

A poster in the window of an empty store caught his eye just then. It advertised a woman's-suffrage rally.

"The girls would paint rally signs on a knight's tin suit these days and send him off on an advertising trip," was his whimsical reflection.

At that moment, with this thought of knight in armor in his mind, he was attracted by a flare of red fire in a blacksmith shop located just off the street. The one worker in the place was revealed by the forge fire. The glow lighted the features of the man. There was no mistaking him—it was Friend Jared Chick. And Farr turned off the street and went into the shop and greeted his one-time traveling companion.

"How does thee do?" replied Jared Chick, quietly, his Quaker calm undisturbed. He drew forth a white-hot iron and deftly hammered it into a circle around the snout of the anvil.

"So you have given up knight-errantry and have gone back to the old job, have you, Friend Chick?"

"No. This is a part of my service. The man who owns this shop is a good man who works hard here all day. And after he has gone home he allows me to work here in the evening."

He pounded away industriously and Farr walked up to the anvil to inspect the nature of the work, for the iron rod was assuming queer shapes.

"A new kind of armor, Friend Chick?"

If there was a bit of sarcasm in Farr's tone the Quaker paid no apparent heed.

"No," he said, quietly and meekly, "this is a brace for the leg of a little lame boy. I have found many children in this city who cannot walk. Their parents are too poor to buy braces. So I come here nights, when the good man is away from the forge, and I make braces and carry them with my blessing. I have some knack with the hammer. I hope to find other ways of doing my bit of good."

"I beg your pardon, Friend Chick," said Farr, a catch in his voice. "I will not bother you in your work. Good night!"

"Good night to thee!" said the Quaker, swinging at the bellows arm.

Farr went back upon the street, his head bowed. "We all have our own way of doing it," he pondered, contritely.

He met a man and greeted him with a friendly handclasp. It was Citizen Drew, that elderly man with the earnest face.

And as he had in the past, he turned, caught step with Farr, and they walked together.

Their stroll took them into the broader avenues of up-town.

As they talked, Farr caught side glances from his companion. The glances were a bit inquisitive.

"Well, Citizen Drew," asked the young man, "what is on your mind this evening?"

"Since I have known you and studied you I have been thinking that you have the spirit of knight-errantry in you," stated Citizen Drew.

Farr laughed boyishly.

"Two very nice old ladies have just got ahead of you with that accusation, my friend."

"Laugh if you feel like it. But there are so few men who can do anything unselfishly in these days that when a chap like you does come along he gets noticed—at any rate, I notice him." He stopped dealing in side glances and stared at Farr fully and frankly. "Other men who would do the things you are doing so quietly in this state have been playing politics—and I have made it my business to watch politicians. And as soon as men have been elected to office by fooling the people—well, those men have simply been set into the Big Machine as new cogs. Are you like the rest, Mr. Farr? Nobody knows where you came from. Everybody who sees you knows you're above the jobs you have been working at. They're talking you up for alderman in our ward. But we have been fooled so many times!"

Farr replied to this wistful inquisition in a way there was no misunderstanding.

"I am not a candidate for anything, Citizen Drew. And I'll tell you how I can prove I am not. I am not a voter here. I have intentionally failed to have myself registered. Whenever you hear another man talking me up for office you tell him that. Therefore, it makes no difference to anybody where I came from or what job I work at."

Citizen Drew accepted the rebuke humbly and walked on in silence.

"You have always been fooled, you say, when you have elected men to office. Haven't you any men in this state whom you can elect to high office, knowing for sure that they'll stay straight?"

"No," returned Citizen Drew.

"I'm a stranger—I don't know your big men—you do know them, and I suppose I ought to take your word. But I don't believe you, Citizen Drew."

"But I told you the truth. We have big men who are honest men. But they won't go into politics. They feel too far above the game. Therefore, how can we elect them to office? I say I told you the truth. The men who go out and hunt for office are the ones who work the thing for their own profit—and that means they stand in with the bunch and the head boss."

It was the same old lament which is everlastingly on the lips of the voters of America! Citizen Drew had again epitomized the average politics of the great Republic!

Walker Farr smiled—and he could express in a smile more than most men can express in speech.

"An original idea has just occurred to me, Citizen Drew," he said, with humorous drawl in his tones. "I'm sure nothing like it has ever been thought of before. There ought to be a new party formed in this country—a party outside all the others. No, not a party, exactly! What should I call it? You see, the idea has just come to me, and I'm floundering a little." His tone was still jocular. "You're right about most of the able and big men staying out of politics except when the highest offices are passed around. Now, how's this for a scheme? Organize a loyal band and call it—well, say the Purified Political Privateers, the Sanctified Kidnappers, the People's Progressive and Public-spirited Press Gang. Go around and grab the Great and the Good who insist on minding their private business and who are letting the country be gobbled up—just go and grab 'em right up by the scruff of the neck and fling them into politics head over heels. They would sputter and froth and flop for a little while—and then they'd strike out and swim. They couldn't help swimming! They'd know that the folks were looking on. And then a lot of the sinking and drowning poor devils, like you and me and the folks in the tenements, could grab onto the Great and the Good and ask 'em to tow us safely ashore; and by that time their pride and their dander would be up and they'd swim all the harder—with the other folks looking on. Hah! An idea, eh? You see, I feel rather imaginative and on the high pressure and in a mood for adventure this evening! Probably because the nice old ladies called me a knight-errant."

Citizen Drew was not ready with comment on this amazing suggestion. He clawed his hand into his sparse hair and wrinkled his forehead in attempt to decide whether or not he ought to resent this playful retort to his lament. The next moment he dealt Farr a swift jab in the ribs with his elbow.

"Take a good look at this man coming," he mumbled.

The oncomer was close upon them, and in spite of the dusk Farr's sharp gaze took him all in.

In garb and mien he was a fine type of the American gentleman who is marked by a touch of the old school. There was a clean-cut crispness about him; the white mustache and the hair which matched it looked as if they would crackle if rubbed. His eyes were steely blue, and he held himself very erect as he walked, and he tapped the pavement briskly with his cane.

He passed them, marched up the steps of a large building, and disappeared through a door which a boy in club uniform held open for him.

"That man," explained Citizen Drew, complacently displaying his boasted knowledge of public men in minute detail, "is the Honorable Archer Converse, whose father was General Aaron Converse, the war governor of this state. Lawyer, old bach, rich, just as crisp in talk as he is in looks, just as straight in his manners and morals and honesty as he is in his back, arrives every night at the Mellicite Club for his dinner on the dot of eight"—Citizen Drew waved his hand at the illuminated circle of the First National clock—"leaves the club exactly at nine for a walk through the park, then marches home, plays three games of solitaire, and goes to bed."

"I know him!" stated Farr.

Citizen Drew's air betrayed a bit of a showman's disappointment.

"I never saw him before—never heard of him. But I mean I know him now after your description—know his nature, his thoughts. You have a fine touch in your size-ups, Citizen Drew."

"I've studied 'em all."

"What has he done in politics?"

"Never a thing. He is one of the kind I was complaining about. Too high-minded."

"But, ho, how a man like that would swim if he were once thrown in!" declared Farr.

"He never even tended out on a caucus."

"I know the style when I see it," pursued Farr. He did not look at Citizen Drew. He was talking as much to himself as to his companion. "Spirit of a crusader harnessed by every-day habit! Righteousness in a rut! Achievement timed to the tick of the clock. But, once in, how he would swim!"

"Think how our affairs would swing along with a man like that at the head of the state!"

"Why hasn't he been put at the head?"

"I have been in delegations that have gone to him"—he waved his hand—"he said he couldn't think of being mixed into political messes."

"He looked on you wallowing in muddy water and you invited him in. I don't blame him for not jumping."

"He's a good man," insisted Citizen Drew. "He gives more money to the poor than any other man in town. The only way I found that out is by having a natural nose for finding out things. He doesn't say anything about it."

"How he would swim!" repeated Farr. "Steady and strong and straight toward the shore, Citizen Drew, and he wouldn't kick away the poor drowning devils, either."

"He probably thinks he has paid his debt to the world when he hands out his money," stated Drew. "When he looks around and sees so many other men holding the poor chaps upside down and shaking the dollars out of their pockets he must think he is doing a mighty sight more than is required of him. But sticking plasters of dollar bills onto sore places in this state ain't curing anything." He stopped. "I've walked with you farther than I intended to, Mr. Farr. But somehow I wanted to talk with you. There's a meeting of the Square Deal Club this evening at Union Hall. I didn't know but in some way we might—It was thought you might be going to run for office."

"The registration-office will prove that I'm not. Pass that word!"

"I'll go back—to the meeting. It doesn't seem to be much use in holding the meetings," said the man. "We hear one another talk—we know we are talking the truth. But nobody listens who can help us poor folks. Well, I'll admit that the politicians come in and listen and promise to help us and we give our votes; but that's all: they give nothing back to us."

Farr broke out with a remark which seemed to have no bearing on what Citizen Drew was saying.

"He comes out at nine o'clock, eh?"

"Who?"

"The Honorable Archer Converse. Leaves that clubhouse then, does he?"

"Regular to the tick of the clock."

"Citizen Drew, hold your club in session until half past nine or a little later. My experience with those meetings is that you always have troubles enough to keep you talking for at least two hours."

Citizen Drew glanced at the face of Farr and then at the big door of the Mellicite Club.

"You don't mean to say—"

"I don't say anything. I seem to be in a queer state of mind to-night, Citizen Drew." Again there was an odd note of raillery in his voice. "A lot of odd ideas keep coming to me. Another one had just popped into my head. That's all! Keep your boys at the hall."

He swung off up the street.

He turned after a few steps and saw the elderly man standing where he had left him. Drew was a rather pathetic figure there in the brilliantly lighted main thoroughfare, a poor, plain man from the Eleventh Ward of the tenement-houses—this man who had been striving and struggling, reading and studying, endeavoring to find some way out for the poor people; some relief—something that would help. Farr knew what sort of men were waiting in the little hall. He had attended their meetings. It was the only resource they understood—a public meeting. They knew that the important folks up-town held public meetings of various sorts, and the poor folks had decided that there must be virtue in assemblages. But nothing had seemed to come out of their efforts in the tenement districts.

Farr stepped back to where Citizen Drew stood.

"I think I will say something to you, after all. Tell the boys in Union Hall to be patient and I'll bring the Honorable Archer Converse around this evening."

He smiled into the stare of blank amazement on the man's face, flung up a hand to check the stammering questions, and went off up the street.

"A decent man's conscience will make him keep a promise he has made to a child or to the simple or to the helpless," Farr told himself. "I have undertaken a big contract, I reckon, but now that I have put myself on record I've got to go ahead and deliver the goods. At any rate, I feel on my mettle." Then he smiled at what seemed to be his sudden folly. "I think I'll have to lay it all to those nice old ladies who were foolish enough to put that knight-errant idea into my head," he said.

XVII
THE MADNESS OF A MIDSUMMER NIGHT

Farr glanced again at the big clock in the First National block.

He had less than one hour to wait, according to the schedule Citizen Drew had promulgated in regard to the unvarying movements of the Honorable Archer Converse. As to how this first coup in the operations of that nascent organization, the Public-spirited Press Gang, was to be managed Farr had little idea at that moment.

He decided to devote that hour to devising a plan, deciding to attempt nothing until he saw the honorable gentleman march down the club steps. A club must be sanctuary—but the streets belonged to the people.

Therefore, Farr took a walk. He went back into that quarter of the city from which he had emerged during his stroll with Citizen Drew; he felt his courage deserting him in those more imposing surroundings of up-town; he went back to the purlieus of the poor, hoping for contact that might charge him afresh with determination. He realized that he needed all the dynamics of courage in the preposterous task he had set himself.

He knew he would find old Etienne sitting on the stoop of Mother Maillet's house where the old man posted himself on pleasant summer evenings and whittled whirligigs for the crowding children—just as his peasant ancestors whittled the same sort of toys in old Normandy.

Mother Maillet's house had a yard. It was narrow and dusty, because the feet of the children had worn away all the grass. Some of the palings were off the fence, and through the spaces the little folks came and went as they liked. It was not much of a yard to boast of, but there were few open spaces in that part of the city where the big land corporation hogged all the available feet of earth in order to stick the tenement-houses closely together. Therefore, because Mother Maillet was kind, the yard was a godsend so far as the little folks were concerned. The high fence kept children off the greensward where the canal flowed. Householders who had managed to save their yards down that way were, in most cases, fussy old people who were hanging on to the ancient cottage homes in spite of the city's growth, and they shooed the children out of their yards where the flower-beds struggled under the coal-dust from the high chimneys.

But Mother Maillet did not mind because she had no flower-beds and because the palings were off and the youngsters made merry in her yard. She had two geraniums and a begonia and a rubber-plant on the window-sill in order to give the canary-bird a comfortable sense of arboreal surroundings; so why have homesick flowers out in a front yard where they must all the time keep begging the breeze to come and dust the grime off their petals? It should be understood that Mother Maillet had known what *real* flower-beds were when she was a girl in the Tadousac country.

Furthermore, Etienne Provancher always came to the yard o' fine evenings and it served as his little realm; and the door-step of the good woman's house was his throne where he sat in state among his little subjects. However, on second thought, this metaphor is not happy description; old Etienne did not rule—he obeyed.

He did not resent familiarity—he welcomed the comradeship of the children. When they called him "Pickaroon" it seemed to him that they were making a play-fellow of him.

He sat and whittled toys for them out of the pine-wood scraps which the yard foreman gave him. There were grotesque heads for rag dolls, and the good woman seemed to have unlimited rags and an excellent taste in doll-dressmaking; there were chunky automobiles with spools for wheels; there were funny little wooden men who jumped in most amusing fashion at the end of wires which were stuck into their backs. Old Etienne was always ready to sit and whittle until the evening settled down and he could see no longer, even though he held the wood and busy knife close to his eyes.

So on that evening he whittled as usual.

Walker Farr came to the yard and sat beside the old man on the door-step and was plainly thinking no agreeable thoughts while he listened to the chatter of the children.

After the darkness had come and the larger boys and girls, custodians of their tiny kin, had dragged away the protesting and whimpering little folks because it was bedtime, Zelie Dionne laid down her needlework over which she had been straining her eyes. The good woman protested often because the girl toiled so steadily with her needle after her day at the mill was ended. And on that summer evening she voiced complaint again.

"You have so many pretty gowns already! You wear one last evening—you wear anodder this evening—and still you make some more! When a young girl nigh kill herself so as to make a picture-book of her dresses I think it is time to look for some young man who seems to like the pictures. Eh?"

"Mother Angelique, I do not relish jokes which are silly," protested the girl. "You know how the girls of our country are taught! We cannot sit with hands in our laps without being very unhappy."

She went out and sat upon the door-step where old Etienne made way for her.

"At first I did not think I would come out, Mr. Farr," she said. "But I have made bold to come."

"I do not think it needs boldness to come where I am," he returned. "I hope you are not going to make a stranger of me because I have not been very neighborly of late. I have been busy and I have been away. The boys have paid my fare up-country, and so I ran about to carry the gospel of the free water. The truckmen have volunteered in half a dozen places. We are doing a great work."

"And yet I am afraid," she confessed. "You are fighting men who can do you much harm. I have been asking questions so as to know more about those men. For they have threatened poor Father Etienne. I wanted to know about them. I cannot help. But can you not help, Mr. Farr? I think you are much more than you seem to be," she added, naively.

"They have threatened Etienne?" demanded Farr, a sharp note in his voice.

"Ah, m'sieu', I have said nottin's to you. I am only poor old man. No matter."

"Why didn't you say something to me?"

"It's because you might feel bad, m'sieu'. P'raps not, for I'm only poor man and don't count."

"What have they said to you?"

"It's nottin's," said Etienne, stubbornly. "You shall not think you got me into trouble. You did not. I would have done it maself as soon as I thought of it."

"I command you to tell me what has been said to you, Etienne."

"They say that I shall be discharge from the rack. They say I have talk too much to my compatriots about the poison water. But I shall talk—yes—jesso!"

"Who says so?"

"The yard boss say to me that. Oh, there's no mistake. He have the power, M'sieu' Farr. The super tell the yard boss, the mill agent tell the super, the alderman tell the mill agent, the mayor he tell the alderman."

"And probably Colonel Symonds Dodd told the mayor," growled Farr. "It's a great system, Etienne. Nobody too small—nobody too big!"

"But I do not care. I shall talk some more—yes, I shall talk in the *hotel de ville* when you shall tell me to talk. I was scare at first and I tol' you I would not talk; but now I have found out I can talk—and I am not scare any more, and I will talk." Pride and determination were in the old man's tones. Since that most wonderful evening in all his life when he had heard his voice as if it were the voice of another man ringing forth denunciation of those in high places, the old rack-tender had referred to that new manifestation of himself as if he were discussing another man whom he had discovered. The memory of his feat was ever fresh within him. And his meek pride was filled with much wonderment that such a being should have been hidden all the years in Etienne Provancher. Many men had called around to shake his hand and increase his wonderment as to his own ability.

"We will wait awhile," counseled Farr, understanding the pride and treating it gently. "Stay at your work and be very quiet, Etienne, and they will not trouble you. You need your money, and I will call on you when you can help again."

"Then I will come. I shall be sorry to see somebody have my rake and pole, but I shall come."

A moment of silence fell between them, and during that moment a young woman passed rapidly along the sidewalk. Walker Farr shut his eyes suddenly, as a man tries to wink away what he considers an illusion, and then opened his eyes and made sure that she was what she seemed; there was no mistaking that face—it was Kate Kilgour.

He stared after her. She halted on the next corner, peered up at the dingy street light to make sure of the sign legend on its globe and then turned down an alley.

"Ba gar!" commented old Etienne, putting Farr's thoughts into words, "that be queer t'ing for such a fine, pretty lady to go down into Rose Alley, because Rose Alley ain't so sweet as what it sounds."

Then two men came hurrying past without paying any attention to the denizens of the neighborhood who were sitting in the gloom on the stoop. The street light revealed the faces of the men as it had shown to them the girl's features. One was Richard Dodd. Unmistakably, they were following the girl. Farr heard Dodd say: "Slow up! Give her time to get there. She's headed all right."

And Farr stared after those men, more than ever amazed.

One of them was obtrusively a clergyman—that is to say, he was cased in a frock-coat that flapped against his calves, wore a white necktie, and carried a book under his arm.

Dodd was attired immaculately in gray, and as he walked he whipped a thin cane nervously. They began to stroll soon after they had hurried past the stoop, and were sauntering leisurely when they turned into Rose Alley.

"I now say two ba gars!" exploded Etienne. "Because I been see the jailbird, Dennis Burke, all dress up like minister, go past here with the nephew of Colonel Dodd. And they go 'long after la belle mam'selle."

"A jailbird!"

"He smart, bad man, that Dennis Burke. But he was hire by the big man to do something with the votes on election-time—so to cheat—and he get caught and so he been in the state prison. But he seem to be out all free now and convert to religion in some funny way. Eh?"

"Etienne, are you sure of what you are talking about?" demanded Farr. His voice trembled. The visit of that handsome girl to that quarter of the city—those men so patently pursuing her—there was a sinister look to the affair.

"Oh, we all know that Burke. He hire many votes in this ward for many years. He known in Marion just so well as the steeple on the *hotel de ville*. And that odder—that young mans, we know him, for his oncle is Colonel Dodd. Oh yes!"

"Good night, Etienne—and to you Miss Zelie!" said Farr, curtly, walking off toward the entrance of Rose Alley. He did not ask the old man to go with him. He was drawn in two directions by his emotions and stopped after he had taken a few steps. This seemed like espionage in a matter which was none of his concern. It was entirely possible that the confidential secretary of Colonel Dodd and the nephew of that gentleman might have common business even in Rose Alley and at that time of evening.

But the matter of that masquerading ballot-falsifier, just out of state prison, overcame Farr's scruples about meddling in the affairs of Kate Kilgour.

He turned the corner into the alley in season to see the two men far ahead of him; they passed out of the radiance shed by a dim light and he saw no more of them. He walked the length of the alley and was not able to locate any of the party. At its lower end the alley was closed in by houses, and it was plain that the people he sought had not passed out into another thoroughfare. He marched back, scrutinizing the outside of buildings, trying to conjecture what business the handsome girl and the two men could have in that section at that hour, and where they had entered to prosecute that business.

"I must continue to blame it all on the nice old ladies," he told himself, smiling at the shamed zest he was finding in this hunt. "But I hope this knight-errantry will not grow to be a habit with me. I mustn't forget that I have another job on hand for nine o'clock—also knight-errantry!"

He paused under the dim light where his men had disappeared and looked at his cheap watch.

Twenty-five minutes of nine!

Then he heard a woman's protesting voice. She cried "No, no, NO!" in crescendo.

He gazed at the house from which the voice seemed to come. It was near at hand, a shabby little cottage with a thin slice of yard closed in by a dilapidated picket fence. He perceived no observers in the alley, and he stepped into the yard. The front windows were open, for the evening was warm, but no lights were visible in the house.

He heard the protesting cry again. It was more earnest.

He head the rumble of a man's voice, but could not catch the words. Whatever was happening was taking place in some rear room.

"No, I say, no! Unlock that door," cried the voice, passionately.

Farr troubled his mind no longer with quixotic considerations about intrusion. He hoisted himself over the window-sill into the darkened front room, passed down a short corridor and, when he heard the voice once again on the inside of a door which he found locked, he immediately kicked the door open. He appeared to those in the room, heralded by an amazing crash and flying splinters.

First of all, he was astonished to find two women there; one was Miss Kilgour and the other was her mother. And there were the two men whom he had followed.

Farr swept off his hat and addressed the girl.

"I happened to be passing and heard your voice," he said. "If you are—" He hesitated, a bit confused, realizing all at once that knight-errantry in modern days is not quite as free and easy a matter as it used to be when damsels were in distress in the ruder times of yore. "I am at your service," he added, a bit curtly.

But she did not reply. Her attitude was tense, her cheeks were flaming, her eyes were like glowing coals.

"You lunatic, you have come slamming in here, disturbing a private wedding," announced the man in the white tie, slapping his palm upon the book he carried.

"Get out of here!" shouted Dodd. He had dodged into a corner of the room, his face whitening, when Farr had burst in. He remained in the corner now, brandishing his cane.

The uninvited guest surveyed the young man with more composure than he had been able to command when he looked at the girl.

Etienne Provancher had fortified him with some valuable information.

"Mr. Richard Dodd, I'll apologize and walk out of here after you have explained to me why you have faked up into a parson one Dennis Burke, late of the state prison, to officiate at weddings."

Upon the silence that followed the girl thrust an "Oh!" into which she put grief, protest, anger, consternation.

"Mother!" she cried. "Did you know? How could you allow—how did you come to do such a terrible thing?"

Her mother put her hands to her face and sat down and began to sob with hysterical display of emotion. Farr scowled a bit as he looked at her. She was overdressed. There was an artificial air about her whole appearance— even her hysterics seemed artificial.

The girl turned from her with a gesture of angry despair as if she realized, from experience, that she could expect, at that juncture, only emotion without explanation.

"Hold on here," cried Dodd, "hold on here, everybody! This is all right. You just let me inform you, Mr. Butter-in, that Mr. Burke has full authority to solemnize a marriage. He is a notary and was commissioned at the last meeting of the governor and council. And I know that," he added, attempting a bit of a swagger, "for I secured the commission for him myself." He came out of his corner and shook his cane at Farr. "I want you to understand that I have political power in this state!"

"I wouldn't brag about that kind of political power, when you can use it to make notaries out of jailbirds. That must be a nice bunch you have up at your State House!"

"On your way!" Again the cane swished in front of Farr's face.

"I beg your pardon, madam," apologized Farr, bowing to the girl. "You seem to be the only one in this room entitled to that courtesy," he added, with a touch of his cynicism. "Am I intruding on your personal business?"

"You are not," she answered, her eyes flashing. "I am glad you came in here. I could have stopped the wretched folly myself, but you have helped me, and I thank you." She delivered that little speech with vigor.

"Kate!" pleaded Dodd. "This isn't fair. I meant it all right. Here's your mother here! You wouldn't be reasonable the other way. We had to do something. For the love of Heaven, be good. You know I—"

She had turned her back on him. Now she whirled and spat furious words at him, commanding him to be silent.

"Do you want to spread all this miserable business before this gentleman?" she demanded. "I am ashamed—ashamed! My mother to consent to such a thing!"

She turned her back on him again and walked to and fro, beating her hands together in her passion. And now ire boiled in Dodd. He directed it all at the man who had interfered.

"This is no business of yours, you loafer. I don't know who you are, but you—"

Farr grabbed the switching cane as he would have swept into his palm an annoying insect. He broke it into many pieces between his sinewy fingers and tossed the bits into Dodd's convulsed face.

"You'll know me better later on—you and your uncle, too. Ask him what I advised him to do about having his weapon loose on his hip—take the same advice for yourself."

Then his expression altered suddenly. A disquieting jog of memory prompted him to yank out the cheap watch.

Twelve minutes to nine.

It was a long way to the foot of the steps of the Mellicite Club! And Union Hall was filled with men who were patiently waiting for him to keep his pledged word!

"I hope you'll be all right now," he said to the girl, haste in his tones. "I'm sorry—I must go—I have an important engagement."

Her eyes met his in level gaze, turned scornful glance at the others in the room, and then came back to his.

"Are you going in the direction of the Boulevard?" she asked him.

"Straight there."

"Will you bother with me as far as the Boulevard?"

"If you are a good walker," he informed her. There was strict business in her tone and cool civility in his.

"I'm going along with this gentleman, mother."

Farr ushered her ahead of him through the shattered door.

"But I want to walk home with you, my child," wailed the sobbing woman.

"You'd better ask Mr. Dodd to escort you. And I trust that the talk you and he will have will bring both of you to your senses."

She hurried away up the alley with Farr, after he had unlocked the front door, finding the key on the inside.

"I am sorry I must hurry you," he apologized, "and if you cannot keep up I must desert you when we get to a well-lighted street."

She drove a sharp side glance at him and did not reply. Probably for the first time in her life she heard a young man declare with determination that he was in a hurry to leave her. Even a sensible young woman who is pretty must feel some sort of momentary pique because a young man can have engagements so summary and so engrossing.

He offered her his arm that they might walk faster. Her touch thrilled him. He was far from feeling the outward calm that he displayed to her.

They did not speak as they hurried.

Both were nearly breathless when they came out on the Boulevard. He saw the big clock—its hands were nearly at the right angle.

"Good night!" she gasped, and she put out her hand to him. "I thank you!"

"It was nothing," he assured her.

When their palms met they looked into each other's eyes. It was a momentary flash which they exchanged, but in that instant both of them were thrilled with the strange, sweet knowledge that no human soul may analyze: it is the mystic conviction which makes this man or that woman different from all the rest of humankind to the one whose heart is touched.

She gave him a smile. "Are you a knight-errant?"

She hurried away before he could reply—and, though all his yearning nature strove against his man's resolution to do his duty, it could not prevail: he did not follow her as he wanted to—running after her, crying his love. But duty won out by a mere hazard of a margin because her face, as she had shown it to him at the moment of parting, possessed not merely the wonderful beauty which had so impressed him when he had first seen her—it shone with a sudden flash of emotion that glorified it.

He turned away and hurried to the foot of the steps of the Mellicite Club.

He had no time to ponder on the nature of that mystery which he had uncovered in the shabby cottage in Rose Alley nor to wonder what sort of persecution it was that could enlist a mother's aid in that grotesque fashion against her own daughter.

He had not time even to frame a plan of campaign against the man whom the patient waiters in Union Hall were expecting him to capture.

The bell in the tower was booming its nine strokes and the Honorable Archer Converse was coming down the steps from his club, erect, crisp, immaculate, dignified—tapping his cane against the stones.

XVIII
CORRALING A CONVERT

Mr. Converse bestowed only a careless glance at the stranger who was waiting at the foot of the club-house steps.

The young man accosted him, not obsequiously, but frankly.

"I know you always take a turn in the park at this hour, Mr. Converse. I beg your pardon, but may I walk for a few steps with you?"

"Why do you want to walk with me?"

"It's a matter—"

"I never discuss business on the street, sir. Come to my office to-morrow."

He marched on and Farr went along behind him.

"You heard?" demanded the attorney.

"I heard." Farr replied very respectfully, but he kept on.

He had rushed away from the girl and had come face to face with Mr. Converse, his mind utterly barren of plan or resource. That interim on which he had counted as a time in which he might devise ways and means had been so crowded with happenings that all consideration of plans in regard to Archer Converse had been swept from his mind.

At all events, he had rendered a service in that time; he had made good use of that forty-five minutes—that reflection comforted him even while he dizzily wondered what he was to do now.

That service had demanded sacrifice from him—why not demand something from that service? An idea, sudden, brazen, undefendable, even outrageous, popped into his head. He had no time for sensible planning. Mr. Converse was glancing about with the air of a citizen who would like to catch the eye of a policeman.

"I know all about you, Mr. Converse, even if you know nothing about me. I'm making a curious appeal—it's to your chivalry!"

That was appeal sufficiently novel, so the demeanor of Mr. Converse announced, to arrest even the attention of a gentleman who usually refused to allow the routine of his life to be interrupted by anything less than an earthquake. He halted and fronted this stranger.

"A man who wears that," proceeded Farr, indicating the rosette of the Military Order of the Loyal Legion in the lapel of Mr. Converse's coat, "and wears it because it came to him by inheritance from General Aaron Converse is bound to listen to that appeal."

"Explain, sir."

"Do you know a Richard Dodd who is the nephew of Colonel Dodd?"

"I do, sir. You aren't asking me to assist him, are you? I will have nothing to do with him—no help from me!"

"Just a moment—wait one moment! Mr. Converse, do you know a man named Dennis Burke who has been in prison for ballot frauds?"

"I helped send him there, sir. Are you reciting the rogues' roster to me?"

"Richard Dodd has dressed Burke up as a parson and is trying to force a young woman into a marriage. I haven't time to tell you how I happened to know about this affair—but it is in Rose Alley and there's no time to waste."

"A preposterous yarn."

"I have just come from that house."

"You're a young man of muscle—why didn't you stop it?"

"The girl's mother is there, backing Dodd. Mr. Converse, the cause needs a man like you—a man of law, of standing, of influence. I appeal to you to follow me."

"A moment—a moment! I scent a ruse. I don't know you. Are you a decoy for blackmailers or robbers?" he inquired, bluntly.

Farr took off his hat and stood before the Honorable Archer Converse, his strange, slow, winning smile dawning on his face.

"I beg your pardon for interrupting your stroll," he said, gently. "I hope you'll look at me! You may see, perhaps, that you're in error. I'll go back and kill Dodd—and come to your office to-morrow—on business—engaging you as counsel for the defense."

"Lead the way to that house," snapped Mr. Converse. The attitude of Farr, his forbearance, his refraining from further solicitation, his frank demeanor, won out for him. "I'm sometimes a little hasty in my remarks," acknowledged Mr. Converse in the tone of one who felt chastened. "Are you a new-comer to our city?" he continued as they hurried away. "You must be. I should certainly have remembered you if I had ever seen you before." It was an indirect compliment—a gentleman's careful approach to an apology.

The young man did not reply. He had conceived for this stately man a sudden hero-worship. What Citizen Drew had told him was added to his own instinct in matters of the understanding of a personality. He did not dare to stop and consider to what despicable extent he was lying to his victim. He knew if he stopped to think he would quit. Now the whole affair seemed a crazy thing. Did even his proposed ends justify this procedure?

"There's a short cut through Sanson Street," stammered Farr, the sense of his own iniquity increasing in the same ratio in which his respect and admiration grew. The honorable gentleman traveled along at a brisk jog, evidently desiring to show his apologetic mood by exhibiting confidence in his guide.

And Farr, stealing side glances at him, was more self-accusatory, more abashed. He cherished the hope that they would be able to anticipate the departure of Dodd and the confederates from the cottage. It was not clear to him just how he would make the incident serve, anyway. He was conscious that he had grasped at any opportunity which would open the ears of the Honorable Archer Converse to a person who had accosted him on the street. Finding somebody in the house would, at least, stamp his story with verity even if it served no purpose in the main intent of Farr's efforts.

But on a well-lighted street corner the young man halted suddenly.

"It's no use," he informed the astonished Mr. Converse. "Conscience has tripped me. I can't do it."

"Do you mean to intimate that you have been tricking me, sir?"

"I mean to say, Mr. Converse, that I had proposed to take a half-hour or so and think up some method of honestly and properly interesting you in a matter which is very dear to me—a public matter, sir. But here is how I spent that half-hour."

Frankly, simply, convincingly he related to his amazed listener the full story of what he had found in the cottage in Rose Alley.

"And therefore I had no time to ponder on my business with you—I simply turned from the young lady, and there you were, sir, coming down the club steps. I did the very best I could on short notice—but what I did was very crude. I apologize. I suppose, under the circumstances, I may as well say 'Good-night'!" He raised his hat.

But there was something in all this which piqued Converse's curiosity.

"Wait one moment. This is getting to be interesting."

A rather hazy conviction began to assure Farr that possibly chance had dealt a better stroke for him than well-considered planning. It was surely something to know that the honorable gentleman was interested.

"If you had had time to think out a method of approaching me—Let me see, your name is—"

"Farr."

"Mr. Farr, supposing I had been amenable to your suggestions, what is it you wanted of me?"

"I wanted you to attend a public meeting," blurted the young man. "They are men who need help—they need—"

"That's sufficient," snapped Converse. "I am not in politics. I do not address public meetings. Mr. Farr, you would have wasted your time planning. Absolutely!"

"But is there not some appeal that—"

"Useless—useless, sir." He tapped his cane, and his tones showed irritation. He whirled on his heels. "It is decidedly evident that you are a stranger in these parts, sir. On that account I forgive your presumption."

At that moment a jigger-wagon rumbled to a halt near them. The corner light had revealed them to the driver.

"Mr. Farr," called the man, "it hasn't taken long for the news of what you did at the meeting to-night to travel around among the boys. And we ain't going to let you get ahead of us, sir."

"The more, the merrier, in a good cause," said Farr; but he was staring regretfully at the back of Mr. Converse, who had begun his retreat.

"I want to tell you I'm on the executive committee of the State Teamsters Union, Mr. Farr. I've been talking the matter up and I can promise you that the union as a body will vote to lend horses and men to carry your spring-water free gratis. And I hope that gent who's starting up-town where the dudes are will tell 'em that there are honest men enough left to protect the poor folks from that poison water him and his rich friends are pumping out of the river to us."

The Honorable Archer Converse halted his departure very suddenly.

"You are not referring to me, are you, my man?"

"I am if you're tied up with that Consolidated Water Company bunch," stated the unterrified member of the proletariat.

Mr. Converse retraced his steps. He shook his cane at the driver.

"I want to inform you very distinctly, sir, that I am *not* interested in the Consolidated."

"Dawson, apologize to this gentleman," Farr admonished the driver.

"I'm sorry I said anything," muttered the man. "But all dudes look alike to me," he told himself under his breath.

Mr. Converse appeared to be considerably disturbed by the humble citizen's sneer in regard to the Consolidated matter. He addressed himself to Farr.

"I have been touched on a point where I am very sensitive," he informed the young man. "I do not condone the policies of the Consolidated in regard to their control of franchises. Their system of operation has introduced a bad element into our finance and politics. I would be sorry to be misunderstood by the people of this state."

"I hope you will not be misunderstood, sir," averred Farr, with humility.

"In order to show you my stand in the matter and so that you may correct any misunderstanding among your friends in these quarters," proceeded Mr. Converse, stiffly, "I will inform you that I am taking the case of the citizens' syndicate of Danburg on appeal up to our highest court. We hope to prove criminal conspiracy. We hope to show up some of the corruption in the state. That is why I have gone into the case."

"I thank you for informing me. I have been trying to fight the Consolidated in my own humble way."

The eminent lawyer came closer and was promptly interested.

"I am in search of information of all kinds, sir. Kindly explain."

Eliminating himself as much as possible, Farr described the operations of the Co-operative Spring Water Association. But he could not eliminate the man on the box-seat of the jigger-wagon. When Farr had finished his brief explanation that loyal admirer gave in some enthusiastic testimony in regard to the man who had devised the plan and had sacrificed his time in efforts to extend the system. He kept on until Farr checked him.

"I will say, Mr. Converse, before you leave, that I'd like to have you carry away a right opinion of me. I was not trying to drag you to a mere political gathering. There are some poor men assembled just now in this quarter who need a sympathetic listener and a little good advice. They are also trying to get justice from the Consolidated and all the general oppression it represents."

"Where are those men?" asked Converse, after a pause during which he wrinkled his brows and tapped his cane.

Farr pointed down the street. Not far away a low-hung transparency heralded "The Square Deal Club."

Mr. Converse gazed in that direction and hesitated a few moments longer.

"You assure me that it's not a mere political rally?"

"I do, sir!"

Then the son of General Converse gallantly extended his arm.

"I'll be glad to be escorted by you, Mr. Farr," he said. "Now that I understand this thing a bit better, I am going to break one of my rules." As they walked along he remarked: "A man's affairs are sometimes directed and controlled for him in a most singular fashion. Little things change preconceived notions very suddenly."

"They do, sir," agreed Walker Farr.

XIX
CONSCIENCE ENLISTING A RECRUIT

A man who stood at the head of the stairs, an outpost, saw them coming and ran and opened a door ahead of them. The door admitted to a hall which was packed with men who were ranged on settees and stood in the aisles and at the sides of the big room.

"Make way for the Honorable Archer Converse," shrieked their *avant courier*, excitedly.

"Three cheers for the Honorable Archer Converse," called a voice, and all the men came on to their feet and yelled lustily.

The distinguished guest climbed upon the platform—Farr close at his heels. The young man placed a chair for the lawyer and remained standing. He raised his hand to command silence.

"This is rather unexpected, boys. But this distinguished man happened to be passing our hall to-night and has dropped in on us in a purely informal manner. It's a great honor, and I want to say to him for all of us that the old Square Deal Club is mighty grateful. I ask you to rise, gentlemen of the club."

All came to their feet again.

"Bow your heads and for thirty seconds of deep silence pay your respect and veneration to the memory of our great war governor, General Aaron Converse."

The Honorable Archer Converse looked forth over those bowed and bared heads. The most of them were gray heads, and toil-worn hands were clasped in front of those men. And when at last the faces were raised to his there was an appealing earnestness in their gaze which touched him poignantly.

"Boys, the son of that great man is present. How will you express your admiration and respect for him?"

They cheered again tumultuously.

Farr walked to the edge of the platform.

"It is kind and generous of Mr. Converse to consent to step in here for a few moments this evening. I will leave the meeting in his hands."

There was a hush for a moment. Then the guest carried his chair to the extreme front edge of the platform.

"I don't know just what sort of meeting this is—I have not been fully informed," he said, very crisply. "But I want it distinctly understood that I am not here to make any speech. Your faces indicate that you are very much in earnest in regard to the business you are met to consider. I am assured that this is no mere political rally?"

"No," somebody replied.

"I'm glad of that. I am not in politics. The political mess grows to be nastier every year. But what are you here for? Come, now! Come! Let's talk it over." He was a bit brusque, but his tone was kindly.

A man who stood up in the middle of the hall was rather shabby in his attire, but he had the deep eyes of one who thinks.

"Honored sir," he said, "I don't stand up as one presuming to speak for all the rest. But I have talked with many men. I know what some of us want. We don't expect that laws or leaders will make lazy men get ahead in the world or that victuals can be legislated into the cupboard without a man gets out and hustles for 'em. I have worked at a bench ever since I was fourteen. I expect to work there until I drop out. I don't want any political office. I couldn't fill one. But why is it that the only men who get into office are the kind who turn around and get rich selling off property which belongs to all of us—I mean the franchises for this, that, and the other?" He sat down.

A thin man in the front row got up.

"Honorable Archer Converse, one franchise that was given away by those men years ago was the right to furnish water to this city. A private concern got hold of that franchise. It holds the right to-day. It saves money by pumping its water out of the Gamonic River. Saves money and wastes lives. The Board of Health's reports show that there were eleven hundred cases of typhoid fever in this city last year. In my family my mother and two of my children died. I shiver every time I touch a tap—but spring-water that can be depended on costs us at the grocer's a dollar for a five-gallon carboy—and my wages are only ten dollars a week. There are lakes twenty miles from this city. Pure water there for all of us! But every tap drips sewage from the Gamonic River. Haven't we got any leaders who will make that water company pump health instead of death?"

"They sent 'Tabulator' Burke up for ballot frauds," said a voter who stood up in a far corner. "But anybody in this city understands well enough that the judge who sent him to state prison knew who the real chaps were, knew how much the real ones paid 'Tabulator' to take the whole blame. And the governor knows it all and has just reappointed that judge."

The Honorable Archer Converse sat very straight in his chair and listened to those men. He continued to sit straight and listened to others. The men dealt in no diatribe. There was no raving, there was no anarchistic sentiments. They arose, uttered their grievances gloomily but without passion, and sat down.

One elderly man stood up and raised both hands.

"I came across the sea to this country, sir. I came because I could have my little share in the government where I paid taxes and labored—I could vote here. It's the only public privilege I have. But, O God, give us some one to vote for!"

"I sympathize with your feelings," replied Mr. Converse. "But you are talking to the wrong man. I'm not in politics."

"By the gods, you will be if my nerve only holds out," Farr told himself.

Another man sprang to his feet. He spoke quietly, but his very repression made him more effective.

"What's the good of voting till men like you do get into politics, Mr. Converse, and give us leaders who will use their power to help the people who voted for them? I'm sick of voting. I'm teamed up to the polls by ward workers—and I know just why those men are in the game and who they're working for. What do you suppose Colonel Dodd cares which side carries this city, or which side carries the state? He and his crowd stand to win, whatever party gets in. You can't beat 'em. Business is business, no matter what politics may be! The city money is wasted just the same, the policy game is let run for the benefit of the rich men who back it, all the grafts go right on. You can't fool me any longer. They stir us poor chaps up at election-time, we rush to the polls and vote, and sometimes think we are accomplishing something. But what we're doing is simply boosting out some fellow who has made his pile and putting in another who wants office so that he can fill his own pockets by selling our common rights out to the same men. I say, you can't beat it!"

The Honorable Archer Converse seemed to find his position on the platform uncomfortable. He rose suddenly and stepped down on the floor. He went among the men. He grasped the hands that were outstretched to him. He realized that he had scant encouragement for these men. The meeting had given him new light. He knew considerable about the old days, and in the old days of politics men flocked to rallies. They harkened humbly to speeches from their leaders, and swallowed the sugar-coated facts, and listened to bands, and joined the torch-light parades, and voted according to party lines, and thought they had done well; the surface of things was nicely slicked over.

He understood that out of the ease with which the mob could be herded, with others doing their thinking for them, had grown politics as a business—with the big interests dominating both parties—and no one realized how it had all come about better than Converse. This new spirit, however, rather surprised him, for he had been keeping aloof from politics. These men who crowded about him were not mere dumb, driven voters in the mass—they were individuals who were thinking, who were demanding, who were seeking a leader that would consider them as citizens to be served, not chattels to be sold to the highest bidder. His keen lawyer's insight understood all this!

"I'm a butcher down in the stock-yards, Mr. Converse," said one man, who pressed forward. "We've got trained bulls there who tole the cattle along into the slaughter-pens. I've got tired of being a steer in politics and following these old trained bulls."

Converse worked his way through the press to the door, Farr at his heels.

When they were on the street the honorable gentleman turned sharply toward the Boulevard.

"I haven't any spirit or taste to-night for moonlight in the park, sir! A nice trick you played on me."

"I wanted you to get a first-hand notion of a state of affairs, Mr. Converse."

"But you ought to understand my temperament better—you ought to know it's going to stick in my mind, worry me, vex me, set me to seeking for remedies. It's just as if I'd been retained on a case. I feel almost duty-bound to pitch in."

"It's strange how a man gets pulled into a thing sometimes—into something he had no idea of meddling with," philosophized Farr, blandly. "That's the way it has happened in my case."

"It has, eh?" demanded Mr. Converse, sharply. He had tacitly accepted the young man's companionship for the walk back to the Boulevard. "Now, look here! Just who are you?"

"My name is Farr and I'm nothing."

"You needn't bluff me—you're a politician—a candidate for something."

"I'm not even a voter in this state. It's men like you, sir, who ought to be candidates for the high offices."

"My sainted father trained me to respect self-sacrifice, Mr. Farr. But for a clean man to try to accomplish things for the people in politics these days isn't self-sacrifice—it's martyrdom. The cheap politicians heap the fagots, the sneering newspapers light the fire and keep blowing it with their bellows, and the people stand around and seem to show a sort of calm relish in watching the operation. And when it is all over not a bit of good has been done."

"I'm afraid I have wasted an evening for you, sir. I'm sorry. I hoped the troubles of those men, when you heard them at first hand, would interest you."

"Interest me! Confound it all, you have wrecked my peace of mind! I knew it all before. But I'm selfish, like almost everybody else. I kept away where I couldn't hear about these things. Now, if I sleep soundly to-night I'll be ashamed to look up at my father's portrait when I walk into my office to-morrow morning. Why didn't you have better sense than to coax me into your infernal meeting?" He rapped his cane angrily against the curbstone as he strode on. "And the trouble with me is," continued Mr. Converse, with much bitterness, "I know the conditions are such in this state that a meeting like that can be assembled in every city and town—and the complaints will be just and demand help. But there's no organization—it's only blind kittens miauling. It's damnable!"

"But this is the kind of country where some mighty quick changes can be made when the people do get their eyes open," suggested the young man.

Mr. Converse merely grunted, tapping his cane more viciously.

They were on the frontier of the Eleventh Ward now. The brighter lights of the avenues of up-town blazed before them.

"Then you will not go into politics?" inquired Farr.

"I'd sooner sail for India with a cargo of hymn-books and give singing-lessons to Bengal tigers."

"Good night, sir," said Farr. He halted on the street corner which marked the boundary of the ward.

"Good night, sir!" replied Mr. Converse, striding on.

The young man watched him out of sight. He heard the angry clack of the cane on the stones long after the Honorable Archer Converse had turned the next corner.

"Maxim in the case of a true gentleman," mused Farr: "tap his conscience on the shoulder, point your finger at the enemy, say nothing, simply stand back and give conscience plenty of elbow-room—it needs no help. There, by the grace of God, goes the next governor of this state."

XX
CONSIDERATION: ONE DAUGHTER

On the morning following his discomfiture Richard Dodd posted himself in a little tobacco-shop opposite the Trelawny Apartment-house. Lurking behind cigar-boxes in the window, he held the door of the house under surly espionage. It was plain to the shopkeeper that "the gent had made a night of it." Dodd's eyes were heavy, his face was flushed, and he lighted one cigarette after another with shaky hands.

Shortly before nine o'clock Kate Kilgour came out and walked down the avenue on the way to her work. Dodd stared after her until she was out of sight. Shame and anger and desire mingled in the steady gaze he leveled on her; in her crisp freshness she represented both the longed-for and the unattainable. He was conscious of a new sentiment in regard to her. In the past his impatience had been tempered by the comforting knowledge that she had promised herself to him—that she was his to own, to possess after a bit of tantalizing procrastination. Now he was not at all sure of her. He had been just a bit patronizing in the past—his successes with women had inflated his conceit—he had exhibited a rather careless air of proprietorship—his manner had said to her and to others, "This is mine; look at it!" But now when he had watched her out of sight jealousy, anger, the sour conviction that he had forfeited her regard combined to make him desperate, and the excesses of the night before kindled a flame which heated all his evil passions.

He threw away his cigarette, cursed roundly aloud, and hurried across the street into the Trelawny.

When Mrs. Kilgour admitted him to her suite she clung to the door-casing, exhibiting much trepidation.

He stepped in, closed the door, and put his back against it.

"Have you got those hysterics out of you so that you can listen to me and then talk sense?" he demanded, coarsely.

She went into her sitting-room and he followed, muttering:

"No wonder you ran away from me last night—no wonder you didn't have the face to stay and take what you deserve. How in tophet I ever allowed you to plan and manage I can't understand."

"You asked me to," she faltered.

"I didn't ask you to rig up a dirty conspiracy to queer me."

"Richard, you are not yourself. You have been drinking!" She tried to exhibit protesting indignation and failed. "Come to me when you are yourself."

"There's no more of this to-morrow business goes with me, Mrs. Kilgour. I'll admit that you're Kate's mother. But just now you are something else. You have tried to do me, and nobody gets by with that stuff—man, woman, or child. We'll have our settlement here and now."

"I did the best I could," she wailed.

"Out of what damnation novel did you get that idea?" he raged.

"It seemed to be a good plan, Richard. I swear by everything sacred I thought it would come out all right. Don't rave at me." Her voice sunk to an appealing whisper. She picked up a book from her table. "If you will only listen—"

"So you did get it out of a novel! My God! what have your fool ideas done to me?"

"How do you dare to talk to Kate's mother like that?"

"I am not talking to Kate's mother, I tell you! I'm talking to a woman who has put me into a hell on earth. I'm talking to you, Mrs. Kilgour, and you don't know the whole story yet."

"All my life it has been the same—only trouble and sorrow and to be misunderstood." She began to sob.

"Is there anything in that novel about ringing in an iceman to break up a marriage? I say it was all a conspiracy. You didn't intend to be square. You intended to rig a scheme so that you could duck out from under. You have always done that, Mrs. Kilgour."

"I had nothing to do with that man coming in."

"Don't try to fool me any more. You told me to come, didn't you? You must have told some yarn to your daughter to have her come."

"I did—it was all—"

"And then you told that plug-ugly to come in, too, and break it up so as to queer me. Why did I ever fall for such lunacy? If I hadn't been desperate I would never have let you drag me into such a devilish scheme. But now you have got to do your part to square me. It's going to be straight talk from now on, Mrs. Kilgour. There must be a settlement between us."

She looked away from him. She was plainly searching her soul for excuses to postpone that settlement.

"That person who came in, Dicky! I swear I did not arrange any such thing. He is only an iceman. I don't know the man. It was some accident. If the matter hadn't been interrupted! It was going along all right."

"What's the matter with your intellect? You know it wasn't going along at all! You simply had us chasing shadows. Good God! I ought to have made you tell me what you were planning. Think of it! Think of me waltzing down there like a boob and thinking you had something real to offer."

"But you frightened her with that jailbird. You should have brought a real clergyman."

"The man I brought has the power to perform marriages! I would have made a nice spectacle towing a clergyman into that mess, wouldn't I?"

She broke in upon his further speech. She wrung her hands, paltering, pleading, trying to explain, trying more desperately to postpone that settlement he was demanding.

"But, honestly, it did seem to be a good plan, Dicky. I'm her mother. I know her nature. You know how some natures have to be handled! She is so self-centered. She has to be taken by surprise. She has to know that she is making a sacrifice. That is why I arranged it all for Rose Alley and borrowed that house. And I had it all planned out what to say to her at the last moment there."

"Well, what was this great thing you were going to say?" He glared at her, disgust and suspicion in his eyes.

She flushed. She hesitated, unable to meet his gaze.

"It's no use to tell you now, Dicky. Somehow, now that I come to think it all over, it sounds rather tame. It all did seem so plausible, what I was going to say when I sat down and planned out the thing. And the romance of it—you know even self-centered girls like to feel that a man wants them so much that he gets desperate—and she said once that she would marry you some time—perhaps—and—"

"Oh, you—you—" He broke in and then stopped, lacking words. "What's the use?" he muttered. "You don't even know your own daughter. She has been enduring me because you have been keeping at her. I understand it now. You told me you could hurry it up. You have made me look like a melodrama villain. You have made her hate me. Now own up! Didn't she rave to you after you got home and tell you she hated me? You have nailed me to the cross for ever where she is concerned—now haven't you? Own up."

"I can win her back, Dicky. Give me a little time." But she was not able to look at him. "Don't scold me any more. I'm her mother. She will obey her own mother in time. Don't hurt my sensitive nature any more." She began to weep, twisting her rings on her trembling fingers.

He scowled at her, narrowing his eyes. "You haven't been playing square with me, Mrs. Kilgour."

"Call me Mother Kilgour, Dicky, just as you always have."

"I won't stand for any more bluffing, Mrs. Kilgour. Kate has sworn to you that she will never marry me—now hasn't she?"

"But I can talk her around—you can win her back. I'll tell her it was my plan—I'll have courage to tell her later—"

"So you have been laying that crazy idea all to me?"

"But I'll get up courage to tell her some day—and your devotion will win her back—devotion always wins. You can—"

"Mrs. Kilgour, I know you pretty well. I repeat, I know you have always ducked out from under—that's your nature. But here's a thing you can't dodge. You've got to come to time. You know how I love Kate. There isn't any reason why she shouldn't marry me. There's no excuse for her holding me off the way she does. You've got to fix it for me—quick! Understand? This fluff talk about 'devotion' and 'some day' doesn't go. I want action. Now hold on! I don't mean to threaten—I've been square with you till now. Good gad, you don't realize what a price I've paid!"

"And now on top of your other insults you are going to twit me again because I have borrowed five thousand dollars from you. Oh, Dicky, I thought you were more of a gentleman?"

"Mrs. Kilgour, I have simply got to make you understand what I have done for you before you'll wake up and do something for me."

"I appreciate what you did, Dicky. Honestly, I do. You save me from losing money on my stocks."

"Where are those stocks?"

She did not look at him. "I have them put away—all safe. They are all right. Just as soon as business is better I will get your money for you, Dicky. You shall have it, every cent."

"Where are those stocks, I say! Mrs. Kilgour, look at me. Were are they?"

"Why are you so particular about knowing where they are?" Protecting herself, she showed a flicker of resentment.

"Because you must sell and hand me that money—at once."

"I—I don't believe I can realize on them just now. They are—are down just at present. They—"

"What are the stocks?"

"I don't care to reveal my private business, Richard."

"It happens to be my business, too. I'm in trouble. I must know. I shall stay here till I find out. You may as well come across."

"As soon as I can arrange it—I will tell you. Very soon now!"

He snapped himself out of his chair and went across the room to her. He put his hands on her shoulders and bent his face to hers.

"You haven't any stocks, Mrs. Kilgour."

"No," she whispered, his eyes dominating her.

"What did you do with that money I loaned you?"

"I paid—a debt."

"What debt? Answer! This thing must be cleared up—*now*!"

She began to weep.

"No more hysterics, Mrs. Kilgour. We are now down to cases. Something bad will happen if you don't confide in me."

Then, cornered, with the impulse of weak natures to seek support from stronger—to appeal to a victor who cannot be eluded—she blurted the truth.

"They got to suspecting me when I was cashier for Dalton & Company. I heard they were going to put experts upon my books, Dicky. I didn't want to go to jail. I would have disgraced Kate. I knew you loved her and would not want her mother to be arrested. I had to have that money. I told you the story about the stocks. So I was saved from being disgraced."

"Oh, you were?" His eyes flamed so furiously that she turned her gaze from him.

"And now I feel better, for I have confided in you and you're going to be my good and true friend from now on. It will be made up to you, Dicky."

"What had you done with all that money you took from Dalton & Company?"

"It costs so much to live—and keep up the position I had when Andrew was alive! A woman needs so many things, Richard. I have always been proud. I was obliged to—"

He swore and swung away from her. "Wasted it on dress and jewelry! You turned the trick on one man and put him underground. And I'm the next victim! I knew I was being played for a sucker, but, oh—"

He battered his fists against the wall in pure ecstasy of rage. Then he sat down and put his face in his hands.

The woman clucked sobs which did not ring true.

"I wonder what Kate would say if she knew how I had come to the scratch. She knew her father was a hero. I wonder whether she would think I am one!" he said, after silence had continued for a long time.

"Are you going to tell her?" the mother gasped.

"I love her too much. But, see here! Do you think I picked that five thousand off a rose-bush?"

"You told me your uncle loaned it to you."

"You think I got it easy—got it for the asking, and that's why you have been loafing on the job," he said, with bitterness. "Ask my uncle for money? I should say not. He never loosened for anybody yet—not even his relatives. Mrs. Kilgour, I love your daughter so much—I was so anxious to help you—I stole that five thousand from the state treasury. I have been covering it in my accounts for more than a year—hell all the time with plenty of white-hot when the legislative committee has been over the accounts. Some day some blasted fool will wake up enough to see that there's a hole in my figures."

He put his elbows on his knees and stared at the carpet. The woman's face grew white.

"That's how it stands with me, Mrs. Kilgour. You know you were not square with me at the start. You said you needed the money for only a few weeks—you said you were pinched in a stock deal. You lied to me. You have wasted the money on fine feathers for your back. I have kept still. You can't pay me. I've got to struggle out of the mess as best I can. But, by the eternal gods, there's something coming to me, and that's your daughter. Now are you going to wake up?"

"I'll do everything I can." Her tone was not convincing, however.

He realized that this woman with the pulpy conscience and the artificial emotions, selfish and a coward, was merely vaguely stirred by his revelation, not spurred by the extent of his sacrifice in her behalf.

"Do what you *can*? Whine to me like that after I have stolen state's money and am standing under my steal? What if this state tips over politically and they investigate the treasury? I tell you, Mrs. Kilgour, I deserve to have Kate. I'm going to have her. You have got to fix it—and right away."

"But I can't marry off a girl of twenty as if she were a Chinese slave." His insistence caused her to display more of her pettish resentment.

"If you can't deliver the goods, Mrs. Kilgour, I shall take a hand in it."

"How?"

"I'll tell her the story."

"You wouldn't dare."

"She has a sense of honor and of obligation even if you haven't. She will pay. She'll pay with herself. That's a devil of a way to get a wife, but if that's the only way I'll take it."

"But you have just owned up that you have embezzled money. As Kate's mother it's my duty to protect her from disgrace."

That amazing declaration fairly took away Dodd's breath.

By the manner in which the woman now looked at him it was plain that he had sunk in her estimation.

"You know, Richard, a mother feels called on to protect a good daughter."

He got up and stamped on the floor in his passion and swore.

"I appreciate what you did for me—but, really, I didn't ask you to steal money—and I supposed your uncle was always liberal with you. You should not have told me falsehoods."

The maddening feature of this calm assumption of superiority was the fact that the woman seemed really to believe for the moment exactly what she was saying and to forget why Dodd had jeopardized his fortunes; her manner showed her shallow estimate of the situation.

"There's another way of doing it," raged the young man, infuriated by this repudiation of obligation. "I'll blow the whole thing about the two of us—and she'll be glad enough to have me after it's all over."

"You haven't any right to bring all this trouble and disgrace into my family."

"You know one way of preventing it and you'd better get busy, Mrs. Kilgour," he advised. "I'm going to give you another chance of keeping your word and paying your debt to me. I want Kate—and I have waited for her long enough."

He clapped on his hat and hurried away.

He left the mother sprawled on a couch, her ringed hands clutched into her dyed hair. She was still clucking sobs which would not have convinced any unprejudiced hearer that she felt real grief.

When Richard Dodd entered his uncle's offices in the First National block a little later he was in the mood to force his affairs a bit. He enjoyed liberties there which the ordinary caller did not have and he walked into Kate Kilgour's little room without attracting attention or comment.

"I know exactly how you feel about last night, Kate." He addressed her respectfully and humbly. "I understand that this is no place to discuss the matter. I haven't come here to do so. I apologize for the affair. I'm going to say this to you—I took your mother's advice. She planned the thing and trumped up the errand which called you to that house. I'm afraid she is rather too romantic. I only say this, Kate: a man's love can make him do foolish things. Please talk with your mother when you go home—and take her advice. If you do, it will be better for all of us." He trembled with the restraint he had put upon himself. "You can see that I have been punished, Kate. I am a different man—you ought to be able to see it. Awful trouble has come to me. I need your love to help me through it."

She gazed at him with level, cold eyes.

"You don't understand. I can't explain, dear! But I'm telling you the truth. Kate, if you don't forget that folly I was guilty of last night and be to me what you have been—if you don't marry me very soon you will be sorry."

"Are you threatening me, Richard?"

"No, I didn't mean it to sound like that. But I know that with your appreciation of what sacrifice means you will be very unhappy if you toss me away and then find out certain things."

"This is not the time for riddles, Richard. What do you mean?"

"I have said all I can say."

"I do not love you well enough to be your wife. I have not meant to play the coquette. I have not known myself. You and my mother—Oh, why rehearse? You know the story. You have understood that my love for you was not what you should have. We may as well end it here and now, Richard. I will forget last night. I will forget all the rest—for it is ended!"

"It cannot be ended," he retorted. "Understand! It cannot be ended. I am trying to hold myself together, Kate. Don't provoke me. I call on you to keep your promise. No other man shall have you." He leaned close. "Do you love any other man?"

She looked up at him and spoke slowly and gravely. "I do not think I do, Richard."

He scowled at her. "You don't *think* you do! What in the name of Judas do you mean by a remark like that?"

"It's because I'm trying to tell the truth," she returned, with simple earnestness.

"This is a sort of new mood you're in?" he persisted.

"Yes."

He hesitated. He started to speak and then was silent for a long time. "Damnation! I won't insult you!" he blurted at last.

"I hope not, Richard."

"It's preposterous!"

"What is preposterous?" Her tone was calm.

"I saw you look at a man last evening."

"Very well!"

"I have seen women look at me like that in my life."

"I was not conscious that I looked at any man in any especial manner."

"You couldn't see yourself. Perhaps you did not realize that you looked at that man with any meaning in your eyes. But the women who looked at me as you looked at him told me that they loved me. I am talking it right out! But if I should hint that you're in love with a tramp I should insult you. I am crazy, that's all. My troubles are affecting my mind. Forgive me, Kate."

"You are, of course, referring to the young man who broke in on our prospective business last evening." There was just a touch of contempt in her demeanor; but her air was coldly business-like; sitting there at her desk she held him, physically and mentally, at arm's-length. Her poise was sure. It seemed perfectly natural for her to be discussing a young man in an impersonal manner.

"I am referring to that low-lived vagrant we met on the road—that iceman—that—well, I don't know what he is except that the devil seems to be kicking him under my feet to trip me. Kate, Kate, it's too ridiculous to talk about—that wretch!"

"Do you mean by that remark that I am taking any interest in that young man outside of mere curiosity?"

"I don't know why you should have any curiosity about a tramp."

"You are not a good student of physiognomy, Richard."

"So you have been studying him, have you? You went away with him and left me. What did he say to you? Where did he leave you? I haven't dared to think about your going away with him. I excused it because you were angry—so angry you'd even pick up a tramp for an escort. But what interest do you take in that renegade?" His tones were acrid with jealousy.

"I did not find him a renegade. I found him a mystery, Richard. And I hope that some day I will know what the mystery is."

"Are you trying to drive me mad?"

"I am merely chatting along in order to keep you off a topic which is distressing. I heard that your uncle intended to have the man investigated after he came into the office here and made that brave stand. I happened to hear the talk the young man made. Perhaps that accounts for my curiosity. Did your uncle find out much about the man?"

"I don't know what he found out," declared Dodd, rapidly losing control of himself. "But I propose to find out for myself."

"Please do, Richard," said the girl, ingenuously and earnestly. She seemed to be losing some of the hauteur she had shown at the first of their meeting.

"I'll find out enough to put him in jail, where he probably belongs. I'm not going to insult you, Kate, by any more talk about a tramp. You can't shift me from the main topic. Go home and talk with your mother, as I have told you. We are going to be married!"

"Richard, our affair is ended."

"Then who is the man?"

"There is no man."

"If you say that and mean it, then you don't know women as well as I know them. You don't know even yourself!" he declared. "I want to say to you, Kate, that we are all walking on mighty thin ice. The sooner you and I take hold of hands and get safely ashore—just you and I—the better it will be. Just let your curiosity about other men fall asleep. I tell you again, go home and talk with your mother."

He bowed, reached his hand to touch hers, but refrained when she turned suddenly to her desk and resumed her work.

Young Dodd hurried out of the building without attempting to see his uncle, and cooled his head and his passion and soothed his physical discomfort by a headlong dash in his car back to the state's capital city.

The girl took her courage in her hands and asked Mr. Peter Briggs, in as matter-of-fact tone as she could muster, whether he did not want any record copy made of his notes in regard to that person who had bearded Colonel Dodd. But Mr. Briggs informed her that the matter was not of sufficient importance.

"The fellow is merely a cheap, loafing sort—here to-day, there to-morrow," said Briggs. "I investigated him thoroughly."

Until then Miss Kilgour had always had a high opinion of Peter Briggs's acumen. She promptly revised that estimate, reflecting that age is bound to dull a person's senses and cloud his judgment.

XXI
THE HONORABLE LION CONFERS
WITH COLONEL TIGER

All his people in the offices of the Honorable Archer Converse noticed that the chief was not amiable that day. His usual dignified composure was wholly lacking. He gave off orders fretfully, he slapped papers about on his desk when he worked there; every now and then he glanced up at the portrait of his distinguished father and muttered under his breath. He had called for more documents relating to state health statistics, reports on water systems, and had despatched a clerk to the capital city to secure certain additional facts, figures, and literature. The junior members of his law firm knew that he had taken much to heart the case of the citizens of Danburg, who had been blocked in their honest efforts to build a water system and who now charged various high interests with conspiracy. The litigation was important—the issues revolutionary. But the juniors had never seen the chief fussed up by any law case before.

Then something really did happen!

The three citizens of Danburg who had occasionally conferred with him came into his office and lined up in front of him. Mr. Davis scratched his chin and blinked meekly, Mr. Erskine exhibited his nervousness by running his fingers around inside his collar, and Mr. Owen fairly oozed unspoken apology.

"Look here, gentlemen," snapped Mr. Converse, "I'm not ready for you. I told you not to come until next week. I have an immense mass of material to study. You're only wasting time—mine and yours—coming here to-day."

"Well, you see, your honor," stammered Davis, "we came to-day so as to save you more trouble and work."

"Work!" echoed Mr. Converse, seizing the arms of his chair and shoving an astonished face forward.

"Why—why—you see we've decided not to push this case any further. And whatever is owing to you—name the sum." He did not relish the glow which was coming into the attorney's eyes, nor the grim wrinkles settling about the thin lips. "So that there won't be any hard feelings, in any way," Davis hastened to say.

"What has happened to you men all of a sudden?" demanded the lawyer. "Explain! Speak up!"

Davis's face was red, and he found much difficulty in replying.

"Well—you see—you know—if you get into law you never know when you're going to get out. We feel that this case is bound to drag! It's an awful big case—and they've got lots of money to fight us."

"I told you I'd take your case for bare expenses and court fees," stormed the lawyer. "It's a case I wanted to prosecute."

"We know—you were mighty fine about it—but we've decided different. You see, the Consolidated—"

Mr. Converse came onto his feet and shook his finger under Davis's nose. "Don't you dare to tell me you have sold out to the Consolidated," he shouted in tones that rang through his offices and brought all his force to the right about and attention.

"That wasn't it—exactly. But they'll take it off our hands—will do the right thing, now that we have shown 'em a few things! Colonel Dodd has seen new light. And it is too good a price for us to throw down."

"You have let those monopolists buy you off. They have paid you a big bribe because they are getting scared. They were afraid they had played the old game once too often. I have them where I want them! No, my men! You've got to fight this thing, I say."

"You can't drag us into law unless we're willing to go," stated Davis, doggedly. "We've taken their money and the papers have been passed—and that settles it. We haven't done anything different than the others have done in this state."

"No, and that's the trouble with this state," cried Converse, with passion. "You came in here at first and talked like men—like honest men who had good reason for righteous anger—and I took your case. And now you sneak back here and give up your fight—bribed after I clubbed them until they were willing to offer you enough money."

"We have only done what straight business men would do Mr. Converse," declared Owen.

"We had a chance to go to the high court with a case that would open up the whole rottenness in this state before we got done fighting, and you have sold out!"

"Good day. We don't have to listen to such talk," said Erskine.

"You wait one minute." The lawyer pulled open a drawer and found his check-book. He wrote hastily and tore out the check. "Here's that retaining-fee you paid me. Now get out of my office."

He drove them ahead of him to the door, shouting insistent commands that they hurry.

When they were gone he gazed about at his astonished associates, his partners, and his clerks.

"I apologize most humbly ladies and gentlemen, for making such a disturbance. I—I hardly seem to be myself to-day."

He went to his desk and sat down and stared up at the portrait of War-Governor Converse for a long time. At last he thumped his fist on his desk and shook his head.

"No," he declared, as if the portrait had been asking him a question and pressing him for a reply, "I can't do it. I could have gone into the courts and fought them as an attorney. I could have maintained my self-respect. But not in politics—no—no! It's too much of a mess in these days."

But he pushed aside the papers which related to the affairs of the big corporations for which he was counsel and kept on studying the reports which his clerks had secured for him—such statements on health and financial affairs as they were able to dig up.

A day later his messenger brought a mass of data back from the State House along with a story about insolent clerks and surly heads of departments who offered all manner of slights and did all they dared to hinder investigation.

"It's a pretty tough condition of affairs, Mr. Converse," complained the clerk, "when a state's hired servants treat citizens as if they were trespassers in the Capitol. It has got so that our State House isn't much of anything except a branch office for Colonel Dodd."

"But you told them from what office you came—from my office?"

"Of course I did, sir."

"Well, what did they say?"

The clerk's face grew red and betrayed sudden embarrassment.

"Oh, they—they—didn't say anything special: just uppish—only—"

"What did they say?" roared Mr. Converse. "You've got a memory! Out with it! Exact words."

Clerks were taught to obey orders in that office.

"They said," choked the man, "that simply because your father was governor of this state once you needn't think you could tell folks in the State House to stand around! They said you didn't cut any ice in politics."

"That's the present code of manners, eh? Insult a citizen and salaam to a politician!"

"Mr. Converse, I waited an hour in the Vital Statistics Bureau while the chief smoked cigars with Alf Symmes, that ward heeler. I had sent in our firm card, and the chief held it in his hand and flipped it and smoked and sat where he could look out at me and grin—and when Symmes had finished his loafing they let me in."

Mr. Converse turned to his desk and plunged again into the data.

The next day he put a clerk at the long-distance telephone to call physicians in all parts of the state—collecting independent information in regard to the past and present prevalence of typhoid; he read certain official reports with puckered brow and little mutters of disbelief, and after he had read for a long time that disbelief was very frank. Mr. Converse had rather keen vision in matters of prevarication, even when the lying was done adroitly with figures.

He was not a pleasant companion for his office force during those days; his irascibility seemed to increase. He knew it himself, and he felt a gentleman's shame because of a state of mind which he could not seem to control.

And finally, out of the complexity of his emotions, he fully realized that he was angry at himself and that his anger at himself was growing more acute from the fact that he realized that the anger was justified. For he woke to the knowledge that he had allowed himself to grow selfish. He resented the fact that anybody should expect him to meddle with public affairs— to get into the muddle of politics. And he knew he ought to be ashamed of such selfishness—and, therefore, he grew more angry at himself as he continued to harbor resentment against any agency which threatened to drag him into public life.

He knew where the shell of that selfishness had been broken—it was cracked in the meeting where his chivalry had received its call to arms in behalf of the helpless. Those men had gazed at him, had told their troubles—and had left it all to his conscience! He did not believe those men were shrewd enough to understand so exactly in what fashion he could be snared in their affairs.

"Confound that rascal who inveigled me there!" ran his mental anathema of the strange young man. "He must have been the devil, wearing that frock-coat to hide his forked tail. And here I am now, fighting for peace of mind!"

And his struggle for his peace of mind drove him, at last, to set his hat very straight on his head and march across the street to Colonel Symonds Dodd's office.

The Honorable Archer Converse had made up his mind that no influence in the world could pull or push him into politics. He held firmly fixed convictions as to what would happen to a good man in politics. To get office this man of principle would be obliged to fight manipulators with their own choice of weapons. And once in office, all his motives would be mocked and his movements assailed. Converse was a keen man who had studied men; he was not one of those amiable theorists who believe that the People always have sense enough in the mass to turn to and elect the right men for rulers. He understood perfectly well that accomplishing real things in politics is not a game of tossing rose-petals.

He went to call on Colonel Dodd. He went with the lofty purpose of a patriotic citizen, resolved to exhort the colonel to clean house. It seemed to be quite the natural thing to do, now that the idea had occurred to him. Certainly Colonel Dodd would listen to reason—would wake up when the thing was presented to him in the right manner; he must understand that new fashions had come to stay in these days of reform.

Thinking it all over, considering that really the matter of this water-supply and attendant monopoly of franchises had become an evil, that the prospects of the party would be endangered if the party leaders continued to nurse this evil, Mr. Converse was certain that he and the colonel would be able to arrange for reform, by letting the colonel do the reforming.

They faced each other. Their respective attitudes told much!

Colonel Dodd filled his chair in front of his desk, using all the space in it, swelling into all its concavities—usurping it all.

The Honorable Archer Converse sat very straight, his shoulders not touching his chair-back.

Physically they represented extremes; mentally, morally, and in political ethics they were as divergent as their physical attributes.

"I'm sorry that you were able to take those Danburg men into camp," said Mr. Converse, couching his lance promptly and in plain sight like an honorable antagonist. "I had been retained and proposed to expose conditions in the management of water systems."

"I don't know what you mean," replied the colonel, following his own code of combat and mentally fumbling at a net to throw over this antagonist.

"Yes, you do," retorted Mr. Converse. "You know better than I do because you own the water systems of this state. But if you need to be reminded, Colonel, I'll say that you are making great profits. You can afford to tap lakes—spend money for mains even if you do have to go fifteen or twenty miles into the hills around the cities and towns."

"Whom do you represent, sir?"

"Colonel Dodd, I think—really—that I'm representing *you* when I give you mighty good advice and do not charge for it."

"I've got my own lawyers, Mr. Converse."

Both men were employing politeness that was grim, and they were swapping glances as duelists slowly chafe swords, awaiting an opening.

Sullen anger was taking possession of the colonel, thus bearded.

Righteous indignation, born from his bitterness of the past few days, made Converse's eyes flash.

"You are one of the richest men in this state, Colonel Dodd, and your money has come to you from the pockets of the people—tolls from thousands of them. Remember that!"

"Huh!" snorted the colonel, looking up at a bouquet.

It is not often given to men to place proper estimate on their own limitations. Otherwise, the Honorable Archer Converse would never have gone in person to prevail upon Colonel Symonds Dodd. In temperament and ethics they were so far asunder that conference between them on a common topic was as hopeless an undertaking as would be argument between a tiger and a lion over the carcass of a sheep.

Mr. Converse rose, unfolding himself with dignified angularity.

"I must remind you, sir, that I belong to the political party of which you assume to be boss. If you refuse to give common justice to the people, then you are using that party to cover iniquity."

Colonel Dodd worked himself out of his chair and stood up. "I am taking no advice from you, sir, as to how I shall manage business or politics."

"Perhaps, sir, in regard to your business I can only exhort you to be honest, but as regards the party which my honored father led to victory in this state I have something to say, by gad! sir, when I see it being led to destruction."

"Well, sir, what have you to say?"

"I will not stand by and allow it to be ruined by men who are using it to protect their methods in business dealings."

"What ice do you think you cut in the politics of this state?" inquired the colonel, dropping into the vernacular of the politician, too angry to deal in any more grim politeness.

"Not the kind you are cutting, sir—your political ice is like the ice you cut from the poisoned rivers."

"It seems to be still popular for cranks to come here and threaten me," sneered the colonel. "It was started a while ago by a shock-headed idiot from the Eleventh Ward."

The Honorable Archer Converse displayed prompt interest which surprised the colonel. "A young man from the Eleventh Ward? Was he tall and rather distinguished-looking?"

Colonel Dodd snorted his disgust. "Distinguished-looking! He threatened me, and I had him followed. He's a ward heeler. Better look him up!" His choler was driving him to extremes. He was pricked by his caller's high-bred stare of disdain. "He seems to be another apostle of the people who wants to tell me how to run my own business. Yes, you better look him up, Converse."

"Very well, sir! If he came in here and tried to tell you the truth about yourself he's worth knowing. Furthermore, I think I do know him."

"Ah, one of those you train with, eh? Do you like him?"

It was biting sarcasm, but to the colonel's disappointment it did not appear to affect his caller in the least. Converse even smiled—a most peculiar sort of smile.

"I must say, sir, that I have been hating him cordially."

The colonel grunted approbation.

"But from now on, sir, for reasons best known to myself, I'm going to make that young man my close and particular friend. You'll hear from us later."

He bowed stiffly and went out, leaving Colonel Dodd staring after him with his square face twisted into an expression of utter astonishment, his little eyes goggling, his tuft of whisker sticking up like an exclamation-point.

"The first appropriation the next legislature makes," he soliloquized, "will have to be money enough to build a new wing on the insane-hospital. They're all going crazy in this state, from aristocrats to tramps."

XXII
ENLISTING A KNIGHT-ERRANT

On his way down the stairs to the street the Honorable Archer Converse, moving more rapidly than was his wont, overtook and passed Kate Kilgour. He was too absorbed to notice even a pretty girl. She had finished her work for the day and was on her way home.

When she reached the street she observed something which interested her immensely: Mr. Converse suddenly flourished his cane to attract the attention of a man on the opposite side of the street. Then Mr. Converse called to him from the curb with the utmost friendliness in his tones. The girl passed near him and heard what he said. It was not a mere hail to an inferior. The eminent lawyer very politely and solicitously asked the tall young man across the way if he could not spare time to come to the Converse office.

She cast a look over her shoulder. The young man came across the street promptly. He was the man who had served her in her time of need!

She went on, but turned again. An uncontrollable impulse prompted her.

They were entering the door of the office-building, and the aristocratic hand of the Honorable Archer Converse was patting the shoulder of this stranger. Her cheeks flushed and she turned away hastily, for the young man caught her backward glance and returned an appealing smile.

"Who is he?" she asked herself, knowing well the chill reserve of Mr. Converse in the matter of mankind.

"Who are you?" demanded Mr. Converse, planting himself in front of the young man when they were in the private office.

The other met the lawyer's searching look with his rare smile. "The same man I was last time we met—Walker Farr."

"I have no right to pry into your private affairs, sir, but I have special reasons for wanting you to volunteer plenty of information about yourself."

For reply the young man spread his palms and silently, by his smile, invited inspection of himself.

"Yes, I see you. But the outside of you doesn't tell me what I want to know."

"It will have to speak for me."

"Look here, I have let myself be tied up most devilishly by a train of circumstances that you started, young man. I was minding my own private business until a little while ago."

"So was I, Mr. Converse."

"You're a moderately humble citizen, judged from outside looks just now. How did I allow myself to be pulled in as I've been?"

The young man's smile departed. "I asked myself that question a little while ago, sir, after I was pulled in, for I am a stranger—not even a voter here."

"Well, did you decide how it was?"

"I was led in by the hand of a helpless child—a poor little orphan girl whom I carried to the cemetery on my knees—a martyr—poisoned by that Consolidated water."

The lawyer was stirred by the intensity of feeling which the man's tones betrayed.

"And it was borne in upon me afresh, Mr. Converse, that the philosophy of the causes by which God moves this world of ours will never be understood by man."

"See here," snapped the son of the war governor, "take off your mask, Walker Farr! There's something behind it I want to see. You are an educated gentleman! What are you? Where did you come from?"

Again Farr spread out his palms and was silent.

"You are right about causes. You are one in my case. There may be some fatalism in me—but I'm impelled to use you in a great fight that I feel honor-bound to take up. Now be frank!"

"For all use you can make of me, Mr. Converse, my life starts from the minute I picked that little girl up from the floor of a tenement-house in this city. For what I was *before* is so different from what I am *now* that I cannot mix that identity with my affairs."

"But I cannot take a man into a matter like this unless I know all about him."

Farr rose and bowed. "I'm sorry you can't accept me at face value, sir. I'm very sorry, because I'd like to serve under such a commander as you. However, I understand your position. I don't blame you. The rule of the world is pretty binding: know a man before you associate with him. But I am as I am. There's nothing more to be said."

"You sit down," commanded Converse. "This is a case where rules of the world can be suspended. For I need the kind of man who dares to face even Symonds Dodd in his office and tell him what he is. Oh, I have just come from there," he explained in reply to Farr's stare. "He told me."

"I went merely as a voice, sir."

"But you seem to have been more than that in getting the confidence of the men in your ward. I know an organizer when I see him. I watched the faces of those men when you stepped before them. They have faith in you. That's a rare quality—the ability to inspire faith in the humble. First, faith— and then they'll follow. The movement I'm going to start needs followers, Mr. Farr! Can you do with other men what you have done with men in the Eleventh?"

"I believe I can, sir."

"Ah, you have led men in the past, have you?" Mr. Converse fired the question at him. But he did not jump Walker Farr from his equipoise. The young man took refuge behind that inscrutable smile.

"Well," sighed the lawyer, after a pause, "it's the dictum that one must be as wise as a serpent in politics, therefore I am picking out a man who will probably give a good account of himself. But it's a crazy performance of mine—going into this thing—and I may as well plunge to the extent of lunacy. Mr. Farr, the rebellious unrest in this state must be organized. We need a house-cleaning. We need the humbler voters! The men with interests are too well taken care of by the Machine to be interested. I want you to go out and hunt for sore spots and get to the voters just as you have in your ward. Find the right men in each town and city to help you. You must know many on account of your work for your water association. The fight will be financed—you need have no worry about that. Perhaps you have organized political revolts before," pursued Converse, still craftily probing. "Then you'll tell me what honorarium you expect."

"My expenses—nothing more, sir. If I had any money laid by I would pay my own way."

"I think," stated Mr. Converse, warming with the spirit of combat, glancing up at the portrait of the war governor, "that we'll be able to surprise some of the fat toads of politicians in this state, sitting so comfortably under their cabbage-leaves. You're a stranger, young man, and as you go about your work the regular politicians will simply blink at you and will not understand, I hope, provided you go softly. It is very silly of me to be in this affair, sir. But a man of my age must have peace of mind, and that infernal meeting in your ward awoke me. Furthermore," he added, displaying the acrimony that even a good man requires to spur him to honest fighting, "a cheap politician only lately flipped my card insolently and referred in slighting tones to my honored father." He rose and gave Farr his hand. "I'll have assembled here in my office at ten o'clock to-morrow morning some gentlemen who will stand for decency in public affairs as soon as they have been waked up. You will please attend that conference, Mr. Farr. We have only a short month before the state convention, and we must bring there at least a respectable number of delegates whom Symonds Dodd cannot bribe or browbeat."

"Most extraordinary—most extraordinary!" mused the Honorable Archer Converse, when he was alone. "From that meeting—to an investigation—from Dodd—to this young man—I have been leaping from crag to crag like a mountain-goat, never stopping to take breath. And here I haven't even been able to find out just who he is—and they do say I'm the best cross-examiner in this state! However, I'll show Symonds Dodd that I'm not to be sneered at, even if I have to hire Patagonians in this campaign."

Even chivalry must needs be spiced with a little strictly personal animosity to achieve its best results!

Colonel Symonds Dodd, laboriously climbing into his limousine in front of the First National block, scowled at a young man because the man grinned at him so broadly as he passed along. In his general indifference and contempt for the humble the colonel did not search his memory and did not recognize this person as the young man who had appealed to him in his office. The face seemed familiar and had some sort of an unpleasant recollection connected with it; therefore the colonel scowled. He was far from realizing that this person carried on his palm the warmth from a handclasp which, just a moment before, had ratified an agreement to dynamite the Dodd political throne.

If some seer had risen beside his chariot to predict disaster the colonel would have shriveled him with a contemptuous look. For the Consolidated Water Company had that day been intrenched more firmly than ever in its autocracy by a decision handed down from the Supreme Court. A city had hired the best of lawyers and had fought desperately for the right to have pure water. But the law, as expounded by the judges, had held as inexorable the provision that no city or town in the state could extend its debt limit above the legal five percent of its valuation, no matter for what purpose. The city sought for some avenue, some plan, some evasion, even, so that it might take over the water system and give its people crystal water from the lakes instead of the polluted river-water. The city pointed to typhoid cases, to slothful torpor on the part of the water syndicate. But the court could only, in the last analysis, point to the law—and that law in regard to debt limit was rooted in the constitution of the state—and a law fortified by the constitution is seldom dislodged.

Backed by law, bulwarked by political power, owning men and money-bags, Colonel Dodd rode home with great serenity. He had even forgotten his rather tempestuous half-hour with the Honorable Archer Converse. As a matter of fact, gentlemen of the aristocracy of the state who prided themselves on their ancestry were considered by Colonel Dodd to be impracticable cranks; he despised the poor and hated the proud—and called himself a self-made man. And Colonel Dodd was firmly convinced that nobody could *unmake* him.

He strolled among his flower-beds that evening.

Walker Farr sat in his narrow chamber and pored over interlined manuscripts. At last he shook the papers above his head, not gaily, but with grim bitterness.

"That plan will stand law, and no other lawyer ever thought of it!" he cried, aloud. "You've got an iron clutch on those cities and towns, Colonel

Dodd, but I've got something that will pry your fingers loose!" He threw the papers from him and set his face in his hands. "And they ask me who I am and I can't tell them," he sobbed.

XXIII
THE PROPHET WHO WAS UNDERRATED

The first sniffer to catch the trail of Walker Farr was the veteran, Daniel Breed, an old political hound who always traveled with muffled paws and nose close to the ground. But when he went to the meeting of the state committee and the Big Boys with his news their reception of him hinted that they suspected he was making up a political bugaboo in order to get a job. He was even told that his services as field man would not be needed in that campaign. And it may be imagined what effect that news had on old Daniel Breed, who had been a trusted pussy-footer and caucus manipulator for a quarter of a century.

"You don't mean to tell me that you're trying to slam me onto the scrap-heap, do you?" he demanded. "I'll scrap before I'll be scrapped."

"Look here, Dan, it's the colonel's orders," explained the chairman. "It has been decided to play politics a little more smoothly. There is too much jaw-gab going among the cranks. If there is any outside work done at all it will be put over by new chaps who are not so well advertised as you old bucks. We want to hide the machinery this year."

"That's a jobeefed nice thing to say to me, a man that would go up in a balloon and troll for hen-hawks, asking no questions, provided the state committee told me it would help in carrying a caucus."

"But we're taking care of the old boys all right, Dan. Vose is in the pension-office; Ambrose and Sturdivant are in the adjutant-general's office patching up the Civil War rolls, with orders to take their time about it. And you'll be used well."

"I want to be in the field," insisted Breed, 'sipping' his lips importantly. "Those fellows are old fuddy-duddies. I'm a natural politician."

He was an interesting figure, this Honorable Daniel Breed. He was entitled to the "Honorable." He had been a state senator from his county. With his slow, side-wheel gait, head too little for his body, nose like a beak, sunken mouth, cavernous eyes, and a light hat perched on the back of his narrow head he suggested a languid, tame, bald-headed eagle. And his voice was a dry, nasal, querulous squawk—a sound more avian than human.

"I tell ye there's yeast a-stirring," he told the state committee. "There's a fellow come up out of the Eleventh Ward in Marion that's some punkins in organizing. He pretends to be a law student in Arch Converse's law-office. He ain't a native. I don't know where he hails from. He ain't a registered voter as yet. But he's a man who needs to be trailed."

"Squire Converse isn't in politics, Dan. You're getting notional in your old age," said the committeeman from Breed's county.

"But good gad! there ain't any statute to keep him out. Something has happened to make him good and mad. Some of these fancy jumping-jacks can make awful leaps when the box is opened, gents! Better take warning from what I tell you!"

The committeemen exchanged smiles.

"We are going to steal a little of the kid-gloved chaps' thunder," explained the chairman. "They have been howling about machine politics and interlocking interests and air-tight methods until the people are growling about the close corporation they say we've got. So we're going to show 'em a thing or two. Nothing like frankness and open house."

"Gor-ram it, you ain't even square with me—after I have worked politics with you for twenty-five years!" He marched up to the table and rapped his hard little knuckles on it. "It's this way, gents," he said, "and I'll be short and sweet. What's the matter with politics when a man like I've always been gets pi-oogled out of the councils?"

"We don't need workers like you any more," stated the chairman.

"But there's politics to play, just the same."

"But in a different way, Breed. There are the new ideas, and new men can operate more efficiently. They won't attract attention."

"Old Maid Orne down in my town came into church late and crawled up the aisle on her hands and knees so as not to attract attention. And she broke up the meeting!"

"We've got to fall in with the new ways, Dan," said the attorney-general. "These are touchy times. We must be careful of the party."

"I 'ain't never disgraced it, have I?"

"Uncle Dan, we want you to take a good, comfortable position and settle down," affirmed Governor Alonzo Harwood, an unctuous, rubicund gentleman who had been listening, smiling his everlasting smile.

"I prefer to hold myself in readiness for a call to the field," squalled Breed. "I'm better'n three of these young snydingles. They don't know how to organize!"

"There isn't much chance for organizing," said a Congressman, placatingly. "The primaries take care of themselves pretty well."

"Yes," sneered old Dan, "a fellow thinks well of himself, or else his neighbors tell him he can save the nation, and he puts a piece in the paper saying how good he is and sets pictures of himself up in store winders like a cussed play-actor, keeps a cash account, and thinks that's politics. I don't care if there ain't ever no more caucuses. This thing ain't going to last. I want to keep in the field. I'll see chances to heave trigs into the spokes of these hallelujah chariots they're rolling to political glory in!"

The mighty ones exchanged glances—deprecating glances—apprehensive glances.

"You don't think I'm dangerous, do you, after I've been in politics as long as I have?"

"No, but we feel that the old war-horses are entitled to run to pasture with their shoes off," coaxed the chairman.

"It seems to me more like tying me up to a stanchion in a stall. I ain't ungrateful, gents. I know this younger element doesn't believe in setting hens in politics any more. It's the incubator nowadays—wholesale job of it. But, by dadder! my settings have always cracked the shells, twelve to the dozen! Then you don't want me, eh?"

"That job in the state land-office—we thought it would just about fit you," suggested the chairman.

"I'd just as soon be sent to state prison—solitary confinement. The state hasn't got any land any more. It has all been peddled out to the grabbers. I've messed and mingled with men all my life. Nobody ever comes into the land-office. You ain't afraid of me to that extent, be you?"

"What do you want?" asked the governor.

"Settled, is it, you don't want me in politics?"

"There isn't anything for you to do," declared his Excellency, and he showed a little impatience, though his smile did not fade.

"Well, then make me state liberian," said old Dan, with an air of resignation.

There was deep and horrified silence.

"I'm developing literary instinks," explained Breed. "I've got a son who owns a printing-office, and my granddaughter can take down anything in shorthand and write it off. I'm going to write a book. She'll take it down and he'll print it."

"I can't appoint you state librarian," said the governor, getting control of his emotions. "It's already tied up, that appointment. Keep it under your hat, but I have selected Reverend Doctor Fletcher, of Cornish, and have notified him."

"Giving a plum like that to a parson who never controlled but one vote, and that's his own—and then voted the way the deacon told him to? I reckon it's about as you say—there are new times in politics. All right! I'll go and climb a sumach-bush. You needn't bother about any job for me, gents. I'll settle down to my literary work."

"What is the book?" asked the chairman.

"I have your word for it that the old days in politics have all gone by," said Breed. "All the old things dead and buried! Very well. That's going to make my book valuable and interesting. No harm in putting it out in these times. I shall entitle it 'Breed's Handbook of Political Deviltry.' I shall tell the story of how it was done when politics was really politics."

"Going to tell all you know?" inquired the governor.

"Of course. Truth, and not poetry, will be my motto. And just for a test of how popular it will be, I'd like to ask you gents how many of you will subscribe for a volume?"

"I think this committee will take the whole edition," said the chairman, dryly.

"Look here, Dan," blurted the attorney-general, "you must be joking."

"I don't know what ever gave you the impression that I'm a humorist," returned Breed. "If there ain't going to be anything more like the old times, then what's the matter with having the story of how it was done? That book will sell like hot cakes. I'll go out and sell it—it will give me a chance to keep on mixing and messing with men."

"Dan, if it wasn't you talking—knowing you well—I'd say this is a piece of blackmail," declared the attorney-general. "Of course you can't put out a book of that kind in this state."

Mr. Breed blinked angrily.

"I'll take all the cases of libel against you and won't charge my clients a cent."

"Fill everybody else's little tin dipper, eh? Passing everybody else a bottle and a rubber nipple! Everybody getting his, and me left out! All right. If that's political gratitude in these new times, go on with you medinkculum! And last year I snapped the six up-country caucuses that gave you your plurality in joint convention!"

"We appreciate all your past services, Dan. If we didn't we wouldn't be trying so hard to place you," said the governor. "We're taking care of all the old boys. You mustn't embarrass us. In these days it's for the good of the party to put in each office the man who is especially fitted for it. We mustn't invite criticism. A librarian needs peculiar qualifications."

"Well, old Jaquish was liberian, wasn't he? And he wouldn't even go vote unless you went and dragged him to the polls by the scruff of his neck. What did he ever do for the party? And look at old Tomdoozle as state treasurer!"

"Jaquish was a bookman, and our state treasurer—but no matter. Now listen! I'm going to put you at the head of a new department in the State House where you won't be lonesome. More people will come there than to the library. You'll have the title of curator."

"What's that?" asked Breed, suspiciously. "And what is the department, anyway?"

"The museum of natural history in the fish-and-game rooms. We're going to make it complete—mounted specimens of all our animals. You'll be curator—you see, you will get a title that sounds well!"

"I'm of a restless and inquiring disposition, and my special forty is politics," stated Breed, sulking. "I don't believe I'm going to relish being ringmaster of a lot of stuffed animals, no matter what kind of a title I get. How much pay goes with the job?"

"Fifteen hundred," said the governor.

"Well," sighed Breed, "it will give me a chance to be around the State House during the session, and I'll take it. Then if I don't like it I can resign after the legislature adjourns."

The Big Ones understood his frame of mind and overlooked his ingratitude.

"And so I'll bid you good day, gents," he said, and straddled out with his hands under his coat-tails.

"So we've got *him* side-tracked and out of mischief," averred the governor. "That takes care of all of 'em, and I'm relieved. It isn't stylish any more to come to town with a lot of old hounds trotting under the tail of the political cart."

But before the end of that week the governor was obliged to call Uncle Dan to a private conference in the Executive Chamber.

"You must remember that you're a state officer," warned his Excellency. "You're a part of the administration. But you are out talking politics all the time. I want you to stay in your department. Just remember that you're curator of our museum."

"I don't like that blamed job," complained Breed. "I don't care what my title is, it only means that I have to dust off that old stuffed loon, keep moths out of that loosivee, and fleas or some kind of insecks off'n that bull moose. It ain't no job for a politician. And there's a steady stream through there asking me all kinds of questions about animals. I don't know nothing about animals. I don't know whether a live moose eats hay or chopped liver. Those questions keep me all hestered up. It puts me in a wrong position before the public. I can't tell 'em which or what, and they think I'm losing my mind."

"Post up! It will keep you busy. Get books out of the library and read. Inform yourself and have a story for the folks!"

A few days later the chairman of the state committee had an indignant report to make to the governor regarding Uncle Dan's natural-history activities.

"He has turned that museum into a circus show, your Excellency. He has named every one of those stuffed animals for somebody in politics he doesn't like, and leads a snickering mob of sight-seers around the room and lectures. When a state officer names a saucer-eyed Canadian lynx for me and then folks come up from that basement and grin at me, it's time a halt was called."

His Excellency called for Breed and called a halt, using forceful language.

"I resign," declared old Dan, nipping his little bunghole of a mouth under the hook of his nose. "Those animals are getting onto my nerves. The whole pack and caboodle are chasing me in a nightmare every time I go to sleep. Their condemned glass eyes are boring me worse than gimlets. I'm going on with that book of mine. I've got a new idea for it. I'm going to put in pictures of animals and name 'em for those tin-horn flukedubbles who could never get an office if it wasn't for the primaries."

"Look here, Breed, you're an old man and you've done a lot of good work in your day, and we're all trying to do something for you. But I have pretty nigh reached the limit of my patience. Politics isn't what it used to be. Different manners, different men. I'm the head of our party and I command you to eliminate yourself. You go back to your job, use common sense, and keep out of things! You are silly—you're senile!"

"You have taken me out of where I belong and have put me in where I don't belong and now you're blaming me because I can't learn a lot of new tricks at my age. I resign, I say!"

"If you give up that job you'll never get another one."

Uncle Dan put his hands under his coat-tails and marched out, his beak in the air.

"The trouble is," he confided to old Sturdivant in the adjutant-general's office, "this younger element that's coming along thinks men like you and I have lost all our ability and influence. They're sally-lavering all over us, telling us how they want us to have an easy job. But it's all a damnation insult—that's what it amounts to."

"All I have to do is lap sticking-paper and gum up the places where these rolls are torn," said old Sturdivant. "I'm perfectly contented."

"Then stay were you're put and swaller the insult," retorted Breed, with disgust. "I thought you had more get-up-and-get. There's a stuffed rabbit in that museum. He'll make a good chum for you in your off hour. Go and sit down with him." He went over to old Ambrose's desk. Ambrose was numbering dog's-eared pages with a rubber stamp and would not admit that he had been insulted by the state committee. "There's nobody got the right to ask me to stop being active and influential in this state," insisted Breed. "They haven't taken my pride into account. I ain't naturally a kicker. I've always obeyed orders. If I've got to go out alone and show 'em that the old guard can't be insulted, then I'll do it."

This time he took the trail of Walker Farr once more and followed that energetic young man until he cornered him.

Farr harkened with interest to the story of the scrapping of the Honorable Daniel Breed as related by that gentleman himself.

"And the moral of the tale is," added Mr. Breed, "when a gang does you dirt turn around and plaster a few gobs onto the dirt-slingers. That ain't the rule in religion, but it's the natural and correct policy in politics. I have been hurt in my tender feelings. If them animals had been alive and savage enough I would have taken 'em up to the state committee-room and ste' boyed 'em onto the ungrateful cusses who have tried to make my last days unhappy. I know every sore spot in this state. You don't know 'em unless you have got second sight. I can take you to every man who has got a political bruise on him. Good gad! I have been poulticing those sore spots for twenty-five years. You need a man like I am."

"I'll admit that I do need such a man. I am a stranger in the state. But I'm going to be perfectly frank with you, Mr. Breed. How do I know but you're a spy who wants to attach himself to me for the benefit of the ring?"

"You don't know," returned Mr. Breed, serenely. "You have to take chances in politics. I'm taking chances when I join in with you. Just who are you and how do you happen to be mixed up in our politics?"

"I am mixing into politics because the men, women, and children are being poisoned by the Consolidated water. That's platform enough, isn't it?"

"Well, I reckon it is, knowing what I know of general conditions. You have got a pretty good head for politics, even if you ain't sincere on the water question," said Breed, with a politician's ready suspicion of motives. "You've got a come-all-ye hoorah there that will make votes."

"As to my personality, that has nothing to do with the matter. I am only an agent. Will you come with me and allow Mr. Converse to ask you some questions?"

"Sure thing!" agreed the Honorable Daniel, with great heartiness. "In politics the first thing to do before you get real busy is to have a nice heart-to-heart talk with the gent who says 'How much?' and laps his forefinger and begins to count. You understand, young man, that I have been in politics a long time. And I ain't an animal-trainer—I'm a field worker and I can earn my pay."

And inside of a week Walker Farr, who had been previously struggling hard against lack of acquaintance in the state, found that Mr. Breed had spoken the truth. The two made a team which excited the full approval—the wondering admiration—of the Honorable Archer Converse.

Farr's power to control and interest men achieved astonishing results with Daniel Breed's exact knowledge of persons and conditions.

But they were rather humble citizens. There was no fanfare about their work. If Colonel Symonds Dodd knew anything at all about the fires they were setting, he made no move to turn on the Consolidated hose.

XXIV
THE STAR CHAMBER IN THE OLD NATIONAL

They did not come furtively, yet they came unobtrusively—these men who drifted into the National Hotel in Marion that day.

At one side of the big rotunda of the National stood Walker Farr, his keen gaze noting the men who came dribbling in, singly, by twos and threes. They were not men of Marion city. A newspaper reporter, happening in at the National, noted that fact. He stood for a time and watched the filtering arrivals. There were some who were plainly men of affairs, others were solid men who bore the stamp of the rural sections. They went to the desk, wrote their names, and were shown up-stairs by bellhops. Most of them, as they crossed the office, nodded greeting to the tall young man who wore a frock coat and a broad-brimmed hat and stood almost motionless at one side of the rotunda.

The National was state Mecca for all kinds of conventions. The reporter studied his date-book. No convention was scheduled for that day. He managed to get a peep at the hotel register. The men who had been signing their names hailed from all portions of the state, but the reporter did not find identities which suggested political activities. It was plainly not a gathering of politicians—none of the old war-horses were in evidence.

The reporter questioned a few of the arrivals, chasing beside them. They all gave the same answer—they had come to Marion on business.

The reply was safe, succinct, and stopped further questions. The reporter did venture to pick out a little man and inquire what kind of business called him to Marion, and the little man informed him with sarcasm that he was a baker from Banbury and had come down to purchase doughnut holes.

The reporter thereupon dodged into the bar to escape the grins of some of the office crew, and his haste was such that he nearly beat the baize doors into the face of Richard Dodd, who was coming out.

"You're the first real politician I've seen in this bunch," affirmed the reporter. "What's it all about?"

"What's what about?"

"This convention that's assembling here."

"I know nothing about it," stated Mr. Dodd, with dignity. "It's nothing of a political nature, I can assure you of that."

The reporter noted that young Mr. Dodd's eyes were red and that his step wavered, and that he exhaled the peculiar odor which emanates from gentlemen who have been prolonging for some time what is known vulgarly as a "toot." In fact, the reporter remembered then the rumor in newspaper circles that the chief clerk of the state treasury had been attending to stimulants instead of to business for almost two weeks.

"I assure you that I know all that's to be known about politics," insisted Mr. Dodd. "If there's a convention here, who's running it?"

They had returned from the bar into the main office.

"I don't know—can't find out. That tall fellow over there seems to know everybody who had been coming in—all the bunch of outsiders. But I never saw him before."

Mr. Dodd closed one eye in order to focus his attention on this unknown across the office.

A deep glow of antipathy and distrust came into the eye which located and identified Walker Farr.

Mr. Dodd cursed without using names, verbs, or information.

"Oh, you know him, do you?"

"No, I don't know him." Mr. Dodd hung to his vengeful secret doggedly. He left the reporter and went and sat down in a chair and continued to stare at Farr, who remained oblivious to this inspection.

The reporter went across the office. There seemed to be more or less mystery about this man who had provoked all those curses from the secretive chief clerk of the treasury.

"Can you give me any information about these men who are meeting here to-day?"

"Meeting of the Independent Corn-Growers' Association." The reporter's gaze was frankly skeptical, but Farr met it without a flicker of the eyelids.

"I never heard of any such association."

"You have now, sir."

"Is it open to the newspapers?"

"Closed doors—absolutely private."

"Who'll give out the statement?"

Farr put his hand on the reporter's shoulder and gave him a smile.

"You see, it's to fight the packers' union and so we are not giving away our ammunition to the enemy. Keep it quiet and when the thing breaks I'll give you our side."

"All right, sir. If it's to be an exclusive for me I'll steer away the other newspaper men. But do you know just why Richard Dodd—that man over there—is damning you into shoe-strings?"

Even at that distance Farr's keen gaze detected the filmy eyes and the flushed face.

"Perhaps it's because the Corn-Growers propose to put their corn into johnny-bread instead of using it for whisky?"

The newspaper man, his suspicions dulled by Farr's radiant good nature and wholesome frankness, went away about his business, but he halted long enough beside Dodd's chair to repeat "the corn-grower's" joke regarding the young man who had been glowering on him.

Dodd got up with as much alacrity as he could command and went across to Farr. Sober, the nephew of Colonel Dodd had treated this person with rather lofty contempt; drunk, he was not so finical in matters of caste— and, besides, this man now wore the garb of a gentleman, and young Mr. Dodd always placed much emphasis on clothes.

"Look here, my fellow, now that I have you where I don't need to consider the presence of ladies, I want to ask you how you dared to mess into my private business?"

Farr, towering above him, beamed down on him with tolerant indifference and did not answer.

"That Lochinvar business may sound good in a poem, but it doesn't go here in Marion—not when it's my business and my girl."

Dodd raised his voice. He seemed about to become a bit hysterical.

Farr set slow, gripping, commanding clutch about the young man's elbow.

"If your business with me can possibly be any talk about a lady," he advised, "you'd better come along into the reading-room."

"It is about a lady," persisted Dodd when they had swung in behind a newspaper-rack. The room was apparently empty. "You understand what you came butting in upon, don't you?"

"I took it to be a rehearsal of a melodrama, crudely conceived and very poorly played."

"Say, you use pretty big words for a low-lived iceman."

"State your business with me if you have any," Farr reminded him. "I have something else to do besides swap talk with a drunken man—and your breath is very offensive."

Dodd began to tap a finger on Farr's breast.

"I want you to understand that I've got a full line on you; you have been chumming with a Canuck rack-tender, you deserted a woman, and she committed suicide, and you took the brat—"

Farr's big hand released the elbow and set itself around Mr. Dodd's neck. Thumb and forefinger bored under the jaw and Mr. Dodd's epiglottis ceased vibrating.

"I don't like to assault a man, but talk doesn't seem to fit your case and I can't stop long enough to talk, anyway. This choking is my comment on your lies." He pushed Mr. Dodd relentlessly down into the nearest chair and spanked his face slowly and deliberately with the flat of his hand. "And this will indicate to you just how much I care for your threats. You'll remember it longer than you will recollect words."

He finished and went away, leaving his victim getting his breath in the chair. Dodd, peering under the rack, saw him hasten and join the Honorable Archer Converse in the hotel lobby and they went up the broad stairs together.

The chief clerk of the state treasury sat there and smoothed his smarting face with trembling hands and worked his jaws to dislodge the grinding ache in his neck. But the stinging, malevolent rancor within him burned hotter and hotter. He started to get up out of the chair and sat back again, much disturbed.

A man who had been hidden by an adjoining rack of newspapers was now leaning forward, jutting his head past the ambuscade. He was an elderly man with an up-cocked gray mustache, and there was a queer little smile in his shrewd blue eyes. Dodd knew him; he was one Mullaney, a state detective.

"What are you doing here—practicing your sneak work?" demanded the young man. As a state official he did not entertain a high opinion of the free-lance organization to which Mullaney belonged.

"I'm here reading a paper—supposed it's what the room is for," returned Detective Mullaney. "But excuse me—I'll get out. Room seems to be reserved for prize-fighters."

"You keep your mouth shut about that—that insult."

"I never talk—it would hurt my business."

"I don't fight in a public place. I'm a gentleman. I want you to remember what you saw, Mullaney! I'll get to that cheap bum in a way he won't forget."

"Do you mind telling me who your friend is?" asked the detective.

Dodd shot him a sour side-glance and muttered profanity.

"I couldn't help wondering what particular kind of business you and he could have, seeing how it was transacted," pursued the detective.

Dodd glowered at the floor. "Look here, Mullaney! There's a whole lot about that man I want to know, if you can help me and keep your mouth closed. I haven't got much confidence in the work you fellows do—they tell me you can't detect mud on your own boots."

Mr. Mullaney pulled his chair out from behind the papers and leaned back in it and crossed his hands over his stomach and smiled without a trace of resentment.

"I might tell you something right now about that tall friend of yours that would jump you, Mr. Dodd—I'm that much of a detective!"

"Tell me, then."

"Just as it stands it's guesswork—considerable guesswork."

"What does that amount to?"

"A great deal in my business. Take this city of one hundred thousand! I'm the only man in it who is making guesswork about strangers his special line of work. The rest of the citizens rub elbows with all passers and don't give a hoot. There are a good many thousand men in this country whom the law wants and whom the law can't find. That fellow may be one of them, for all I know. I guess he is, for instance. Then I make it my business to prove guesswork."

"You must be doing a devil of a rushing business!" sneered Dodd.

"I manage to make a good living. I don't talk about my business, for if I should blow it I wouldn't have any. I say, I *guess*! Then I spend my spare time hunting through my books of pointers. For ten years I have read every newspaper I could get hold of. I come in here and study papers from all over. Every crime that has been committed, every man wanted, every chap who has got away, I write down all I can find out about him. Then, if anything comes up to make me guess about a man I begin to hunt my books through."

"Well, if I'm any good on a guess," snorted Dodd, "that renegade who just insulted me is down in your books, somewhere. You'd better hunt."

"It's slow work and eats up time," sighed Mr. Mullaney.

Dodd looked at him for a time and then began to pull crumpled bills from his waistcoat pocket. He straightened five ten-dollar bills, creased them into a trough, and stuck the end toward the detective.

"Follow his trail back. I never heard of your book scheme before. Take this money for a starter. If you can't find him in your books, pick out half a dozen of the worst crimes any man can commit and hitch 'em on to him somehow," urged Dodd, with fury. "Go after him. And when we get him good and proper I want to do some gloating through the bars. He's the first man who ever smacked my face for me—and I'll see that he gets his."

He left Mr. Mullaney stowing the money away in a big wallet which was stuffed with newspaper clippings. He hurried in to the bar, gulped down a drink, and then went to the office desk and examined the hotel register. Anger and zest for revenge were stimulating in him a lively interest in that meeting which Farr seemed to be promoting. Mr. Dodd did not care especially what kind of meeting it was. He had set forth to camp on Walker Farr's trail and do him what hurt he could.

Dodd was a well-posted political worker. The names of the men were not names especially prominent in state politics, but his suspicions were stirred when he saw that all counties in the state were represented. And no more were arriving. He decided that the conference must be in session.

Dodd avoided the elevator. He tramped up the broad stairs to the floor above the office. The doors of the large parlor were closed. He turned the knob cautiously; the doors were locked. He heard within the dull mumble of many voices—men in conversation. It was evident that the formal meeting, whatever it might be, had not begun its session. He tiptoed away from the door and climbed another flight of stairs.

There were no nooks and corners of the old National Hotel which Richard Dodd did not understand in all their intricacies. As his uncle's political scout it had been his business to know them.

He hunted along the corridor until he found a maid.

"Is there anybody in Number 29?" he asked.

"Two of that new crowd that just came in have it, Mr. Dodd. But they have gone down-stairs again."

He wadded a bill in his palm and jammed it into her hand. "Let me in with your pass-key, that's a good girl. It's all right. I won't disturb their stuff. I only want to listen. You understand! There's a political game on. I want to get to that ventilator in the closet—you know it!"

"Oh, if it's only politics, Mr. Dodd!" she sniffed, with the scorn of a girl who has seen many conventions come and go, knew the little tricks, and had developed for the whole herd of politicians lofty disdain; she knew them merely as loud-talking men who had little consideration for hotel maids, men who littered their rooms with cigar stubs and whisky-bottles. She started for the door, swinging the pass-key on its cord. "If it's just politics, sure you can go in. Many a buck I've let in to listen to their old palaver down in that parlor."

Dodd bolted the door behind him.

He felt entirely safe, for he understood that the rightful tenants of that room were locked into the parlor below. He climbed upon a chair in the closet and put his ear to the grating of the ventilator.

He heard only one man's voice. He recognized its crisp tones—it was the Honorable Archer Converse.

"I repeat, gentlemen, that this interest of yours would amaze me if I had not been prepared by reports from our agents who have been so well captained by Mr. Walker Farr. Remember that this is simply a conference, prior to organization. Every man of you is a chief in it. Let us be calm, discreet, sensible, and silent.

"I'm not going over the details of the unrest in this state. The fact that so many of you are present here from all sections is sufficient commentary on that unrest. We understand perfectly well that a certain clique of self-seekers has arrogated to itself supreme control of the party. A party must be controlled, I admit. If that control were in the hands of honest and patriotic men we would not be here today.

"I'm not going to bother you with details of what has been going on in departments in our State House. The employees are the tools of the ring and they have misused their power. I'm afraid of what may be uncovered there when the house-cleaning begins. But the honor of our party demands such a house-cleaning."

Richard Dodd's hands trembled as he clung to the ventilator bars.

"However, we are faced by something in the way of an issue that's bigger than graft."

Now his earnestness impressed more than ever the listener at the grating.

"Gentlemen, to a certain extent graft is bound to be fostered and protected by any party; but when a party is used to protect and aggrandize those who monopolize the people's franchise rights it's time for the honest men in that party to be *men* instead of partisans. Don't you allow those monopolists to hold you in line by whining about party loyalty. And don't let them whip you into line by their threats, either. I refuse, for one, as much as I love my party, to have its tag tied into my ear if that tag isn't clean!"

The assemblage applauded that sentiment.

"I'm going to call names, gentlemen. Colonel Symonds Dodd has this state by its throat. With Colonel Dodd stand all the financial interests— the railroads, the corporations, even the savings-banks. He is intrenched behind that law which limits the indebtedness of our cities and towns. Municipalities cannot own their own plants under present conditions. Those men are even using the people's own money against them! They scare depositors by threats of financial havoc if present conditions and the big interest are bothered by any legislation.

"I must warn you, gentlemen, that it's a long and difficult road ahead of us. But we must start. I have not intended to discourage you by stating the obstacles to be overcome.

"I have explained them so that, if we make slow progress at first, we shall not be discouraged.

"We will organize prevailing unrest and the innate honesty in this state. We will establish a branch of the Square Deal Club in every town and city. It must be done carefully, conservatively, and as secretly as possible." The lawyer's cautious fear of too much haste now displayed itself. "The most we can hope to do is send to the state convention some men who will leaven that lump of ring politics. Party usage and tradition are so strong that we must renominate Governor Harwood, I suppose, for a complimentary second term."

"I think we can do better," cried a voice.

"Possibly," returned Mr. Converse, dryly, "but we must do that 'better' carefully and slowly. In politics, gentlemen, we cannot transform the ogre into the saint merely by waving the magic wand and expecting the charm to operate instantly. Possibly we can control the next legislature. I do not know just what legislation we may be able to devise and pass, but I hope for inspiration.

"I will say now that I am with you. My purse is open. Command my services for all questions of law. I will establish myself at the capital for the legislative session.

"But there is one thing I will not do under any circumstances—I will not accept political office."

"You bet you won't," muttered young Dodd, at the grating. "You wouldn't be elected a pound-keeper in the town of Bean Center."

But if Mr. Dodd could have seen through that grating as well as hear he would have been greatly interested just then in the expression on the face of Walker Farr. The face was not exactly the face of a prophet, but it had a large amount of resolution written over it.

"I don't want to be the first one to throw any cold water on our prospects," declared a voice, after Mr. Converse had announced that the meeting was open for general discussion; "it really does seem to me that we stand a good show of getting control of the next legislature. But after we do get control what prospect is there of passing any legislation that will help us? Wherever there is a water system in this state the municipality has been so loaded down with debts our machine politics have plastered into it that the legal debt limit has been reached. The only way this water question can be cleared up is by taking the systems away from those monopolists— making them the property of towns and cities. But if towns and cities can't borrow any more money, just how is this to be done? Mr. Converse hasn't told us! We can clean up politics, perhaps, but it seems to me that we'll never be able to clean up the dirtiest and most dangerous mess."

On the silence that followed broke a voice which made Dodd, his ear to the grating, grate his teeth. His hatred recognized this speaker. It was Walker Farr.

"I apologize for venturing to speak in this meeting," he said. "But if that gentleman's question isn't answered here and now in some way I'm afraid men will go away discouraged. I have heard the same question, Mr. Converse, as I have traveled about the state lately. I have thought about this matter constantly, in my poor fashion. And because I went into that job of pondering with an open mind is the reason, perhaps, why a strange idea has come to me. You know they say that strange notions are born out of ignorance. The better way would have been, possibly, to submit the plan first of all to your legal mind, Mr. Converse. I will keep silence now and confer with you, sir, if you think best." His tone was wistful.

"Talk it out in open meeting," cried the cordial voice of Mr. Converse. "Free speech and all of us taken into confidence—that's the spirit of this movement of ours!"

"Has it ever occurred to anybody to form a new municipality for water purposes only? I have studied your state constitution, and the language in which the debt limit of five percent is provided I find applies strictly to towns and cities. Suppose the citizens of Marion, together with the adjoining towns of Weston and Turner, all of them now served by the Consolidated, should unite simply as individuals for the common purpose of owning and operating their own water-plant—form, say a water district?"

"An independent body politic and corporate?" It was Converse's voice and it betrayed quick interest and some astonishment.

"I suppose that would be the legal name, sir. Wouldn't it be possible to organize such a combination of the people, distinct from other municipal responsibilities? Then if we can elect the right men to our legislature we can go to the State House and ask for some legislation that will enable us to take over systems by the right of eminent domain, provide a plan of fair appraisal, give us a law which will make water-district bonds a legal investment for savings-banks. In short, gentlemen, I repeat, this plan is nothing more than an organization of the desired territory and people into a new, distinct, and separate municipality for water purposes only, leaving all other forms of municipal government to pursue their accustomed functions precisely as though the district had not been organized. That's the idea as best I can state it in few words."

There was a long period of silence.

Dodd, listening to the mutterings of a revolt which threatened the whole political fabric which protected him, his interest clearing his brain of the liquor fog, could imagine the scene below. That assemblage was staring wide-eyed at Archer Converse, the law's best-grounded man in the state.

"It is very modest to call that suggestion an idea," stated Mr. Converse, at last. "Mr. Farr, if I can find the necessary law in our statutes to back it up, it's an inspiration."

There was the ring of conviction in his tones.

Mr. Dodd left the grating and escaped from the hotel.

He fairly cantered to headquarters in the First National block; he felt a politician's frightened conviction that he had something mighty important to tell his uncle.

XXV
A GIRL AND A MATTER OF HONOR

It had been a protracted session.

Judge Ambrose Warren, corporation counsel for the Consolidated, leaned back in his chair and gazed at the ceiling over the peak of the skeleton structure he had erected in front of his nose with his fingers.

Colonel Dodd squinted first at his nephew and then at the bouquet on his desk.

The nephew had been attempting by all the methods known to the appealing male to win only one return glance from Kate Kilgour; but the young lady held her eyes on her note-book, poised her pencil above the page, and waited for more of that conversation and statement of which she had been the silent recorder.

"You think you have given us all the main points of what you overheard, do you, Mr. Dodd?" inquired the judge, turning sharp gaze on the young man.

"I can't remember any more."

"You think you recognized voices sufficiently well to be sure that this person named Farr made that novel suggestion in regard to what was called a 'water district'?"

"There was no mistaking his voice," said Dodd, with the malevolence of bitter recollection.

Another prolonged silence. Then the judge asked, his eyes again on the ceiling, "Just who is this Walker Farr?"

Richard Dodd, keeping jealous espionage on all the girl's emotions and movements saw a flush suffuse her cheeks; her hands trembled. She raised her eyes in a quick glance and he detected eager inquiry.

"I don't know who he is," growled the colonel.

"You'd better find out," advised the corporation counsel.

"Why?"

"Of course this thing has been put up to me very suddenly. I can give you only a snap judgment. But that scheme has possibilities."

"As a lawyer you don't mean to tell me that a crazy idea like that can be put through in this state against the combination we control?"

"It will not be a case of combination and money and politics, Colonel, when it gets to the high court. It will be *law*. And I'm sorry you can't tell me any more about the man who has devised the plan. I'd like to know how he dug it out."

"But a gang of pirates can't organize like that and confiscate our property! We're going to tap the lakes. We're going ahead right away. But can that fool's scheme scoop in the Consolidated Water Company?"

"That's to be found out. I am going to tell you now that I believe an organization of citizens into an independent water district can be made legally and be independent of other debts. Colonel Dodd, if that opposition gets control of the next legislature you can depend upon it that the necessary legislation will be passed. We may as well look facts in the face: they're getting mighty restive in this state; the people have been penned in by the Machine very effectually to date—but show 'em a place now where they can jump the fence and they're going to do it."

"But what's the good of paying you twenty-five thousand dollars a year for law if you can't keep the bars up?" The tone was that of the impatient tyrant.

"You'll please remember that this thing is likely to go to the United States court. When you go in there you've got to leave your side-arms of politics—pull and pocket-book—at the door. I will say this: the Federal Constitution guarantees protection against any irregular, illegal, or confiscatory action under state authority. That is, no states shall pass any law impairing the obligation of contracts nor shall any state deprive any person of life, liberty, or property without due process of law nor deny to any person within its jurisdiction the equal protection of the laws. Now, of course, a corporation is a person in the meaning of the law, and therefore we can carry the matter to the United States Supreme Court, but I want to tell you that if the next legislature enacts law permitting water districts, and the state authorities proceed to condemn your plants, you may as well get ready to step out from under. You are a shrewd man and you understand the spirit of these times in regard to giving to the people their full rights in public utilities. I say again, you'd better get a line on this Walker Farr, because it's either a case of ignorance inspired or else he's a deep one. He has started with a plan that can be defended by law—and the judges in these days are handing the people's rights and property back to them when there is a legal opportunity."

"Why, this Farr is a nothing—nobody. Dug in our trenches for a while until he was discharged. Briggs looked him up for me. The only man in this city he has been at all intimate with is an old Canuck named Provancher who tends the rack down at Gamonic Mill. You can judge him by the company he keeps."

"Well, he seems to be fraternizing with better men just now," drawled the judge. "Archer Converse, for instance!"

"The thing to do," suggested young Dodd, still watching the girl, "is get something on that hobo and boot him out of town or put him in jail. It ought to be easy enough."

"And it will be attended to," declared the colonel, with venom. "We'll kill that one crow and hang him up in full view of the rest of those croakers! I'll put something over on that fellow and have all the papers in the state print it—and high-and-mighty Converse will be so disgusted that he'll quit and the rest of the crowd will be ashamed to keep on. Disgrace a reformer! That's the surest play in politics! We must get Farr!"

He turned his scowling gaze away from the flowers and found Miss Kilgour looking at him with an expression in her eyes he had never seen there before. Reproach and scorn seemed to mingle in the stare she gave him. He blinked, and when he looked again she was examining the point of her pencil; he decided that his eyesight had played him a strange prank.

"By the way, Miss Kilgour," he informed her, "you need not remain. Make two typewritten copies—the judge will need one."

Richard Dodd arose when she left her chair, but she did not glance at him. He began to speak before she had reached the door, unable to restrain his jealous temper longer.

"Uncle Symonds, pass the word to that old Provancher, through the superintendent of the Gamonic, that unless he comes across with all the stuff he knows about that Farr he'll be fired. And I've got a hunter out on my own account. It will be easy enough to catch the skunk and strip off his pelt."

Miss Kilgour closed the door behind her with a sharper click than she had ever given its latch before. She hurried to her typewriter in her little room and began to work with all her energy.

She was so busy and her machine clattered so viciously that she did not hear Richard Dodd when he entered. He leaned over her.

"Have you talked with your mother yet? Has she given you some advice?" he asked. His jealousy still fired him and his tone was not conciliatory.

The contempt in the glance she flung upward at him roused him to passion. In the state of mind in which he then was he made no allowances for her ignorance of conditions in her mother's case. He knew what he had done for Mrs. Kilgour's sake, and this attitude on the daughter's part pricked him like wilful ingratitude.

He put his hands on the keyboard of the typewriter and stopped her work. "I love you, Kate, and you have known it for a long time. I tried to show you how much I loved you. I know I did a foolish thing. But I loved you." He almost sobbed the protestation. "I've been in hell's torment since it happened. I've been a fool all the way through, but I won't be a fool any more if you'll take pity on me."

She did not speak. Her silent, utter contempt stung more deeply and surely than words.

"If you insist on being so high above, I'm going to bring you down a little," he sneered. "I hate to do it, but you've got to be shown where your real friends are. I have given your mother a chance to say something to you, and say it right. But she hasn't done it, and I don't propose to be made the goat." In his anger he was not choice in his language. "You go home and ask her whether or not she owes me five thousand dollars. Oh, you needn't open your eyes at me in that style! It's time we all got down to cases in this thing, Kate. I've waited for her long enough. She has simply fluffed me along. Now she has got to do her part."

"Have you lost your mind?" she demanded.

"No! But I lost five thousand dollars when I loaned it to your mother. Kate, she told me she had a stock deal on—that she would be able to pay it back. Listen! I may as well go the limit with you. I took money that wasn't mine so that I could help your mother out—it was because I loved you. Now you realize how much I have loved you. I protected your mother. And now, by the gods, if you and she don't come to the scratch in this thing and do right by me I'll show up why she had to be protected, and after that you'll never draw a happy breath again in your life. I advised you to talk with your mother once before. This time you'd better to it."

She leaned back in her chair, white and trembling, for his tones carried conviction.

"I have hated to open this thing up, Kate. I have waited a long time, hoping you'd understand that I would make a good husband—that I deserved to have you. I'm only speaking out now so that you'll wake up. You've got to stand by the man who has stood by you. Go talk with your mother!"

After he had hurried out she went back to her work, but her fingers could only fumble at the keys. By effort of will persons of strong character can compose themselves after disaster has been confirmed; but impending disaster that is hinted at—guessed at—is a menace which paralyzes. She was endeavoring to write down what Richard Dodd had revealed of the plans of Walker Farr. She understood that the mighty power of the state machine was now doubling its fist over the head of the stranger who had come into her life in such peculiar fashion. At the same moment she was cowering under the threat of something she did not fully understand.

And from the Dodds—uncle and nephew—came the menace which loomed over both of them.

Then to her came Peter Briggs, who had been summoned to a conference in the inner office; by direction of his chief he had been reading to Judge Warren certain entries penciled in the note-book which he guarded with the elastic band.

"The governor wants you to add these items to the record, so that the judge can have a copy," said Mr. Briggs to the confidential secretary. "The subject isn't a very genteel one, Miss Kilgour, but orders are orders, and you'll have to excuse me."

And Mr. Briggs kept snapping the elastic band nervously while he dictated, carefully looking away from the young woman.

In such manner Kate Kilgour learned of the existence of Zelie Dionne and of the child whom Walker Farr had protected; Mr. Briggs's zeal in the interest of his employer had made him a partisan in that affair, with easy conscience regarding the matter of the details. The bald record showed that Farr and the girl had cared for the child between them, had nursed it with grief and solicitude, had borne it to the plot of land where the little graves were crowded so closely. Mr. Briggs complacently avoided dates and age and the minuter details. He even pleaded the case, having caught a cue from Colonel Dodd; his record left the impression that Walker Farr, who had come from nowhere—nobody knew when—had lived in Marion unknown and unnoticed at the time when he had compassed the ruin of a confiding girl.

"A scalawag, and a bad one!" commented Mr. Briggs, closing his notebook. "And of course there's worse to come! Posing as a reformer—that's the way such renegades work the thing. A new game for every new place!"

And Kate Kilgour, remembering the vagrant on the broad highway, wrote down the arraignment of this person, trying to understand her emotions.

Her own eyes had seen him garbed as a tramp, plainly a homeless nomad.

Her ears had just listened to the story of his shame.

But after a time, in spite of what she had seen and heard, that strange instinct which dominates the feminine mind in spite of what the mere senses affirm took possession of her.

She had known from the first that Richard Dodd's garments, his attitude, his professions, his position did not make him what her woman's heart desired.

But, somehow, this other man, no matter what he seemed to be from outward appearance, stood forth for her from all the world. At times, in her ponderings, she had disgustedly termed her mood regarding him pure lunacy. Then she gave rein to the domination of her intuition; the man was not what he seemed to be!

She determined to put him out of her thoughts for ever.

Just then, however, writing out the story of his turpitude, she must needs have him in her mind.

She wondered whether he were honest in his attempts to help the poor people.

She had believed that he was when he had faced Colonel Dodd.

She determined that she would make some investigation of her own in regard to the mysterious person who had taken such possession of her thoughts since she had met him in the highway—whose personality had so pricked her curiosity. She comforted herself by calling her interest mere curiosity. That was it! If this man were what they claimed he was she might help in revealing him as an enemy of the poor folks.

And then to her came another thought.

She looked around the offices where she worked and bitter lines were etched in her forehead and about her mouth.

The place had become hateful. She was conscious of a passionate desire to be free from the atmosphere of that central web of the Great Spider.

She bent over her work and hurried.

What was the shadow over her home?

She realized that she was not thinking clearly in the matter. She knew that impulse was driving her. But it was impulse which was uncontrollable. For a long time she had understood the sinister influence which had radiated from that office in the First National block. But it had been rather the impersonal influence of partisan politics and she had had little knowledge of the persons concerned. But, now that the situation had been so sharply pointed by recent happenings, she understood better what had gone on in the past.

This stranger, whoever he was, seemed to be fighting for the good of the people. She had heard him declare his principles boldly; she knew the selfishness of the men who opposed him. She resolved to know more.

It was close upon six o'clock when she finished the transcription.

She had given much thought to her own affairs while she had been working. And now she allowed impulse to dominate. She resolved to leave that employment which brought her into contact with Richard Dodd and where her duties required her to prepare material for the ruin of a man who seemed to be doing an unselfish duty, no matter what they said. She did not try to analyze that quixotic impulse; she merely obeyed.

She tied up the packet of manuscript, addressed it to Colonel Dodd, and slipped under the string a sealed note. In that note she resigned her position, stating that a matter of personal honor demanded that she leave instantly. She did not qualify that statement by any explanation. But she knew in her own heart just what it meant. For when she left the office she did not hasten straight home as her anxious fears prompted her; she made a detour around by Gamonic Mill in search of one Provancher, who, she had learned, tended the rack of the canal.

The thought that dominated all other thoughts and comforted her was the reflection that she was no longer the confidential secretary of Colonel Symonds Dodd, and that now she might obey certain promptings of both curiosity and conscience.

The rumble of the big turbines was stilled when she came to the fence which surrounded the rack, and old Etienne was starting away with rake and pike-pole. But when she called he came to her—wondering, much abashed, for she was by far the prettiest lady he had ever seen.

"Are you the friend of Mr. Walker Farr?" she asked, and she was even more embarrassed than he.

"I am too poor mans to be call a friend, ma'm'selle. I can just say that he is grand mans that I love."

"Then you are the one to give him this message. Tell him that men who are fighting him in politics intend to do him great harm and that he must be very careful. Tell him that he will understand who these men are."

"*Oui*, ma'm'selle. But will he understand who tell me that thing?"

Her cheeks were crimson. "No, no! He mustn't know that."

"Then he will tell me, 'Poh, old Etienne, you know nottings what you talk about.' He is very bold mans, and he not scare very easy."

"But he must be cautious, for these men have power. He need not be afraid of them, but he must watch carefully. You tell him that they want to make out bad things about him so that they can print them in the papers and hurt the cause he is working for. Can you remember?"

"*Oui*, ma'm'selle! I never forget anything what may be for his good. I will tell him."

She hesitated for a long time and stared wistfully at the old man. She started to go away and then returned to the fence, plainly mustering her courage.

"Do you know whether there is anything—about him—which wicked men can use to hurt him?" she stammered.

"I only know about him what I know, ma'm'selle," he replied, with a gentle smile nestling in the wrinkles of his withered face.

"Could you tell me some of the things you know?" she asked, after much effort, striving to make her voice calmly inquiring.

Old Etienne set the rake and the pike-pole against the fence. "I will be quick in what I tell you, ma'm'selle, for I have no place to ask you to take the seat. But I'm sure you will listen very well to this what I say."

And he told her the story of Rosemarie.

But he did not go back as far as the pitiful figure on the canal bank, he made no mention of the water-soaked wad of paper which bore a mother's appeal to the world, he did not mention the key to Block Ten. He told the story of Walker Farr's devotion to a child. He did not dare to reveal to this stranger the identity of that child, because the telltale letter had been hidden from the coroner, and old Etienne stood in awe of the curt and domineering men who enforced the laws. But with simple earnestness and in halting speech he revealed the tenderness of Farr's nature and gave further testimony to her woman's understanding that this man who had come into her life possessed depths which she longed to probe.

"But the child!" she ventured, after Etienne had finished the story of how the two of them, voices in the wilderness of careless greed, had faced the masters of the city in the *hotel de ville*; "it seems strange that a man—that anybody should take a child and—" She hesitated.

"*Oui*, ma'm'selle, it seemed strange," agreed the old man, studying her with sharp glance of suspicion—a gaze so strange that she shifted her eyes uneasily.

Ah, Etienne told himself, the law sometimes sent queer emissaries to probe for it—and he feared the law very much.

He must be very careful how he told any of the secrets which might trouble his good friend, who was now such a friend of the mighty folks; as for himself—well, he would willingly be a martyr if the law demanded—but he did fear that law!

"But he loved the child very much," she hinted.

"So much that he will fight them because they have poisoned her—he will fight them and not be scare."

"It is strange!" she repeated.

"*Oui*, ma'm'selle," he said, regarding her with still more suspicion.

"But before that morning—when you found them here under the tree! He told you—"

"He walk the street with her in his arm. I don't tell you some more about dat t'ing what I do not know!"

But she knew that he was withholding something from her. She mustered her courage.

"Mr. Provancher, the bad men are making threats that they will print stories about the child—and its mamma—to hurt your friend. And the stories will make the mamma very sad."

"No stories can make her sad," said old Etienne, solemnly. But he did not say that he had raked the mother from the canal. The law must not know!

"But I have heard about her," she insisted.

The old man's mouth trembled; he was frightened. "What you hear?" he faltered.

"Only good things. That she was very tender and went with you to the grave."

"*Oui*," admitted Etienne, visibly relieved and grasping at this opportunity. "She's sweet and good. She's play-mamma."

"And her name is Zelie Dionne?" she asked, her face growing white in the dusk.

"*Oui*, ma'm'selle—she live across in the little house where there are plant in the window—she live with the good Mother Maillet what I told you about." He pointed to the cottage. "You go some time and talk with her—but not now," he added, his fears flaming. He was anxious to be the first to talk to Zelie Dionne, in order that she might help him to protect their friend. "You shall talk with her—soon—p'raps. I will tell her so that she will not be afraid. Yes, you shall hear the play-mamma say good things of poor Rosemarie."

She bowed and hurried away.

And before her tear-wet eyes the words "play-mamma" danced in letters of fire. It seemed to be only another sordid story.

But she remembered the face of Walker Farr, and in her heart she wondered why she still refused to condemn him.

XXVI
THE DRIVEN BARGAIN

The Honorable Daniel Breed, "sipping" his thin lips and propping his coat-tails on his gaunt fingers, patrolled the lobby of the National Hotel and his complacency was not a whit disturbed when Richard Dodd passed in front of him and sneered in his face.

"Keep on practising making up faces," advised the old man, amiably. "Perhaps in the course of time your uncle will give you a job making up faces as his understudy, seeing that his physog is getting so tough he can't manage it very well these days."

Young Dodd whirled on his heel and returned. "We've got a line on you and your amateur angels, Breed."

"Don't consider me an amateur, do you?" asked the old politician, smacking his lips complacently.

"You're a has-been."

"Sure thing!" agreed Mr. Breed. "The state committee told me so, and the state committee never made a mistake."

"We've got so much of a line on your crowd that my uncle has called off the organizers. There's no need of our wasting money in this campaign. You're that!" He clacked a finger smartly into his palm.

"Oh yes! You're right! Some snap to us."

"I mean you're nothing."

"Run in and take another drink, sonny," advised Breed, giving slow cant of his head to denote the baize door through which Dodd had emerged. "What you have had up to date seems to be making you optimistic—and there's nothing like being optimistic in politics. I'm always optimistic—but naturally so. Don't need torching!"

"Look here, Breed, we've got enough dope on that ex-hobo who is doing your errand-boy work—we know enough about him to kill your whole sorehead proposition. But I don't believe my uncle will even use it. No need of it."

"Probably not," said Mr. Breed, without resentment. "And I wouldn't if I were he."

"We won't descend to it. Now that we have got rid of a lot of old battle-axes of politicians—and I'm calling no names—we can conduct a campaign with dignity."

"So do! So do! And it will save a lot of trouble, son; that's why the newspapers wouldn't print that stuff about Mr. Farr after your uncle got it ready. Libel cases make a lot of trouble."

Dodd grew red and scowled. "Look here, Breed, you're licked before the start, and as a good politician you know you are. My uncle wants you to drop in and see him. He told me to tell you so. This is no official order, you understand. Just drop in informally, and he'll probably have something interesting to say to you."

"I'm terribly rushed up—shall be till after convention," averred Mr. Breed, piercing the end of a cigar with a peg he had whittled from a match.

"What's the good of your being a fool any longer?"

"Always have been, so I've found out from that state committee who never told a lie—and it's comfortable to keep on being one," he said, with great serenity.

"You don't think for a minute that you are going to get control of the next legislature, do you?"

"How much money have you got—your own money, I mean?" inquired Mr. Breed, guilelessly, his eyes centered carefully on the lighted tip of his cigar.

"Say—you—you—What do you mean by that?" rasped Dodd, putting the cracker of a good round oath on the question.

"I meant that I wanted to bet something—and I wouldn't want you to go out and borrow money—or—or—anything else." From the cavernous depths where his eyes were set Mr. Breed turned a slow and solemn stare on the enraged chief clerk of the state treasury.

"What do you want to bet?"

"Any amount in reason that after the first of next January there'll be a fresh deal in the way of state officers in every department in the Capitol.

Arguing futures don't get you anywhere, son. If you've got money to back that opinion you just gave me it will express your notions without any more talk. But don't go borrow—or—or anything else."

Dodd stared at the shrewd old political manipulator for a long time.

"You have money to bet, have you?" he asked.

Mr. Breed languidly drew forth a wallet which would make a valise for some men and carelessly displayed a thick packet of bills.

"There it is," he said, "and I earned it myself and so I ain't poking it down any rat-hole without being condemned sure that I'll be able to pull it all back again with just as much more sticking to it. That wouldn't be sooavable—and from what you know of me I'm always sooavable."

Dodd looked at the bills, carefully straightened in their packet, and giving every evidence of having been hoarded with an old man's caution.

There was something about that money which impressed him with the sincerity of Mr. Breed's belief in his own cause. The young man grew visibly white around the mouth.

"I'll see you later, Breed," he gulped. "I don't believe you know what you are talking about—but I'm not national bank on legs. I'll be around and cover your cash."

He went back into the bar, swallowed a glass of whisky, and went out and hailed a cab. He directed the driver to carry him to the Trelawny Apartment.

Mrs. Kilgour admitted him to the vestibule of the suite.

"Is Kate at home?" he demanded.

"Yes, Richard!" She shrank away from him, for his aspect was not reassuring. "You know—she has given up her work—she is—"

"I know all about it, Mrs. Kilgour. But I want to ask you whether she has given up her work in order to marry me at once?"

"Why, I—She said—I think it will come about all right, Dicky." She was pitifully unnerved.

"Have you told her why she must marry me?"

"It is not time to tell her—it is not right—I can't—"

He seized her arm and pulled her into the sitting-room. The daughter rose and faced them, reproof and astonishment mingling in her expression.

"This thing is going to be settled here and now," said the lover, roughly. "There is going to be no more fooling. Has your mother put this matter up to you so that you understand it, Kate?"

"She has told me that she owes you five thousand dollars," returned the girl. Her eyes flashed her contempt. "You told me that yourself. I repeated the statement to her and she admits it."

"But did she tell you how it happens that she owes me that money?"

"For God's sake, Richard, have some pity! This is my own daughter. I will sell everything. I will slave. I will pay you. Kate, for my sake—for your own sake, tell him that you will marry him."

"I will not marry this man," declared the girl. "It has been a mistake from the beginning. As to your business with him, mother, that is not my affair. You must settle it."

"You belong in the settlement," declared Dodd. "Hold on! Don't leave this room, Kate."

He reached out his hands to intercept her, and Mrs. Kilgour, released, fell upon the floor and began to grovel and cry entreaties.

But his raucous tones overrode her appeals.

"We're all together in this. I am five thousand dollars shy in the state treasury, Kate. I took that money and loaned it to your mother when she begged me to save her stocks. But she didn't have any stocks."

Mrs. Kilgour grasped his knees and shook him. But he kept on.

"She had embezzled from Dalton & Company. What I did saved her from prison and you from disgrace, Kate. And now I am in the hole! Listen here! There's hell to pay in this state just now! The soreheads are banding together. A man has just offered to bet me big money that there's going to be an overturn in the State House departments. I don't know whether it will happen—but you can understand what kind of torment I'm in. Kate, are you going to let me stand this thing all alone?"

The girl stood silent and motionless in the middle of the room.

She did not weep or faint. Her face displayed no emotion. It was as white as marble.

"Do you want to drag my daughter down with you?" cried Mrs. Kilgour.

"You'd better not talk about dragging down," he shouted, passionately. "I didn't steal for myself. Give me your love, Kate! Give me yourself to encourage me, and I'll get out of the scrape somehow. I'll find ways. But if you don't come with me I won't have the courage or the desire to fight my way through. I'll not disgrace you if you marry me—I swear I will not! With you to protect from everything I'll make good. Symonds Dodd is my uncle. He won't see the family name pulled in. But you must marry me!"

"And if I do not?" she asked.

"We'll all go to damnation together. I don't care! I'll blow it all. I won't be disgraced alone because of something I did for your mother. I may sound like a cur. I don't care, I say! I'm going to have you, and I don't care how I get you!"

"We need not be so dramatic," said the girl. Some wonderful influence seemed to be controlling her. "Mother, stop your noise and go and sit in that chair. You demand, do you, Mr. Dodd, that to save my mother from exposure as a woman who has stolen, I must be your wife?"

"I do."

"Do you really want a wife who has been won in that fashion?"

"I want you."

"You realize, fully, don't you, the spirit in which I shall marry you?"

"We'll take care of that matter after we are married, Kate. You have liked me. You will care for me more when you come to your senses in this thing."

"You remember what my father did in the way of sacrifice, I suppose? It was no secret in this state."

"Yes," he muttered, abashed under her steady gaze.

"I am like my father in many ways—in many of my thoughts. Perhaps if he had not set me such an example in the way of sacrifice I should say something else to you, Mr. Dodd. But as the matter stands between us, considering the demand you make on me, I will marry you."

The concession was flung at him so suddenly—he had expected so much more of rebellion—that he staggered where he stood. He advanced toward her. But she waved him back.

"Sit down!" she commanded. "This matter has gone far outside romance. It has become one of business. It is a matter of barter. I have had some experience in business. You say that mother owes you five thousand dollars which you took from the state treasury?"

"Yes, Kate."

"And your books will be examined very carefully, of course, if there is an overturn in your office?"

"Yes. It won't be any mere legislative auditing."

"I know something about politics as well as about business, Mr. Dodd. I cannot very well help knowing, after my experience in your uncle's office. I suppose the next state convention will determine pretty effectually whether there will be an overturn or not?"

"If we renominate Harwood it ought to give us a good line on the control of the next legislature," he told her. "A hobo and a goody-goody," he added, with scorn, "think they have stirred up a revolution, but they have another think coming." He had been calmed by her outwardly matter-of-fact acceptance of the situation. But he did not perceive the fires of her soul gleaming deep in her eyes.

"If Governor Harwood is renominated and the next legislature is in the hands of your uncle, as usual, you will be sure to remain in your position?"

"Of course!"

"And you can hide the discrepancy on your books from the auditing committee?"

"I am pretty sure I can."

"You appreciate fully, don't you, Mr. Dodd, why, after all my troubles in this life up till now, I should hesitate to marry a man with state prison hanging over him?"

"Yes."

"If Governor Harwood is not renominated I shall expect you to defer our marriage until you can work out of your difficulties. There will be danger and it is not in the bargain of my sacrifice that I shall pass through such disgrace with you; at any rate, I do not consider that added suffering is in the trade and will not agree to it. I prefer to remain as I am and share the disgrace of my mother. Do you agree to that?"

"I don't like it, but I suppose I've got to be decent in the matter."

"But if Governor Harwood is renominated at the convention I will concede a point on my part and will marry you at once, taking it for granted that you will be able to clear yourself. In that way both of us are making concessions—and such things should be considered in a bargain." She was coldly polite.

He bowed, not knowing exactly what reply to make to her.

"You have accused me of trifling in the past," she continued. "I will now try to show you that I can conduct straight business as it should be handled. Shall I make a memo of our agreement and hand it to you?"

"There is no need of it," he stammered.

"Thank you, Mr. Dodd. And now that the matter has been settled to our mutual satisfaction, I will ask you to go. I think my mother needs my attention. And I am reminded that our bargain does not dispose of the fact that my mother owes you five thousand dollars. I will reflect on how that debt may be paid—by insurance"—her face grew whiter still—"or by some arrangement."

"I wish you wouldn't say such—" But she interrupted him.

"On my part, this is strictly business, Mr. Dodd, and I must consider all sides. I will give the money matter careful thought. I'm sure we can arrange it. I have merely bought my mother's good name with *myself!*"

He stumbled out of the room and went on his way.

"Mother, you and I have some long, long thoughts to busy ourselves with before we attempt to talk to each other," said the girl when the two were alone. "I am going to my room. Please do not disturb me until to-morrow."

For an hour Kate Kilgour was a girl once more, sobbing her heart out against her pillow, stretched upon her bed in abandon of woe, torn by the bitter knowledge that she was alone in her pitiful fight. She was more frank with herself in her sorrow than she ever had been before. She owned to her heart that a few days before even a mother's desperate plight would hardly have won such a sacrifice as she had made.

She was ready to own that she loved that tall young man of mystery whose face had refuted the suspicion that he was a mere vagrant. It was strange—it was unaccountable. But she had ceased to wonder at the vagaries of love. In her prostration of mental energies and of hope she confessed to herself that she had loved him.

But now between his face and hers, as she shut her eyes and reproduced his features, limned in her memory, those fiery words danced—there was a "play-mamma" who with him had loved the little girl named Rosemarie.

Checking her sobs, she sighed, and her heart surrendered him.

Her sacrifice had been made both easier and yet more difficult.

Then she snuggled close to her pillows and gazed out into the gathering night, and pondered on the fact that if Walker Farr won his fight in the state convention that victory put an end to her poor little truce in the matter of Richard Dodd.

Then she was sure that she had put Walker Farr out of her heart for ever, because she found herself hoping that he would win. The girl had not yet grown into full knowledge of the dynamics of a true and unselfish love—she did not fully know herself.

XXVII
A DICKER FOR A MAN'S SOUL

The populace came first and packed solidly into the galleries of the great auditorium of Marion city.

For years the state conventions of the dominant party had attracted but little public attention. They had been simple affairs of routine, indorsing the men and the principles of the Big Machine. The next governor had been groomed and announced to the patient people long months before the date of the convention; platforms protecting the interests were glued placidly and secretly and brought forth from the star chamber to be admired; and no delegate was expected or allowed to joggle a plank or nick the smooth varnish which had been smoothed over selfish privilege.

But this year came all the people who could pack themselves into galleries and aisles.

Below on the main floor were more than two thousand delegates. Every town and city sent the full number accredited. After these men had been seated the men and women who thronged the corridors and stairways were allowed to enter and stand in the rear of the great hall.

Strange stories, rumors, predictions, had been running from lip to lip all over the big commonwealth. It was reported that the throne of the tyrant was menaced at last by rebellion which was not mere vaporings of the restless and resentful; organized revolt had appeared, marching in grim silence, not revealing all its strength, and therefore all the more ominous.

A military band brayed music unceasingly into the high arches of the hall. The music served as obbligato for the mighty diapason of men's voices; the thousands talked as they waited.

The broad platform of the stage was untenanted. The speakers, the chairman, the clerks, the members of the state committee, did not appear, though the hour named as the time of calling the meeting to order arrived and passed.

In an anteroom, so far removed from the main hall that only the dull rumble of voices and the shredded echoes of the blaring music reached there, was assembled the state's oligarchy awaiting the pleasure of Colonel Symonds Dodd.

He sat in a big chair, his squat figure crowding its confines.

The state committee and the rest of his entourage were gathered about him.

There was a committeeman from every county in the state—the men who formed the motive cogs of his machine.

One after the other they had reported to him.

And each time a man finished talking the colonel drove a solid fist down on the arm of the chair and roared: "I say again I don't believe it's as bad as you figure it. It can't be as bad. Do you tell me that this party is going to be turned upside down by a kid-glove aristocrat who has hardly stirred out of his office during this campaign?"

"He has had a chap to do his stirring for him," stated one of the group.

"A hobo, scum of the rough-scruff, hailing from nowhere! Shown up in our newspapers as a ditch-digger—a fly-by-night—a nobody! I'm ashamed of this state committee, coming here and telling me that he has been allowed to influence anybody."

"Colonel Dodd, what I'm going to say to you may not sound like politics as we usually talk it," declared a committeeman, a gray-haired and spectacled person who had the grave mien of a student, "and it is not admitted very often by regular politicians who run with the machine. But we are up against something which has happened in this queer old world of ours a good many times. We have had the best organization here in this state that a machine ever put together. But in American politics it's always just when the machine is running best that something happens. Something is dropped into the gear, and it's usually done by the last man you'd expect to do it. The fellows who are tending the machine are too busy watching that part of the crowd they think is dangerous, and then the inconspicuous chap slips one over."

"I don't want any lecture on politics," snapped the boss. "Do you mean to insinuate that that low-lived Farr has put *this* over on *us*?"

"I have hunted to the bottom of things and I do say so, Colonel Dodd."

"How in blazes did that fellow ever get any influence? I haven't been able to believe that he has been accomplishing anything."

"You ought to have listened a little more closely to us, Colonel," insisted the committeeman. "Every once in a while there comes forward a man whom the people will follow. And he is never the rich man nor the proud man, but he is one who knows how to reach the hearts of the crowd. A shrewd politician can get power by building up his machine. And then some fellow in overalls who has some kind of a God-given quality that has never been explained yet so that we can understand, smashes into sight like a comet. It may be his way of talking to men, it may be his personality— it is more likely a divine spark in him that neither he himself nor other men understand. But every now and again some humble chap like that has changed the history of the world, and I reckon it's pretty easy for such a man to change the politics of a mere state."

His associates were staring at him and Colonel Dodd was giving him furious glances. He had spoken with enthusiasm. He broke off suddenly.

"I beg your pardon. I don't mean to go quite so far. But I'm a student of history and I've read a lot about natural-born leaders."

"You evidently know more about history than you do about politics," growled the colonel. "This whole state committee doesn't seem to know much politics. If you have allowed that Farr to slime his way around under cover and do you up in your own counties, I'll see to it that we have a new state committee."

"I have an idea that that convention out there will attend to the matter of a new state committee for us."

The new speaker's voice was very soft. His nickname in state politics was "Whispering Saunders." He was known as being the most artistic political "pussy-foot" in the party. It was averred that he could put on rubber boots and run twice around the State House on a fresh fall of light snow and not leave a track.

"If I'm any kind of a smeller—and I reckon it's admitted that I am," purred Saunders, "we are walloped before the start-off in every county delegation out on that floor."

"But what has been the matter with you fellows all the time?" blazed the boss. "Up to now you have been reporting simply that the soreheads were growling and were not getting together so as to be dangerous."

"Did you ever try to shovel up soft soap from a cellar floor with a knitting-needle?" inquired the politician. "That's how it's been in this case. Every man I talked with was slippery. I know slippery times when I see 'em.

I've been afraid, but I hoped for the best. Now that they are here, with this convention due to be called to order, they are not slippery any longer. They don't need to be. I've just been through the convention hall. They are out and open—and they're against us."

"That Farr has a proxy from a delegate in the Eleventh Ward and is on the floor," stated another.

"But he isn't a voter."

"He wasn't a little while ago, but he is to-day, Colonel. The board of registration had to put his name on the books—he has lived here long enough to become a voter."

Colonel Dodd glared from face to face. It was plain that he was angered rather than dismayed; he was like a bull at bay, shaking the pricking darts out of his shoulders. He took a hasty glance at his watch. 'Twas twenty minutes past the hour appointed for the calling of the convention. He could hear the distant band still bellowing bravely to kill time.

A giant of a man stood up—a cool man, rather cynical. He was the chairman of the state committee.

"I have been waiting till all these gentlemen got the panic worked out of their systems—or, at least, had said all they could think of about that panic, Colonel. Now we can go ahead and do real business. We have not had a battle in this state for a long time, and this panic may be excusable. They say that the men who are the worst frightened before the battle do the best fighting after they get into the real scrap. I will admit that the situation in the state has been a little slippery, as Saunders has said. And some men have dared to do a lot of loud talking since they have arrived here in this city. It is so strange a thing that it has got everybody in a panic. The Chinese are wise—they show dragons to the enemy, but the dragons are only paper. Wouldn't think the enemy could be scared that way, eh? But look at this bunch of state committeemen! A pasteboard 'natural-born leader' set up, and Archer Converse puffing smoke through the nostrils of that effigy! Gentlemen, you ought to be ashamed of yourselves!"

Colonel Dodd snorted emphatic approval.

"You are talking like children. Guff and growls can't carry this convention. That crowd hasn't even got a candidate for governor. Have you heard one mentioned?"

"I don't suppose they would dare to go as far as that," said one of the committeemen. "Governor Harwood, by party usage, is entitled to a renomination, of course. What they figure on is a new state committee and a platform that will include reforms."

"Huh! Yes! So much striped candy! Give it to 'em. Then we've got only twenty-four men to handle in the way we have always handled state committees—and even that crowd can't find saints and archangels for their candidates! And as for a political platform—bah!"

It was the practical politician's caustic estimate of conditions.

Then the chairman joined in, bolstering this supercilious view: "As for that legislature—how many bills were ever passed in our legislature over a governor's veto after we had got in our work? We are going to have a safe man for governor. That band's lungs won't last for ever. Colonel Dodd, are you ready?"

If revolt and the spirit of resentment and rebellion did exist in that assemblage, which the magnates of the party faced when they marched upon the platform, the tumult of applause covered all sinister outward aspects. The routine of the convention was entered upon: the secretary read the convention call, the organization was perfected without protest, and the orator of the day, as president pro tem, a conservative United States Senator, began his "key-note speech." It was a document which had been in proof slips for a week, and which all the party workers from Colonel Dodd down had read and approved. Therefore, when Richard Dodd entered from one of the side doors and came tiptoeing across the platform and touched the colonel's arm and jerked energetic request for the colonel to follow, the colonel followed, glad of an excuse to be absent while the Senator fulminated.

Young Dodd's face was flushed and working with excitement. He hurried his uncle into a small retiring-room and locked the door.

"I've got your man, uncle," he declared.

"What man?" The colonel was grouchy and indifferent.

"Your man Farr."

"I don't claim him."

"But you said you wanted him. You said you wanted to hang him like a dead crow in the political bean-patch."

"Merely momentary insanity on my part, Richard. There seems to have been a little run of it in this state, and when Judge Warren caught it and gave it to me I talked like a fool, I suppose. But you must remember that a polecat can give the most level-headed man an almighty start—and then the level-headed man walks out around the polecat and goes on his way very calmly."

"But don't you consider that Farr is a dangerous man?"

The colonel held up his pudgy hand and snapped a finger into his palm. "He amounts to that in front of the muzzle of a ten-inch gun."

"But I went ahead after what you said. I have put out time and money. I hired a detective. I figured I was doing a good job for the machine." Young Dodd's voice trembled and disappointment was etched into his anxious features.

"Well, what have you found out?"

"I can't tell you. It's another man's secret, and he's got to have cash or a guaranty before he'll come across with it."

"What's the price?"

Richard Dodd exhibited confusion and hesitation. "I made some promises to him, uncle, because I know what has been paid in the past for things which didn't seem to be as important as this—judging from the way you and the judge talked. So I—well, I—"

"Price, price, I say! I'm used to hearing money talked," harked the colonel. "I've got to get back into that convention. Out with it!" He made two steps toward the door.

"Five thousand!" blurted the young man.

Colonel Dodd whirled and whipped off his eye-glasses so as to give his nephew the full effect of his contemptuous fury.

"Why, you young lunatic, I wouldn't pay that price if they were going to elect Farr the governor of this state, and make him a present of the Consolidated, and you could bring proof that he is the reincarnation of Judas Iscariot."

A roar of voices and a thunder of thudding feet announced that the Senator had finished.

Colonel Dodd hurried away.

The nephew found Detective Mullaney in the alley behind the auditorium, and the young man's air of discomfiture and the sagging shake of his head told the story of his errand without words.

"If they're getting too mean in their old age to hand me a fair price for a good job then let 'em get licked," declared the detective. "You stuck to our original figure of five hundred dollars, didn't you?"

The young man looked over the detective's head and lied. "Five hundred—that's what I told him."

"And he wouldn't consider it?"

"Something has braced him so that he isn't afraid of the man any longer. Perhaps he has got a line of his own on him. It doesn't seem to be worth anything any longer. Suppose you tell me just who he is and what about him?"

"Not on your life!" retorted Detective Mullaney, sharply. "I ain't saying anything against your family, of course, but when I give a Dodd something for nothing—even a hint—it will be when I'm talking in my sleep and don't know it. But I'll tell you what I *will* do. Give me my two hundred and fifty and I'll hand you the whole proposition and you may go ahead and make what you can of it. I swear to you again that I've got it on him. Seeing what he did to *you*, you ought to feel that the story is worth that much of a gamble even for private purposes."

Dodd hesitated, put his hand in his pocket—then withdrew it empty.

"No, Mullaney. What's the good? He says Farr isn't dangerous, and has turned down the whole thing flat. I may as well keep my money. If you want to sit on the platform, come along with me. I can find a place for you."

Detective Mullaney followed willingly, for he knew that people were fairly piling over one another in an attempt to get into the hall by the main entrance.

He sat down in one of the square chairs on the platform and searched with his sharp little eyes until he found the face of Walker Farr in the terraced rows of humanity. It was not difficult to locate him, for his physique made him loom among other men and he was posted under the banner which marked the location of Moosac County.

The detective found the eyes of the young man directed toward the gallery with such intentness and for so long a time that he endeavored to trace that earnest scrutiny to its object. The detective was not exactly certain, but he finally picked out a very handsome young lady who occupied a front chair in the balcony; she seemed to be returning the young man's intent regard.

"You have the reputation of knowing all the pretty girls in the state," whispered Mullaney, drawing Dodd's attention with a nudge. "Who is that up there in the gallery, front row, fifth from the aisle; blue feather, and so handsome she hurts my eyes?"

To have his attention drawn thus rudely to the one girl in all the world gave Dodd a sensation which he did not relish—and his face showed his astonished resentment.

"That is Miss Kilgour, who used to be my uncle's secretary. Why do you want to know who she is?"

"Because there seems to be something very especial on between her and the man we thought was worth five hundred dollars to us."

"That young lady, Mr. Mullaney, is engaged to me," stated Dodd, acridly. "You'd better drop the topic."

But he did not display either the joy or the pride of the accepted suitor as he looked up at her.

"I'll simply say that you're a mighty lucky chap and I congratulate you," returned Mr. Mullaney, hiding his confusion by getting very busy with newspaper clippings and papers which he drew from his breast pocket.

The detective was wholly unconscious of the irony of that remark. But it brought a flush of shame to Dodd's cheek, for the sorrow and sting and ignominy of that part which he had played had not departed from his soul nor did even the fervor of his passion for her help him forgive himself; he stared at her guiltily as the thief gloats over his loot and is conscious of his degradation without feeling sufficient contrition to give up the object he has stolen.

For he remembered with fresh and poignant recollection the circumstances under which that girl had given her promise to him so recently: she had stood over a mother who had abased herself before them, had cast herself down and had writhed and screamed and implored her to consent; and the mother was driven to do this by the lash of his threats. He had stood there and demanded, and the woman on the floor had confessed her frailty, owned to her misdeeds, acknowledged her debt, and had frantically begged her daughter to sacrifice herself.

The girl had given her "Yes," paying the debt with herself; but her eyes had been wide and dry and her face was white and set and she had looked past the man to whom she promised herself when she had murmured that promise.

Dodd swept cold sweat from his forehead as he remembered; he found almost the same expression now on her face as she gazed down on Walker Farr, who stared back at her anxiously, perceiving a grief that he could not understand.

In that vast assemblage those three, thus wordlessly, no one marking them, fought a tragic battle of hopeless love with their eyes.

Detective Mullaney pored over his papers. "By gad," he mused, "I haven't kept my books all this time for nothing. I know my card. I've got him right—it's dead open and shut. But I swear he doesn't look the part he played, even if the description does fit him. Well, law is law! If I can't sell him to Symonds Dodd, I'll find out how much those will pay who do want him."

The routine of the great convention had been proceeding.

"And the gentleman from Danton, Mr. Gray, moves that we do now proceed with the nomination of a candidate for governor," intoned the chairman in sing-song tones.

XXVIII
THE MAN WHO WAS NOT AFRAID

One after the other, dignified and decorous, three men of the Big Machine, representing three of the large counties of the state, came upon the platform and put in nomination the name of Governor Harwood to succeed himself.

These speakers had been carefully selected. They were elderly gentlemen whose reputations, tones, and demeanor bespoke safe and sane conservatism. They took occasion to rebuke the new spirit of unrest in the old party, and their tremolo notes of protest were extremely effective. While these men talked, a listener was compelled to feel that rebellion against the established order of things could only be rank sedition; for many years have these arts of oratory been employed to appeal to the average man's party loyalty; voters have listened and have been ashamed to revolt—as a son dutifully bows his head under a father's reprimand and responds to a father's appeal—for, after all, in matters where appeal is made to loyalty the human emotions are not so very complex.

The elderly gentlemen put great stress on the fact that not in twenty years had a faithful governor been refused the honor of renomination for a second term. Would their convention deny that compliment to Governor Harwood? It was the same appeal that had been made for twoscore years in order to perpetuate the dynasty of gubernatorial figureheads who had obeyed the ring's orders.

Walker Farr heard *sotto voce* murmurings of men in his vicinity. They were men who had joined the new revolt and had stood bravely enough for a change in county political managers. But these men revealed that they were timorous about altering long party custom. They said, one to another, that it would be going too far to refuse renomination to Governor Harwood. It might split their party so widely that the rival political party would be able to carry the state—and that would never do.

Farr was in no wise surprised to hear these murmurings.

He had sounded men before that convention as he had traveled about the state.

He had found them ready to begin house-cleaning in the smaller affairs of county management, and by assault on the little wheels of the gear of the machine which had so long ground political grist; but they were unwilling to tempt fate by venturing on such a general overturn as putting up for governor a man who had not been selected and groomed for high office during the accustomed term of apprenticeship—legislature, senate, and council.

He realized how well the great ring had intrenched itself in absolute power by appealing to conservatism in matters of safe men for high office. Safe men meant those who protected the big interests and saw that no raids were made on capital—no matter how many abuses capital might be fostering.

Mumble and grumble all about him, and men's faces showing that they were agreeing with the tremolo appeals of the elderly orators!

Even the Honorable Archer Converse, his legal cautiousness governing his opinion, knowing the temper of conditions in his state, had emphatically discouraged Farr when the young man had timidly questioned him in regard to the advisability of securing a candidate for governor outside the ring's dynasty.

Mr. Converse's discouragement of such hopes would have been even more emphatic had he ever dreamed that this apostle whom he had sent out into the field was coddling the audacious hope that Mr. Converse himself by some miracle might be put into the governor's chair.

The orators proceeded, one after the other. They were applauded. They retired.

Walker Farr was oppressed by the lugubrious conviction that he was the only man in that great assemblage who felt enough of the zealot's fire to be willing to put all his hopes to the test.

He looked at the faces on the platform. There sat Colonel Dodd, wearing his expression assumed for that day and date—smug political hypocrisy.

His henchmen winged out to right and left of him. They represented finance and respectability.

Sometimes political rebels will gallantly and audaciously venture when they rail behind the backs of their leaders; but when those leaders appear and fill the foreground with their personalities the rebels subside; they are impressed by the men whom they behold. They defer, even when they are stung by knowledge of their leaders' principles.

Colonel Dodd and those with him were the accredited leaders.

Delegates glared, but were cowed and silent.

Farr pondered. Perhaps the advice of Mr. Converse was best:

"Take what we can get in our first skirmish. Keep it for the nucleus of what we hope to get later. If we put all to the test in our first fight against forces that have been in power for all the years and lose, then the cause gets a setback which may discourage our men for ever."

And Mr. Converse, having so declared, had remained away from the convention that day, feeling that no more was to be gained.

"And I move you, Mr. Chairman," called a voice, "that the nominations for governor do now close."

This had been the custom in the past.

It was not in the minds of that convention that another candidate would be put forward. Governor Harwood was waiting in an anteroom, thumbing the leaves of his speech, and all the delegates knew it. All desired to expedite matters, nominate by acclamation, hear the inevitable speech, and go home.

"One moment before that motion is seconded!"

The voice was so loud, so clear, so dominant, so ringing, that the effect on the convention was as galvanically intense as if somebody had blown upon a bugle.

Walker Farr had risen to his feet.

Colonel Dodd set his curved palm at his mouth and from behind the chairman shot a few words at the presiding officer as one might shoot pellets from a bean-shooter. The chairman scowled impatiently at Farr, and a delegate among those who watched eagerly for signals from the throne rose half-way to his feet and bellowed, "Question!" The cry was taken up by other delegates, just as the unthinking mob follows a cheer-master.

Farr climbed upon a settee. He stood there, silent and waiting, and his expression, poise, and mien wrought for him more effectively than speech.

He towered over all the heads. He was markedly not one of those New-Englanders there assembled. His mass of dark-brown hair, his garb, the very set of his head on his shoulders, differed from the physical attributes of all others in the hall. And, as the delegates continued to shout for the question to be put, he turned slowly so that his expression of dignified and mild protest and appeal was visible to all. And as he turned he gave the girl in the gallery a long look.

The chairman pounded with his gavel.

"I second the motion," called a delegate, taking advantage of the first moment of silence.

There was another roaring chorus of, "Question!"

But Walker Farr remained standing on the settee, waiting patiently. He showed no confusion. There was added dignity as well as appeal in his attitude and expression.

"Before that vote is taken I want to say one word as a man to men," shouted a delegate. "It's plain to be seen that that man standing there is a gentleman. We are sent here to attend a meeting for the good of our party. If, as delegates, we refuse to listen to a gentleman because we're in too much of a hurry, we'd ought to be ashamed of ourselves. If, on the other hand, we're *afraid* to listen to him, whatever it is he wants to say, then God save this party of ours!"

That was a sentiment which promptly struck fire in that assemblage.

There before their eyes stood the subject of that challenge, stalwart, modest, appealing silently—the sort of appeal which won.

The galleries broke into applause first. Then the delegates took up the demonstration in behalf of fair play. They beat their hands and pounded their feet. The applause from the galleries had more or less of rebuke in it, because it began while the challenger's voice still echoed in the great hall.

The chairman's gavel thumped ferociously.

Colonel Dodd cursed under his breath. He had been on the trail of that convention, its movements, its progress, as a hound dog would follow the trail of a fox. He had seen it safely headed for the corner where it would be run to earth. He detected sudden peril in this threat of a detour.

"Good Jericho!" gasped a committeeman near him. "The chairman ain't letting this convention get away from him, is he?"

It was natural alarm in the case of a man who feared to allow any expression in a convention except such as had been arranged for previously and had been passed upon by those in power.

"This isn't the kind of convention that will get away!" hissed the colonel in reply, bolstering his own convictions that all was safely harnessed. "But I don't want any fooling."

He caught the eye of his nephew and summoned him with an impatient jerk of the head.

Richard Dodd hastened across the platform and bent his ear close to his uncle's mouth—the colonel pulling him down.

"If your man can stop that fool now—quick—for five hundred dollars, I'll pay."

Young Dodd gulped. He needed five thousand dollars!

"He won't consider less than I told you."

"Well, let the idiot talk to us—he can't do any harm."

The colonel pushed his nephew away. In spite of that applause he still half expected that the convention would close the nominations. What else was there to do?

"The vote is upon the motion to close the nominations for governor," stated the chairman. "Those in favor will say 'Aye!'"

Every delegate in that hall was looking at Farr. They were staring at him with curiosity and interest. But even curiosity does not always prompt politicians to open a convention to a person who may prove to be a bomb that will upset plans and precedent.

Then Farr gave them that wonderful smile!

The "Ayes" were scattered and sporadic! Men did not relish shutting off a chap who stood there and smiled upon them in that fashion.

At the call for the "Noes" a bellow of voices shook the hall.

The convention had given this stranger permission to speak by that refusal to subscribe to the cut-and-dried plans. Colonel Dodd was no longer smug. He scowled ferociously.

"Gentlemen of the convention, I am grateful," cried Walker Farr. "And I will not abuse your patience."

"Platform—take the platform!" called many of the delegates.

He smiled and shook his head. "Let me talk to you standing here where I can look into your eyes, gentlemen. I feel pretty much alone in this convention. I *am* alone! I represent no faction, no interest except the cause of the humble who have asked for help from the masters who have been set over them. Perhaps I ought to have remained silent here to-day. My cowardice has been prompting me to keep still. It is no easy matter for me to stand up here and disturb the order of events which had been arranged by the gentlemen who have managed your public affairs for you so many years. But it would be much more difficult for some of the others here to speak, because the gentlemen who manage politics have methods by which they can discredit a man in his profession, ruin him in his business, stop his credit at banks and in other ways make him pay dearly for his boldness in speech. I have no money in banks, no business which can be ruined."

"I rise to a point of order!" shouted a delegate, obeying a nod from the stage. "The business in hand is the nomination of a governor."

"That is my business," stated Farr, calmly.

With political scent sharpened by his apprehension, Colonel Dodd narrowed his eyes, sat straight in his chair, and desperately endeavored to fathom the intentions of this rank outsider.

In spite of his bluster to the state committee he was worried. He had not felt comfortable since his conference with Judge Ambrose Warren. He did not like the "feel" of political conditions. There was some indefinable slipperiness about matters.

He could not bring himself to consider the impossible idea that the convention would bolt—would run amuck, no matter who addressed it— no matter what contingency arose. But to have the convention even tolerate this brazen interloper troubled his sense of mastery; the convention had been too ready to permit the stranger to speak. It wasn't politics as the colonel had been accustomed to play the game. And this—this man from nowhere—it was preposterous!

He snapped his head around and found his nephew close behind him.

"You young whelp," gritted Colonel Dodd, visiting his anger on the nearest object, "where's your political loyalty? This isn't any time to drive bargains. If you can stop that fellow hustle and do it."

"It's another man's secret, I tell you. I've got to buy it."

"I'll make it a thousand."

Young Dodd's face was white, but he knew how desperate his case was and how vitally necessary it was to play his cards as he held them.

"I gave you final figures," he whispered.

"Where is that man? Let me deal with him."

"It must be done through me."

"If you wasn't my nephew I'd think this was blackmail."

Young Dodd stepped back to avoid the glare in his uncle's eyes.

The colonel turned away and listened. Farr's voice was raised now in solemn appeal.

"The idea of my letting myself get rattled by a crack-brained demagogue," muttered the colonel. He had been fondling the outside of his coat furtively, locating his check-book. Now he took his hand away.

"It is well to respect service and to show courtesy, gentlemen. I have listened with interest to the eulogies which have been given Governor Harwood. He is, without doubt, an amiable gentleman. But let me tell you that the next legislature is going to be asked to pass a law which will be a club with which the people will rap the knuckles of Greed till that unholy clutch on the water systems of this state will be loosened for ever."

The delegates stared at him for a few seconds when he paused, and then a tumult of applause greeted his utterance.

"I ask you, gentlemen, whether Governor Harwood—and you know him well and how he has been chosen—will ever sign a bill that will take profit from the hands of his political makers even to give that profit to the people who are the rightful owners?"

This time men were silent, but he knew what they thought from the manner in which they looked at him.

"I do not need to tell you that the veto of a bill by a governor means, in most cases, its death. Gentlemen, it would be polite and kind and gracious of you to bow low here to-day and hand up the nomination to the amiable Governor Harwood. But with the conditions as they are in this state are you going to be polite, merely, while the hearses are rumbling down your streets? I have no way of knowing how many of you into whose eyes I am looking have seen death enter your own homes from the taps of this much-promising, little-accomplishing water syndicate. But if you have seen death touch your loved ones, or if you go home from here and behold fever ravaging your community, it will be poor consolation to your soul to remember that at least you were polite to an amiable man who desired the honor of a renomination."

The faces of the convention showed that this blunt yet shrewd appeal to the individual antagonism of men had produced profound effect.

"But that is only one feature of what this state demands and needs, gentlemen," was Farr's ringing declaration. "This struggle for pure water has opened a broad avenue. The towns and cities of this state must take back into their own hands the properties and franchises which have been mismanaged by the men to whose hands unwise gift by the people has intrusted the people's own. We need a man in the Big Chair of State who will stand with the people in this crusade!"

This amazing declaration in open convention produced as much consternation on the platform as if Farr had dropped a bomb there.

He uttered something which was worse than mere political rebellion: he was proposing to take for the people properties which constituted the backbone of the oligarchy's power in state affairs.

Colonel Dodd had been growling behind the chairman, angrily endeavoring to get the ear of that gentleman. But the chairman seemed to be as wholly absorbed by this astonishing arraignment as were the delegates.

The head of the state machine, for the first time in his career, was compelled to come into the open instead of through the mouth of a lieutenant. He could not wait to give orders.

He rose and stamped to the front of the platform. His voice rang hoarse and loud.

"There can be no more of this unparliamentary and irregular nonsense. What has got into this convention? Don't you understand that no speaker is allowed to break the rules and attack a man under guise of nominating another? Mr. Chairman, I demand that this slanderer be removed from the hall and that we proceed to the nomination of a governor."

There was a hush during which Farr and Colonel Dodd looked at each other, crossing their stares like long rapiers over the terraced heads.

"I fear I was wrong," confessed Farr, gently. "But we poor folks down in the ranks don't know much about the rules, and when we are struggling to save the ones we love we are apt to forget and talk to the heart of things. I am not trying to show that I am a skilful orator, gentlemen of the convention." He held up his arms. "I am crying for *Justice!*"

The delegates broke into applause once more.

And Walker Farr sent a queer look straight into the eyes of the colonel.

Conviction slapped Colonel Symonds Dodd in his mental face with a violence that made him blink!

This man was no amateur in understanding how to sway an audience. To be sure, he had transgressed parliamentary usage, but in those words he had driven home facts that all knew to be truths—truths which others had been afraid to voice, but which, once put into words in public, tied the hideous stamp of ring favoritism upon Governor Harwood, made him a candidate who could not be trusted.

The colonel understood, and he also saw plainly that the most of the audience had accepted the apology, and held no prejudice against the speaker.

"Now that I understand what the rules governing nominations are I will not break them again," declared Farr.

But like a shrewd and not over-scrupulous lawyer he had jabbed into the proceedings a stinging truth which, though excluded by the rules, nevertheless served vitally the big purpose of his efforts; the colonel understood that, too, and turned back to his chair fairly livid with rage.

"There is a man in this state who knows true law," continued the speaker, "and that you may be assured that he will sign a bill which is passed for the good of the people, let me tell you a little about his character."

Colonel Dodd cursed without trying to moderate his tones very much.

"There's no telling what tack that renegade will take next. This infernal convention is getting to be a nightmare. Those fools out there are listening as if they expected that cheap demagogue to bring 'em a new Messiah," he told the committeemen near him.

"There's a funny noise going on out there among 'em," ventured "Whispering Saunders." "Round-up fellows say they hear something like it when a herd is getting ready to stampede. It's the same thing in a political convention sometimes. The reason for it is: the crowd is ripe and the head steer gives the right bellow—and off they go!"

Colonel Dodd grabbed his nephew by the elbow and rushed him off the stage and into an anteroom.

"Is that matter on the hair-trigger, Richard?" he demanded.

"It's ready to be snapped any minute."

The colonel whipped out his check-book and began to write. "It's as old Saunders said," he muttered as he wrote. "And we've got to rope, throw, and tie that one steer."

The check was for five thousand dollars!

Young Dodd seized it, and when his uncle hurried back upon the stage the nephew, through the door which was left open, beckoned to Mullaney. The detective came, hurrying past Colonel Dodd, who stared until the door had closed behind young Dodd and the officer.

"But he's my own nephew!" he assured himself, as if he were replying to an accusation laid against Richard Dodd. He shook his head and sat down in his chair. "I wonder how long it has been since old Bob Mullaney put a price of that size on his secrets! I'm afraid Richard hasn't the Dodd ability to drive a sharp trade."

But Richard was showing considerable ability in that line behind the door of the anteroom.

He jammed two hundred and fifty dollars in crumpled bills into the detective's hands, cleaning out his pockets for the purpose. He had slipped the check into his deepest pocket the moment his uncle had handed it to him.

"It was hard work to screw him up, Mullaney. You have seen how I worked him. This is all he gave me—two hundred and fifty. Take it and spring your trap."

"You don't look honest," grumbled the detective. "If I'm any kind of a guesser you're holding out on me."

"That's your price. You agreed. There isn't any time to argue this. Give me back the money." He grabbed the bills from Mullaney's clutch. It was magnificent bluff. "I'll hand it to my uncle. He isn't very keen on the thing, anyway."

"I'll take it—give it back. I'll apologize," pleaded Mullaney.

"Will you swear to keep all this under your hat—the whole thing? Uncle says if you dare to speak to him about it—hint to him or anybody that he paid money for anything on Farr—he'll deny the story and have your license taken away."

"I promise—swear it," Mullaney agreed.

Dodd returned the money, and the detective started out on the trot.

"You come, too, and I'll tell you on the way. Time is short. You'd better help me," he advised Dodd. They hurried away together, rushed out into the alley and around to the front of the hall, the detective pouring certain information into Dodd's ear as they made their way to the big door and into the main corridor.

Then they bored through the crowds.

The detective led the way and showed his badge to compel the people to give them a lane.

They entered the rear of the auditorium.

"You take the left side and I'll take the right," commanded Mullaney. "We need to paralyze him first. That's all there's time for just now—I've had short notice. But get that name to every man of your crowd you can, and when the howl is started tell 'em all to join in."

Dodd had had scant time to digest the knowledge which the detective had imparted on the run. But his eyes gleamed wickedly as he began to whisper to men among the delegates. And as he moved about he noticed that the girl in the gallery had marked his activity, even to the extent of turning her gaze from Walker Farr, whose voice was ringing through the spacious hall.

XXIX
THE BOMB

Walker Farr, towering over their heads, talked to the men in whose midst he stood.

Mere eloquence no longer avails in these days of cynical disbelief in the motives of political orators. But this young man who stood there was sincerity incarnate. The wonderful and mystic magnetic quality which wins men and inspires confidence radiated from him. And every now and then, as he glanced up at one face in the gallery his voice took on new tones of appeal and pathos. He was one crying from the depths to those in authority! By the marvel of his language he made the men who sat there as delegates understand that theirs was the power to make or mar—to save or sacrifice their state in the crisis which was upon them. He made them feel their responsibility after he made them understand their power.

And he also made their duty plain.

The crux of the situation rested on such a man as they should place in the highest office in the state.

In other times, under other conditions, some pliant and amiable figurehead might serve them well.

He told them, with outstretched finger and vibrant voice, what must be the masterful qualifications of the man who should assume the cross of public service and carry it up the steeps where he would be lashed at every step of his weary way by the thongs in the hands of privileged capital.

Colonel Symonds Dodd had come back to the platform, cursing himself for a fool. The moment the check had left his hands he was angry because he had allowed circumstances to stampede him.

He wondered what was getting into him and into politics.

Was he afraid of mere talk from a demagogue! But after he had sat there for a few moments and listened, and had watched the faces of the delegates, he decided that if five thousand dollars would stop the mouth of that man he had spent money wisely. It was borne in upon him that he had spent greater sums many times for lesser service.

He saw Richard Dodd and Mullaney circulating among the delegates. He restrained with difficulty an impulse to rise and shout to them to hurry. He felt that danger to his program and his political structure was imminent. Because once again were true eloquence and masterly appeal winning men.

All the listeners in the vast hall were as still as death. All eyes were on this speaker who seemed to be clothing with effective speech all the hidden convictions of the delegates themselves who had nursed protest without being able to put it into force.

Colonel Dodd had seen conventions in similar mood in the old days before the saddle of party had been as securely cinched as it had been in late years.

The chairman of the state committee uttered the colonel's rising fears. The chairman had lost his sneer and his bumptious confidence. His face was red, he was sweating, he was staring out over the convention and snapping his fingers impatiently.

"Good gad!" he informed those in hearing on the platform, "what kind of a turn is this thing taking? We have let this convention get away from us. That chap has got the whole crowd marching to the mourners' bench. He can wind up by nominating a yellow dog and they'll rise and howl him into office by acclamation!"

Farr paused for a moment to give effect to his next words.

"Such in character, in honest impulse, in honor, in ability, in devotion, and in God-given nobility must be the man who will lead you. Has God given such a man to this state? He has!"

"Yes and the devil has given us Nelson Sinkler to speak for that man!"

The voice was shrill and agitated and it came from a section of the hall where the rabid adherents of the machine were massed; it was an amazing and shocking interruption.

"I said Nelson Sinkler—that's you!" screamed the voice.

And on that, from here and there in the hall, like snipers posted in ambush, men shouted the name "Nelson Sinkler"—the words popping like rifles.

There was uproar. Part of it was protest, part hysterical demonstration of excitement in an assemblage which did not in the least understand.

Then after a time came quiet, for the object of the attack stood in his elevated position, unruffled, stern, turning bold front to right and left as men barked at him.

"I am here where all may look on me," he said. "Let one or all of those who are attacking me stand forth in view, too."

No one stood up.

"It's a cowardly man who will not put his name to a letter or show his face when he makes an accusation," cried Farr.

"How about a man who doesn't dare to use his own name?" This questioner remained in ambush.

"Your right name isn't Walker Farr and you know it isn't," bellowed a voice on the opposite side of the hall.

Other voices pot-shotted at him with the words, "Nelson Sinkler."

"Will one man in this convention stand up and show himself so that I can talk to him face to face?" shouted the man at bay.

Detective Mullaney and Richard Dodd could not find seats. The others were sitting, and the two were marked men.

"Well, Dodd, you have been whispering. What have you to say aloud?" demanded the man they were baiting.

"I say your name is not Walker Farr."

"You!" The tall young man darted a finger at Mullaney.

"I say you're Nelson Sinkler."

"And what of him?"

"He is wanted by the state of Nebraska for murder."

A sound that was mingled sigh and groan ran and throbbed from galleries to floor; it filled the great hall and seemed to vibrate back and forth over the assemblage. And for the long minute that the dreadful sound continued until it had breathed itself out into horrified silence the man who stood on the settee looked straight into the white face of the girl in the gallery.

But those of the throng who devoured him with eager stares could not discern one trace of confession on his countenance.

Then he did a strange thing.

He held his arms out toward Detective Mullaney and crossed them, wrist over wrist, and he smiled.

"If you are certain enough of your man to dare to arrest me, sir, I stand here waiting for the handcuffs."

The detective hesitated, visibly embarrassed. He had been looking for confusion, confession by manner, even collapse.

"This is a put-up political job," declared a delegate. "That's no murderer—that man."

"I am waiting," repeated Farr.

Detective Mullaney flushed. There were murmurs of hostility in the throng about him. He ran over swiftly in his mind the contents of his notebook and fortified his courage.

"I haven't secured a warrant yet—but I'll take your dare," he announced. He started to come down the aisle.

"Just one moment," called a stentorian voice in the gallery. "You're wrong, my man, down there. I don't want to see an innocent person disgraced in public nor an officer get himself into a scrape. That man is not Nelson Sinkler."

"What are we running here—a state convention or a police court?" Colonel Dodd demanded, leaping up and grabbing the arm of the presiding officer. "Order all those men ejected from the hall."

But at that moment the convention was not in the control of the chairman. Irregular as it all was, human nature demanded to be shown there and then.

Delegates arose, shouting, and surrounded Farr, making effectual bulwarks against Mullaney with their bodies. Voices asked the stranger in the gallery for information, and he motioned the vociferous mob into silence.

"I am a United States post-office inspector, and I can easily prove my identity, gentlemen. I'm here in this convention merely as a spectator, killing time till my train leaves. But I know Nelson Sinkler because I arrested him a month or so ago after he had been a fugitive for two years. He killed a mail clerk. He is now awaiting trial. If that man down there is arrested as being Nelson Sinkler it will mean a lot of trouble for somebody." He sat down.

"Who are you?" yelled a chorus of the ring's henchmen. They pressed as near to Farr as his body-guard would permit and shook their fists at him.

"I am a man and not a spirit," he said in the first silence—and silence came quickly, for they were eager to hear. "You can see that for yourselves. But just now I am less a man than a *Voice*." He shouted that last word. "The Voice calls you to rebuke the kind of politics that has just been attempted here. You have seen, you have heard! Will you indorse it by your votes? Will you keep in power that gang that has attempted it in the desperation of defeat?"

"No," the voices of men tumultuously replied.

Reckless and unjust attack had never tossed a more golden opportunity into a man's hands.

"Then come over to the side of decency, my men. Nominate a champion who will be spotless and unafraid. There is war in this commonwealth instead of politics. Through one war the great patriot of this state led his people with high chivalry. For the next governor of this state, in these trying times, I nominate the son of that patriot—the Honorable Archer Converse of this city—God bless him!"

"We're licked," gasped Colonel Dodd, trying to make the state chairman hear him, for the roar that rocked the great hall was deafening. "A boomerang has come back and mowed us flatter than an oven door in tophet."

In the rout, in the retreat—horse, foot and dragoons—crisp orders were issued and obeyed. The friends of Governor Harwood had only one resource—it was to save that gentleman's face. His nomination was withdrawn.

That convention had run amuck, it was a mass of wild men who were feeling liberty from oppression for the first time and gloried in their new and sudden freedom from ring rule.

Then the delegates who came upon their feet roared the unanimous nomination of Archer Converse.

In the gale of that acclaim the opposition uttered no protest; the delegates who still remained loyal to the machine scowled and kept their seats.

Ducking under the tossing arms of men who flung aloft their hats and cheered with the frenzy of delight that the amazing victory inspired, Richard

Dodd escaped to the rear of the hall and jammed himself into the press of the spectators. He hid behind a hedge of bodies and then dared to look at Colonel Dodd's face. The mighty passion which flamed on the uncle's countenance was revealed to the nephew's gaze even at that distance. The colonel was at the edge of the platform and was beckoning imperiously to some one. Young Dodd saw Detective Mullaney work his way out of the throng which surrounded Walker Farr; the officer was obviously obeying the summons of Colonel Dodd and marched to the platform and climbed on a chair in order to converse with the angry man who had beckoned.

And when Richard Dodd saw that conference begin overwhelming fear swept out of his soul all other emotions. He no longer had eyes for that girl in the gallery. Not even love and the promise she had made availed to stay him. Panic allowed him no time for planning an excuse or framing a lie. In playing for the stakes he had exacted he had felt that his uncle would hold no autopsy on the price of success. But five thousand dollars plucked from the Dodd pocket by a falsehood for which no excuse could be offered! And on top of that a crushing defeat which had been made definite and final by the work which Colonel Dodd had paid for!

The nephew saw Mullaney shake his head and throw up his hands in appeal and protest.

That spectacle made Richard Dodd a fugitive who thought only of saving himself. He fought his way through the crowd and ran out of the hall. The thought of facing Symonds Dodd in that crisis or of waiting to be dragged before the furious tyrant—that thought lashed the traitor into mad flight.

He glanced up at the clock in the First National tower. He had three minutes before the bank's closing time. He controlled his emotions as best he could and presented the check at the paying-teller's grill. The money was counted out to him without question, and when he held the thick packet in his hand he realized still more acutely in what position he stood in his affairs with Symonds Dodd.

He rushed to a garage, secured his car, and fled.

"I tell you I gave my nephew a check for five thousand dollars," insisted the colonel. "And the Dodds don't lie to each other!"

"Then they have begun to do it," declared Mullaney. "He has double-crossed the two of us. There was never any talk between us of more than five hundred for the job."

Colonel Dodd hurried into the anteroom and called the bank on the telephone. "Almighty Herod!" he yelped, when he was informed that the check had been cashed. He banged the receiver upon its hook. "Even my own nephew has joined the pack of those damnation wolves!"

Then with the air of a man recovering from a blow and wondering dizzily what had struck him, he left the convention hall by a rear door and went to his office.

Those whom he passed on his way out made no attempt to stop him, did not urge him to remain. That convention seemed to be doing very well without calling upon Colonel Symonds Dodd for help or suggestions.

XXX
A GIRL'S IMPULSE

Herald unofficial, *avant courier*, Mr. Daniel Breed squeezed himself through the pack of people while they were still cheering the name of the Honorable Archer Converse.

"Giving candy to youngsters and good news to grown folks never made anybody specially unpopular," Mr. Breed assured himself with politician's sagacity.

Therefore, he jog-trotted down to the Converse law-offices and shot himself into the presence of the estimable gentleman who had remained aloof from the distracting business of a convention.

"He's done it," proclaimed Mr. Breed, making his sentences short and his message to the point because he was out of breath.

"Who has done what?" demanded Mr. Converse, with equal crispness.

"Farr. You're nominated for governor. Acclamation! He's a wiz with his tongue." Mr. Breed pursed his little mouth and "sipped" with gusto. "Some talker! Don't ever tell me that good talk doesn't win when the right man makes it at the right time."

Mr. Converse rose and stood—a rigid statue of consternation and protest. "Do you mean to come in here and tell me that I have been nominated by that state convention? Without my sanction? Without my consent?"

"Sure thing! Easy work! Played all the tricks. Made believe he was green. Poked rights and lefts to Harwood's jaw. Had himself paged as a murderer—at least, I reckon it was his own get-up. It cinched the thing, anyway. He understands human nature."

But Mr. Converse did not in the least understand this talk. "Look here, Breed, you haven't gone crazy yourself, along with the rest, have you?"

"Nobody's crazy. People have simply woke up."

"I'll be eternally condemned if I—"

"That's right! You will be if you don't button up your coat and go over to the hall along with that notification committee that's probably on the way, give the folks your best bow, and say you'll take the job. We're some little team when we get started."

"You're an infernal steer team, and you have dragged me into a mess of trouble," declared Mr. Converse, with venom.

"Glad you're in," retorted the imperturbable Breed. "A man needs more or less trouble so as to round himself out; I've been having some troubles of my own. Whatever job you give me after you're elected, don't put me back with them stuffed animals. Harwood made his mistake right there!"

"It has begun already, has it?" asked Converse, indignantly. "Office-seekers at it?"

"Sure thing!" responded Mr. Breed, amiably. "When you cool down you'll remember that I got to you first with the good news."

Five minutes later the Honorable Archer Converse, muttering, but more calm, was marching toward the convention hall in the company of a proud committee of notification.

He walked out upon the platform and waited for the wild tumult of greeting to subside, and while he waited he searched the assemblage with stern scrutiny to find the face of Walker Farr.

But that young worker of miracles was not in evidence.

He had risen with the others when the band began to blare the music which signaled the approach of the nominee.

Once more he turned his gaze toward the girl in the gallery.

There was nothing in his demeanor to suggest that he had been a victor. His face was white, and after his eyes had held hers for a long time he gave her a wistful little smile which expressed regret, sorrow, renunciation, rather than pride. She no longer wondered at the interest she felt in this man; she knew that she loved him. She was able to own that truth to herself, and to view it calmly because she had made her promise to Richard Dodd and was resolved to keep it. That determination made of this love a precious possession that she could put away for ever out of the sight of all the world. Such a poor, meager, little story of love it was! A few meetings—a hand-touch—a word or two.

There in that packed forum had been their only real love-making. Over the heads of angry men they had told each other with their eyes. There was no misunderstanding on the part of either. Both knew the truth.

And yet, after he had told her, this enigma of a man bowed his head and edged his way to the door, moving unobtrusively through the press of humanity, taking advantage of the confusion which marked the entrance of Archer Converse.

Impulse goaded Kate Kilgour at that moment. She did not reason or reflect. Something in the air of this man told her that sorrow instead of triumph was dominating him; his whole demeanor had said "Farewell" when he had turned from her. The instinct of the woman who loves and longs to comfort the object of that affection drove her out of the hall, and she followed him—ashamed, marveling at herself, searching her soul for words with which to excuse her madness, should he turn and behold her.

But the autumn dusk was early and she was grateful because it shrouded her.

Farr, leaving the din of the convention, going forth alone, looked more like the vanquished than the victor. He walked slowly, his head was lowered, and he turned off the Boulevard at once, seeking deserted streets which led him down toward the big mills.

Their myriad lights shone from dusty windows, row upon row, and the staccato chatter of the looms sounded ceaselessly.

Farr climbed the fence where old Etienne was everlastingly raking. The young man had not seen much of the old rack-tender for some weeks, and now he greeted Etienne rather curtly as he passed on his way to the tree. But Etienne seemed to understand.

"Ah, I will not talk, m'sieu'. I will not bodder you. I hear how much you have work and run about, and you must be very tire."

There was a crackle of autumn chill in the air, but Farr took off his hat and sat down and leaned his head against the tree. He closed his eyes. One might have thought that he wished to sleep.

When the rack-tender made his next turn toward the street he saw a woman at the fence, and as he peered she beckoned to him. He went close and saw it was the pretty lady to whom he had told the story of Rosemarie. She trembled as she clutched the top of the high fence, and when she spoke to him he understood that she was very near to tears.

"Is there not some way—some gate by which I may come in?" she pleaded.

"That is not allow, ma'm'selle. It is trespass."

"But I want to speak—to—tell him—We can talk over there beside the tree and will not be heard. It is to Mr. Farr I wish to speak. I saw him when he climbed the fence." She hurried her appeal with pitiful eagerness.

"Ah yes, I have one little gate for maself—for my frien'—for hees frien', ma'm'selle. I will break the rule. You shall come in."

She went softly and stood before Farr for some minutes before he opened his eyes.

Then he looked up and saw her and he did not speak. He seemed to accept her presence as a natural matter. She was clasping her hands tightly to steady herself. His calm demeanor helped her.

"I don't know why I came here," she murmured.

"I know. It's because you are sorry for me."

"But I followed you. I dared to do that. I don't know why. I haven't the words—I can't explain."

"I understand. You wondered why I came away from the convention. You want to ask me why."

"Yes, that's it. I am interested in the fight. I have left the office where so many bad things were planned."

"I know. It was good of you to warn me."

"And now I am afraid you are in trouble."

"I am."

"But you have many good friends now, sir."

"I fear they cannot help me. When I left that hall I tried to tell you with my eyes that I was going away."

"I—I think I understood," she stammered. "It was wrong—it was folly—but I followed you without knowing why I did so."

"I am glad you did. I can say farewell to you here."

"But you must not go away, Mr. Farr. You are needed."

"I am going because I can best help the work in that way. If I stay here I may be the cause of great harm."

"I cannot understand."

"I do not want you to understand."

"Why?"

"It is a matter which concerns others besides myself."

"Does Mr. Converse know that you are going away?"

"I shall tell him to-night before I leave town."

"He will not allow you to do."

"Yes—he will," the young man returned, quietly.

There was a long silence.

"Coming here—following you—it was a mad thing for me to do," said the girl, still striving to find explanation for her act. "But I have had so much trouble in my own life—I am sorry for others who are in trouble. I want to tell you that I am sorry."

"I understand," he repeated.

Another period of silence followed.

"That is all," said the girl. "I only wanted to tell you what a grand battle you won to-day—and then I saw your face there in the hall and I knew that you did not want praise—you wanted somebody to say to you, 'I'm sorry.'" She dwelt upon the word which expressed her sympathy, putting all her heart into her voice. "And now I'll be going," she said, "and I hope you understand and will forgive me."

Farr had been sitting with head against the trunk of the tree. When he had started to rise she requested him to remain seated. Now he stood up so quickly that she gasped. She was plainly still less at ease when he stood and came close to her.

"Wait a moment. You think that I am a very strange sort of man, do you not?"

She was silent.

"You need not answer—it doesn't need answer. You naturally must think that. You met me when I was a vagrant. You have seen me selling ice from a cart-tail. But—I will be very frank, for this is a time which demands frankness—you have seen me in other circumstances which have been a bit more creditable. You do not know who I am or what to make of me. But with all your heart and soul you know that I love you," he declared, his tones low and tense and thrilling. "That love has needed no words. It has been strange love-making. Wait! This isn't going to be what you think. If I were simply going to say I love you I would have said it to you long ago—I am not a coward—and I had seen the one mate of all the world; I knew it when I saw you in the dust of the long highway. And after you went on I picked a rose beside the way, and the ashes of that rose are in my pocket now. I called you the little sister of the rose and plodded along after you, playing with a dream. And I threw the rose away after I saw you in the woods with your lover—and understood. But I went back and hunted on my knees for your sister. I didn't intend to say any of this to you. For it is of no use."

"No; I am promised to Richard Dodd," she sobbed.

"If that was all that stood between us I'd reach now and take you in my arms," he said, with bitterness.

"It is more than a mere promise—he owns me—it was bargain and sale—it's sacrifice—for—But I must not tell you." She went to the tree and put her forehead on her crossed arms and wept with a child's pitiful abandon. He came close and put tender hand upon her shoulder.

"Sacrifice, little sister of the rose! Then there is another bond between us! Sacrifice! My God! the curse that is sometimes put upon the innocent!" He put the tip of his forefinger under her chin and lifted her face from her arms. "I haven't any right to tell you that I love you. I must march on. I cannot even explain to you why I cannot take you in my arms and plead for your love."

Her eyes told him what answer his pleading would win, and he trembled and stepped away from her.

"Since it can never be," she said, brokenly, "you may as well know that I—that I do—I couldn't help it. I am forward—I am bold—it is shameless—but I never loved anybody before." She put out both her hands, and he took them.

Old Etienne dragged doggedly at his work, his lantern lighting his toil. The looms clacked behind the dusty windows which splashed their radiance upon the gloom.

"It is a bit strange that now another wonderful but bitter experience should come into my life on this spot where we are standing," he told her. He spoke quietly, trying to calm her; striving to crowd back his own emotions. "I guess fate picked this spot as the right place for us to say farewell to each other. I stood here one day and saw old Etienne draw a dead woman to the surface of the water, and I found a letter in her breast and I took her key and went and found little Rosemarie."

She stared at him, her eyes very wide in the darkness.

"And that dead woman—she was the mother of the little girl?"

"Yes, a poor weaver that the mills had broken. And Rosemarie and I sat all night under this tree. It is too long a story for you now. No matter about that, but I—"

"I know about Rosemarie," she confessed.

"And my heart opened and something new came into it, little sister of the rose. And now on this spot I stand, and all joy and hope and love are dead for me when I give back to you these dear little hands."

She was still staring at him.

"But I must not—I dare not speak of it," he proceeded. His grasp grew tense. "See how I am trying to be calm? I will not loose my grip on myself. Our doom was written for us by other hands, dear heart. When it was summer I walked here with Rosemarie and play-mamma. Now it is autumn and—"

"Play-mamma!" she gasped.

"Yes, a dear, good girl who worked hard in the mill and who was very good to our Rosemarie; I was making poor shifts at buying a little girl's clothes, and Zelie Dionne was wise in those matters and was busy with her needle."

"I hope you been excuse me," broke in old Etienne. "I overheard the name of Zelie Dionne, but I don't mean to listen. I have some good news for you, M'sieu' Farr, what you don't hear because you ain't been on this place for long time. And it is not good news for you, ma'm'selle, for now you can't get acquaint with very nice Canadian girl. The big beau Jean have come down here from Tadousac and now he own nice farm and they will get marry and be very happy up in the habitant country."

"Thank God, there's some happiness in this world," said Farr. "She is a good girl."

There was almost joy on Kate Kilgour's face when she looked up at Farr.

Her god had been restored to his pedestal.

"Farewell," he said at the little gate through which she had stepped into the street.

"No," she cried as she turned and hurried away; "I'll not say it—not now!" And he wondered because there was joy in her tones.

XXXI
THE MASK OF CYNICISM

Old Etienne came to the gate with his lantern; the big turbines were stilling their rumble and growl in the deep pits and his day's work was ended.

"P'r'aps you may walk to Mother Maillet's with me and say the good word to Jean from Tadousac and to Zelie Dionne, who is now so very glad," suggested the old man, humbly. "The good priest he marry them very soon and they will go home."

"Yes, I will go, Etienne. I can say good-by there to you and to Miss Dionne."

"So you go visit some place, eh, after your hard work? That will be very good for you, M'sieu' Farr. You shall come back much rest up and then you will show the poor folks how you will help them some more."

"I shall not come back—I am going away to stay."

"But you promise under the big light at the *hotel de ville*—I hear you promise that you will stay," protested the old man.

"My work is finished."

"That is not so, M'sieu' Farr. For many men come to talk to me over the fence since I stand up in the big hall. They are wiser than such a fool as I am. They say that you have just begin to do great things for the poor folks. You shall take the water-pipes away from the men who have poison them. Ah, that is what they say. I do not understand, but they say it shall be so."

"Other men can do it," said Farr, curtly.

"And yet you will come back—when?" The old man was struggling with his bewilderment and doubt.

"Never."

He understood how he was hurting that old man, but bitterness and hopelessness were crowding all tender feelings out of Farr at that moment.

Once more he put on the mask of cynicism. He feared to show anybody the depths of his soul.

In the good woman's little sitting-room they found Zelie Dionne.

"I have stopped in to say good-by, Miss Zelie. I am going away. I'm sorry that the grand young man from Tadousac is not here."

"He comes to sit with me in the evening. You shall wait and see him."

"No, I must hurry on."

"I have been reading about you." She tapped the newspaper in her hand. "The boy just passed, crying the news. It is very wonderful what you have done. Now you will be the great man. But I knew all the time that you were much more than you seemed to be."

"However, you don't seem to understand me just now," he declared. "I am going away from this city—from this state. I am going to stay away."

"*Oui*, he have say that thing to me," said old Etienne, brokenly. "And I do not understand."

"And *I* do not understand."

"I'm tired—put it that way."

"Ah no, that is not it."

"Well, I am more or less of a sneak and a quitter when it comes to a pinch. I don't want you two good folks to feel sorry about me. Forget me. That will be the best way. I hope you will be very happy in Tadousac, Miss Zelie."

"I hoped we were better friends," she said simply. "I am very sad to find you do not trust us."

"Oh, I'm selfish—that's it. Remember me as a selfish man who was tired and ran away."

"We have talked about you, Uncle Etienne and I, and we have never said that you are selfish."

"That shows you don't know me," said Farr, roughly.

"But we know what you have done," insisted the old man, with patient confidence. "For what you say you shall not do we do not care about that. For we have seen what you have done—ah, we know about that and care about it very much. You are wiser than we are, and if you say you must go we can only look at you very sad and bow the head. I wish I had some language so to tell you how very sorry! But the Yankee words—I know not those which tell how sorry I shall be. It is not much I can do for the poor little childs—only whittle and save pennies for the fresh air."

Another man, another tone, might have put rebuke, indirectly, into those words. But old Etienne, rasping his hard palms nervously, was merely vowing himself to sacrifice because there was no one else left to do so. Farr understood and was softened.

"And now I must go to the bed for my sleep, because the rack must be cleared before the wheel start to go roompy-roomp in the big pit asking for its water." He was showing nervousness, haste, his voice trembled; he staggered when he lifted himself out of his chair.

"You'd better say good-by to me now," said Farr, rising with the old man. "It's a good night under the stars. I shall probably be far out on the road by daylight."

"Good-bye," muttered old Etienne, fumbling his hat and bowing.

"But aren't you going to say something else to me—say you're sorry to have me go?" demanded the young man. "We have been close together in some things we shall never forget."

"I have told you. I cannot say how sorry." The old man's voice was little more than a husky whisper.

"I like you, Uncle Etienne. I want you to know it. You are an old saint." He put out his hand, but the rack-tender turned and hurried to the door. "Not take my hand?" cried Farr. "Am I as much of a traitor as all that?"

"Oh, I cannot speak! I have no word," wailed the old man from the gloom in the street. His voice rose in shrill, cracked tones. He began to weep aloud. He had been restraining his feelings with all the strength of his will since Farr had announced his intentions. His departure was flight. He began to run away down the sidewalk. "Saint Joseph, guard my tongue!" he gasped over and over. "I'll go very fast so that I not say it, for I am only old Pickaroon, and he is fine gentlemans!" He continued to weep broken-heartedly.

"Mr. Farr, he was afraid he would tell you how much he loved you— afraid that you would be insulted if he presumed to tell you of it."

"I don't think I just understand that," commented Farr, staring into the night, peering to get another glimpse of Etienne.

"I understand!" said the girl. "It would be too bad for you to go away and think that at parting he was not polite to you. I would not like to have you suppose that fault is in one from Tadousac. He has told me. If you will not follow him and frighten him by saying that you know it, I will tell you."

"I will not follow him. Probably I shall never see him again."

"It may be a bit hard for you to understand, for you do not know the French nature, perhaps. But since little Rosemarie went away for ever he has loved you. You made something more of him than the old rack-tender when you took him into partnership. When you made him your friend before all the big men at the City Hall something bloomed in him, m'sieu'—something that before had been only a withered bud! Ah, you think I am fanciful? Very well! I cannot think how to say it any other way. You are a token for him from little Rosemarie who has gone away; you are friend, you are son, you are in his eyes destined savior of these poor people."

"I am glad I am going away. I would hate to betray such childlike faith. Good-by, Miss Zelie!"

He heard her call to him when he was in the street. He turned and halted and saw her slim, white figure at the gate, and he stepped back half-way.

She was girlish sympathy incarnate, and his troubled, hungry, self-accusatory soul caught the radiation of that womanly solace.

"It's not what you say to me you are," she said, her breath coming fast, her tones low. "It's what I know you are! That you will be when at last you shall come to yourself. I do not care what you say. I shall not remember! To the world—to me—to poor Etienne, just now, you lied about yourself, M'sieu' Farr—about your real self. But you did not lie to a little girl when she asked you to show your true self to her. Of yourself—with little Rosemarie—that shall I remember!"

"I thank you," he said, gratefully.

"Some day some woman will love you," she continued. "And when you are sure that she does love you, then you will tell her your troubles and she will know what to say to make things right for you. For that is the mission of good women. They understand how to listen and how to help the men they love. You shall see!" She hurried into the house.

Farr was promptly admitted when he presented himself at the door of Archer Converse's residence, and he was conducted to that gentleman's library, and came face to face with his patron, whom he found sitting very erect in a high-backed chair.

"I have been waiting for you, sir," said Converse.

"I expected that you would be waiting, sir."

"Be seated."

"I will stand, if you please. I have only a few words to say."

"Then your nature must have changed very suddenly," said the lawyer, dryly. "Or did you pump your reservoir dry of language when you put my name in nomination to-day?"

Farr bowed without reply.

"I hear that speech commended very highly. Among opportunists you deserve high rank, Mr. Farr. You have tipped a state upside down very effectively, and I am upside down along with the rest."

"I will stand here very patiently, sir, and take my punishment. As between ourselves, I had no right to do what I did to-day without consulting you. As regards conditions in the state, I had a right to seize that opportunity and give to the people a man who can be depended on. I did so. Go ahead, now, Mr. Converse!"

To the young man's surprise, the nominee arose and came to him with hand outstretched. A smile broke through the grimness of the lawyer's countenance. "I have accepted a public trust with pride, I am obeying my plain duty with satisfaction, and I shall work to be elected with all my might. Otherwise I wouldn't be the son of my father. My boy, I have had a talk with Citizen Drew to-day. He told me about your idea of kicking honest men into politics. I want you to understand that I thank you heartily because you have kicked me in. I'm going to swim!"

"'Then God's in His Heaven and the world's all right,'" declared Farr.

The lawyer's quizzical and searching gaze was rather disquieting; the young man had found Converse eyeing him with peculiar interest during their meetings in the recent past. Now Converse bestowed particularly intent scrutiny on his caller.

"I feel that I have done my work, sir," Farr hastened to say, anxious to terminate this interview. "I am going away—out of the state. I shall not return."

Mr. Converse did not break out into protest. He eyed Farr more closely. Then he reached a button and turned on the full light of the chandelier. "You have a good reason for deserting just when you are most needed, I presume, sir?"

"I have. It is a reason which especially concerns the success of the legislation which we have discussed. If I stay I shall hamper you."

"I will ask you to stand where you are for a few minutes, sir," said the lawyer, commanding rather than requesting. He went to a cabinet and drew forth a package. He brought that packet to the table and began to sort photographs.

He selected one, regarded it with careful gaze, and shifted his eyes to the young man's face.

"Um!" he commented, with judicial tone. "Now—suppose you tell me—just how your continued presence in this state will hamper me"—he paused; he drawled the next words, emphasizing them—"Mr. Bristol!"

Farr had begun nervous retreat when the lawyer had begun comparison of the living features with the photograph. It was plain that he feared rather than understood.

"Hold on, there!" shouted the investigator. "You may as well stay and settle this matter, Bristol. You look at this picture! You recognize it, do you? If you are in any doubt I'll inform you that it's a picture of your father when he and I were in law-school together."

"I deny any relationship to that man."

"Your tone and your manner convict you, my boy. I jumped you with that name purposely. I am no fool when it comes to examining a witness. When I first laid eyes on you I thought I had seen you, yourself, somewhere, and I have been puzzling my brains. Then it occurred to me that I had known in my youth a fellow who looked like you. You're the son of your father, all right. Don't stultify yourself by lying to me. You are Morgan Bristol's boy! Hah?"

"I am," confessed the young man, with resignation.

"What is your first name?"

"Thornton."

"Sit down, Thornton!"

The visitor obeyed.

"What have you done that you're ashamed of, my boy?"

"I cannot tell you," said Bristol, firmly.

"Oh, but you're going to," insisted the lawyer, with just as much firmness. "You are now retaining me as your attorney and counsel—whether you know it or not. And when a man talks to his lawyer and tells the truth it's no betrayal of confidence. Out with it!"

"There's nothing to be done, Mr. Converse."

"There's always something which can be done when a man is in trouble. You are Morgan Bristol's son. I was in school with your father. He went West and settled. Is he alive?"

"I think so."

"How is it that you don't know?"

Mr. Converse settled himself into the tone and pose of the cross-examiner.

"I have been a vagrant, hiding myself in the highways and byways of this country, for a long time."

"What happened to drive you out like that?"

"Right there, Mr. Converse, is where I must halt. It is a family matter. I cannot go into it."

"Look here, Thornton, you are in trouble. If you are in trouble, so is your father. He has lost a boy! You can tell me now what it's all about, or I'll drop my affairs and go and hunt up Morgan Bristol and ask him about it. You may just as well save me all that time and trouble. You're a lawyer, yourself—I know it."

"Yes."

"And you're a good one and know our code when it comes to secrets. I am not asking you to expose a family skeleton—I'm demanding that you treat me as your attorney and trust to my discretion. You are in trouble and need a helper, and, by gad! you have got to take me into this thing."

Thornton Bristol set his elbows on his knees and clutched his shaking fingers into his hair.

"I have been meaning to keep it all to myself, sir," he stammered.

"Quite likely. You have done mighty well at it, I should judge. But you know that any man who acts as his own lawyer usually does a mighty poor job. He lacks perspective."

Bristol did not reply.

"I have been studying you a little since I have known you," the lawyer went on. "You are a very strange mixture, my boy. I much fear that in some things in this life you are too quixotic in your views. We had a case here in town—a man named Andrew Kilgour—"

"I have heard about that man, sir."

"Thornton, from what glimpses I have had of your nature, I'm going to tell you here and now that you are covering somebody else's fault. You are no coward. You would face your own delinquency just as bravely as you came here and faced me to-night. Now, what did your father do?"

"Speculated with trust funds of estates."

"Old story, eh? Too bad, Morgan. I liked you when you were young."

"But I want you to understand it," cried the son. "It is hard for me to talk about it, sir, but it isn't exactly the old story. My father was too indulgent where I was concerned. He tried to do more for me than he could afford. He didn't tell me the truth about his affairs—I supposed he was a rich man. I always had everything that money could furnish. When he found that I was interested in the law he sent me to schools at home and abroad and ordered me to take my time and go to the bottom of all."

"Well, I reckon you did," stated Converse. "If ever I saw a chap with the true legal mind you have it, polished and pointed. You came into this state and saw a solution for a problem which has blocked us for twenty-five years. It's good law! And we will have a legislature that will pass it. But when did you find out that your father had taken other folks' money?"

"I came home and insisted on going to work in the office. Then he told me. The settlement was due and had been called for. He was obliged to tell me. And he tried to convince me that he had not taken the money for my sake. He was willing to appear in my eyes a thief without excuse. But I knew. I had selfishly accepted it all without thought—and only half grateful. Young men are thoughtless, sir."

"Your father seems to have been quixotic after his own fashion, Thornton. I think I remember some of his traits when he was in school. But as old Hard-Times Brewster used to say, 'We are all poor, queer critters and some be queerer than the others!' So you were a little queerer than your father, eh, and tried to square matters by a worse piece of folly?"

"It may have been folly. Perhaps it was. But I did not stop to argue or reason. That money had been spent on me. I accepted the blame. I said nothing to my father. I wrote letters to the persons who had lost. I told them that I had taken the money as my father's agent—without his knowledge. I said I had deceived him as well as them. And then, so that I might not perjure myself on the witness-stand or have the truth gimleted out of me by lawyers, I put on rags and hid myself among the thousands who trudge the highways and ride the trusses of freight-cars. And no one has come to me and put heavy hand on my shoulder and said, 'I want you!' But some one will come if I remain here. I am going to hide myself again."

"I say it has all been a piece of folly," insisted Converse. "Dear folly! Yes, almost noble folly! But it must end, my boy. I suppose your father is back there toiling to repay those men from whom he took money."

"I suppose so, Mr. Converse. But he has not been disgraced in the eyes of the public."

"There's where your noble folly has made its mistake. You have doubled his grief, Thornton. Just sit there a moment and ponder. You will understand what I mean."

"I have understood—I have pondered—but I have not had the courage to go back. At least, they could not say to him that his son was in prison. He has escaped that grief."

"And has endured a heavier one, my boy. I'm afraid you're a poor counselor in your own affairs." He came across the room to Bristol and slapped the bowed shoulder. "Now you have found a better one. I have taken your case."

The young man looked up into the kindly features of his adviser and was only half convinced.

"Don't you realize how easy it will be for you to make money from this time on? You don't? Well, let me tell you. As soon as you can be admitted to the bar in this state I'm going to make you my law partner. Hold on! I'm doing you no especial favor—I'm putting into my office a man who had the legal acumen to devise a plan to break the unholy clutch of plunderers who have had this state by the throat for a quarter of a century. I'm simply grabbing you before somebody else gets you. I expect to be governor of this state, and I want my law business looked after by a man who is able to keep up the reputation of the firm. But first of all, my boy, you and I are going back to your home. I think you'll find me a fairly good lawyer in straightening out tangles. I'll know just how to talk to those folks out there. And then you're coming back here with me and face this state as yourself and help me fight the legislation we want put through to enactment—and be damned to 'em!" He put his arm about the young man's shoulders and drew him to his feet. "It has been a hard day for you, my boy. There are some hard things ahead of you. You must go to bed. The morning will bring comfort and good counsel."

But when Bristol started toward the door Converse restrained him gently and led him toward the stairs which led up from the big vestibule.

"You're home, my boy—right here—you're home here from this time on! This is your other home until your father needs you more than I do. I have been pretty lonely in this house for a good many years without realizing just what was the matter with me."

"After all, you have only my word for what I am and what I have done," expostulated Bristol.

"Oh no, I have the evidence of my eyes and ears and my own common sense."

Bristol pressed the hand stretched forth to him.

"I'm not going to talk to you any more to-night," stated the host, when they were on the upper landing. "It will all seem different in the morning. It's going to be all right after this, Thornton. I'm sorry I haven't a wife. A woman understands how to listen to troubles better than a man. Is your mother alive?"

"No, Mr. Converse."

"I might have known that. You would not have allowed a mother to suffer—your folly would never have gone so far. You would have been home long before this. Ah, well, my boy, some woman will know how to comfort you some day for all you have endured. Good night!"

The young man knew that Zelie Dionne had been right in what she said; he did not require the added opinion of the state's most eminent lawyer.

XXXII
THE DEBT

Colonel Symonds Dodd sat at his desk in the First National block and clutched helplessly at the dragging ends of events. He failed to get firm hold on anything and irefully informed Judge Warren that the whole situation was a "damnation nightmare."

"Well," affirmed the judge, who had been pricked in his legal pride by his master's tongue, "the Consolidated has eaten some pretty hearty meals. It's no wonder it is having bad dreams right now."

"You're squatting down like an old rooster in a dust-heap," raged the colonel, too angry to be choice in his language. "You, a twenty-five-thousand-dollar lawyer, come in here to me and say that you can't block the confiscatory scheme of a bounder—a nobody—a black-leg stranger in this state!"

"I'll carry on the fight if you order me to do so," said the corporation lawyer. "That's my business. We can lobby in the next legislature. We can fight the laws that Archer Converse's legislature is bound to pass, for they're after us, Colonel Dodd. We can carry the thing to the highest tribunal—and then we can fight the appraisals on every water-plant in the state, but—"

"Well, but what?"

"One by one they'll pry loose every finger we have got hooked on to our proposition. I have submitted that water-district plan to the acid test, Colonel. It was my duty to do it. A lawyer must keep cool while his bosses curse and disparage. I have the opinions of the law departments of three leading colleges on the scheme. They all say that such a plan, if properly safeguarded by constitutional law, will get by every blockade we can erect. Now if you want to spend money I'll help you spend all you care to appropriate," concluded the judge, grimly.

"We'll fight," was the dictum of the master.

"Then I take it that you have definitely decided to give up your political control, Colonel! A certain amount of popularity is needed to cinch any man in politics. You're going to be the most unpopular man in this state if you start in to fight every town and city simply for the purpose of piling up costs and clubbing them away from their own as long as you have the muscle to do it."

"I don't care about politics—politics has gone to the devil in this state already. They'll get tired of chasing fox-fires through a swamp following after such lah-de-dahs as Arch Converse, and will come back and be good. I'll wait for 'em to come back. But in the mean time I'm going to have the courts say whether our property can be confiscated. I'll take a few pelts while they're trying it on!"

Judge Warren bowed stiffly and retired from the interview.

Day after day passed and Colonel Dodd was more than ever convinced that the nightmare was continuing. Politicians agreed with him—all of them with amazement, many of them with wrath.

Because the Honorable Archer Converse and the man who had called himself Walker Farr had dropped completely out of sight, leaving no explanation of any sort.

"They didn't even tell *me*," confessed Daniel Breed, "and I'm their chief fugler, and here's the November election right plunk on top of us—and even the Apostle Paul would have to do at least four weeks of spry campaigning in this state to be sure of being elected if a state committee was getting ready to lay down on him like ours seems to be doing. I'm jogafferbasted. I can't express myself no other way."

Mr. Breed, in moments of especial anxiety and despondency when he reviewed the situation, darkly hinted that the grand jury ought to look into the thing. The Consolidated had done about everything up to date except assassinate and abduct, he averred, and everybody knew Colonel Dodd's present state of mind.

However, Colonel Dodd did receive Miss Kate Kilgour politely when she came to him; he had always held her in estimation next to the bouquets in his office.

"I have come to you," she explained, "because I could not get the information anywhere else. I have tried. I do not want to bother you, sir."

The girl was pitifully broken, her voice trembled.

"Well, well, what is it?" he demanded, impatiently, and yet with a touch of kindly tolerance. "You needn't be afraid of me even if you did leave me in hop-and-jump style, Miss Kilgour."

"Where is your nephew, Richard?"

And then, in spite of his assuring statement, Miss Kilgour *was* afraid of him.

His square face was suffused with red, he thwacked his fist on his desk and leaped out of his chair and stamped away from her, cursing viciously.

"Who sent you here to ask me that question?" he shouted, advancing on her from the window.

"It's my own business—I came on my own account," she stammered.

"How comes it to be your business, miss?"

"I gave him my promise to marry him."

"If you did you made a devil of a mistake; I can tell you that, young woman!"

"I realize it, Colonel Dodd. I want to know where he is. I want to take back that promise."

He controlled himself and stared at her. "Take my advice and consider your contract with Richard Dodd annulled—for good and sufficient reasons, Miss Kilgour. I don't want to say any more. I can't say any more. This thing touches me on a sore spot. Don't be afraid. I'm not angry at you. But just forget that fellow and go on about your own business."

"I will do so, Colonel Dodd, after I have settled certain business with him."

"What business?"

"I cannot tell you."

"You'll have to tell me," he insisted, roughly. "I'm now engaged in looking into my nephew's affairs. I want all the information I can get."

"I can only ask you—implore you to tell me where he is."

"I'd like to know, myself," he retorted, bluntly. "I'd give considerable to know. You needn't look at me as if you think I'm lying! Now you may as well be frank with me, Miss Kilgour. I'm going to be frank with you. I have always found you to be a young woman of prudence and caution. I'll take a chance and tell you something which I have been keeping to myself. I want you to know why you needn't feel bound to keep any promise you have made to my nephew. He has played a despicable trick on me, his own uncle, after all the help I have given him. He practically stole five thousand dollars from me and has run away, and I don't know where he is. Now, what have you to tell me?"

"I want to put this in his hands, sir." She produced a packet, at which the colonel peered with curiosity. "You will certainly find out where he is. I want you to give it to him."

"Oh, love-letters, eh?"

"No, sir!"

With shaking fingers she untied the cord and displayed the contents. The packet was money, many bills stacked neatly, and the size of the bundle made the colonel open his eyes very wide.

"We—I—we owe it to him, sir. There are five thousand dollars here."

"So that's what he did with my money, eh? Well, I'll take it."

"I don't think it is your money, Colonel Dodd. I have good reason to feel sure that it is not. I have not seen your nephew since the day of the convention, and then only at a distance. And this money—it was borrowed a long time ago."

"Borrowed by whom—by you?"

"No, sir. I cannot tell you the circumstances. I simply want you to give it back to him. I shall feel that I am released from my obligation."

"Look here, my dear young woman," said the colonel, with all his masterful firmness, "there are going to be no more riddles here. You must tell me the truth. I must have it—hear? Otherwise I shall take steps to make you tell—and that may not be as confidential as a chat here with me. I propose to know about my nephew's affairs, I inform you once again!"

"My mother borrowed this money from him. She was in trouble. He helped her."

"Your mother needs a guardian. I beg your pardon! But I thought she had had her lesson once before in her life. So my nephew loaned money to your mother! Where did he get that money?"

"I do not—"

"Hold on! Wait before you say that, Miss Kilgour. I'll not endure falsehoods from anybody just now. I have been lied to too much lately. This is a matter of my own nephew. I command you to tell me the truth."

She hesitated a long time, her countenance expressing her agony. "I haven't any right to betray him, sir."

"He did not get five thousand dollars by any honest means. The reputation of the family is in jeopardy just now, Miss Kilgour. I want to protect it for my own sake. He confessed to you, didn't he?"

"Yes."

"I can better understand your sense of obligation now. When a man commits a crime for a woman she gets some fool notions into her head about standing by him. I know my nephew's extravagances, Miss Kilgour. He had to steal to get five thousand dollars for your mother. There is just one handy place where he could steal. He took that money from the state treasury. He has told you so. Am I not right?"

"Yes."

Colonel Dodd turned his back on her and looked up at his bouquets.

Perspiration streaked his thick neck. His jowls trembled. She pitied this man, even in her own tribulation. She had never seen him moved before.

"How did you get this money, Miss Kilgour?" he asked, after a time, his voice very low.

"Must I tell you?"

"Certainly. We are going to the bottom of this thing."

"I received a little legacy from my aunt a few years ago—I had put it away in the bank. I had saved some money from the wages I got here. My mother—I am sorry to say that she has been vain and extravagant, sir—she had wasted money on jewels and dress, and now she has sold everything. We have disposed of all our furniture and have gone to board in a very cheap place. I have been able to make out the amount of the debt. Here it is!" She placed it on his desk beside the flabby hand which lay there.

He did not speak for a long time. "I am sorry for you," he said at last. "This is a wicked thing. But I know better than to tell you to keep this money."

"Thank you," she said, quietly. "I know you understand!"

"I will put it in the place where it belongs. That's all!"

And when he kept his broad back to her she went out of the office, her feet making no sound on the thick carpet.

XXXIII
ALL THE WORLD OUTSIDE

A good lawyer can accomplish much when men are willing to listen to reason and to accept the proffer of reparation!

"All going to show," declared the Honorable Archer Converse to his young protege, after they had parted at last from Morgan Bristol in the Western city, "that a thistle doesn't hurt much, after all, if you grab it with all your might and vim. We have found honest gentlemen here, thank God! It has been made plain to me, my boy, that they all knew you better than you knew yourself and that's why they waited so patiently. But, oh, that folly of yours!" However, he patted Thornton Bristol's shoulder when he said it. "It's a good thing for a young man to have a healthy debt when he starts out—a debt that's a joy to pay. Just look on it as an incentive, boy! You simply mortgaged your future!"

"I am glad that I have been called on to pay for what I wasted," declared Bristol. "And I am not sorry, Mr. Converse, that my folly led me out into the byways of this world. I'll know how to appreciate the rest of life more highly."

"Needs a hot fire to make good steel—that's so," agreed his mentor. "And speaking of fire—I reckon we're going to find it almighty hot when we get back to the place where we're expected. Now that we're leaving affairs all serene behind us, you must let me do a little careful thinking about how to meet the situation that's ahead of us."

Archer Converse reappeared in his home city as unobtrusively as he had left it and he held the polished shield of his urbane reserve over any vulnerable points which darts of questions might attack.

Mr. Breed, assuring himself that he had certain personal rights in the matter, came with a veritable lance of interrogation, and thrust tirelessly.

"It is the custom when a man has been nominated never to close an eye or leave the job for a minute. You have broke over all rules and I have been doing my best to fix up a story to account for it," stated Mr. Breed.

"Thank you," returned Mr. Converse. "No doubt you have done a very good job."

"I done the best I could without knowing what I was talking about."

"And the general comment—the run of talk was—what?"

"General talk was that you didn't seem to be worrying much about the election."

Mr. Converse turned a benignant smile on his new law partner.

"It's generally conceded, then, that I feel sure of being elected?"

"Why, they think you wouldn't have skyhooted off unless you were confident."

"Exactly! That attitude of mine takes care of the band-wagon crowd. They have climbed aboard, I'm told."

"Yes," admitted Mr. Breed. "But the state committee has taken advantage and has laid down on ye!"

"Breed, you run along and tell the chairman of that committee—from me—that unless he gets busy with his crowd in every county of this state inside of twenty-four hours I'll come out with a public statement that I have been forced to run my own campaign in behalf of the people. You don't think there'd be any doubt about my election after that statement, do you?"

"Not a bit," confessed Mr. Breed. "You're more of a politician than I had any idea of. Excuse me for any other kind of remarks. I'll go shoot a little hot lead in that chairman's left ear."

"Ordinary intelligence and common honesty," commented the Honorable Archer Converse when Mr. Breed had departed. "They are such new elements in running politics in this state that they seem to the crowd to be a brand-new variety of political astuteness, Thornton! I'm not going to be quite as frank and honest in some other statements I'm about to make, under the circumstances. I don't believe my conscience is going to trouble me a bit. We'll go over, if you please, and have a word or two with Colonel Symonds Dodd."

Mr. Converse's secretary prefaced that call by a telephoned request for an appointment, and therefore Mr. Peter Briggs led them directly into the presence of the colonel.

"This is my friend and law partner, Mr. Thornton Bristol," said Converse, apparently and blandly unconscious that he was tossing at the magnate something much in the nature of a bomb.

Colonel Dodd came forward in his chair, his hands clutching the carved mahogany of the desk in front of him.

"Oh, I beg your pardon, Colonel," purred Mr. Converse, amiably. "I forget that you are not as familiar with Mr. Bristol's identity as I am. You have known him merely as a stranger who has called himself Walker Farr."

"Yes, and he has registered himself on the voting-lists as Walker Farr," blustered Colonel Dodd. "Mr. Converse, something will drop in your camp before long—and it won't be rose-leaves!"

Mr. Converse fixed a penetrating gaze on the angry man.

"Colonel," he said, with meaning, "you are probably well aware that in politics many things are done for a certain purpose—and many of those things are a bit off color so far as the strict law is concerned. If you particularly care about digging up the past of politics in this state I will come with my own little shovel and assist with great pleasure."

"You're making an ass of me with this peek-a-boo business."

"Mr. Bristol," continued the nominee, with composure, "after long study abroad and at home has devoted himself enthusiastically to study in sociology and economics, and has preferred to gain his knowledge about conditions by first-hand observation. He came into this state in pursuit of his object, and by force of circumstances was drawn into our state upheaval."

"Much more deeply than I intended to be drawn, Colonel Dodd," stated the young man, with dignity. "I think you will remember that I said as much to you in an interview we had. I called myself a Voice, if you will recollect, and humbly begged you to attend to certain reforms. Your refusal, and the manner with which you refused, rather forced me into your affairs."

"And I give you warning right here and now," blustered the colonel, "that I'm going to force myself into *your* affairs. I'm going to have you investigated from puppyhood to the present, Mr. Whatever-your-name is."

"We may as well issue general warnings—all of us," said Mr. Converse. "I have prepared a statement for the newspapers regarding my friend, Mr. Bristol, and he will add a statement of his own relative to his project in regard to water districts. If you care to malign Mr. Bristol on the heels of that, Colonel, you may go ahead. But if you choose weapons of that sort in the conduct of this campaign we shall be forced to use a few cudgels of our own—for instance, we might be able to give the people considerable information as to how the state departments have been managed under your general direction. The funds of the state treasury—"

Converse was about to mention the matter of the usufruct of the state's money deposited in the colonel's banks for the benefit of the syndicate.

Colonel Dodd pulled himself out of his chair and exhibited instant and alarmed confusion. "We'd better make it a gentlemen's campaign," he broke in.

"Very well," agreed Mr. Converse, politely. "And now that we are proceeding toward such an amicable understanding, will you allow me to express the hope that the Consolidated will meet us half-way in regard to the legislation that is inevitable? I have no desire to use any of my powers as the governor of this state to embarrass your interests; let us trust that we can get to a prompt adjustment in the matter of the water-plants. As a lawyer of some experience, I have to inform you, Colonel Dodd, that the cities and towns of this state are going to own their own systems. The city of Marion proposes to fight the first test case through. You are a heavy taxpayer—I trust you will not help to run your city into debt which is needless."

"I will confer with you," admitted the colonel, his manner subdued.

"I will ask you to confer with Mr. Bristol, my partner. He will have full charge of the litigation. I am assured that the next city government meeting will attend to the matter of choosing him as counsel, with a suitable retaining fee," said Mr. Converse, with pride. "I will appreciate it personally and as chief executive if your interests will favor the matter. It will be better all around."

Colonel Dodd did not reply. But there was much significance in his bow as they retired.

"I trust I did not intimate that I was employing any sort of threats," said Mr. Converse, when he and Bristol were on their way down-stairs.

"I think he understood, sir."

"His suggestion that we have a gentlemen's campaign was very significant, coming from Colonel Symonds Dodd. The outlook is very hopeful," stated the nominee. "We'll see the state committee chairman to-morrow, Thornton. I feel quite sure that he will have our speechmaking routes laid out. Mr. Breed is very convincing—sometimes—when he discusses the political situation."

When they were at the foot of the steps of the Mellicite Club, the young man begged permission to go about some affairs of his own.

"But your own affairs must wait, my boy," insisted Converse. "The party claims you from now on."

"I will do my duty, sir," said Bristol, smiling; "but this evening I must have for myself."

"I have invited some gentlemen to dine with us. It's an important conference."

"The conference I hope to have, Mr. Converse, will be the most important one of my life."

The lawyer blinked, trying to understand.

"I will tell you to-morrow—I trust it will be the happiest news I ever told to any person—I will tell you first." He hesitated. "You have always given me good advice, sir. One night you told me that only a woman can listen with perfect sympathy and comfort a man's troubles surely."

Converse came close, put his hands on the young man's shoulders and studied him with intent regard. "My boy," he said, "go along—and God go with you!"

Bristol tore his hand from the lawyer's clasp and hurried away.

But at the Trelawny he did not find the Kilgours' name on the directory board. The elevator man, the janitor, the manager, told him the same story with the same indifference. The Kilgours had sold their possessions and had removed—they had left no address.

Bristol walked the streets and cursed the stilted folly that had made his farewell to her a parting in which he had pledged nothing, had promised nothing, had left no hopes for the future. He was not consoled by the thought that his farewell to her had been for her own sake, as he had viewed his situation. In the depths of his despair, when he had released her hand at the little gate, he had grimly sacrificed himself—had resolved to save her from himself by final and complete separation.

And thinking of that parting at the little gate, hardly realizing where his wanderings led him, he went down to the great mills which were dark and silent under the shadows of the evening.

Old Etienne had brought a lamp from Mother Maillet's kitchen and had set it on the stoop. He was whittling, and a little boy snuggled close, fixing intent regard on the work.

The evening was bland after a balmy day of Indian summer.

Bristol stopped at the fence and called greeting.

The old man peered anxiously, shielding his eyes from the light of the lamp.

"M'sieu'! M'sieu'!" He stammered, brokenly, gasping as he spoke the words. His wrinkled face worked as if he were trying to keep back the tears. His voice choked.

"You are surprised to see me back here, Etienne—is that it?"

"I am not surprised, m'sieu'. I knew you would come back. I am glad—that's why the tear come up in my eye. I cannot help that."

"You are working late, Uncle Etienne."

"*Oui*, the odders are gone home. But this leetle boy—I take care till his modder come from the shop. But you shall come in here, m'sieu'."

"I cannot stop, Etienne. I am—" He could not finish the sentence. He turned to go.

"I say you shall come in. You must come queeck!" The old man spoke in a shrill whisper. He put aside his knife and stick and hurried to the fence. He reached and caught Bristol's sleeve. "Ba gar!" he declared, with as much impatience as anybody had ever heard in the tone of Etienne Provancher, "even the poor habitant boy in the Tadousac country know better how to love the nice girl as what you do, M'sieu' Farr."

"My name is not Farr; it is—"

"I don't care what your name be," snapped the old man. "Tell me that some odder time. It's what *you* be—that's what I care! And you don't be good to nice girl."

"I don't understand."

"You go back there and rap on Modder Maillet's front door and then you understand! I'm only poor mans, m'sieu', but I shall talk to you like I spoke to the mans in the *hotel de ville*—and I shall not be scare when I am right."

"Look here, Etienne! What do you mean?"

"*La belle* ma'm'selle—ba gar! you have to be hit with brick bang—dat fine, pretty lady—she what tell me the good word to say to you about the bad folks—you must know she leeve now in the good woman's house."

Now it was Bristol's turn to grasp Etienne's arm. He shook the old man.

"Miss Kilgour—here? Speak up! Don't be so slow!"

"I have speak up. Odderwise you go off and be a big fool some more," retorted the rack-tender, boldly. "She's in there. She come here to live because somet'ing has made her very poor—and very sad. And her modder she cry all the time. And *la belle* ma'm'selle she come to the big tree and she ask me many things—"

While the old man chattered Bristol was yanking impatiently at the catch of the gate. He could not find the latch in the dark and so he kicked off a few more pickets from Mother Maillet's much-abused fence. He crawled through and bumped against old Etienne, thrusting him from the path, checking the flow of information.

The young man leaped up the steps, to the plain dismay of the little boy, and beat upon the door.

"It is I, Kate!" he called. "I have come back."

When she opened the door—half timorous, half eager, wholly beside herself—he took her in his arms and kissed her, paying no heed to the goggling eyes of childhood or the averted gaze of old age.

"But you left no word for me. Did you believe me when I said I would not come back?"

"I knew you would come back," she sobbed. "So I came here. I knew you would find me here."

Etienne drew near apologetically and picked up the little boy.

"Oh, my own girl, I have so much to tell you!" the lover murmured. "I know you will listen."

"We have so much to tell each other," she said, her hands against his cheeks.

The old man puffed out the lamp and set it to one side and tiptoed away, the child in his arms.

"You ke'p your head under my coat—just so," he commanded the struggling and inquisitive youngster. "Your modder would not like to have you breath in so much night air. We go find her!"

He heard the murmur of eager voices behind him, and then the door of Mother Maillet's house was shut softly—and that left all the world outside.